Roderick Mountain

Priceless Union

Worldwize Limited

This edition published 2022 by Worldwize Limited
Delta 606, Welton Rd, Swindon SN5 7XF
info@worldwize.com
020 8004 7775

ISBN: 978-1-9163984-0-5

Copyediting by Sara Magness
Cover design by Paola Bertozzi

Visit roderickmountain.com for details of other books, events, book
signings and e-newsletters for information on new releases.

For Ingrid

Acknowledgments

My eternal thanks go to the several people whose wise counsel helped make this adventure more readable: my ever-patient wife, Ingrid, Karol Griffiths at The Literary Consultancy, Sara Magness for her eagle-eyed editorial observation, Paola Bertozzi for her cover design genius.

My thanks also go to the authors, Zofia Duszynska, Fisayo Eniolorunda, Lucy Grace, Jessica Norrie, Carla Pryce, Margaret Wells and Bill Ryan at Bloomsbury.

Once in a lifetime, if you are lucky, you fall in love so deeply that oceans, natural disasters and murderous treachery cannot divide you. This love is empowering, honest, humorous, poignant, playful. Challenges crumble; together you achieve anything your hearts desire.

In 1858, the renowned artist Jasper Cropsey set out to paint a four-season set of landscapes in New England. As part of the Hudson River School, his paintings had already gained huge favour in cultured society; he commanded large fees and his paintings sold extremely quickly.

So quickly in fact, Cropsey never saw his stunning four-season set side-by-side – nor had anyone else ....

1

John Baxter turned the rental car left into Arlington Street, glancing at the Ritz Hotel to his right. Seconds later, he pulled into his private space in the car park at the end. As he took the keys from the ignition, a red dot appeared on the windscreen. He wrenched his chest sideways and downwards, not hearing the click of the breaking glass. The windscreen was now opaque, a small tidy hole telling John the bullet had been aimed at his chest. The red dot, now larger and diffuse, was shifting left and right in its sinister search. John gazed up at the dot of light, his heart thumping so hard he could actually hear it. Motionless, he remained crouched to the left, straining to hear any clues that might tell him the threat had passed.

Another bullet zipped into the back of the driver's seat. The windscreen disintegrated, raining its tiny cubes of glass into the car. John stayed motionless, wondering if the gunman might approach the car to ascertain the kill. Total silence. He waited. Then, the squeal of tyres. Tentatively, John straightened up, slowly lifting his head above the dashboard. The car park was deserted. He got out of the car and looked at his cobalt-blue Jaguar parked in the adjacent space. It was unharmed. Satisfied, he looked at his watch; he had ten minutes for the two-minute walk back to the Ritz.

Lucy Howard looked again at the photo – and squinched the image larger. She studied his face. Was that sadness in his eyes?

The black cab stopped on Piccadilly outside the Ritz. She smiled – when had she last dressed like this?

Lucy thanked the driver, gave him twenty pounds for the ten-pound fare and stepped under the stone colonnade to the jewellery window of the hotel. Passers-by might have assumed she was gazing at the pearl necklaces on display. But Lucy was focussed on her reflection – and was grudgingly satisfied with her appearance.

She felt younger than her forty-three years. His emails had made her laugh; they seemed to speak the same language. As a lawyer, Lucy had suggested the meeting for professional reasons – but John Baxter intrigued her. In the phone calls that followed, he had offered to pay for her flight from Boston's Logan to London's Heathrow – in first class. She politely refused the offer but wondered why their meeting was so important to him. Her subsequent online search showed his art collection to be spectacular. Several of the works were valued at more than ten million pounds.

Their years at Oxford had overlapped. More interesting was his extremely generous donation to Women's Aid. What was the story there? Could he be one of very few men not threatened by her wealth? Nor did it hurt that he was taller than her; even fewer qualified in this department.

Her long, thick honey-blonde hair was gathered into a ponytail with a black scrunch-tie that matched her silk, figure-tight, off-the-shoulder cocktail dress. She walked to her left under the colonnade a few yards, then right into Arlington Street, almost immediately coming to the entrance to the hotel.

Climbing the steps, she smiled at the doorman who cleared her way.

As she strode towards reception, the carpet reminded her of the New England fall; its caramel, red and rust colours triggered memories of her home in Massachusetts. The warm tones of the stone walls and columns created a welcome intimacy perfect for this evening. The gentle murmur and occasional clink of wine glasses reminded her she was approaching the tea-room, a raised area that in the evening served as a cocktail lounge.

Lucy had always enjoyed the civilised ambiance of the Ritz, but tonight there was more – an excitement she had not felt in years.

She recognised John Baxter as he rose to his feet, smiling. 'John?'

'Wow. Lucy. It's good to meet you at last.'

She smiled. His strong, warm hands engulfed hers. He kissed her on each cheek. 'Shall we sit down? I hope you think the Ritz was the right place?'

Something inside her was starting to melt. 'It's perfect. I love white orchids. I don't think I've ever seen so many.' She looked at the pianist in his black tie, faultless fingers manifesting the romance of Piano Concerto No. 2 from one of her favourite composers. 'And I love the Chopin.'

John's masculinity was obvious. But she'd been right; beside the kindness in his dark-brown eyes Lucy detected some melancholy.

She relished the feel of his hand on the small of her back; his touch was gently firm. The small, curved blue sofa, just outside the tea-room, allowed little distance between them as they settled, John to her left, half-turned towards her. She noticed his darting look at the scar on her jaw.

She touched his arm. 'It's OK,' she smiled.

'How was your flight?' he asked.

'Bumpy,' she grinned. 'But I had yesterday to recover.'

'Well, I'm glad you came. You believe a painting given to one of your clients is a fake.'

'Yes. It's a portrait of John F. Kennedy done by Norman Rockwell. It was given to one of the clients I've been representing in her divorce. Actually, it was she who questioned its authenticity and I had my doubts the minute I saw it. She had planned to sell it to pay my firm's legal bills. She knows I have a small art collection, so she asked my opinion. I told her I would get it authenticated properly.'

'Hence why you wanted to see me?' John replied.

'Exactly. But if the perpetrators are who— is something wrong?' she asked.

'I thought I saw something near the entrance.'

He stared at the door with the intensity of a stalking cat. 'I'm sorry, Lucy – would you excuse me for a minute?'

'John, what's wrong?'

'Please, just give me a few seconds.'

A minute later, Lucy watched as he returned. She guessed him to be six feet, four inches. His strong, athletic frame moved easily with a presence she found highly attractive. Thick, dark-brown hair was swept back from a forehead that suggested considerable intellect. Yet his face hinted strength of character and quiet determination.

She looked again into his eyes. He had rowed for Oxford in the varsity boat race in 1989. But only two days after the

10

gruelling race on 25th March, he was on a rowing machine doing a sponsored row of 100,000 metres for Women's Aid.

The *Oxford Times* asked why he had chosen this particular charity. As a child, John had witnessed his uncle's violence to his wife. When asked why he had chosen to row, he told the reporter he had 'done a bit of rowing on a river'.

A week later, the reporter returned to ask why he had not mentioned rowing in the winning Oxford boat two days before his 100,000-metre double-marathon. According to his crew mates, John's answer was typical.

'You never asked.'

The reporter returned to her desk at the *Oxford Times*, still unaware that John Baxter had rowed his 100,000 metres in a world record time of four hours, twenty-four minutes.

Lucy smiled. *I'll enjoy getting to know this man.*

'Is everything alright?' she asked.

'It may be nothing – but I've been followed recently.'

'I have too. Your art interests. My client's potential art fraud. Perhaps we shouldn't be surprised. But my sources agree – if anyone can unravel an art mystery, it's you.'

'Rockwell's not really my niche; I'm far better on the early American landscapes.'

'You were clear about that in your emails,' she replied. 'You probably know I was married into the Black family. I think the Blacks are involved.'

A wine waiter approached. Lucy smiled up at the man in his crisp burgundy uniform. She turned to John and asked what he was drinking.

'It's a really smooth Bordeaux.'

'That sounds perfect, thank you,' Lucy said to the waiter.

'The Blacks who own the coal and oil in Montana and Wyoming?' John asked.

'Yes.'

'Didn't they lose their Chief Financial Officer recently?'

'Yes. Larry Black was one of the cousins – and unusually honest for a Black. He was poisoned, but they couldn't find enough evidence to convict.'

'From what I've heard about the Blacks, it's a miracle you got away with your life.'

Lucy smiled. *If only you knew.*

'There are decisions I would now make differently.' She paused. 'But if I can prove fraud, it would cut off the head of a very large and greedy snake.'

'That's quite a fight. The energy industry operates with the collusion of very senior politicians. You're going to bump up against huge, vested interests.'

'You're right. The fossil-fools are old white climate change deniers, several of them senators. But Larry was murdered down in Tennessee – which still has the death penalty.'

'Is there something else?'

She smiled. 'Actually, the stakes are even higher. John Black is the CEO of Black Industries and one of the two senators in Massachusetts. With the US Senate balanced so finely, if the Republicans lose one senator, the Democrats have the majority. They could – and would – pass laws that would make big oil and coal much less profitable.'

'So, there are fortunes to be lost.'

Lucy nodded. 'Not just fortunes. When share prices and dividends plummet, directors can lose their places on the boards – which is why they get so vindictive in protecting their interests.'

'Yes – at the expense of all living creatures on the planet who need oxygen. Fossil fuels are woven into the economic fabric of the largest energy-consuming countries. Saving our breathable atmosphere will depend on our collective abilities to make the transitions needed.'

'I saw your enthusiasm for the environment on your website, John. You built a wind farm in Scotland – 120 megawatts – if my research was correct.' She paused.

'John, I may as well be open with you upfront. I've started to extrapolate what could happen if we play our eco-cards right. Suppose the four climate change deniers in the US Senate who run the largest oil and coal extractors could be made to change the directions of their companies?'

'What do you mean?' John asked.

'Well – suppose we uncover felonies perpetrated by the CEOs of these companies? And suppose we use that leverage on those four CEOs? Exposure would lose them their Senate seats. The Majority Speaker in the Senate finds out. The last thing he wants is to see a 51–49 majority for the Republicans turn into a 47–53 minority. He would put huge pressure on those Republicans to do whatever it takes to keep their seats – the kind of pressure that makes diamonds.'

John grinned. 'I love it – but it's dangerous.'

Lucy nodded. 'Either they change the objectives of their companies from extracting fossil fuels to generating wind and solar energy, or – they don't, in which case the Democrats have a majority in the Senate and Obama can pass all the eco-legislation he's been itching to; either way the environment wins.

'But the profits from the wind and solar companies will be vast – more than two trillion dollars per year. What if those profits could be diverted to fund an enhanced version of the Affordable Care Act – a version that Obama only dreamt about happening in generations to come?'

'Wow, Lucy! Two trillion dollars per year into healthcare – all generated by new jobs created by renewable energy. I am *in*. These felonies you talk about – do I take it you already have some information?'

Lucy smiled. 'I mentioned John Black as being one of those CEO-senators. And I believe his Chief Operating Officer, Kelly Black – his only daughter – has commissioned at least two murders.'

2

'Tell me about the Blacks.'

'John Black had nine offspring. I married Billy, the middle one. The atmosphere was always so poisonous; except for Andrew and Peter, they felt like angry rattlesnakes coiled for a strike.'

'Do you feel you're in danger?'

'They've not threatened me directly, but I get the feeling I'm being followed. Billy's not the main problem; Kelly did an MBA at Princeton. Graduated "magna cum laude". She's the only daughter. With eight brothers, five of whom are older, she grew up crafty and vicious.

'In fact, Billy calls her "V".'

John looked at Lucy, quizzically.

'Billy says she is vicious, vindictive, vengeful and violent.'

'Yikes. If she's one of your fossil-fool opponents, you're going to have to be very careful.'

'Especially as she's no fool. People say she's even more ruthless than she is bright. Billy told me each sibling was given a million dollars on their twenty-first birthday. On her twenty-fourth birthday, Kelly went to see her father. She'd turned a million dollars into two and a half million – and took bank statements as proof.

'He told her that if she could turn it into five million, he would make her Chief Operating Officer.'

'And she did?' John asked.

'Took her only twenty months – and Billy told me how.'

Lucy paused. 'But I have to be careful not to prejudice the case.'

John smiled. 'Talking cases. My time's pro bono on this. You've crossed the pond. Seems the least I can do.'

'Thank you, John. I never assumed ...'

'I know. But I'm more than happy to help. Tell me how you came by your art, Lucy.'

'Quite simple, really – my second marriage was to the only son of Lord and Lady Howard. Tim inherited the art along with the estate. He died four years ago; pancreatic cancer.

'He made sure the American works came to me. They had more than two hundred works of art, many of them family portraits. They weren't going to miss a dozen New England landscapes. I expect your entry to the art world was much more interesting.'

'Well – my first job was restoring paintings at the National Gallery in Trafalgar Square.'

The wine waiter returned. 'I think you'll find this *exceptional*, madam.'

Lucy turned to John, just catching his glance at her figure. For the first time in years, she was enjoying her femininity.

She collected herself. 'You were telling me your story.'

'It was luck really. The gallery sent me out to look at some landscapes at a huge place in Kent. "Simpson", the butler, showed me twenty paintings they wanted cleaned and sold. The lady of the house, Victoria Markham, needed money for maintenance of the estate.

'I was completely overawed; the building was enormous. Scores of twisted Tudor chimney stacks. Beautiful five-hundred-year-old stained glass. One window commemorated a visit by Henry VIII and Catherine of Aragon in 1525. There were thirty-five rooms on each of the four floors. And the living rooms still had the original English oak panelling.

'Twenty of the works were American landscapes – but there were two Mrs Markham particularly liked, part of a four-season set from New England. They were done by Frank Cropsey, from the Hudson River School. Twenty-five years ago, a Cropsey sold for ten thousand dollars. Now, you'd be lucky to pay ten million. I've been looking for the missing two ever since. If I find them, I'll give her the whole set.'

Interesting – he's going to give twenty million dollars' worth of art to Mrs Markham.

'Mrs M was so sad to be losing the paintings; she likened it to having family pets put to sleep.

'So I offered to help her keep her favourite pet. Instead of her paying the 17.5 per cent auction commission, I'd put the word out to the collectors I'd met. The money we raised from

4

the first one would cover the restoration of all twenty paintings. She'd save the 17.5 per cent so she could afford to keep two or three. If I couldn't sell them all, she could always sell the rest at auction as planned – and they'd all have been cleaned.

'I liked Mrs Markham – she reminded me of my Scottish Petrie grandmother, lots of spirit, and a twinkle in her eye. Anyway – knowing the stakes made me determined to justify her faith in me.'

He said Petrie!

Lucy pondered for a moment. 'She fixed the house, then?'

John nodded. 'We'd be left with two or three of the works. She'd keep one and I'd keep one, as payment for my services. It was going to take a while, so the process would be gentler on her.

'Mrs M agreed. "I like you, young Baxter," she said. "We have a deal."

'Then she asked if I did the *Times* crossword. This felt odd, given the conversation. But a year later I was in her library, admiring her paintings. On the table was the *Times* crossword facing upwards, completed. I was very impressed, and I remembered her question a year earlier.'

The waiter approached.

Lucy looked up at him. 'This is exquisite. It's my favourite Médoc.'

His lips pursed in appreciation. 'It is indeed Château Largaux '78, Madam. Perhaps in a while you would like another?'

'Seventy-eight? I would *love* another.'

Little do they know.

'Don't I know you from somewhere?' John asked the waiter.

5

'I've been here five years, sir. And I believe this is not your first visit.'

'You're right – but I get the feeling we've met somewhere else.'

'I'm sorry, sir. I don't think I can help you,' he said, politely withdrawing.

'I take it you sold her pictures?' Lucy asked.

'Actually, only sixteen. But we sold several for ten thousand pounds each, so it didn't matter. Mrs M was pleased for three reasons. She could keep three paintings, not one – and some of the excess could keep her beloved Simpson on till he retired in eighteen months.'

'But you got your start in the art world?'

'Absolutely; Mrs M kept Cropsey's spring landscape and gave me Cropsey's summer. They're stunning – six feet wide, four feet tall; the colours are vivid without being gaudy. The peace in the landscapes is just – from another age.

'We'd done better than our initial plan, and she invited me to her dinner parties so that everyone knew me. But right from that day, I've wanted to get the whole set together for her.

'Anyway, a year later, I'd accumulated three pieces, and one I sold for twenty thousand pounds. I resigned my job to buy and sell art.'

'Your website has some great paintings.'

'It only shows the pieces I would sell. But – I've been lucky.'

'You're very modest. Most of the works are priced over a million pounds. Several are more than ten million each. That can't be luck.'

'You've been doing your homework,' he replied, hesitating. 'But actually … I do feel lucky. Buying a painting for two thousand pounds and waking up ten years later to find it's worth twenty thousand is a bit like getting up on a surfboard expecting an ordinary wave – then finding you're riding a tsunami a hundred feet tall. I feel like it's all a dream – a kind of bubble that could burst at any moment. But instead of riding a wave you know cannot last more than five minutes, I'm still on the same wave twenty years later – and the crazy prices in the art world just keep getting more and more ridiculous.'

She smiled.

He's worth two hundred and fifty million but he's more interested in the art. When did I ever meet a man whose ego isn't threatened by a lawyer's salary?

'Three reasons. You said Mrs Markham was happy for three reasons, but you only mentioned two.'

'You're right – I've sometimes wondered what the third was.'

3

John looked at Lucy. *Why the nickname, Mona Lisa? And how could anyone scar that pretty face?*

'So – tell me about you, Lucy, and why you chose law.'

'Dad was a professor of law. Mum wanted me to do languages. They spoke nine or ten. "You pick up languages easily," my father said. "You'll learn more. But you don't pick up the law like that. It's a training that will always pay the bills."'

'So, you chose law.'

'Yes – family law, estate planning, divorce, prenups, wills, etcetera.'

'So how come you live in the US?' John asked.

7

'Our chambers opened an office in Hartford, Connecticut.'

'You must be surrounded by lots of eligible men. So ...'

'Why marry Billy Black?'

'Well – it's not as if you are unattractive, or unsuccessful.'

Understatement of the year, Baxter – she's gorgeous, and successful enough in her own right not to be dazzled by money.

Lucy blushed. 'I fell in love with Billy; he was the kind of original thinker I have always found attractive. He was not the slightest bit interested in the family oil business, for one thing. He was one of only two siblings who did not look uncomfortable in a suit and tie. He was good-looking, athletic, witty – and seemed to have all the time in the world to show me around New England and make me feel at home.'

Lucy paused. 'He knew I loved art; he took me to the Isabella Stewart Gardner Museum ... and the Rockwell ... and the Museum of Fine Arts. It seemed we had so much in common. I was not the person I am now. I was lonely, all that way from home and my friends. That made me vulnerable. And there was Mary Black, Billy's mum.'

Lucy smiled. '"Ma", we call her, mother of nine. Very kind and welcoming; we had some lovely chats. Her only real daughter, Kelly, was so like her malevolent father, maybe Mary looked at me as someone to adopt. Our chats were more honest and intimate than I've had with anyone.'

'So, Kelly thought of you as a threat?'

'Possibly, especially as she coveted her mother's jewellery so much – and she was the only daughter. She couldn't stand me in the house.

'Anyway, Mark and Oliver arrived. Mary wanted to see the kids at every opportunity, so we had lots of time to get close. I miss those chats. Mary's very special.

'But it wasn't easy in the early years – having to be on top of my game when I'd only had two hours' sleep because one or other of the kids was teething. I tell you – I learnt new respect for mothers everywhere.'

'Tell me about the Black ranch – it's supposed to be quite something.'

'It's a beautiful place just outside Marlborough, near Boston, high up on a ridge that overlooks a lot of Massachusetts. There's four hundred acres of lush pasture and stabling for over a hundred horses.

'The family ranch houses are dotted around the perimeter of a huge circular piece of grass. Most of the brothers lived there – some with families. The main house has a cavernous living room – complete with Egyptian red-granite statues eight feet tall, either side of the fireplace.

'They owned another house up on Beacon Hill in Boston. It was the cause of one almighty row I had with Billy; they were paranoid about it.'

'Why?' John asked.

'It's where they store their business information. His father had Billy install a huge safe in the basement. The Old Man wanted the safe encased in concrete two feet thick.'

John raised his eyebrows. 'Makes you wonder what he's so afraid of losing.'

4

Lucy showed outstanding ability very early. Her Norwegian mother spoke several languages, four fluently. Lucy's Swedish father was Professor of Law at Dartmouth College in Hanover, New Hampshire. Years of travel, including periods in Europe and England, had necessitated teaching in several different native tongues.

Academically, Lucy was ready to enter Oxford University at the age of sixteen. She had achieved four language A-levels in only one year, not the usual two. But her teachers knew an extra year at school would give her two more languages and a little more maturity. A year later, with six grade As, she sat the Oxford entrance examinations.

As the autumn progressed and Lucy worked towards her exams, she became aware of a tension around her. She wondered why, until one day a friend showed her a newspaper clipping.

St Catherine's College student – the youngest in 25 years to sit for Oxford.

St Catherine's College was abuzz with their new celebrity. But Lucy continued her studies, ignoring the commotion, often putting in twelve-hour days in the school library. For these crucial autumn weeks, continuous exhaustion diminished her usual beaming grin to a kind of half-smile. This, combined with her implacably calm nature, prompted her friends to call her The Mona Lisa.

Three months later, Lucy was creating other news. The *Daily Telegraph* announced:

'Mona Lisa', youngest ever student to read law, awarded scholarship to Oxford – aged 17.

In 1990, armed with First-Class Honours, Lucy joined the Honourable Society of the Inner Temple and began training for the Bar. The quality of her degree was not exceptional in her new environment. What impressed her senior colleagues was her unique ability to translate the nuances of law into any of the leading European languages.

One morning in court, after a sleepless night spent reading a complicated legal brief, her Senior was struggling. They were defending their female client from a divorce claim of nearly £75,000,000 and the case was more than usually loaded with animosity. Lucy and her Senior found themselves falsely accused of colluding with the corrupt practices of their client.

Lucy felt her body tighten. Nobody told her this could happen! How could all the years of study be wasted? How could her career be so cruelly curtailed before it had even started?

In the seconds that followed, Lucy discovered that in crucial moments, her mind never let her down. She had also read the ninety-page brief overnight and had slept very little. With clinical precision she moved quickly to the page her Senior needed and put her finger to the relevant phrase. This proved crucial to winning the settlement for their client – and the fee of £15,000,000. Lucy was elated; no words could describe her discovery. Instead of becoming smug about her efficiency, all she showed of these feelings to the outside world was a grateful half-smile.

Lucy's cool half-smile widened slightly at the end of the year when she achieved another landmark in London's legal profession – the first ever Bar trainee to be paid a bonus. For her crucial part in winning the £15,000,000 fee, the Head of Chambers approved a Christmas bonus of £1,500,000. She had only recently celebrated her twenty-first birthday.

Lucy's continuing modesty and quiet determination caused her chambers to re-adopt the nickname she had been given at school. Whenever a senior lawyer in chambers needed the sharpest support in the most lucrative cases, she or he called for The Mona Lisa.

Lucy duly passed her Bar exams and worked closely with the Head of Chambers. After three short years, she was offered the chance to open an office in Hartford, Connecticut. She found herself at a cocktail party given by America's richest oil tycoon, John Black. She was introduced to Billy Black, one of nine heirs to a fortune worth in excess of $60,000,000,000.

Lucy was not easily dazzled. But a certain loneliness, so far from her friends back in England, made her vulnerable to a whirlwind romance, a proposal of marriage and the gift of one of the most extravagant engagement rings ever made in North America.

Within three years Lucy produced two children: Mark, and then Oliver. Life was hectic with a job that required her to be at the top of her game. Initially, and often tearfully, she struggled with these conflicting demands, feeling guilty about the long hours that took her away from her children. In her tears of exhaustion, she determined to justify the faith her chambers had placed in her.

Eventually, life settled into a routine made easier when her children started to talk. Some of the tiredness was replaced with the joy of relating to little people who made her laugh – and cry. Mark's first words were 'Mummy love'.

Life seemed so full. But Lucy was uneasy. She was over-hearing pieces of conversation her husband Billy was having with his family. Why was he being so secretive? What was he withholding from her?

These doubts became more insistent. Then came the conversation she heard Billy having with his father.

'Pa, if the Chinese official won't play ball, why don't we get Kelly to kill him like we did in India?'

Lucy stiffened. She felt immersed in ice. How could she spend her life with people like this?

At the same time, Lucy was aware of another yearning – something she had not experienced since her last days at Oxford. Where were the men of unimpeachable values, men with the moral, emotional and physical strength to take complete possession of her? Where was the man who deserved the unconditional love she offered, the man into whose love and strength she could melt?

5

As a child, John Baxter showed exceptional curiosity and energy. Simple pleasures, like gazing at the night sky, he experienced differently to his friends. John wondered if stars ever stopped shining and how long their light had taken to reach him.

His intense curiosity sometimes made him seem a little odd to others, but they liked his generosity. On one occasion, his friend had been saving his pocket money for a Slinky and needed the last fifty pence for the purchase. Without hesitating, John gave him the money. This meant a little less went into his telescope savings account that week, although he never mentioned it.

John's insatiable thirst for knowledge gave him an unusual breadth of interests. Only the more perceptive teachers at school judged him brilliant, but he passed quietly into Christchurch College, Oxford in 1986.

Soon after John had started his Maths course, his father died of a stroke. The doctors told him it was smoking related, as with most strokes. For days after his father's death, John kept remembering what his father had said to him recently.

'Do what you love; follow your passions; be true to yourself. Life's too short to do anything else.'

Within two weeks of his father's death, John switched to read History of Art – and never looked back. He had an appreciation for the exquisite detail and patience required to create the classical masterpieces. It seemed to John that manifest in a Michelangelo or a Canaletto was the highest essence of humanity.

Though he was happy with his degree course, John Baxter was acutely aware of a tension emerging in his life. Enthralled as he was with the great artists, John became interested in his own ancestors. One had been the first man to circumnavigate and map the entire coastline of a land he called Terra Australis – a country he eventually named Australia. Another had been a famous and well-published Egyptologist. Both had been larger-than-life mavericks, sharply focussed on their endeavours. John identified with their curiosity and found himself torn between researching them and getting on with his course.

But, with the self-discipline his friends respected, he chose to refocus on his degree. He would come back to the explorers in his family later. In August 1989, armed with First-Class Honours, he beat more than two hundred other applicants for a job at the National Gallery in Trafalgar Square, restoring classical paintings.

The other tension in John's life was his inability to find the girl who could keep his interest. John Baxter's athletic six-foot, four-inch frame and his easy-going, gentle manner caught the attention of the girls at Oxford. But his passions for art history and ancient Egypt made him appear selfish and boring. Within months, every relationship melted. One by one, his girlfriends left him, looking for someone to make them feel special. John felt so lonely, he wondered if he should settle for someone less than exciting.

Even on his wedding day, he knew the woman standing next to him was not his perfect match. Two children arrived – first Charlotte, then Emma. For a time, life had new meaning and he doted on his daughters. So, on one level it came as a shock when his wife announced she was leaving him – on another, he had always half-expected it.

John Baxter knew something had been missing. It all become clear when he woke one night from a vivid dream. A tall blonde woman was smiling, as if expecting him. She was draped in white, the see-through gauze her only garment. She stretched out her arms, beckoning, open. She started to communicate wordlessly – conveying her meaning as clearly as if she were speaking.

'The woman stands before you, a yearning in her eyes.
Possess me, John, I beg you, our dreams to realise.'

6

Lucy studied John closely. The warmth in his smile was genuine. 'Well, sitting here in the Ritz Hotel, three and a half thousand miles distanced from Boston and the Black family and Old Man Black's safe, does give me a certain perspective.'

John grinned. 'Give it your best shot.'

'Billy told me the safe is eight foot wide, eight foot deep and eight foot high. It took him a month to cast the two-foot-thick wall of reinforced concrete that encases it. Apparently, the safe combination has a twelve-digit code that changes daily. I'd have to guess the Old Man had more than just information to protect; it's probably where he keeps his ill-gotten gains.'

John pondered for a moment. 'An eight-foot cube could certainly contain a lot of art ... And the Blacks live in the Boston area ... I wonder ...

'Are you hungry, Lucy?'

'I am actually.'

'We could eat here if you like? I want to know about the real Lucy, not Lucy Black or Lucy the lawyer.'

Lucy, when was the last time a man gave you the tummy-flutters?

She smiled back at him, glad he could not read her thoughts and very glad he'd chosen a table with chairs on adjacent sides.

'The picture you emailed doesn't do you justice. I love your dress, by the way.'

He glanced briefly at her chest – and seemed not to mind that she noticed. Lucy could feel her face and neck blush again. He was genuine – and unapologetically masculine. She knew from her PA he had been divorced five years.

16

'Thank you. And you obviously keep fit. How do you manage it with all the travelling you do?'

'A bit of rowing every week – and as much skiing as I can manage. Do you ski?' he asked.

'Love it.' Lucy paused. 'Actually, it was in Killington, up in Vermont that I first knew Billy to be tricky. I'd arranged to meet him after skiing. He had to make some business calls, he said, and had to miss our afternoon session.

'But I was tired, so I stopped earlier than usual. When I arrived, he was kissing a girl at the other end of the bar. I watched them, at a distance, feeling totally lost. I went back to our hotel and cried.'

'I'm sorry,' John said. 'I know what *that* feels like.'

That was said with feeling. There's a story there, Lucy.

She looked into his eyes. All she could see was kindness now. She allowed herself a fleeting look at his mouth, risking he might see. How she had longed for a man with his warmth, his modesty, his ability, his obvious masculinity. What a contrast to the puny, cold, Machiavellian career men in her firm's legal chambers.

'I take it Billy's infidelity was the main problem, then?'

'One of them – but he was always stealing. Crazy, when you think they'd each received a million dollars. It was him stealing a painting that finished our marriage. Billy and two of his brothers came to me in the kitchen to persuade me not to tell anyone.'

Lucy paused. 'It's how I got my scar.'

She shuddered at the memory. He put his hand on hers as she rested the tips of her fingers on the base of her wine glass. She smiled at the warmth and strength in his hand.

'There's kindness in your eyes,' she said. 'I was hoping there would be. You can never quite tell from a photo, can you?'

She glanced again at his lips and rested her other hand on his, stroking it gently.

It feels so natural ...

'So, Lucy – there are other art specialists. Why choose me?'

Lucy smiled. For the second time, she was glad he could not read her thoughts.

'I was impressed by your passion for American art and your enthusiasm for finding the two missing paintings. And I noticed you rowed for Oxford – in the winning boat in '89.'

'In your emails, you never mentioned your college,' John replied.

'Somerville.'

'One of the hardest to get into,' he replied.

'I don't know about that. I do know I was too young when I first went up.'

'Did you stay in touch with any of your friends at Oxford?'

'A few. A lot of the lawyers ended up in politics – or the civil service.'

'No one gets into Somerville without impressing some very clever people at interview.'

Lucy grimaced. 'Maybe,' she said. 'And no one gets into the varsity boat without fighting for it. And then wins the race when the opposition are twelve pounds heavier per man.'

'I was just one of a team of nine. Historically, it was the biggest mismatch weight for weight in any varsity race, ever. No one gave us a chance. But it was also the very first race where both coxes were girls. Ali did us proud.'

They laughed – and picked up their wine glasses at the same time.

'We seem to have come to a similar place. So, what motivates John Baxter to get out of bed each morning?'

For the third time in ten minutes, she was glad he could not read her mind.

'Learning and writing, I suppose. I wake up each morning really grateful; grateful to be doing things I love.'

'Learning?'

'Yes, I've been learning the ancient Egyptian hieroglyphs – all seven hundred. It's fascinating.'

'So, why so sad?' Lucy asked.

'My friends envy my wealth. And that I don't have to set an alarm clock, even though I do. They think I'm lucky to be rich, to travel the world in search of beautiful things ...'

'But?' Lucy asked.

'But I miss something my friends have always had – someone special to share it with.

'Enough about me. Tell me, Lucy, have your marriages put you off men for ever?'

'No way. My two marriages were opposites, actually. Billy Black was unfaithful and cruel. But Tim Howard was gentle ... kind ... respectful ... a real gentleman and completely unassuming. Which, considering he was a lord from one of England's oldest families, was quite remarkable.

'Now, I've had a bit of time. My girlfriends tell me four years is much too long, that I need some romance in my life.'

'But what do *you* think you need,' John replied.

Lucy smiled. *When was the last time someone actually asked me what I want?*

19

'A kind touch ... a best friend ... someone genuine ... educated ... someone who loves me unconditionally ... a man who knows when to use his strength and when to be gentle ... someone who understands a girl needs roses and chocolate every so often.'

She darted him a look. There was a knowing air in his smile, a gentleness she could trust, something that elicited honesty.

'What about you – what kinda gal does it for you?'

He smiled. 'She's kind, caring, very bright. She wants lively conversation. She uses her abilities for the good of others. She wants to leave the world a better place. She's sensuously female.'

John paused. He took both her hands in his and looked her in the eyes.

'She trusts that I will use my strength to make her feel loved, desired, delighted to be a woman – delighted to be *my* woman.'

Oh, my god, Lucy.

She held his gaze. Her heart started to pound; the butterflies in her abdomen were becoming more insistent. 'But strength has to go with kindness. Can you do that?'

'You'll have to be the judge of that,' he replied.

She felt his hand on the small of her back once more as he gathered her a little closer.

Can he possibly know?

He moved his face closer to hers – and looked into her blue-grey eyes.

Lucy put her lips very gently to his.

7

'John, it's been so long.'

'Me too,' he replied.

He squeezed her hand softly. 'Let's eat,' he said, changing the subject. 'You said you keep the art in Wimbledon?'

'In Wimbledon Village. My work takes me backwards and forwards over the pond, so I need somewhere to call home when I'm here.

'John, I'm curious – of all the paintings you could have looked at in the US, you never told me why my paintings are of such interest. Surely you'd have more success in the States?'

'You'd think so. But I've been looking in the States, off and on, for well over ten years. And a couple of your winter landscapes intrigued me. As I mentioned, Mrs Markham's "Winter" was stolen from her some years before I met her. And she never owned "Autumn". So I never miss a chance to see an autumn or a winter that might complete her set.'

'John, I'm pretty sure none of mine are Cropseys. So, I don't see how they could help.'

'You probably know that a canvas is occasionally started by the accomplished artist, then completed by a relative novice in the school ... or the other way round – the novice starts the canvas, then the master completes it.'

'And sometimes those canvases go unsigned,' Lucy said, thinking.

'Exactly – and it's unlikely Cropsey spent so much time in New England, yet failed to paint the most famous mountains – especially with his record of painting landmarks.

'But more than that, a Cropsey, on its own, fetches at least ten million dollars at auction. If I could collect all four seasons, even if one was an excellent painting partly done by one of his better pupils, they'd be unique in the art world ... and priceless.'

'Don't I remember Poussin painted the four seasons,' Lucy replied.

John smiled. 'You're right. And there've been other artists who've done it. Michetti the Italian did it – and Monet did it, but in his impressionist style – and Grabar the Russian did it.'

'So, what makes the Cropsey set so special?'

'Michetti, Grabar, Monet, Poussin are really the only famous artists who accomplished all four seasons. One or two lesser-known artists did it, but they're not a patch on the Cropseys.

'Anyway – it's something very few artists have done well. The special thing about the Cropsey set is the size of the canvases. Michetti, Poussin and the others painted in thirty by eighteen inches. Cropsey painted his set seventy-two by forty-eight inches. They're literally six times larger. But he kept the detail as refined as if he was painting something a sixth of the size. It requires much more work, and he pulled it off – seemingly effortlessly. They're absolutely stunning.'

'Now, I understand,' Lucy replied.

'Maybe not quite. Grabar's set has been broken up – and Winter has been so badly damaged it's worthless. Monet's impressionist style doesn't show the seasons very distinctly – and the four paintings are owned by three different owners. Michetti's are in pretty poor condition and he's not the most well-known of artists. And Poussin's set is owned by the Louvre – and not available to private buyers.

'So, the Cropsey paintings are literally the only ones of this artistic merit or size in the world. He painted them photoaccurate and it's the only set on earth a collector could hope to own privately.'

'How do you know one of the missing two is not owned by a museum somewhere?'

'I've scoured the catalogues of all the collections and all the auctions over twenty years. Autumn and Winter are not on public view.

'If I could get the whole set together, it would be unique in so many ways. The only other world-class four-season set still together is the Poussin set – currently insured for a hundred million euros. But it's nowhere near as impressive as the Cropseys – and it's in the Louvre.'

'Amazing,' Lucy replied, pausing.

'I can see why you might be interested in mine then,' Lucy continued. 'But they're going to seem quite ordinary compared to your Cropsey.'

'You never know,' he replied.

The waiter approached and they chose the salmon and new potatoes.

'Would you mind if I choose the wine?' Lucy asked. 'There's a pink from the Château Largaux that's perfect with salmon.'

'Sounds great,' John replied.

'It seems I've invited you to see my treasure, Mr Baxter.'

'Well – gorgeous and beautiful treasure merits an inch-by-inch examination.'

Oh, I do hope so. I can hardly wait.

Lucy's blush deepened. She knew his likely sensitivity to subtle changes of colour tone would give her away. She felt as exposed as if he had already removed her dress.

They ate their salmon in the most highly charged atmosphere. He asked if she wanted any dessert.

Lucy smiled and shook her head. *The only dessert I want is not on the menu.*

He gestured for the bill, and leant towards Lucy to kiss her again.

The bill arrived almost immediately and Lucy reached for it.

'It's very kind of you, but this one's mine,' he replied.

As they stepped out of the lift onto the fourth-floor corridor, Lucy was shaking.

'Are you OK, Lucy?'

'You can probably hear my heart, John. I've never been so nervous.'

Or so ready to give myself.

'Me too,' he replied, gently placing her hand on his chest.

It was comforting to hold his hand as they approached the room. Once inside, he pushed the door firmly shut, an act that set her heart racing faster. She looked up into his eyes as he cupped her head in his hands. Their mouths met – passionate, searching. She pressed her hips to his. He took the scrunch-tie from her ponytail and ran his fingers up her neck and into her thick blonde hair.

How did he know I love that?

He held her head again – tender kisses finding the scar beneath her left ear.

24

Lucy – you're melting – in all the right places – how delicious to feel like this again.

She was being led into the more open area of the room. They kissed again, this time more relaxed, exploring, playful. His hands felt so good on her bare shoulders. She was ceding control – what bliss. She tilted her head back, offering her throat – and her surrender. Then, the caress of his lips on her neck, the unzipping of her dress. He paused, allowing her the dizzy anticipation of the moment.

She looked again into his eyes, her face and chest blushing. He held her waist firmly to his – and she held his gaze, knowing that when she stepped back, her falling dress would leave her completely naked.

8

Sunday – 30th September

Lucy woke the next morning feeling like a goddess – powerful, excited, at peace. She looked across at John, still sleeping. His broad chest moved slowly and powerfully with the ebb and flow of his breathing. It had been an act of love. He had given all of himself – and she smiled as she remembered.

A few minutes later, Lucy emerged from the shower to find her lover awake.

'Good morning, gorgeous,' he said.

She smiled and asked if she could treat him to a room service breakfast. 'Only scrambled eggs and smoked salmon will do,' she said. 'And fresh croissants and orange juice and black coffee.'

'Perfect,' John said. I'll get it ordered before I shower … last night was out of this world.'

'It was – both times.'

He took the towel from her body and held her. His kiss emptied her mind; there were only her feelings – feelings so intense, they could only be expressed one way.

John broke the silence. 'Come on – let's have breakfast. You have more treasures we need to examine, I think.'

Lucy went to the hand luggage she had brought over the Atlantic. She unrolled a little peach-coloured, mid-thigh-length dress with a frilly hem.

'Will this do?'

'It will look fabulous with you in it,' he smiled. Otherwise naked, Lucy slipped it over her head and held out her arms for him to approve.

Easy on, easy off. I hope he takes advantage.

They wolfed breakfast and made their way down to reception. He took her hand. It felt good to hold his hand in public. They turned right out of the Ritz and walked the short distance down Arlington Street to the car park.

Lucy wondered why John was looking at the floor of the empty parking space next to his car. She noticed him flick a tiny cube of glass to the wall with his foot. He opened the passenger door to his cobalt-blue Jaguar and she lowered herself into the soft tan leather. He closed the door slowly but firmly, enveloping her in its protective luxury. As Lucy watched him walk around the front of the car, his feline ease reminded her of their sleepless night. He seemed to embody the effortless, explosive power of a cat – sensuous, silent, like the Jaguar itself.

As they made their way out to her home in Wimbledon, it seemed so natural to be together; the long silences had no need of meaningless chatter.

'How long are you over here?' John asked.

'As long as I need. The boys look after themselves; they don't need me for the everyday things anymore. And I don't think I mentioned, I'm on a short sabbatical. Our Head of Chambers wanted to make a gesture for the long hours we did recently for two consecutive divorce clients in the entertainment business. Especially the last one – we saved her tens of millions.'

'Was she a famous singer?'

Lucy looked at John. 'In the interests of client confidentiality, let's just say she was more than happy to pay twenty per cent of what we saved her.'

John smiled. He knew from his lawyer friends that Lucy could have been paid half of her firm's fees on a case of that size.

'Turn right into Belvoir Square, just here. I'm down near the end on the left.'

'I can't wait to see inside,' John said, looking at Lucy's home.

They sat in the car for a few moments, taking in the events of the last few hours.

'Does your persistence always get you the objects of your desire?' she asked.

'I've always admired great beauty – and it does sometimes require great persistence to obtain – but I don't remember needing too much persistence last night.'

She kissed him. *Nor will you this morning.*

9

John could not remember ever feeling so welcomed by a home. Lucy had created a soft, pastel colour scheme with long, velvet raspberry drapes and pale-yellow walls. She turned on the table lamps from the main wall switch. This gave the room a warming glow.

A large brick-built inglenook with stone mantelpiece dominated the room. Facing the fireplace was a dusky-pink sofa, flanked on each side by matching armchairs. The colour of the sofa and chairs echoed perfectly their enveloping cosiness.

John imagined evenings with Lucy curled up in front of the fire, with plenty of red wine and dark chocolate.

'It's just like you,' he said. 'It's gorgeous. Very feminine … and warm … and inviting.'

She kissed him. 'Thank you, John.'

Each side of the fireplace was a four-foot-wide canvas hung at head height. John approached the one on the left. The famous view of the bend in the River Thames from Richmond Hill was a painting many artists had attempted over the centuries. But this one was vivid, real, photo accurate. On the other side of the fireplace was another London scene. The merging, pastel shades of the pink-and-yellow sky made John think of Turner. His eye went immediately to the signature.

'Turner, no less. How did you get this?'

'That's a long story,' Lucy said, taking his hand. 'But you can see what inspired the colour scheme in here. Come ...'

She led him into her dining room. On the two longest walls were six paintings, all American art, mostly from the 1800s.

'The others are in the study through there. As you can see, most of them are landscapes. But, as I said, I don't believe any of them are particularly noteworthy.'

John looked at Lucy's collection. 'You've got to be kidding. You told me about the Copley and the Sargent. But you never mentioned the Rockwell.'

She stood at his side, gazing at her paintings, as if for the first time.

'Come through to the study,' she said. 'The other six are in here.' He followed her through. 'None of them are in the sun at any time.'

'They're fabulous. But why didn't you mention the Rockwell?'

'To be honest – it looks unfinished to me,' she said.

'But that's how he worked. Mostly, he took photographs so he could remember the detail. If you look at his finished work, it's painstakingly accurate. But sometimes he did prelim drawings instead of taking photos. These drawings very rarely see the light of day. Have you seen his painting *The Ungrateful Man*?'

'No.'

'I think this is a prelim sketch for it. If it is, it's really rare. What's through that door?'

'Oh, just a cupboard. Actually, there's another painting in there, but I couldn't find space for it on the walls.'

'Do you mind?' John replied.

'Be my guest.'

'It's large,' John said. He slid the six-foot-wide canvas out of the box and leant it up against the wall.

'It can't be,' he said.

'What do you mean?'

'It's got the same frame as my Cropsey Summer – and it's the same size. If I could do something as accomplished as this, I'd definitely want to sign it with more than just "L"', he said. 'Whoever "L" is captured the New England autumn beautifully.'

In silence, they continued to look at the paintings.

'It's strange, isn't it?' she said. 'After a while, you stop noticing even the most beautiful things. Such a shame we stop seeing.'

Lucy walked back into the sitting room, murmuring something about Fairtrade and shade-grown Arabica beans. John hardly heard her; he was too preoccupied.

Two minutes later, the aroma of freshly ground coffee wafted through. He could hear noises from the kitchen, so he turned towards the door into Lucy's sitting room. Her peach-coloured dress was thrown casually over one of the armchairs, her four-inch heels abandoned on the floor.

He turned into the kitchen to find Lucy standing, her back to him. He paused at the door, admiring her, and her lack of inhibition.

She turned. 'Come on in.'

'That could have two meanings,' he replied.

'You should decide what it means.'

Here she is – every last inch – all woman – willing and wanting.

He took her in his arms, her vulnerability inciting his strongest protective instincts.

Wake up, Baxter. She is but a dream; why does this sensuously unselfconscious goddess give herself so freely?

'Are these the rower's arms holding me so tight?' she said.

'Let's just say – they're strong enough to hold you for as long as I want.'

'And how long would that be?'

'Suppose I don't ever want to let you go?'

She reached up on tiptoes to kiss him – lingering, longing.

'Yes, John – here – in the kitchen.'

10

Lucy and John spent the day in bed, sometimes chatting, mostly sleeping. She had never been this happy merely to be with a man.

He is dreamy – why couldn't we have met at Oxford?

Lucy found herself recalling her days at university. How vulnerable she'd felt when she first arrived, only just seventeen. How the men stared at her. How the women in her year group, all two years older, struggled with her presence.

More than twenty-five years on, she knew she could only have offered John Baxter the girl she was, not the woman she'd become. She wondered how many women would now judge her harshly. Would they regard her as old-fashioned?

31

She wondered how many privately shared her longings for a stronger man, even if they could never admit it.

She didn't care now; she was confident of her place in the world, of the value she added to friends, to her children. In her legal capacity, she was one of only a small handful of people worldwide who could negotiate in so many different languages. Why had this confidence taken so long to arrive?

John empowered a clarity and a confidence in herself. She felt so strong with him; she could do and be whatever she wanted. He understood her needs, without judgement. She was wrapping the most intimate, profound gift to him – the unequivocal gift of all of herself and anything he wanted of her.

It was something she had chosen to offer, without it being demanded of her. It came from the strength acquired from contented self-acceptance, from her feelings for him – and from the chromosomal need only he ignited in her.

As afternoon turned to evening, she asked if he was hungry. 'Ravenous.'

'This calls for the Fire Stables then.'

He looked at her quizzically. 'Ms Howard?'

'The Fire Stables,' she repeated. 'It's a restaurant just over there, in Church Road. I'll see if we can get a booking. But we do have to talk about my name.'

'What's on your mind?'

She sat down on the bed beside him. 'After Tim died, all my financial affairs stayed in the name Howard; it made it less complicated while we enacted Tim's will.'

'What do you mean?' John asked.

'Tim was the only child of Lord and Lady Howard. Tim's will was "all to wife". The cousins had to listen to the lawyers read out what they'd feared – that the house and estate had all been left to me. They told me on the spot they would challenge the will.

'Tim's parents were already deceased, so the only legitimate heirs were male cousins, not yet of majority age. So, under the terms of the will, priority had been given to the wife of Tim Howard, Lord Hathersham.'

'You.'

'Yes, me.'

'So I've been bedding Lady Hathersham? I feel like the woodman in *Lady Chatterley's Lover*.'

Lucy giggled. 'For the record – I love what you do in my woodshed.'

John smiled.

'Anyway, I resolved the issue over the house and title quite easily,' she continued.

'How so?'

'Well, Tim knew I had no desire to take the estate from his family. But to make it easier for me, he left it all to me initially. That way I was in the strongest possible negotiating position.

'I parted with the title and the estate in return for three items that were already legally mine, under the terms of the will. One was a painting. The other two were the house in Boston and the little place in SW1.

'I deliberately chose non-cash items that were not important to the family. Their fear was that I'd turn the estate into an animal park. When they discovered I had no such intention, they were so relieved they agreed to my wishes. I'd gone into the meeting as prepared as they were unprepared. The cousins had never been to Boston. And they thought the painting was a copy.'

'What's the painting?' John asked.

Lucy stood away from the bed, naked, her arms outstretched, as if to encourage a search of the walls. The paintings were exquisite originals of tigers by David Shepherd and Alan Hunt – but not what Lucy meant to show him.

Then he noticed an archway off the bedroom. Lucy took him through the doorway into a large dressing room. Once inside, John looked to his right. She waited for his reaction …

11

John Baxter stood speechless, admiring the six-foot canvas. He looked at Lucy in disbelief, then back at the painting he had last seen in the Harvard Art Museum in Cambridge, Massachusetts, fifteen years ago.

'You own *The Piazza San Marco*? This is one of the most prized Canalettos in the *world*. You better not tell the Italians.'

'They already know. Come on – I'll tell you over supper.'

He continued to gaze at the iconic Canaletto, the classic view over St Mark's Square in Venice towards the Basilica di San Marco.

John knew what made art good – subtle colours, patient and intricate detail, lack of compromise on every aspect of its composition. But what made a piece of art great was that intangible quality that would demand respect for all time. This canvas had it all. He was lost in admiration – for the painting, and Lucy for acquiring it.

While John admired *The Piazza San Marco*, Lucy donned a pair of heels. Wearing nothing else, she approached her mirror wardrobe, slid the door open and selected a tiny cocktail dress.

John felt enveloped in beauty – only feet from one of the world's most respected paintings, yet close enough to touch its gorgeous owner. He wanted to savour the moment. 'Don't move, Lucy.'

The little dress she had selected, she draped over a chair. They stood rooted, his eyes gorging alternately on Lucy and the painting. Now he knew she was the woman in his recurrent dream. He kissed her as if repossessing a long-lost soulmate.

Lucy tore her lips from his. 'We'd better be quick, then. The booking is for ten minutes and it'll take us at least a minute to get there.'

She grabbed her dress and led him from the room. As they left, he noticed the door that slid over the entrance archway along the inside of the dressing room wall. The steel of the door was fully four inches thick.

'You keep it safe, then.'

Lucy tapped a combination into a keypad on the wall by the bed. They watched the door close and witnessed the reassuring sound of huge steel bolts locking into the door frame.

She lay back on the bed.

'I'll explain later,' she said. 'One door shuts, another one opens.'

Fifteen minutes later they walked over to the Fire Stables. A waitress suggested they took a seat on one of the sofas while she cleared a table.

'This could get to be a habit,' Lucy said.

John was curious. 'Tell me about the secure room and how you obtained the painting in the box.'

'The walls, floor and ceiling are all eighteen inches of reinforced concrete. I call it my strongbox. There's air filtration to eliminate incoming poisonous gases and viruses and spores. There's secure electricity and phone cabling and TV and internet. It enters the box in special steel casing, wrapped in a lead outer liner, embedded in the concrete.

'The separate electricity supply has its own fuse box and connection inside the strongbox itself. So even if an intruder finds the house fuses, the electricity supply to the strongbox can't be disconnected.

'With the food and water provisions I could live in there with the boys for three months, if I had to. I only moved the painting here when it was all finished and nobody would know the contents.'

'Were you building it to protect the painting or yourselves?' John asked.

'To answer that, I'd need to tell you how I got my scar ... and I don't think I'm ready quite yet ... is that OK?'

John hesitated. 'I'm sorry, I didn't mean to pry. It's obviously a painful memory.'

How could anyone want to harm this angel? Whatever it was must have been horrendous.

'There's a lot more violence in the Black family than ever comes to light. Sometime, I'll tell you what Old Man

36

Black did to his senior officer to get dishonourably discharged from the US Army – and how Jack Black got his nickname "Skull-Cruncher".'

John winced. 'Wow.'

Lucy took a sip of her wine. 'And then there was the divorce settlement meeting. I was surrounded by the three most vicious and impulsive people I've ever come across. Let's just say it has given Billy five million reasons to hate me.'

John was pensive. 'Gotcha.'

'And don't forget – these are people prepared to ruin beautiful tracts of Montana and Wyoming in order to sell filthy fossil fuels which then ruin our atmosphere – double whammy.

'So now you can see the other reasons for the strongbox – Old Man Black and his vicious daughter, Kelly – and Billy – and Jack, the Skull-Cruncher. I had to feel I could protect us all.'

They ambled back across the road from the restaurant. John put his arm around her waist.

How do we possibly make this work? She lives most of her time in America. Whatever it takes, I will protect this angel. I only hope I'm worthy of the task. Got to find out about the little man who shot at me?

Lucy opened her front door. They climbed the stairs and fell into bed.

'I don't even know where you were born,' John asked.

'Putney,' she murmured.

'So was I,' he replied. But Lucy was already asleep.

As he drifted off to sleep, John remembered his recurring dream … a tall blonde woman, draped in white, the see-through gauze, beckoning, communicating wordlessly.

'The woman stands before you, a yearning in her eyes.
Possess me, John, I beg you, our dreams to realise.'

12

Monday – 1st October

Lucy woke early, still slightly jet-lagged. As her eyes adjusted to the darkness, she looked across at her lover sleeping peacefully.

She knew his feelings for her were as powerful as her own for him. She felt complete; free to be the woman she had always known existed, free to be honest with herself and with him without fear of judgement; free to express her feelings as and when she needed. She could be his sensual seductress, whatever he wanted – so long as she was *his*.

John was stirring and she left the bed to percolate some coffee. When she returned to the bedroom, he was awake.

'That smells great,' he said.

'John, I was hoping we could talk about the copy painting my client's been given.'

'Well – it *is* the reason for your trip. And you've not been to my place yet.'

'Let's go today,' she grinned. 'Who knows, there may even be some decent art on the walls.'

'Let's go after breakfast. Don't I remember a sandwich shop on the high street?'

'You do. We have every brand of coffee shop in the Village,' she replied.

Lucy zipped up a very tight pair of stretch jeans which showed her long legs exquisitely. Her white T-shirt pulled taut over her chest, she tucked neatly into the faded blue denim.

'Will I do?' she asked.

'The word "ample" doesn't come close,' he grinned. 'But, yes, you'll definitely "do".'

She smiled as she brushed on the final touches of some blue eyeshadow. She looked in the mirror at him. She could see his fascination as she parted her lips to apply the pink lipstick she knew set off her blonde hair.

'Lucy – before we go, do you mind if I take another look at the pictures downstairs? There's something bothering me.'

A minute later they were in her dining room. He looked again at the one on the floor. Then, habit made him turn it to look at the back.

'That's odd. Have you ever noticed this?'

The canvas was double-sided, a paintable surface on each side. The reverse side of the painting had brown oil paint washed over it.

'Look. It's got some paint missing in this top left corner,' John said. 'There's different paint underneath. And look at this …'

On the bottom of the frame, written in a dark-blue ink, were the words:

Ill health? Cocoa, all mixed up and covered with cream

Lucy's face lit up. 'That's Mary Black's writing. She sends the kids presents in the post.'

39

'You said she gave this to you. It's very good. Did she tell you anything about it?'

'Not really. She kept saying that I should never get rid of it.'

'Lucy, this is a crossword clue. The words "all mixed up" tell you it's an anagram.'

'Let's write it down so we can solve it over breakfast.'

As they left Lucy's house, John put his arm round her. She smiled up at him.

If only you knew how good it feels to be in your arms. Can you possibly know how completely you have taken my heart, Mr Baxter?

She placed his hand into the denim pocket on her bottom.

They turned left out of the close onto Church Road, turning left again into the Wimbledon Village high street almost immediately.

'This'll do,' Lucy said, as she led him into her favourite sandwich shop. 'I love the atmosphere in here; the photos of the players all over the walls; the olde world decorations, straight out of a 1930s Agatha Christie novel. I love this picture of Steffi with Martina.'

'Have you ever been here in Wimbledon fortnight?' John asked.

'What, in the village, or in this particular shop?'

'Either,' he replied. 'Normally the players are looking for anywhere they can eat during the Championships, especially as the Club is just down the hill.'

'Funny you say that. I was in here in June this year. Andy was sitting over there in the corner with Boris. Little did we know that a week later Andy was going to be in the final.'

Lucy paused. 'You do seem to have an appetite for this, Mr Baxter.'

'Three, sweetheart,' he muttered, as he pondered the clue.

'Now *that* is significant.'

He kissed her. 'What?'

'This is the first time you've called me "sweetheart" – and why three, anyway?' she said.

'Appetites? One for solving the puzzle, one for breakfast, and the biggest of all three – the insatiable one I have for you.'

She giggled. *How long has it been since I've laughed with a man?*

She kissed him on the cheek. 'In view of where we are, let's concentrate on the first two, shall we?'

The waiter asked how they took their coffee. John looked up at him. 'Black as night, strong as death and sweet as love.' The waiter smiled as he retreated.

'Very poetic this morning,' Lucy said.

'We have to mix up the letters: *Ill health Cocoa.* The best anagrams give you a clue from the words themselves. If this anagram is one of the better ones, then the clue's in front of us, actually in the words we can see.'

He paused for a moment. 'Come on, Lucy. With all your languages, you should be good at wordplay.'

She knew from the grin on his face, where his use of words was intended to lead. How could she not – after the way he had taken so long making love to her last night? She decided to indulge him.

'If I was half as good at wordplay as you are at …' She cut herself short, looking around her. She lowered her voice to a whisper. 'I'd have got there already.'

He smiled at his lover. 'It takes two.'

'OK, then, Mr B. On your premise, let's take *health* – or even *Ill health* – or *Cocoa*. What can we make from that?'

He picked up a paper napkin and wrote the letters at random all over the napkin.

'Isn't cocoa supposed to have medicinal properties? The ancient Mayans took it for extra strength,' Lucy ventured. 'Perhaps the reference to ill health is linked to cocoa as a cure.'

Lucy suddenly sat up straight.

'John, we have to consider the anagram and the picture at the same time. It's a peak, probably in New England, if the painting was done in one of those schools.'

'Well, the word "hill" can be made from these letters,' he suggested. They looked at the letters again for a few seconds ...

'A Chocolate Hill,' they blurted, at the same time. Several people in the restaurant were now staring. John apologised to the next table – then turned back to Lucy.

'Lucy, if it's the Mount ...'

She looked at him, puzzled.

'The missing one Frank Cropsey was supposed to have painted – one of the two I've been looking for – Mount Chocorua, in New England, in winter. Apart from that one, there's never been a single painting of Mount Chocorua ever credited to Cropsey – even though he spent lots of time there. It was painted in 1858, along with Spring and Summer. But no one's ever found it.'

Her face lit up. 'Covered in cream – a snow-capped mountain – winter. It all fits.'

He nodded. 'Lucy, if you have *Mount Chocorua in Winter* ...'

'We'd better find out before we get too carried away,' Lucy said. 'And you said Mrs Markham had one stolen.'

'Absolutely – the irony – after all these years of searching for it in North America, I find it in England, almost on my doorstep.'

He waved for the bill. They gulped their remaining coffee. John thrust a ten-pound note at the waiter as they rushed out. 'The coffee was great,' John said.

Two minutes later Lucy unlocked her front door.

They stood. Admiring the painting. John turned it round to look more closely at the section of paint missing in the top corner.

'What do you feel about having this taken out of the frame and having the brown layer removed?'

'It's been in the dark all these years. It's not as if it's a family heirloom … let's do it.'

'Let's get it over to my old gallery. And let's hope lots of time elapsed between the painting of the two different layers.'

Lucy was curious. 'Why so?'

'Because if the layers are of the same material, and they went on in the same four or five years, they could have done some merging. The top layer of the first coat could have mixed slightly with the bottom layer of the second coat. That makes it impossible to take off the top layer without ruining the base layer – unless there's a coat of varnish in between, in which case the two layers of paint would never have come in contact.'

Lucy was thinking. 'How can we find out?'

'The gallery will take minute samples in this corner without damaging the rest of the painting. They have their own analytical equipment – they'll get an answer in minutes.'

John added, 'If the worst comes to the worst, you still have a very good autumn landscape on the front of the canvas that we can get cleaned and put back in the frame.'

John dialled the National Gallery, but had to leave a message.

'So, when do I get to see your place, Mr Baxter?'

'Why don't we go now? But let me look at *The Piazza* again, before we go.'

They climbed the stairs and entered Lucy's dressing room.

'Girl done good – girl done very good,' John said.

They exited the strongbox. Lucy walked to the bed and sat down. She entered a six-digit code into the keypad on the wall. As the door slid tightly shut, it occurred to Lucy that the painting of Mount Chocorua might need protecting as much as *The Piazza*.

Could this be the reason we are being followed? Do the Blacks want the picture? What will they do to get it back?

13

Lucy smiled as John opened the passenger door of his Jaguar for her.

You must be one of the few gentlemen left in England.

'It's a pity you won't meet Charlotte and Emma,' John said.

'That's a shame.'

'They went to Rome and Florence with their mother.'

'It'd be nice to meet them before I go back.'

Twenty minutes later, they approached Whitehills Close, just outside Esher. The heavy wrought-iron bars of the black gates were tipped in gold. John pressed a key fob and the gates to the private road slowly swung open. He trickled the car two hundred yards to the left-hand dog-leg in the road, then a further two hundred yards to the driveway of his home and a second set of gates.

Lucy looked up at the house. Its log cabin exterior was completed by the generous overhang of the Swiss chalet-style roof. Each of the horizontal beams of the exterior were at least a foot wide, giving the building a rugged, forest feel. On the front of the building, protruding from what Lucy guessed was the main bedroom, was a balcony made from wood that matched the rest of the exterior.

'You did say you liked skiing,' she smiled.

'It's the grey remote this time,' he apologised. 'You might know the code, actually. If I tell you it's the birthday of our favourite Giovanni, would that help?'

'Unfortunately not,' Lucy replied. 'But we're talking about Giovanni Antonio Canal, yes?'

'97-10-28 – his birthday in 1697.'

Lucy entered the digits and the dark-green sliding gate retracted. John drove in and tapped a few keys on the grey remote again for the garage doors to open. 'Another birthday?' she asked.

'Actually, it's the date Mother Teresa died – my way of re-membering a person who personifies two of the highest quali-ties: selflessness and modesty. Some believe the highest humans choose the moment of their death. If you were as modest as

Mother Teresa, which day would you choose to die – when fewest people would notice?'

'Go on, then.'

'The night before Diana's funeral – when the world was nearing its maximum grief, 5th September 1997. The *Times* newspaper gave Mother Teresa only fifty words … disgraceful, after that long and selfless life.

'I'm sorry about the security,' he said. 'Occasionally, I've been followed home from auctions. Living beyond the dog-leg in the road means you can't see the house from the entrance to the close.'

'Anyone might think you had some treasure to protect.'

John looked at her. 'I do. The log cabin appearance is deceptive. Actually, it's just a façade to the insulated concrete walls. It had to be made of concrete to take the weight of the door and window frames.'

'So you do have treasures to protect, then?' Lucy grinned.

'I couldn't get insurance, otherwise.'

The next few minutes should be interesting, Lucy.

Once inside the garage, John opened Lucy's door for her. Something seemed odd. The space was the width of a double garage, but from the outside it looked wide enough to accommodate at least three cars.

They emerged from the garage into the house and then into the hallway. There was one painting that seemed to stand out from the rest. Immediately, Lucy moved towards the wall opposite the front door.

'Another Canaletto. *Old Walton Bridge* – 1754. Look at those threatening clouds,' she offered. 'I don't think I've ever seen clouds painted that dark. Isn't that very near here?'

'Yes. Would you like to see it?'

'It can't still look like that?' Lucy asked.

'No, unfortunately. Now, it's a rusty old steel bridge they're about to replace. When the kids were little, we used to go there when I picked them up from school. They used to feed the ducks by the river.

'Actually, it was Charlotte who told me it was coming up for auction. She was thumbing through a Sotheby's sale catalogue I'd left around. She told me we absolutely *had* to have the picture. I told her it would cost at least a million pounds.'

'No problem then,' she said. 'And anyway, you can always sell it for two million in a few years. That is what you do, isn't it?'

'I had to laugh at her positivity, but I thought about it.'

'Well, what happened?' Lucy asked.

'I went to the auction – and waited for the two Italians who are my normal competition for the Canalettos. But they weren't there. I went upstairs to the gallery they convert to an auction room. When the Italian art came up, the bidding was quite subdued.'

'Why?'

'My main competition for the Italian art is a chap from the Galleria Nazionale d'Arte Antica, in Rome. The Italians are trying to retrieve their national treasures.'

'Like the Greeks and the Elgin Marbles,' Lucy suggested.

'Right. So I expected him to be there. But he wasn't. Nor was the private collector who collects Canalettos and Titians.

'The bidding started at the reserve of two hundred and fifty thousand pounds. There were only two of us bidding; I got it for only three hundred and one thousand. The kids were due back from school in a week, so I had it hung and lit immediately. You should've heard the squeals when Charlotte saw it.'

Lucy grinned. 'What happened to the buyers?'

'They were on the same flight from Rome. It was two hours late – and their luggage was delayed off the plane.'

'So here it is,' Lucy frowned.

'What's up?'

'I was just wondering how you knew the plane was late.'

'As I exited the gallery after the sale, I turned just in time to see a little guy taking my photo. He followed me. So I turned left, down New Bond Street, checked he was still following me, turned left onto Conduit Street, checked again, turned left onto Regent Street, left onto Oxford Street and then left onto New Bond Street again.'

'You mean back to where you started?' Lucy asked.

'Yes. That way I was sure he was following me. Anyway, I was hungry, so I went back into Sotheby's to have tea in their cafe. As I turned into the building, I got my phone ready. When he rounded the corner into the front entrance, I got a photo of him before he could turn away. I actually got a good look in his eyes – he has one brown eye and one green eye.'

'Creepy. What happened next?'

'He turned and left – so I had my cream tea.'

'You seem very calm about it.'

'He was only about five foot six. He didn't mind me seeing him – until I took the photo.'

'And this happened before we even met,' Lucy said. 'It's almost as if someone's trying to warn you. But I still don't understand how you knew the "galleria guy" had his flight delayed.'

'Well, the Sotheby's Cafe is about twenty yards into the building on the left. You walk past it to the stairs that take you up to the auction room; I knew I'd see the two Italians if they entered the building. They'd always been cautiously friendly whenever I'd seen them at galleries or auctions. But I waved at them and they approached me. The auction was long over, so I asked them if I could treat them to a cream tea. It was then I found out about their flight.

'It's odd. You see people several times as competitors. But when I chatted to them, they were not the aloof academics I'd always believed; they were really friendly – and art was far from the only thing we talked about.' John paused.

'What is it?'

'Well – two things. Domenico asked for my home address. He said – when I get an envelope from Italy, it will be the most important letter I will ever receive in my life.

'I next met Benito – he's the one collecting for the Italian National Gallery – at an auction in Paris a couple of months later. He told me that Domenico had been killed by a car.'

Lucy frowned. *Surely, this couldn't be Jack Black again – could it?*

'It's such a terrible waste. It takes a lifetime to build up his depth of knowledge, knowledge that will die with him. It's very sad; he seemed kind ... you could tell from the way he spoke to the waitress.

'But there was something else when I met Benito,' John continued. 'He told me that Domenico had a theory about Menkaure's pyramid on the Giza Plateau and would share this information through his solicitor.

'Anyway, would you like to see the spot in Walton this particular picture was painted from?' John said.

'Aren't you going to show me the rest of the house?' Lucy asked.

He took her hand and led her into his living room. Lucy guessed the room to be more than forty feet in both directions.

Impressive. He has managed to make a large room feel cosy.

The room was dominated by an impressive grey stone fireplace, which offset perfectly the semi-circular grey soft-leather sofa that faced it. On each side of the fireplace were two huge candles, four inches thick, each one mounted in its own four-foot-tall candlestick. The lush deep-pile cream-coloured carpet added the warmth that made Lucy feel at home.

Lucy smiled at her next thought.

The perfect place for you to make love to me – in front of the fire – in the candlelight – champagne and strawberries and dark chocolate.

Her eyes were drawn immediately to the summer landscape by Frank Cropsey, given to him by Mrs Markham. Measuring six feet wide and four feet tall, the painting would have dominated a smaller room. In the classical composition format, an eggshell-blue sky nestled the single peak one third the way across the canvas. In the foreground were three horses, their heads lowered to drink from a stream. Cropsey had captured the remote tranquillity of the scene beautifully.

'It's absolutely gorgeous. Now I see why you want to complete the set so much,' Lucy said.

'Yes, but have you noticed how similar the style is to your autumn landscape?'

She nodded. 'And what other treasures have we here,' she said, as she walked over to the wall to the left of the fireplace. 'So – you have Venice too.'

Lucy looked round at John. She turned again to look at the painting by Thomas Moran – *Sunset Venice*. Then she glanced to the right of the fireplace. *Sunset in the Rockies*. Two sunsets. Perfect together in this room. 'I imagine these large red-orange sunsets look absolutely stunning when you have the same colours of a log fire burning here in the winter.'

He walked up behind her, enveloping her body.

The irony made Lucy smile – his arms were far too powerful to escape. And now that he had her wrapped in them, she had no wish even to try. He kissed her neck gently as she continued to gaze at the atmospheric sunset of Venice.

'Did you ever do any painting yourself?' Lucy asked.

'Only a little at school. I had the daily humiliation of being in a class of people who had talent, which I decidedly did not.'

Lucy spotted John's rowing machine in the gym beyond the living room. 'Do you ever get out on the water?' she asked.

'Not anymore.' He held her. 'Ms Howard, it's time you saw the bedroom.'

Why do I get the feeling this is going to be significant?

He held her hand up the stairs and into the bedroom. Lucy's gaze was drawn to the painting of a woman hung above the bed. She stood rooted, imagining herself in the woman's place. Her heart quickened.

Not for the first time in John's presence, she was aware of a longing not satisfied since her very last day at Oxford. Her kiss left him in no doubt of her approval.

14

Tuesday – 2nd October

John looked across at Lucy, her hair spread over the pillow. He studied the scar on her face. He wondered how it had happened and what it said about the Blacks. It had not put her off men – if her appetites for him were any indication.

He adored her mannerisms, her mischief, her sense of humour, her exceptional intelligence, her extreme femininity – and the way they locked eyes in their most intimate moments.

He sat up on the edge of the bed to dial the National Gallery again and was offered an appointment at ten on Friday. If he and Lucy had solved Mary Black's clue correctly, they had found the first of two paintings he needed for Mrs Markham's four-season set.

John's voice had woken Lucy; he could feel the warmth of her hand on his back.

'Good morning, sleepy,' he said.

'It is a good morning, as you mention it,' she replied. 'Or it was a hundred and forty-three years ago,' she grinned. 'You're into birthdays, John. Here's a clue. He was a lawyer who used his legal brain then his huge moral courage to make a lasting difference to humanity.'

'Well, when you put it like that, I'd have to say Mahatma Gandhi,' John replied.

Lucy smiled. 'On the 2nd of October I always remember him; he's my favourite lawyer, an example to us all.'

On Friday morning, Trafalgar Square was bathed in sunshine. John took Lucy's hand as they stood at the foot of Nelson's column. They admired the National Gallery, its imposing width dominating the square. Recent rain had left small fresh pools of water dotted across the concourse – as if cleansing the square of the past. Tourists fed the pigeons and climbed on the great bronze lions. As lovers took selfies, John wondered if any of the carefree visitors enjoying the sunshine knew or cared about the history of Lord Nelson.

John and Lucy approached the gallery from the rear to go through the door he had used more than twenty years ago. As John held the door open for Lucy it seemed he was opening the door to his world, a world he had never shared so profoundly with anyone.

He smiled – and kissed her.

'What?' she enquired.

'Oh, nothing. Nothing more important than the fact that I'm head over heels in love with the brightest, most giving, sexiest thing on legs.'

Lucy kissed him. 'Come on; we're here on a mission.'

John grinned. 'And you think talk about "coming" – and "missions" – will take my mind off your legs?'

'You're insatiable … thank god,' she retorted.

He put his arm around her as they started down a long corridor.

'Is that the "Oh my god" you appealed to repeatedly last night, sweetheart?'

Lucy giggled. 'That's below the belt.'

'As I remember from last night, that's exactly where your god seemed to reside.'

Lucy shook her head, smirking.

They walked a few steps more. John's mind returned to the reason for today's trip.

'If this painting is Cropsey's Winter, have you thought about selling it to me?'

If this is Cropsey's Winter, I'll donate it to the cause. Don't forget – I've never really had the painting anyway, as I've never seen it.'

'Maybe I take you to the Bahamas for a couple of weeks,' he replied.

She kissed him. 'Right now, you could take me anywhere. But the Bahamas does sound good after the caseload we've had recently.'

They were greeted by a woman in her mid-forties. The heavy black frames of her glasses made her look severe, an effect not helped by her thick black hair.

'Mr Baxter, this is an honour. I'm Vanessa Thompson,' she said, handing them both a business card. 'You are John and Lucy Baxter?'

Lucy looked at John, her puzzled frown yielding to a grin.

'Actually, we're not married,' he smiled at Vanessa.

'I'm so sorry,' Vanessa said.

'No worries,' John replied. 'But talking names – when I worked here twenty years ago I learnt the restoration business from Dr Gary Thompson. Any relation?'

'He's my father,' Vanessa replied. 'But he's retired now.'

'So,' John replied, 'I'm the one who should feel honoured; your father is revered all over the art world.' He looked at her card. 'Where did you do your PhD?'

'Oxford – Somerville, in fact.'

'In that case, I ought to leave you Somerville brains to catch up,' John said, grinning.

Vanessa looked at Lucy. 'Really?'

'I read law – guilty as charged,' Lucy said.

'At Somerville?'

'Still guilty,' Lucy replied, smiling.

Vanessa studied Lucy's face more closely. 'Boff – The Mona Lisa! You're the one who caused all the rumpus when you got to Oxford.'

Lucy blushed. Vanessa looked at John. 'The Mona Lisa was the youngest ever scholar to enter Oxford. You must have heard about her, Mr Baxter? She was a legend, almost from the day she went up. She was nicknamed Isis – and The Mona Lisa – amongst other things.'

'Lucy, you never mentioned all that.'

'You never asked.'

Vanessa recalled, 'If the rumours are correct, you spoke seven languages fluently when you arrived at Oxford – at the age of only seventeen – and nine when you left, including Mandarin.'

'Why Mona Lisa and Isis?' John asked. 'And why Boff?'

'Later, John. Vanessa's busy.'

Vanessa pursed her lips, suppressing a smile. John detected a flicker of amusement between the two women.

Vanessa interrupted his thoughts. 'It's such a shame; I have another appointment at eleven. Perhaps we could catch up sometime soon. Would you like to follow me?'

Dr Thompson led them through to the Restoration Laboratory. Around the perimeter of the room were various futuristic machines, some with digital displays, some humming.

John looked upwards. In the middle of the fifteen-foot-high ceiling were the words *Michelangelo era qui*, in four-inch-tall, cobalt-blue characters. Lucy followed John's gaze upwards.

'So, Michelangelo *was* here! There's obviously a higher calibre of graffiti in a place like this,' she said.

He smiled. 'We have to suspend our disbelief a little. For Michelangelo to have been here, he'd have needed to be three hundred and fifty years old. This place was only built in 1824.'

Vanessa looked up. 'We left it there – it's a kind of reminder of why we come to work, what it's all for. We have no idea who put it there, but we kind of like it.'

Lucy took a photo, smiled and whispered into John's ear. 'I know who put it there.'

'It's changed a fair bit; the layout's all different,' John said, changing the subject.

He took Lucy's painting out of its box and laid it brown side upwards.

'We need to see what's underneath this brown layer.'

Vanessa removed the six-foot canvas from its frame. She pulled the overhead camera to three feet above the centre of the painting. Looking at a screen offset to her right, she clicked the mouse to take a digital photo. She moved the camera above each of the four corners, taking a photo each time. Finally, she positioned the camera to within a foot of the upper right-hand corner to take a closer image.

'With the basics out of the way, we can do a bit of investigating. Have you any idea what's covered?' Vanessa asked.

'We have an idea it's a Cropsey.'

'So – let's take a look.'

She swung the camera out of the way and brought in the overhead microscope to replace it. Adjusting its position using the screen once more, she focussed in on the top right corner very closely.

'This section is where we work initially; it's hidden by the frame anyway.'

Using what looked like a dentist's metal pick, she took minute samples of the top layer of brown paint and tiny samples of the layer that had been slightly exposed by a very small scratch. She passed the samples to her assistant, Sophie, who put a couple of drops of a clear liquid onto each sample separately.

'Do you need the painting on the reverse dated?' Vanessa asked.

'If you could,' John replied.

Vanessa turned the canvas over and took another sample from the very top corner. 'As you've seen, we take samples so small you can only just see them with the naked eye. It's all possible now we have the digital microscopes.'

Sophie inserted the sample dishes into a machine that hummed slightly.

'The paint-dater has completely revolutionised our work. My father developed it,' Vanessa said, as she read the labels her assistant had attached to the sides of each dish.

'The brown wash is the most recent. About 1986. The layer of varnish underneath it is mid-1850s. Ditto the painting underneath. And the picture of autumn on the other side is 1880s.'

'How much margin of error is there in those dates?' John asked her.

'It's to within a year on recent samples, but to within three to five years on samples from the 1800s,' Vanessa replied.

'How can you be so precise?' Lucy asked.

'The Stereo Binocular Microscope allows us to see depth, whereas previously we couldn't see how deep we were digging for samples. This is particularly useful when you have paint that went on in different layers – and a hundred and fifty years apart. Only six of these machines exist – so you came to the right place. So, on this canvas done in the 1880s, there is no way it could've been done within twenty years of the one done in the 1850s on the other side.'

'Brilliant,' John replied. 'It's time Lucy told you our intentions.'

'We have nothing to lose. If we don't try, the painting will never see daylight. If it's a Cropsey, his signature is normally two inches in from the right and two inches up from the bottom.'

'We would never start where it's most important,' Vanessa replied. 'Before going onto the important patches, we start somewhere else – to see how easily the brown comes away, and how delicate we need to be to preserve the paint. If we go too strong we could compromise the signature. So we start very gently – and away from the important parts. In this case, it should be relatively easy since the layers are oil over varnish. That's most unusual, by the way – almost as if the person applying the brown layer knew it would be easy to remove without damaging the varnish layer or the oil painting under that.'

Sophie approached the group, looking at Vanessa.

'Your eleven o'clock has postponed till next week,' she said.

Vanessa Thompson looked at the couple.

'Why don't I show you what to do. We'll see what pressure to use. Then, while I sort out a couple of admin things, you can continue to clean the painting. Anyone up for that?'

Lucy put her hand up.

'OK. A cleaning job for you then, after all those years of study,' Vanessa smiled.

Vanessa emptied a small vessel of acetone into a wider beaker and added an equal volume of water to it. She said this was to ensure the initial solution was not too strong. She dipped a cotton bud into the beaker of acetone and applied it to the canvas in a rolling motion. As she rolled the head of the bud across the extreme upper right, the brown paint came off easily. She took a fresh bud and repeated the motion, applying slightly more pressure.

'I'm just seeing how much pressure I can use. The brown looks to be coming off quite easily so far. But notice – I'm not rubbing; I'm rolling the bud across the surface to see how much comes off.'

She took a third bud and eased off more of the brown paint. Pinching a small piece of white cotton cloth with a pair of tweezers, she dampened an area of the painting about one inch square.

'If you dampen an area in advance, it makes it easier ten minutes later to take the paint away. But so far, so good. And don't worry about the cotton buds; each restorer here uses about a hundred tubs every week.'

Lucy sat at Vanessa's stool and repeated the procedure a few times. Vanessa seemed happy.

'Let me have a look through the microscope,' she intervened. 'Just have to make sure we're not damaging the varnish underneath, before we do too much.'

She peered into the twin glasses of the stereoscope for a few seconds. 'Seems fine. Now you continue for what should be no more than eighty hours and two hundred tubs of buds – and you'll be good.'

Lucy frowned her disbelief.

'And when we've done that, we have to do the same thing all over again to remove the varnish covering the oil. It's the varnish layer that takes the real time.'

Vanessa could see the incredulity on Lucy's face. 'But I'll be back in fifteen minutes to save you from all that,' she said, grinning. 'Have fun.'

Vanessa walked out of the lab. Lucy looked up at John, stood behind her.

'Whatever they're paid, it's not enough,' she winced.

'It's enough – believe me. You pay a fortune for this – but then, having done the job for two years, I can tell you it takes ages.'

Lucy looked around her. 'It all seems very modern in here – all the latest equipment and everything. I wonder what this microscope cost, if there are only six in the world.'

'Yes, I wonder. They had a benefactor who donated two and a half million pounds a few years back. They completely rebuilt and re-equipped the lab.'

Lucy dipped a cotton bud into the acetone. She worked in silence for a few minutes, edging towards the area she and John knew might reveal the signature. John took the chance to explore the laboratory. He looked across at Lucy, on the other side of the lab. 'This paint-dater is a carbon-dating machine.

All paint contains an organic element, even if only in traces. This dates the carbon in those traces – fascinating.'

'Ah,' Lucy said. 'If you want fascinating, get over here.'

Lucy had revealed the characters *y '58* in the lower right-hand corner of the canvas.

Lucy continued cleaning, a little to the left of the letter 'y' she had uncovered. A minute later she had revealed the letter 'e'. She looked up at John.

'Could still be a "Copley",' he said. 'He painted in the 1850s too.'

'Clever clogs,' Lucy frowned. 'Still – we won't have long to wait. The next letter is either an 'l' or an 's'. She continued rolling cotton buds across the canvas. A few minutes later she uncovered an 's'.

'Now who's the clever one,' he said.

'I take it you've found something,' Vanessa said, re-entering the lab.

Dr Thompson could see immediately what had been revealed. She positioned the microscope to discover if any of the oil beneath had been damaged. 'It seems you've done a great job.'

'I have to hand it to you, even doing this tiny fraction, I can appreciate the patience you need,' Lucy said.

'Well – the tricky bit is not the removal of the brown layer; the more skilled process is taking off the varnish layer. If the owner smoked, the varnish becomes yellow. We have to remove the whole varnish layer before re-protecting it again.'

'So, you think this varnish layer will have to come off?' Lucy asked.

Vanessa smiled. 'Definitely. When I looked at it closely, I could see the yellow; I knew the colours underneath would come alive if we removed it. You might be amazed when you see the difference. Artists varnished their work precisely so the protective varnish could be replaced.'

'So, you knew the varnish would protect the painting from any mistakes I made?'

Vanessa smiled. 'You didn't think I'd trust a beginner with a Cropsey, if there'd been no varnish to protect it?'

Lucy entrusted her Cropsey to Vanessa's team for cleaning. As they made their farewells, Vanessa suggested they all met up sometime for a glass of wine.

'Let's go through to the Gallery, John; we're not here very often.'

'In that case, it's a different door,' John said, as he led Lucy from the restoration lab. John ushered Lucy through the door ahead of him. As she turned slightly, her eye was caught by a plaque above the outside of the door. It read: *The Baxter Laboratory*.

'Is that you?' Lucy asked.

'Guilty as charged.'

Lucy shook her head in mock disapproval.

'You gonna tell me why they call you The Mona Lisa? Or Isis for that matter? Or Boff?'

'To the first question, all I would say is you're the art expert, Mr Baxter. To the second I would say you're the Egyptologist, not me. To the third, I would say that you have the disadvantage of being a man.

'I'm sure you'll figure them all out. Anyway, you have two weeks in the Bahamas to bring a half-smile to my face.'

15

Sunday – 7th October

Tiny waves were gently lapping the shoreline. Of only two hotels on this remote island in the Bahamas, John had chosen the one with old-world colonial charm. The honeymoon apartment was the largest in the hotel, comprising vast bathroom, separate dressing room and forty-foot-wide bedroom. The waist-high wood panelling was painted mushroom white; the dark-blue-and-mushroom-striped curtains matched the bedspread. Two sofas and two separate armchairs created a homely feel, and a large writing desk had been placed beneath a six-foot-wide mirror. Adorning the coffee table was a huge arrangement of flowers in Lucy's favourite combination of pinks and blues.

Their first-floor suite faced east, directly overlooking the turquoise expanse of the Atlantic. Beneath their balcony, an expanse of lush green grass, elevated twenty feet above the beach, was fringed with palm trees and a generous display of pink and purple bougainvillea. From the lawn, a stone stairway descended to the beach, its pink sand visible through the shrubbery.

Lucy and John gazed down in silence. He put his arm around her waist as they took in the scene. Lucy was the first to speak. 'Wow ... I've done some research. Apparently, the beach is tiny particles of coral, ground to a very fine, faintly pink powder by five million years of Atlantic waves.

'It's gorgeous; I love it.' *Boy done good, boy done very good.* 'Can you smell the flowers? Aren't they glorious?'

This island paradise is so romantic – perfect for the retreat we need from the real world.

They went back into the room. John took the bottle of Laurent-Perrier pink champagne from the ice bucket; it was her favourite. He opened it, poured two generous glasses, put one on the writing desk near Lucy and sat on the sofa nearest to her.

'The flowers and the champagne,' she smiled. 'They're perfect – thank you.'

Lucy wanted to look her best for their first meal in the hotel. She was using the writing desk as a dressing table and had spilled some tubes and tiny tubs from her make-up bag onto it. She knew how much he enjoyed watching her put on her face.

'You hungry, sweetheart? You look gorgeous, by the way.'

Lucy was putting the last touches to her mascara. 'I'm still naked, silly,' she replied.

'Exactly.'

Lucy giggled.

'I hope you like the little something I'm going to wear,' she said.

She watched as he approached her.

He bent down to kiss her neck.

Can you possibly know what that does to me?

Lucy felt tears coming.

'What's the matter, sweetheart?'

'I worried about my face – and you – you take me, scar and everything.'

64

'You're far more interesting for your battle scars – the woman is far sexier than the girl.'

He paused.

'What?' she asked.

'Actually, it's a real turn-on; it shows strength – you've come through whatever he did and survived – strong and proud. That strength is very sexy.'

Lucy stood up and fixed her mouth firmly to his. She could feel her very being merging with his own. But today the process felt more complete – she was dissolving into his desire for her – a passion so powerful it was intoxicating.

Can you really be this strong and this sensitive at the same time? Are you for real? Pinch yourself, Lucy.

She sighed. 'I have a little job for you I think you'll enjoy,' she said.

'Oh?'

'This little dress is halter neck. If you stand behind me while I hold my hair out of the way, you can nestle me into the halters – then tie them at the back of my neck. Do you think you could do that?'

'I do,' he said.

Lucy smiled at him in the mirror – and wondered how deliberately he had chosen those two words.

'Then follow me.' Lucy picked up the dress and took hold of his hand. She led him out onto the balcony, checking no one was on the lawn below. She put her dress on the coffee table and turned towards the gentle evening breeze coming off the sea. She lifted her arms above her head – allowing overly familiar fingers of cool air to explore as they wished.

65

John grinned as Lucy enjoyed her bliss. She looked at him. 'The breeze can't have all the fun. It's time to nestle me in. But I need the job done … manfully.'

They woke before dawn. Lucy had always wanted to swim as the sun rose out of the sea. In dim light, they walked along the beach, admiring the few houses overlooking the sea, elevated on top of the dunes. The occasional tree extended long, swooping boughs over the pink sand, their large, waxy green leaves gently wafting in the slightest early morning breeze. A hundred yards past the last house, they stopped to look out over the sea.

They were alone.

She held his hand as they walked across the cool, pink, powder-fine sand to within fifteen feet of the waterline. She loved the feel of his strong hands gently pushing the robe from her shoulders.

Lucy treasured these moments of vulnerability; from their first night, she had loved being naked while he was clothed. It was her total surrender – her unconditional gift to him, to his masculinity, an act of love.

She knew what it meant for him too; he loved the trust she was showing him with this gift of her body. It magnified an already powerful need he had to protect her. His kiss was longing, urgent. She responded, her mouth opening to him, certain of the only outcome, that would quench what they needed from each other.

John Baxter. I love you more than you can possibly know.

She undid the cord on his robe and looked down.

'Can't wait any longer,' she said, taking the robe from him. 'And by the looks of things, nor can you,' she said.

He took her hand as they walked into the sea.

In chest-high water, Lucy wrapped her long legs firmly around his waist. She lay back in the water. 'Show me how deep your love goes, Mr Baxter.'

He lifted her shoulders towards him. Lucy looked into his eyes as she impaled herself – his warm invasion timeless, beautiful.

In their union, they watched an orange sun float slowly from the sea.

16

Monday – 8th October

John and Lucy emerged from the water and returned to the hotel. They sat down to breakfast on the hotel veranda overlooking the beach.

'If you were going to paint over an existing painting, you wouldn't put a brown layer over the oil. You'd use a very pale layer, usually white, because white is the easiest pigment to overpaint.'

'So – whoever covered it up had no intention of painting over it?' Lucy asked.

'Possibly. And why would it be painted on the reverse of a painting already there? Frank Cropsey was no Van Gogh – he sold hundreds of paintings, and built a large mansion he called "Aladdin". We have to assume he could afford all the canvases he wanted.'

Back on the beach, Lucy sat on the edge of her sun lounger. 'There's *Sugarloaf Mountain in Autumn*, signed "L" on the front - and *Mount Chocorua in Winter*, signed "J Cropsey '58" on the back, covered with brown paint.'

John nodded.

Lucy continued. 'We know the paintings were done twenty years apart – and a long time before *Chocorua* was covered up in 1986. If you owned the only picture of Chocorua done by a famous painter, surely you'd be proud to own it?'

Lucy was picking up handfuls of the coral sand and letting it slip slowly through her fingers. 'But if you wanted to hide a stolen painting – it would be very convenient that another painting was on the back. Nobody would think of looking for another painting – especially as *Autumn* was done so beautifully.'

'We know Billy stole at least one. What if the family has to cover up his misdemeanours continuously?'

Lucy frowned. 'What if whoever covered the canvas in brown paint was trying to send a message?'

'What do you mean?'

'If to paint over a canvas, you'd normally create a white background, and yet you painted it brown – you might be trying to tell the informed observer there was something underneath.'

'I love your brains, sweetheart.'

'So, why do you keep trying to fuck them out of me?' Lucy replied.

John grinned. 'Didn't you say Billy's brother, Peter, did some painting?'

'Yup.'

'If Peter knows about art, why couldn't he cover up another piece of Billy's stupidity? But do it in such a way that the right person would know it was there.'

Lucy googled 'Black industries news'.

Black family accused of robbery –
Paintings removed for evidence

'*In response to allegations made against my family, we repeat that we are not involved in the robberies, which we believe were carried out by ex-wives with a grudge.*'

'That's a joke, John. Kelly never thought of them as family. But there are only two ex-wives, and I'm one of them.'

John was thinking. *I wonder what it'll take to put this lot away.*

17

Wednesday – 17th October

Lucy took John's hand as they walked lazily along the shore. They had often walked the mile of beach either side of the hotel.

'Penny for them, sweetheart,' John said.

'I was thinking how much I love just being with you.'

'Me too – whiskers on kittens,' he replied.

Lucy smiled. 'Tell me some of your other favourite things.'

'Right – first thing that comes into our heads? You game?'

Lucy agreed.

'OK. Let's start with kittens, then.'

'Puppies,' Lucy replied.

'Walks in the woods, with my dog when I was a kid.'

'Walking in the country,' she replied.

'A highly charged picnic in the country – where you and I know we'll make love,' he replied.

'Mmmm,' she smiled. 'In the sunshine, in a meadow – very naughty.'

'The art of Jandri Nowi.'

Lucy – nota bene – *she did the erotic painting above his bed.*

'Your openness,' she said.

'You opening yourself to me,' he replied.

Oh, my god, Lucy – sexy doesn't start to describe this.

'You, telling me to get naked, Mr Baxter.'

They kissed where they stood on the beach.

'If this gets any more explicit, Mr Baxter, you'll have to take me into the sea.'

'That mischievous look I love so much,' he replied. 'Take off your bikini top and give it to me.'

'Men who listen properly,' she laughed.

Lucy looked into his eyes as she removed her top. She handed it to him, pulling her shoulders back for full effect.

His gaze dropped unapologetically. 'Your fabulous tits.'

'The way you play with them. Sometimes so gentle, some-times greedy and squeezy.'

'Like with your halter neck dress?'

'You, turning me on so much I get the shakes,' Lucy replied.

'Like the Ritz on our first night.'

'Now, I *definitely* need you to take me into the sea, John.'

'We're only a hundred yards from the hotel, sweetheart; can you wait two minutes?'

'Barely, Mr Baxter. Barely.'

'You, baring yourself to me emotionally – and physically whenever when I want you.'

She looked into his eyes. 'I've never wanted to so much.'

He smiled. 'We're nearly at the Hotel. Here's your top.'

'How lovely it feels to trust you with my body,' she replied.

'How lovely it is to be trusted so completely.'

'Kindred spirits, then,' she said.

'Generous spirits.'

'Caring people.'

'The RSPCA,' John said.

'Whiskers on kittens,' she retorted, triumphantly.

He took her in his arms and kissed her. 'I love you so much.'

A minute later, Lucy started to shake as they walked briskly through the hotel.

'You remember I described how this pink sand was ground so fine?' she asked.

'Yes, sweetheart – something about relentless Atlantic pounding.'

He shut their door. They were alone at last. Strong hands turned her body away from his – undoing the bows on her hips, her back, behind her neck.

She climbed on the bed – no longer able to watch him. She positioned herself, blissful in her elevated accessibility, listening for his approach …

71

18

Thursday – 18th October

The next morning Lucy woke first. She left the bed as gently as she could so as not to disturb him – and started on the first of two tasks. She googled Jandri Nowi, the artist, and found the website. She obviously loved animals – she captured their essences, their fur, their playfulness so perfectly.

Then Lucy found what she was looking for. The erotica explored female sexuality with such mischief that Lucy identified with the subjects. She smiled at the extra possibilities she and John could explore.

She exchanged emails with Jandri. This culminated in an appointment for Lucy to pose. The resulting painting would be John's Christmas present – and could only be hung in his bedroom.

She turned as John stirred.

'Whiskers on kittens,' he said.

'What?'

'You – sitting in front of your computer – au naturel.'

Lucy smiled and exited the artist's website. 'Come and look at the latest news, lover.'

John joined her on the sofa and gazed at her tablet.

Kelly Black had announced the disappearance of two of her eight brothers, Matthew and Billy.

'Time to find out the early indicators,' Lucy said. 'I never practised criminal law, but there are often indicators that extrapolate into worse behaviours later. It's used as a future-behaviour map by criminal psychologists.

'Ah. Matthew was convicted of assault in 1990 – served six months in the Federal Correctional Institution in Berlin, New Hampshire.'

She looked up, frowning. 'Billy told me that conviction was quashed on appeal. Another of his lies.'

'And here's something about a jewel theft – yes, look. Several valuable items of jewellery were taken from the ranch. Police have not been able to specify when the items were stolen.'

'That's curious,' John said. 'If there were no obvious signs of a break-in …'

'Then a family member stole the jewellery,' Lucy replied. 'The best jewels in the family were owned by Mary. Most of the jewellery the Old Man bought her was lavishly expensive. I think it made her feel that he was not as bad as everyone believed.'

John walked onto their balcony to gaze out on the view they would be leaving tomorrow. As his gaze swung to his left, he saw something move in the shrubs – and the unmistakable circular reflection from the glass of a camera lens …

'You hungry, lover?' Lucy asked, as he re-entered the apartment.

'Very. D'you find anything?'

'Possibly – Mary met her old man as a junior reporter on the *Boston Times*.'

Lucy watched as John walked back onto the balcony with his phone.

What's he up to?

She followed him onto the balcony. 'What's up?'

John took a photo. 'I didn't want to alarm you, sweetheart.'

73

'Let's put the picture on the larger screen. Come on, I have the connecting cable.'

Taking John's phone, she sat down again at her tablet and tapped a few keys. She reached the last photo in the gallery. 'Look.'

The photo had captured a dark shape, just clear enough to see the face was very fair.

'John, whoever this is in the bushes looks pretty small.'

Lucy's face changed. 'If he's been watching us from the moment we got here …'

'Highly unlikely he was ever up as early as we were,' John replied.

'But if he was, John?'

'If he was, sweetheart – he saw a goddess walk naked into the sea. He then witnessed something even more beautiful – lovers enacting feelings that words cannot express.'

'Mr Baxter?'

'Yes, sweetheart?'

'I love you so much – that's all,' she smiled.

'That's everything, lover. Your love is more than any man on earth ever deserved. One day, maybe I'll deserve it.'

She reached up to kiss him. 'You already deserve it – you just don't know how much. I can see I'll have to prove it to you – at every opportunity.'

He kissed her. 'I love you, Lucy.'

'Here's my promise, Mr Baxter. Whenever you need me, we will enact the feelings that words cannot express.'

As they sat down to lunch, they were met with the widest smile from the waitress who had served them for ten days. Occasionally, Grace had shared snippets about her husband and children. She was always happy to see Lucy and John whenever they appeared for meals.

Lucy looked at Grace – and thought she detected the exhaustion of a struggling mother. She asked Grace more about her children.

'The children are very athletic,' Grace told her. 'Must have got it from their father, 'cos look at me,' she laughed. Her younger son, Martin, aged only fourteen, had won the Bahamas Under-18, 400 Metres Championships.

Grace related how her son had been injured and needed surgery on his foot. She and Joseph were working all available hours to save the money for the trip to the US for the operation. It was why she had been on duty for sixteen hours of every day.

As Grace poured the wine, John mentioned it was their last full day on the island. Lucy asked if they would see her next morning to say goodbye. Grace looked at them, tears welling in her eyes.

'Grace, you never told us your last name.'

'It's Freeman, why do you ask?'

'Just curious,' Lucy responded.

John looked at Grace. 'Grace, have you seen anyone on the island recently that struck you as unusual?'

Grace paused – looking to see if any of her colleagues could hear them. She leant forward and lowered her voice.

'Yesterday, there was a funny thing down at the harbour. A man got angry with my Joseph when he wouldn't let him on the shuttle to come back across the water. The boat was too full. I told you my Joseph drives the boats over here.'

'What happened?' John asked.

'The little man – he was making so much noise that one of the passengers offered to give up her seat and wait for the next shuttle. So it was all OK – but the man had eyes with different colours.'

John put his forefinger to his lips. 'Grace, can you lend me some paper and something to write with?'

Grace nodded. She returned less than a minute later with a sheet of paper and a hotel-branded pencil. John nodded at her. He wrote:

Did Joseph find out where the man is staying?

Grace wrote: *Next hotel up beach – north.*

'Thanks, Grace,' John said, smiling at her.

John showed the note to Lucy. He wrote on the paper:

Why, ten years after your divorce from Billy, are the Blacks now feeling vulnerable, if it's not about the art?

John and Lucy usually walked the few hundred yards from the hotel on the east of the island to the harbour on the west side. Today, so as not to be overheard, they climbed into their rental moke.

Lucy parked outside The Landing Cafe at the marina and looked around to discover if they had been followed. John took her hand as they walked through the marina. They found a table overlooking the boats and a waiter approached them with a cocktail menu.

Lucy looked at the menu and leant over to whisper in John's ear. 'I'll have what you did to me in the sea.'

He suppressed his smile as he looked at the waiter. 'Could we have two "Slow, Comfortable Screws", please?'

John looked back at Lucy, who was looking away, a Mona Lisa smile on her face.

The waiter withdrew and Lucy turned back to John. 'What a lucky girl I am.'

John noticed something – and turned his head quickly to his left.

Lucy could see he was thinking. He dialled Eleuthera Airport and asked them to confirm their flights to Fort Lauderdale for noon the following day.

'The line's not very good.' John raised his voice quite loudly to the airport official.

'Yes, Lucy Howard and John Baxter on the twelve-noon flight from Eleuthera to Miami on the nineteenth. Yes, twelve noon, thank you,' he repeated, almost shouting.

Twenty minutes later, they finished their cocktails and returned to the moke.

'Do you mind if I drive this time?' John asked.

He drove for a couple of minutes. Once he knew they were not being followed, he took a quick left, then a sharp right, and parked the moke. They were alone.

He dialled the airline desk at the airport again. He lowered his voice. 'What is the ten a.m. flight to Miami looking like on the nineteenth?' he asked.

'OK, let's see … plenty of seats on that one, sir. Only four seats taken. You could turn up and pay at the desk here.'

'OK, thanks,' he said, ending the call.

'I like your thinking,' Lucy said.

'Just in case …'

19

Friday – 19th October

L ucy wanted to see the sunrise on their last morning. There was just the faintest chill at five o'clock as she and John walked down to the beach. She welcomed his arm around her shoulders.

Lucy's tears fell silently, little crimson pear-drops that reflected the sunrise and her feelings for the man who made her feel so safe.

How is it possible to be so happy – and so sad at the same time?

He cupped her head in his hands and gently licked the tears from her face.

How can a man be so masculine and so sensitive at the same time?

Later that morning, as they boarded the boat that would take them to Eleuthera, a large man extended his hand to Lucy. He was wearing dark baggy trousers and a white cheesecloth shirt. She took his hand gratefully and stepped down into the boat. 'You must be Joseph,' she smiled.

'Ah,' the big man said, in his gravelly voice. 'You must be Lucy … and you must be John,' he beamed. 'My Grace, she tol' me all about you. She says you have the most smiling faces she has seen this year. It's nice to meet you.'

He stood there, awkward, not knowing what to do. 'I have to be getting all these folks on here. Water's pretty smooth today.'

Three minutes later Joseph landed his passengers on Eleuthera Island. Lucy and John were the last to step onto the jetty. Lucy turned to Joseph, an envelope in her hand.

'Joseph – will you promise me something?'

He hesitated. 'Yes, miss?'

Lucy looked around to make sure she could not be overheard. 'Promise me not to open this envelope till after ten this morning. Can you do that for me?'

'Yes, miss. But what …'

'Just promise?'

'I promise.'

'Goodbye, Joseph, and give our love to Grace for us.'

At ten o'clock, Joseph walked into the hotel. He wanted to open the envelope with Grace, who was surprised to see him.

They opened the envelope together. For a moment, neither of them could quite believe what they saw. The cheque would comfortably pay for her son's foot operation.

Grace found the nearest chair, sat down and wept – and wept.

Lucy looked at John uneasily as they boarded their seventy-minute flight from Eleuthera to Fort Lauderdale.

What if the little spy has anticipated our earlier take-off?

There were only six passengers. As they left the ground, Lucy squeezed John's hand three times in quick succession, a silent message that had become their private shorthand for the three words *I love you*. A few seconds later they passed over their hotel.

'Look, John. The big guy with the white shirt. He's waving up at the plane.'

Forty minutes into their journey, they started to relax. Even though they were seated right at the back, several rows behind the nearest passengers, she lowered her voice. 'Surely, John, if something nasty was going to happen, it would've happened by now.'

'You're probably right ... but we have to be a lot more proactive – a lot more.'

Thirty minutes later they were safely on the ground at Fort Lauderdale.

John dialled Eleuthera Airport. 'Can you put me through to airport security?'

'He's on a break right now.'

'Airport security, on a break?'

'Yes, sir. We only have nine people here. You can call back a little later; he shouldn't be too long.'

'It's urgent. Can I speak to anyone in authority?'

'There's no one here right now. I can leave a message?'

'There must be someone – is the pilot for the noon flight there yet?' John persisted.

'The pilot won't be here till just before the flight,' she answered.

'I need to leave an urgent message – it's very important. Do you see the pilot before he takes off?'

'Oh, yes, sir.'

'Can I leave an important message then? Can you ask him to double-check the hold and everything in the aeroplane cabin before he takes off? Have you got that?'

'Yes, sir. But can I say who's calling?'

'John Baxter. I'm on another flight soon, so I won't be able to call again – it's very important – will you tell him please?'

'I will.'

Lucy sensed something was wrong. 'What's up?'

'Something in that lady's voice,' he replied. 'A kind of tired resignation, maybe.'

It was only 11.20 in Fort Lauderdale and the noon flight from Eleuthera would not take off for another forty minutes. He googled the number for Bahamas Air Head Office. Not able to reach anyone, he left his name and mobile number, with the time and date of his message, explaining why he believed it was worth checking the plane.

At Eleuthera Airport, Diane was due on her break. How dare the caller assume the pilot was male? What kind of sexist pig would make that assumption? Diane put a quick note on her noticeboard for the next shift.

White man-pig called. Wants you to check hold before you fly to Fort L. at 12.00.

Twenty minutes later, Carol Jackson walked into Eleuthera Airport. A native Bahamian, and a highly experienced pilot, she put the message in her trouser pocket. There was nobody around to explain. As she walked out onto the tarmac, her phone buzzed with a sext from her husband.

She smiled – and texted him something even more explicit in return. She then started the first of thirty-six routine flight checks.

The checks complete, she watched her eight passengers walk from the small airport terminal building. A few minutes later she was taxiing down the runway to position the small twin-prop aircraft for take-off into a slight headwind.

At 11.50, Lucy sensed John's continued unease. They were sitting in the plane waiting to leave Fort Lauderdale for Boston.

He decided to try Eleuthera one more time and reached for his phone.

'You'll have to turn that off now,' the cabin hostess instructed.

'Just thirty seconds?' he asked. 'It's very important.'

The hostess looked at him. 'I'm sorry sir, we're ready to leave now. I must insist.'

'Just one call?' he asked.

'Sir, if you insist on being difficult, I'll have to ask you to leave the plane.'

She raised her voice so that nearby passengers could hear what she said next. 'That will hold all the other passengers up because we have to get your luggage off too. That could take half an hour.'

John looked at his fellow passengers, now staring at him.

His phone beeped. Its screen was completely dark.

He looked up at the cabin hostess. 'Battery's dead anyway.'

20

'Welcome home, Miss Lucy. How was the flight?'

Steve was always glad to chauffeur Lucy to and from Logan. He had purchased his first Mercedes only a year after emigrating from the Bahamas in 1962. He kept his cars immaculate, inside and out, so that his clients would always feel they were riding in luxury. His easy-going style had endeared him to Lucy from her very first trip with him.

Miss Lucy had none of the aloof arrogance many of his rich clients exuded. There was something about this very tall, elegant blonde with her genuinely warm smile that made him feel important when she was in his car. It was only a short drive to Concord and he wished she lived further from the airport.

'I'm sorry, sweetheart,' John said. 'I should be excited to be going to your home. But I've got bad feelings about that noon flight. I feel a bit sick, actually.'

'Google it, then,' Lucy replied. 'My phone's in my hand luggage in the trunk.'

'My battery's dead, remember?'

Lucy squeezed his hand.

Thirty minutes later they were approaching her home.

'This is me, about a hundred yards on the left.'

John looked ahead to the large white, weather-boarded house with a blue-grey slate roof. The first floor, at the front of the house, boasted nine identical Georgian sash windows, each group of three topped by a large gable above. On the ground floor were another eight windows, four each side of the white front door and porch. Two hundred feet from each end of the house was an enormous, mature cedar tree, each one contrasting with the much paler green of the expansive flat lawn that surrounded the house on all sides.

'I'm glad we got on the earlier flight. Two hours later and I wouldn't have been able to see this; it's absolutely gorgeous.'

Lucy beamed a wide smile at Steve as she thanked him. She and John watched him pull away. 'He has never kept me waiting at the airport – not once. He's always there waiting. He always looks pleased to see me.'

She opened the front door and flicked some lights on. John retrieved the cases from the doorstep and closed the heavy oak door. The hallway was thirty feet square with a large stone-built fireplace opposite the front door. Two oak staircases ascended from the granite flagstone floor, accessing the two ends of the landing upstairs that formed a minstrel gallery above the fireplace.

'It's just as I always imagined the classic Boston house. If this was mine, I'd be living here all the time. He paused. 'The lights – they look like they could be the originals?'

'You're right; these are the brass originals, with the original frosted glass shades – installed in 1888 by the Edison Electric Company, only ten years after electricity was first used in homes.'

She took his hand and led him through to the sitting room. The rose-white painted panelling extended from floor to ceiling and gave the large room a warm glow. The floor consisted of the original twelve-inch-wide planks, partially covered by long, woven cotton rugs of multiple pastel shades that stretched from the doorway to the fireplace.

Was Aphrodite ever this bright? Was Venus ever this feminine?

'In the 1820s most of the houses here had brick-built fireplaces. But as you can see, this one was built of stone. The wooden mantel is a famous part of Boston's early history ...' Lucy paused as John made his way to the fireplace and spotted an indented carving in the huge piece of oak at the right-hand end.

'Harwich 1608!' He turned to Lucy, incredulous.

She smiled. 'I think you've got it.'

'This is one of the timbers from the *Mayflower*! Wow. Talk about a piece of Boston history.'

Then he noticed a painting hung on the north wall. His eyes lit up. 'Do you know how this picture came into being?'

Lucy shrugged her shoulders.

'I take it you know these are the initials of George Henry Durrie?'

Lucy nodded.

'*Ketcham Farm in Winter* was painted in the late 1850s – about the time Cropsey was painting his four-season set. He was staying with the Ketcham family in his period of poverty. He painted this as a thank-you for putting him up. But more significantly, Ketcham Farm is in New Haven, near your home in Farmington.

'I love it … I just love the colour and the light.' John paused for a moment.

'Last time this came up for auction it fetched more than four hundred and fifty thousand dollars.'

'Didn't realise,' Lucy said nonchalantly, looking at the painting again.

'Now, I see why you've been so keen to get me back here.'

'Well, Mr Baxter, you've not seen it all yet. Come with me.'

She led the way up the stairs into the bedroom. Dominating the room was an antique, eight-foot-wide four-poster bed. Its canopy, a rich, dark-blue velvet edged with gold embroidery, matched the bedspread, which reached to the floor.

John stood spellbound. 'I've only seen anything like this in royal palaces. Did you get it like this?' he asked.

'No. I got the bed frame from the Warren Store in Vermont. The owner of the store said it would look great when it was "dressed". A local lady did the dressing.'

John smiled. 'All I can see is undressing in this room.'

Lucy grinned. 'Would you like to see the undressing room, then?'

She led him through, as she had in Wimbledon. But this room was even larger.

'*The Piazza San Marco* lives again,' John said.

'One of them is a copy – you have to tell me which.'

John approached the painting. 'This is the copy, but it's absolutely fantastic.'

'I went back to the gallery where Lady Howard had obtained the original in Harvard. They referred me to the young artist who'd painted a copy of *The Piazza San Marco* before they let Lady Howard take away the original.'

'Makes you wonder what other paintings he's copied,' John replied. 'Anyway, now I get why you wanted us here.'

'The kids are here in New England. If the Blacks are going to get nasty about my divorce settlement, the obvious way to get at me is through the kids. Four people can live in here for a year.'

'I've never heard of a safe room this well provisioned,' John replied. 'Or so well decorated with art; I love your use of this left-hand wall. It looks like a kind of rogues' gallery.'

'More like a heroes' gallery; some of my favourite people; two of them, lawyers,' Lucy replied.

John took a moment to admire the four portraits on the long wall opposite the cupboards. Lucy had arranged her heroes in chronological order of their birthdays: Mahatma Gandhi, Mother Teresa, Nelson Mandela and Martin Luther King.

Then John's eye was caught by an open cupboard, opposite. 'And so many vitamin supplements.'

'Mother Bear needs to feed the cubs. And the cubs eat a lot of food.'

John looked at Lucy. 'Well ... let's hope we never have to use it.'

21

John and Lucy walked back downstairs and into the kitchen. The table with its oak benches either side matched perfectly the ten-foot-wide dresser that John guessed to be at least two hundred years old. The granite flagstone floor extending from the hallway showed very little wear for its two centuries and completed the feeling of authenticity and permanence.

Lucy had adorned the dresser with a mixture of rose pink and blue glass goblets on one shelf and some old pewter plates and tankards on the shelf below. John noticed that the pewter was decorated with etchings of Viking longboats. He looked at Lucy. 'Your ancestry. It all makes sense; blonde hair, blue eyes.'

Lucy grinned.

'Let's find out about the noon flight,' he said. 'Where's your tablet?'

Lucy accessed her news feed. She looked at John, horrified. 'It exploded just after take-off. Everyone killed, including the pilot.'

'What? Lucy!' John held his head in his hands. 'I should've had my battery charged – you remember – on the plane. Lucy, what've I done?'

The TV reporter was interviewing a lady from Eleuthera Airport. Diane Smith was being asked if she had seen anything unusual.

'Nothing. It's been a day like all the rest, really. We only get four flights a day and only five days a week. We had no warning or anything.'

'So, your hunch … I'm going to be sick.' Lucy left quickly for the bathroom, the colour gone from her face. John remained standing and pondered the last twenty-four hours.

How are we going to keep the kids safe? How can I keep Lucy safe? This needs some serious thought.

A minute or two later, Lucy emerged.

'How are you feeling, sweetheart?'

Lucy said nothing.

'Why would the Blacks bother themselves with all this? It seems way out of perspective.'

'Nine people have died, John – just because someone wanted to kill us. This is *way* beyond perspective.'

Tears were coming to her eyes. 'Five million dollars is less than a hundredth of one per cent of their wealth.'

Lucy put her arms round him. 'I love you so much, John – but I'm afraid for us. What if being together has made us a target?'

'And I love you too.' He held her tight. 'What makes you think this is about your divorce settlement?'

88

Lucy looked at him. 'I think it's time you knew about the divorce settlement meeting – and the episode that persuaded me I needed the protection I lined up for it.'

John said nothing as Lucy paused. 'If I tell you what I call this episode, can we leave it at that? One day I'll be able to tell you all of it.'

'Fair enough,' he replied.

'OK, then … I call it the "knife incident".'

John looked at her, horror all over his face. He held her tight, cupping her head to his shoulder.

'So let me tell you about the precautions I took for the meeting.

'I knew Old Man Black would make the meeting intimidating. He'd gather around him the most violent members of the family. So, I chose a security firm to go with me. They wanted details of the Black siblings and photos of the whole family and the layout of the ranch and Old Man Black's office. Their preparation was nearly as impressive as their physical size. Two of them were about six feet nine or ten inches tall; the third was only a bit shorter.

'I'd never seen guys this big – let alone three in one place. Talk about intimidating; when I first met them they were in full battledress. I got nervous just looking at them – and they were working for me.

'I asked them what their mothers fed them. The leader told me "Hacker" was "the largest dude ever to serve in the US Army. Three hundred pounds of muscle." Survived three tours in Afghanistan.

'He told me the stronger they appeared to be, the less risk there was of confrontation. "As you can see – our aim is no confrontation at all," he said.

'I paid them nine thousand dollars. Hacker drove the jeep to the meeting. I was in the back, wedged between the two others. I felt absolutely tiny. When we got to the ranch, one of the guys stayed outside. He turned the jeep so that its tow bar was towards the window of Black's office. The other two arranged themselves in front of me. Simon opened the door – and wet himself – literally.

'I tell you, John, when I saw Simon's reaction, I wondered if I'd overdone the security – until I remembered what he and his brothers did to me in my kitchen.

'Anyway, we went through to Black's office. The Old Man laughed. He said he ought to have known I'd come prepared.

'The leader told him, "Prepared is for losers – *decisively* prepared is how we operate. You'll find the phones and your security link to the police have been disconnected. They'll be reconnected when we leave the premises."

'He threw a pre-formed noose over the oak beam and passed the rope out of the window. He walked up to Billy, Jack and Simon. "You little boys know all about ropes from overhead beams."

'He was referring to the knife incident I'd told them about. You should've seen their faces when the rope was tied to the tow bar of the jeep. He told the three little boys to stand back-to-back.

'Old Man Black stood up. "You guys blow in here like the storm on the Sea of Galilee and use a noose to negotiate? This is outrageous."

'The leader released the safety catch on his semi-automatic. "Listen up, Old Man," he said. "These three came into our client's home and assaulted her using knives. The noose is to remove them from the negotiations. If they say nothing for the next five minutes, the jeep stays parked."

'He tightened the noose around their necks. He told them the jeep did zero to sixty in five seconds – and that if any one of them said a single word, the jeep would snap all their necks together.

'Then he turned to Kelly. "We've heard all about you. So, if I see any mobile phone before we leave here, we will string you up from this beam – in full view of your brothers – and you will be dressed exactly like my client was when they left her hanging from the beam in her kitchen … Like I said – decisively prepared."

'Then he turned to me. "Over to you, ma'am. The meeting's all yours."

'I pointed out that Billy would not want a lot to do with the kids. The raising of the children would fall to me.

'Black suspects I know a lot about the family. I asked for $5,831,400. He stared at me – long and cold – then signed a cheque for five million. He slid it across the desk, completely unemotional.

'He said the money would come off what he was going to leave Billy in his will. The anger in Billy's eyes told me I was now in danger – exactly what the Old Man intended.

'I told them I would keep out of their way. They knew what I meant. The Old Man asked me the significance of the amount I'd asked for.

'Kelly interrupted. "Daddy, I'm surprised at you. It's all their birthdays – 29, 15 and 7. If you multiply 29157 by two hundred, you get 5,831,400."

'John, at that moment I registered just how quick Kelly is. I promised myself I'd never underestimate her.

'Anyway, I reminded them that the cheque is a legal contract under law. I told them that if it was not honoured by the bank, I'd line up so many subpoenas for their financial information, they'd get no work done for months.

'As I was leaving the meeting, the Old Man looked up at Kelly, grinning. Then he looked at me with a kind of arrogant triumph on his face.

'"I'd have paid you ten," he said.

'I said nothing – but I'd have taken two.'

22

' Sweetheart, we need to get on the front foot before it's too late. We need much more information about the Blacks – and their intentions.'

They were suddenly bathed in blue and red light coming from the driveway.

'The police,' John said. 'They've tracked us from the flight list.'

The sound of the doorbell ringing twice was followed by a loud thumping on the door itself.

Lucy opened the door, John at her shoulder.

Three machine pistols were aimed at them, held by shaven-headed men in blue uniform.

'Is this the Howard residence?' one of the men asked.

'Yes,' Lucy said.

'We have a warrant to search this house.'

Lucy and John led the three uniformed men through to the kitchen.

'I expect you were alerted by my answer-machine message.'

'You're John Baxter, I take it?'

'Yes, I am.'

'So why did you leave the message?'

'Someone's been following us. Lucy was married into a family who bear long-term grudges. I believe you know the Blacks?'

'The Blacks.' He flicked his gun to gesture to his men to get on with the search. They disappeared upstairs.

John could see Lucy was nervous about the guns. 'You won't need the guns, Officer. We don't own any. Would you like some coffee?'

The officer lowered his machine pistol slightly, recognising it looked out of place.

'We need you to give a statement down at the precinct,' he said.

'Are we being charged with anything?'

'Not exactly.'

Lucy interjected. 'In that case, Officer, we're not obliged to attend the precinct under Massachusetts law; but we're happy to give you a statement here.'

'And how come you know so much about the law, ma'am?'

'I'm a practising lawyer, licensed in Connecticut and Massachusetts. Perhaps you can tell us what's been done about the woman who denied taking a message about the security threat at Eleuthera? Is she going to be charged?'

'And why there is no permanently staffed security desk at the airline?' John added.

Lucy was curious. 'Does BH Air record incoming phone conversations made to Eleuthera Airport? Because if they do, you have proof that the woman at the airport lied about not having any warning. You need to interview her – not John, who left his name and warned of the threat, forty minutes before take-off.'

'I've got to get the statement, ma'am. I think you understand.'

John gestured to the officer to take a seat. 'That's your urgency, Officer. Ours is different – how the *hell* do we keep us all safe from these killers?'

Fifty minutes later, Lucy and John finished dictating their statements. The police seemed satisfied as they returned to their vehicle.

Lucy poured two fingers of whisky into each of two heavy lead-crystal tumblers.

'Wow,' John said. 'That should do it.'

Lucy took a large sip. 'John, when the police arrived you were talking about getting on the front foot.'

John put his forefinger to his lips. He picked up Lucy's tablet. He typed:

First, we hire private help to find out if we're being listened to here. Second, we hire someone who knows about art.

Lucy typed. *Where do we get people like this?*

Nat. Gallery knew investigators who made sure insurance claims were not fraudulent attempts to raise £. I know one of them v well.

Let's do it. But let's get someone to find out if we can ever have gd chat again in our own hse.

John showed Lucy his screen, opened on the *Boston Globe* newsfeed page.

Body of Peter Black discovered in forest.

Lucy looked at John in horror. She typed, *Peter was one of only two decent brothers. Matthew and Billy went missing. Do you suppose M and B killed him? Poor Mary – got to call her.*

They searched down, eager to see more.

Jack Black held for murder.

Lucy typed, *Let's see if Matthew and Billy are still missing.* 'Look at this,' she said out loud. Her own screen read:

Billy Black released on $1,000,000 bail as brother Jack is charged with murder. Malvito decision follows.

John typed. *Who is Malvito?*

Lucy replied, *Old Man Black is one of the two Massachusetts senators; Senator Malvito is the other. Malvito has a hotel chain – most of them licensed casinos as well. Very rich – started 1970 with $80, so story goes – self-made man – now employs several hundred people all over US.*

Lucy dialled Mary Black – but had to leave a message on voicemail.

Then she typed. *We do need that help you talked about.*

John dialled William Ritchey.

'John – great to hear from you.'

'Likewise. William, I'm in Boston – can we meet?'

'Definitely. I'm finishing an investigation in Boston, and I have to get the report finished. Can we meet up Thursday? I'm at the Oaks Hotel.'

'That's great, William. Three p.m. in reception?'

'Three is great. Looking forward to it.'

John whispered to Lucy. 'William is the "go-to guy" if the insurance people suspect any kind of funny business. He has a huge knowledge of art – and he misses nothing. The insurance companies work with him when they need someone really sharp – and he's one of the good guys in the business.'

Lucy nodded. 'In that case, would you mind if he looked at the painting that fetched me over to London to see you?'

'Good idea. William is used as an expert witness; he'll give you the kind of forensic accuracy that stands up in court.

'But we also need a different kind of investigator – let's see …'

He typed *private investigators in New England* and got a long list straight away.

Is your strongbox upstairs the same as your Wimbledon one?

Electronically – yes. This one much bigger. And one year's food and drink for four people.

John paused. *So, if four people could live a year, then six of us could survive eight months.*

96

23

Saturday – 20th October

George Bellows had served in the Boston Police for twenty-eight years. He had received nineteen commendations in his sixteen years as a detective but had never been given the promotion his colleagues knew he deserved. George's mother was African American; his father was descended from the English settlers who had crossed the Atlantic in 1855. Neither had benefitted from any formal schooling but both had encouraged their son to nurture his natural ability and his insatiable curiosity.

At the time of his resignation from the police, he had completed an online Master's degree in criminal psychology. He bore no grudges about his lack of promotion. Some of his ex-colleagues consulted him on tricky cases, enabling him to earn more in a week than his ex-boss did in a month.

Now out of the police force and self-employed, he sat at his desk at home, wondering why no one had called for two weeks. But then his phone buzzed with a call from someone calling himself John Baxter. They arranged to meet at the Holiday Inn in Boston.

Thirty minutes later, George watched a couple enter the hotel lobby and look around. The woman was stunning – nearly six foot tall with long blonde hair tied in a thick ponytail. The man was at least four inches taller and carried himself like an athlete.

George got to his feet.

'John Baxter?'

'Yes, George. Nice to meet you. This is Lucy.'

George gestured to the seats. 'What can I do for you folks?'

'Mr Bellows, I've been followed out of an art gallery in London – and Lucy and I have been spied on in the Bahamas recently.'

Lucy was studying George. 'And we were booked on a flight from Eleuthera that was bombed.'

'I saw that on CNN. Do you mind me asking what business you folks are in?'

'I'm an art dealer and Lucy's a lawyer. Are you any relation of the artist George Bellows?'

'My great-great-grandfather.'

'I know some of his work ... but he didn't paint very long; there aren't many paintings of his coming up for sale.'

'He died early. And you're right, not many get out of private hands. And, no, I can't paint to save my life.'

Lucy was curious. 'Mr Bellows, can you tell us about the work you've done in this kind of security situation?'

'Yes, ma'am. One of my recent assignments was to look after the kids of an Arab sheikh. The sheikh had some enemies in the arms trade – something he had understated when I agreed to the work.

'Anyway, I saved the kids from a nasty fate in a boat, so everyone was OK. I got the work because the father had been referred to me from someone else I prevented from being shot. It's all been word of mouth – but they're all still alive and well.'

George continued to talk about the surveillance and anti-surveillance work he had been doing. He described how his years in the police had enabled him to understand the minds of some of the most vicious and persistent criminals in New England.

He noticed Lucy relax back into her chair.

John also picked up on her approval and broke the silence. 'Well, George, how do you feel about helping us? And what are your rates?'

George looked at John. *These people look honest.*

'It can be four hundred dollars a day, plus expenses, or a flat four seventy-five a day with no expenses.'

John looked at Lucy. She nodded almost imperceptibly. 'Is this seven-days-a-week help?'

'How long do you think you'll need me?'

'Maybe ten days initially – then to review it for each further ten days,' John replied.

'What kind of help do you need?'

'I need to tell you about the plane yesterday – the one that blew up after take-off. We need to check we're not being listened to.'

George was unfazed. 'Anti-surveillance is no problem with my federal background. Has anyone has been into your home?'

'It's unlikely,' answered Lucy. 'I have six-figure combination security on all exit doors and the downstairs windows are triple-glazed and bulletproof.'

John looked at Lucy. 'Wow.'

'I can tell you – if you have three glazings, audio surveillance won't work because voices are too disturbed by three distortions.'

John studied Lucy's face. She turned to John and nodded.

'George – Lucy and I would like to engage your services for what could be as much as three months. Would you be able to work with us for that time?'

George studied the couple. 'How about four twenty-five a day including expenses, not four seventy-five. You pay plane fares. First ten days paid in advance, thereafter each ten days paid in arrears?'

John extended his hand to George, who shook it firmly. 'Give me your bank details, George, and we can transfer the first instalment.'

George went home to collect the electronic equipment he needed. He checked his bank account. John Baxter had paid him $5,000 for the first ten days, not the $4,250 they had agreed. He had never been overpaid before.

George knew that the failed attempt to bomb the plane would result in more attempts on their lives. He packed the gear he needed into his long olive-green Buick and made straight for Lucy's address in Concord.

'Where do you spend most of the time in the house?' he asked.

'Probably the kitchen, the living room, and the bedroom, I guess,' Lucy replied.

George electronically swept the living rooms and the main bedroom. Lucy and John watched as he checked ceiling light fittings individually, and the fuse box. 'I need to check out the back of the property.'

Lucy let George out of the kitchen door. He walked the fifty yards across the lawn to the perimeter fence and took photos as he walked the entire boundary of the plot. Ten minutes later, he knocked on the kitchen door before re-entering.

'I need to ask you about your dressing room,' George said.

Lucy showed George how the strongbox worked. He wanted to see how fast it could close behind them when they entered it.

'If it's alright with you folks, I'll start surveillance here this evening. I'll split my time between checking if anyone is watching you here and being over at the Black place in Back Bay.'

George returned to his car, feeling uneasy. He knew how relentless the Blacks were …

24

Lucy was worried. *The fact we need a team merely to survive does not augur well.*

'Sweetheart, if the Blacks plan to get you implicated, we need information we can negotiate with – some insurance.'

'Let's see what George turns up then,' Lucy said. 'At least we know we can talk. Let's see if there's anything else about the family?'

Lucy set her tablet on the kitchen table. A few seconds later she was transfixed.

Billy Black accused of jewel theft at the Ridge Ranch
Matthew Black in bar brawl in Farmington

'What the hell's he doing over there?' Lucy asked. 'He was always getting drunk. I wonder if he's with Billy, if Billy's out on bail.'

Lucy dialled her younger son, Oliver.

'What's up, Mom? How was the rest of the trip?'

'It was fine thanks, sweetie. Listen, have you seen your father?'

'No. Why?'

'Billy's up to no good in the Farmington area and I want you to be careful.'

'Mom. We're both bigger than him; he wouldn't try anything.'

'One or two of the Blacks carry guns. If Billy calls, will you let me know immediately?'

'Yep, sure thing.'

Lucy turned to John. 'I look at the boys sometimes and wonder at how those hunks came from inside me. Oliver is right – both of them are much bigger than their father – but that won't matter if the Blacks call round with guns.'

'Would the family harm your guys?' John asked.

'Would you take the risk? In criminal law Matthew was classified as a delinquent recidivist when he was sixteen. By the time I met him, he was the most impulsive and angry idiot I'd ever encountered.'

Lucy's phone buzzed. 'Hey, Mom. Guess who called when I was out back?'

'Billy?'

'Yep. Dropped a bench off for us. Looks like a lot of work. It's a kind of garden bench. He carved our initials in the seat of it. Kind of looks nice. Really heavy piece of oak.'

'You didn't speak to him, then?'

'He was in a rush. Said he was running late.'

'Can you tell Mark not to take any packages from your dad? There's been a robbery at the ranch and I don't want you guys arrested for handling anything stolen. Promise me?'

'Got it. I'll tell him.'

'Thank you. And the most important of all, Oliver ...'

'I know, Mom. You love us.'

Lucy's smile turned to concern as Oliver ended the call.

'What's up, sweetheart?'

'John – the bench – Billy never does anything that isn't for his own good.'

John looked at Lucy. 'Does seem a bit random; just turning up like that. Makes you think of Greeks bearing gifts.'

Lucy's thoughts were interrupted by her cell phone.

'Jane. It must be one a.m. in England. What on earth is this important?'

Lucy listened for a few seconds.

'Well, I could go at the beginning of next week. Could you book me first class? I can go from Logan any time after noon on Monday.'

She looked at John. 'The office want me in Atlanta for a "prelim". Jane's the office manager in London. The client's in Atlanta and it's easier for me to see him, rather than get someone from the London office to cross the pond – and the time zones.'

Lucy paused. 'The fee will be eight figures and the office have offered me fifty per cent – I reminded her I'm on sabbatical – but I'm the only one in the firm who speaks Mandarin.'

'There's a couple of auctions in London next week. Christie's are selling a few pieces of nineteenth-century American.

Perhaps, after your prelim, you could join me in London – give you a chance to see me hard at work?'

'Mmm, that might work,' Lucy pondered. 'Let me see how quick Jane can get me back to London. She's probably still awake. Talking of Chinese, this leaflet is the best Chinese food delivery in the area – why don't you call them while I call Jane back?'

Lucy talked to Jane while John ordered the food.

'Jane won't be able to book either flight till the morning. What did you order for us?'

'Duck. We'd better tell George someone is coming to the house.'

'If you've ordered duck …' Lucy pulled a bottle from the wooden frame. 'I think you'll find this *exceptional*.'

'What – Château Largaux? How the …'

The TV news interrupted him with a news bulletin.

Matthew and Christopher Black found dead at family ranch – Suspected poisoning.

Lucy stared again at the screen. 'Dear god – let's see if this is on the local news.'

Twenty minutes later, the doorbell chimed. Lucy looked through the spyhole in her front door. The large frame of George Bellows dwarfed the Chinese-food-delivery man.

John joined Lucy at the door. 'Sorry, George, we were going to tell you we had a delivery coming but we got distracted by the news. Come on in, both of you.'

George put his hand on the small man's shoulder as they followed Lucy back into the kitchen. 'I saw the news too – suspected poisoning. I figured you and your lady were next.'

The delivery driver turned, anxious about being shut in. 'Not so fast, boy,' George interjected.

'That's OK. I better be on my way.'

George insisted. 'Tell you what, boy – you start first. We're going to put a little bit on this plate, and you can tell us if it's good enough for these folks to eat.'

The delivery man ran for the hallway. George spun round, grabbing the man's fleece. 'What's your name?'

The young man said nothing, obviously nervous.

George persisted. 'And whose car was that you just got out of?'

Lucy looked at the delivery boy. There was something about his face and his dark-brown eyes that reminded her of Billy. He continued to say nothing. George poked him sharply with a very large forefinger.

'And why did the delivery boy from the Concord Chinese get into the car you got out of?'

'Look, I just make the deliveries, that's all.'

'Well, I want you to eat some of this food.' George continued to hold onto him. 'Ma'am, let's get some of this on a plate. He looks like he could do with a good feed.'

Lucy put a little food from each of the white cardboard boxes onto the plate and set a fork to the side of the plate. George boomed at the little man. 'EAT.'

'Please don't make me eat it, I hate Chinese. Please.'

'You're eating it whether you like it or not,' George replied.

'Please, no, please.'

'Have you got any very sharp kitchen scissors, ma'am? Sharp enough to cut ears off?'

The delivery man started whimpering. 'I'm feeling kind,' George continued. 'I'm going to give you three choices. One – you eat this food. Two – I cut your ears off. Three – you give us two bits of information and you get on your way, unharmed.'

'Information?'

George lowered his voice and very slowly uttered the words, 'Two bits of information. If you lie, I remove half of one ear each time. Do you understand?'

'Yes.'

'First question, then. Who are you working for?'

The man hesitated.

'Mr Baxter, the scissors please.'

'No, please. He said he'd kill me if I told. Said it would look like an accident – a car accident.'

'Describe him to us, then,' John insisted.

The man gave a description and Lucy pushed back from the kitchen bar. 'That's Jack.'

'You folks know something I don't?' George asked.

'It's one of the brothers of my ex-husband, Billy. His name is Jack. He killed his ex-girlfriend and her new boyfriend some years back by hitting them with a rental car.'

Lucy looked at John. 'That's how Jack became known as the Skull-Cruncher – he drove back and forth over the bodies so many times, he eventually flattened their skulls.'

'What a lovely family,' John said.

George nodded. 'I remember the case. We had to pick the teeth out of the mush to identify the bodies.' He turned back to the delivery boy. 'Now there's three questions, boy, not two.'

John pushed the scissors across the table to George.

George looked at Lucy. 'We're gonna need some old, large towels, ma'am. Ears lose a lot of blood. You're probably not gonna want to watch this.'

Lucy looked at John, appalled. *Surely, he's not actually going to do it.*

'Question two. We know you're not a delivery boy for Concord Chinese. They all have uniforms round here, and proper ID.'

He opened and closed the scissors, clipping quickly to the side of the man's face. 'Because it's dark, I couldn't see what car he was driving. But I think you know.'

Again, the man hesitated.

Lucy put two large towels on the table.

George took the scissors to the man's ear.

'Gold Cadillac convertible with Massachusetts plates,' the young man blurted.

'Good boy. Does that car ring any bells, ma'am?'

Lucy shrugged her shoulders. 'It's been a few years.'

'Question three. What's your name?'

'Jim ... Black.'

Lucy's mind was racing. *The Blacks have used their own brother to do their dirty work – what will happen to him when the Blacks discover he has failed?*

25

Lucy grabbed her phone. 'Hi, Mark. Don't eat any takeout. The Blacks have just tried to poison our Chinese.'

'You're kidding me.'

'Listen, Mark. Make sure you tell Oliver. He gets takeout with Colin sometimes when you're not there. Will you tell him anyway, in case I don't get him on his cell?'

'Will do. But what the —?'

Lucy cut him off. 'Sorry, Mark. I have to try Oliver. But please try to get him on his cell, 'cos if he's up at Colin's I may not get hold of him right now.'

'Got it.'

Lucy tried Oliver's cell phone and got no reply, so she left a message. She then texted him with an additional warning. She then dialled again so he would know it was urgent.

John dialled his daughter Charlotte.

'Hi, Dad. It's the middle of the night.'

'Listen, Charlotte. The Blacks have just tried to poison us with a delivery of Chinese. Can you tell Emma straight away; it's urgent. We've got to be really careful about what we eat – everything – do you understand – not just takeaways.'

'OK, Dad. I thought you were back soon anyway?'

'I am. But this is too important. Will you tell her now?'

'OK. I will; I promise.'

George had released James and sat him at Lucy's kitchen table.

Lucy's attention returned to James. 'You're the one I never met. James, do you know who I am?'

He looked suspiciously at her.

'James, I used to be married to your brother, Billy. I'm Lucy.'

He continued to stare.

'Where do you live, James?'

'We live on Beacon Hill, near the top.'

'Who is "we"? George asked.

'Me and my brother, Simon. You can't tell anyone I told you. They'll hurt me. Please.'

'What do you mean, hurt you?' Lucy enquired.

'They hold me down ... and Billy burns me with his lighter. He has a lighter but he doesn't smoke.'

Lucy shuddered. 'I know.' She hesitated, glancing at John. 'Billy and his brothers did it to me.'

John winced. 'Hell's bells, sweetheart. You never said.'

Lucy turned back to James. 'How old are you, James?'

'Twenty-two, tomorrow.'

'You're much younger than your brothers, aren't you, James?' she asked.

'Mom said I was a gift from God, but they say I was a mistake that should've been drowned at birth. They don't know.'

'What don't they know, James?'

'I remember things.'

'What things?' Lucy persisted.

'Everything.'

'When you say everything, what do you mean?'

'Numbers. They have all their numbers in their phones. But I have all their numbers in my head. Simon leaves his phone around and I look at the numbers. There's bad people in his phone. You mustn't tell him I know.'

'Can you tell us some of the numbers, James?'

The three of them listened as James recited, in perfect alphabetic order, ten names with their phone numbers.

Lucy interrupted him. 'OK, James, thank you. I've heard about these memories … What's your favourite thing to remember, James?'

'Music. They don't know I take piano lessons.'

'James, how many lessons have you had?' Lucy asked.

'One hundred and ninety-six.'

'You must be good at the piano,' she replied. 'Why so many lessons?'

'Recently, my piano teacher gets all these people. I play the piano and they pay her ten dollars to listen to me. I don't need the sheet, see. I play from memory.'

Lucy looked up at John. She took James's hand in hers as she looked back at him. 'Has Ma heard you play?'

'Once, in the beginning, when I played the scales my teacher told me.'

There's no way I'm letting you out of our sight, tonight. How many other lethal visits have you had to make?

'You should stay with us tonight, James. Tomorrow, it's your birthday and we're going to do something special.'

26

'Maybe I shouldn't go to Atlanta, John? Maybe we're in over our heads. The Black family is thick with thieves and thugs. I should never have got you into all of this.'

John held her in his arms – then glanced at George.

'George, can you guard Lucy's kids while she's in Atlanta?'

George paused. 'It actually makes it easier if you're in Atlanta because they can't fight the war everywhere.'

'Is that how you see this, George – some kind of war?' Lucy asked.

'Absolutely, ma'am. We're in a fight for your lives – two attempts, and counting. But we have some advantages. I still have ten or more friends on the force who'd help at a moment's notice – all of them armed. Our opponents can't expand their numbers like that. We've got a much bigger team if we need it.

'And to introduce some random patterns, we move your young men to Boston for two days, then return them to Connecticut.'

'These friends you talk about, George – are you sure they'd help us?' Lucy asked.

'Ma'am – one or two of them have saved my life, and vice versa. When you go through that with people, you're closer than brothers. They would definitely help us, especially 'cos it's the Blacks. Boston's been trying to put 'em away for years.'

Lucy picked up her phone.

'Jane, so sorry to call you again in the middle of the night, but plans have changed. I need first class to Atlanta, then back to London on the twenty-eighth at the end of the day. Can you do that? … Yes, in my name … thanks Jane.'

John looked at George. 'Not bad, for your first thirty minutes on the job, George.'

Lucy gestured to the TV news. Old Man Black was being asked about the death of three of his sons, Peter, then Christopher and Matthew.

Black was unemotional. 'No comment,' he shrugged.

Then came the next question from another journalist: 'Is it true that Christopher and Matthew died from poisoning?'

111

Black said nothing.

John stared at the screen. 'He's lost three of his sons and he's cold as an Arctic wind.'

George started for the front door. 'I'll hang around in case there's any other surprises. And if you're booking a table anywhere, don't book it in your real names.'

John lowered his voice. 'Why James's ears, George?'

'You're the art expert, Mr Baxter. I'm sure you'll figure it out.'

'That's the second time ...'

Lucy was hungry. 'Let's go to the Grotto, in Concord. Do you like Italian, James?'

'I like pizza.'

On the way to the restaurant, James described how his brothers and sister had persuaded him to carry the Chinese food into Lucy's home. Aside from her cigarette lighter, Kelly had brought a four-foot-long piece of heavy electrical flex for the occasion. James lifted his T-shirt and twisted in his seat to show John the welts he still carried four days later.

John winced. 'Hell's bells, James. Have you seen a doctor about this?'

John looked sideways at Lucy, who kept her eyes on the road.

'He never does anything ... Anyways, there's a piano at the house.'

'I don't follow your logic, James.' Lucy looked at John, puzzled.

'When I got to go to college, Ma said to stay in our house in Boston 'cos it's near the college. I play the piano whenever I want. She told me how to cook and everything. She told

Simon not to hurt me. She said if he hurt me, she would get the police.'

Lucy frowned at John. 'Would you like to see Ma tomorrow, on your birthday, James?'

'Yes, but can I play Steinway?' he asked.

'Tomorrow, you can play all you like.'

An hour later, Lucy drove them back to the house and showed James his bedroom.

Lucy walked down the landing to the main bedroom, where John was admiring the pictures on the walls. He turned to face her. 'Quite a day, sweetheart.'

'No kidding – that family is unbelievable.'

'But getting smaller.'

Lucy sat on the bed. 'Yes. What do you make of George? He knew the food was poisoned – and acted immediately.'

John was thinking. 'Something interests me though. Matthew and Peter and Christopher are all gone. James seems not to have a mean cell in his body. Jack is not the subtle type to use poisoning; we know his style is to use the car. That leaves Billy and Simon, Kelly and Andrew who could've used poison to kill us.'

'Andrew's not the type. I always liked him. He's a doctor here in Boston. He and Louise have two daughters. She's a sweetie. She and Mary spent two days helping me find a wedding dress when I married Billy. It was two of the most fun days I can remember. Over the years I got to know her and Andrew quite well. He's not capable of murder.'

'OK, well that leaves Billy, Simon and Kelly,' John said.

113

'Yes, if we assume the murderer is one of the siblings. Who else has anything to gain from those deaths?'

'Maybe that's not the only question we should ask, sweetheart,' John replied.

'What's on your mind?'

John looked at Lucy. 'You said "one of the siblings". Did you ever read the Agatha Christie book *Murder on the Orient Express*?'

'Yes, the murder was carried out by the whole group; each of them had their own reasons,' Lucy replied.

'Whatever it is, sweetheart, we have to make sure we and the kids are not on the successful hit list.'

27

Sunday – 21st October

James Black woke up with his brother Peter foremost in his mind. He replayed Peter's visit to Kelly in her house in Boston. Peter had been excited by the painting Kelly told him she had bought for him – but was nervous enough about the visit to have told James about it. Entering Kelly's house, Peter had dialled James on his phone and left the line open – just in case.

James knew the memories of Peter's screams would never leave him. He had never seen Peter alive again. He had lost his only friend – one of only three people who had never laughed at him.

As he walked into Lucy's kitchen, James's mind moved back to the visit he had made with his mother to a psychologist. The doctor told him he was someone very special – a super-functioning autistic. It came with gifts that other people neither had, nor could ever understand. The doctor suggested that he should nurture these gifts, not try to deny or ignore them.

More recently James had experienced new abilities; he seemed able to pick up on the intentions of those around him. He noticed that his brain surrounded these people with colours that told him their personalities – and their intentions.

He took in the scene in an instant. John was pouring coffee. Lucy was making pancakes. But they were one person moving in two different bodies, encapsulated by a sheath of the same colour. Their movements in the kitchen were a kind of dance, the one always conscious of the other, each moving in synchronised purpose. It fascinated him that distance did not separate them.

'Good morning, James. Did you sleep well?' Lucy asked.

'I slept a long time for me.'

'Happy birthday, James. Twenty-two years old,' Lucy replied.

John looked at Lucy, questioning. James noticed John's awkwardness.

She nodded.

John continued. 'James, do you still want to see your ma?'

James said nothing, mesmerised by the purple light surrounding Lucy and John and which seemed to be getting deeper. It looked like a soft casing, enveloping them, changing shape with the movement of their bodies.

115

She smiled at him. There was no judgement – only gentle acceptance, the same feeling he got from his mother. Lucy put a plate of wholemeal pancakes in front of him.

'Tuck in, boys,' she said. 'There's some local maple syrup if you want it.'

'Peter was the fisherman in the Bible.'

'James?' Lucy asked.

'Peter – always fishing – fishing for answers – painting, fishing, painting, fishing. Peter never hurt me. Peter and Andrew never hurt me. Andrew wanted to give me the puppy. He said that someone at his work was trying to find him a home. Andrew asked me if I could look after him. Matthew told me that if I took the puppy, he would find it and kill it.'

'Was Peter fishing for answers too hard then, James?' Lucy asked.

'Kelly and Billy have lighters, but they never smoke. They did Peter too.'

Lucy shot a glance at John. 'Well, if we're visiting Mary out on the ranch, we should call her. Otherwise, she'll come out here.'

Lucy dialled the number. 'The Ridge,' came a voice.

James was sitting adjacent to Lucy and could hear his mother's words.

Lucy smiled. 'Ma, it's Lucy.'

'Lucy. It's great to hear from you. How are you and the boys?'

'They're fine. But that's not the reason I'm calling. It's James's birthday and we didn't know your plans.'

There was a pause. 'So you've met James. Lucy … I can't say anything over the phone. The Ridge has had some terrible upsets.'

'I know, Ma. I'm so, so sorry. I left a message on your machine. I guessed you were organising things. We only got back from Eleuthera the night before last. I'm so sorry, Ma; we thought it might cheer you up to see James on his birthday. If it's OK, we could bring him over to see you?'

'Of course, Lucy. But you keep saying "we". Who is "we"?'

'John, Ma. I know you'll love him. We could be with you before noon? James has a nice surprise for you.'

'OK, then. I guess I'll see you soon.'

Lucy took her tablet and keyed in a few strokes. She smiled as she picked up her phone. 'Ma is not expecting us before twelve, which means we can have breakfast without rushing.'

She keyed in a few more strokes. James noticed her wink at John as she walked out of the kitchen. Returning two minutes later, she nodded to John. 'Anyone for more coffee?'

James watched closely as John spoke to Lucy. 'I look at you and know what it means to love so much it hurts.'

He continued to stare as Lucy put her hand on John's chest over his heart. She moved her hand in little circular movements and looked up into his eyes.

John kissed her. 'What if my presence in your life is endangering all of you?'

'You only survive this together,' James said.

28

Mary Black was ablaze with emotions. She looked forward to seeing Jim on his birthday and always relished Lucy's visits to the ranch. Meeting Lucy's new man might enable her briefly to forget the sadness at losing three of her sons.

She had always expected something terrible to happen at the ranch. Her husband John had always been so angry – angry with everyone except her. He had told her once that she calmed him down – that she enabled him to believe that not everyone was out to harm him.

But Mary knew his anger had infused itself into six of their nine children – and now three of them were gone. She had spent the last thirty-six hours oscillating between despair and disbelief. Poison was a female weapon. She tried to bury the thought that her only daughter could kill three of her brothers; Kelly was so like her father.

Now, as on several occasions recently, she had only a couple of hours to compose a coded message, this time to Lucy. Her phone calls were probably being tapped and that she could never put any of her beliefs and fears on paper. She would have to prepare a message – and do it fast.

She went to her library for the crossword puzzle book she had bought recently in Marlborough. She would have to work quickly. Tears were coming again – tears that would have to wait if she was to use what might be her only chance to tell Lucy what she needed to know.

Mary wrote the briefest of letters first. She would find the words in the crossword book next. Fighting back the tears for Matthew, Christopher and Peter, Mary found her brain working surprisingly fast.

Then the guilt – feelings of guilt that her sadness was more for Peter than for the other two. Was a mother supposed to have favourites?

No time for self-indulgence, Mary. Got to get this message ready for Lucy.

The answers to the clues came faster than ever before. It was only thirty minutes later that she had the words she needed. She wrapped the book in ordinary brown parcel paper. If the wrong people turned up, it would look like a present she was giving to Jim for his birthday.

As the tears started again, she realised she was still in her nightdress.

Mary, get yourself together. Lucy, Jim and John will be here in a couple of hours.

Twenty minutes later, she descended the stairs. She put some coffee on to brew and sat in her favourite chair. For the first time in days, she smiled. Lucy had given it to her only days after discovering that Mary loved rocking chairs.

She felt light-headed – then remembered she had eaten nothing since the discovery of the death of her three sons nearly two days ago. She had been too busy organising death certificates and the myriad of other things that seemed urgent.

Those wretched memories came again – memories of the three bodies of her sons being put ignominiously into black zip-up plastic bags before being dumped insensitively into the back of the collection van.

You have to write it down.

Mary took her coffee to her library, trying to make sense of it all. She knew that getting it into her journal would help the process.

She went to a shelf of books that looked the same as any other. She had obtained twenty-four antique leather-backed ledgers, completely unused, from an old book dealer in Boston.

It was with some irony that Mary recalled it was the tenth anniversary of the assassination of John Kennedy that autumn that had prompted her to start these diaries. Here she was recording the murder of her own sons.

No one else knew that these old ledgers contained her diarised notes going back to November 1973. Mary started to write.

Sunday – October 21st 2012

Peter, then Matthew and Christopher – all poisoned – why?

Saddest two days of my life.

None of them had any involvement in Black Industries.

Kelly? Only one who knows contents of John's will.

Who next?

Still not clear as to Kelly's goals.

Andrew and Louise came over yesterday to be with me – she's so sweet.

Andrew asked about Jim's safety – NB: only sibling to do so.

Lucy coming over before lunch today – with her new man – and Jim.

Never a cross word between us.

All remaining brothers suspects – Police don't know that Billy adored Chris and Matt.

Kelly conspicuous by her absence – as cold as her father.

Simon and Jack gone for two days – again.

Where do they go in these two-day absences? Too dangerous to try to find out?

How callously the funeral people treated my boys when they took them away.

Horrible – don't they know these are the things people remember – for ever!

Mary stopped writing – her mind emptied, for now. She replaced the book in the long row of anonymous, leather-backed volumes, forming an unobtrusive continuation of a twelve-foot-long line of similar books.

Her thoughts returned to Lucy.

What if whoever killed my sons tried to kill Lucy? That would be a loss too heavy to bear. What if the killer is already planning it?

29

Lucy, John and James finished breakfast. As John got up to clear the plates, his phone buzzed with a call from George.

'Mr Baxter – listen hard. Lock all the windows and doors, shut the curtains in the downstairs rooms and get under the oak table in the kitchen. Only after you've done that, turn on the news. I'm coming to you. Do *not* leave the house till I get there. Have you got all that?'

'Yes, George. Got it.'

John looked at Lucy. 'Are all the windows and doors locked?' he asked, drawing the blinds down in the kitchen. 'Are all the curtains still closed from last night?'

'What the hell is going on?' Lucy asked.

John raised his voice. 'Are the windows and doors all shut and locked?'

'Yes; they haven't been opened since we were away.'

'And the curtains?'

'Still closed from last night.'

'Get under the table, both of you.'

Lucy hesitated.

'NOW.'

John grabbed the TV remote and sat down next to them.

The news images were of a house with smoke coming from a bedroom window. Fire officers were leaving the building.

James pointed at the screen. 'That's my bedroom.'

A reporter was talking into her microphone.

'Residents say they've never seen anything like it in this sleepy quarter of Boston. Police think the explosion was caused by a hand grenade thrown from a passing car … we'll update you when we have more.'

'George is on the way over.'

'That's my bedroom,' James repeated. 'That's Kelly. She's black.'

Lucy looked at him for a moment – and put her hand on his shoulder.

How long can we hold them off? It was pure luck James was not at home.

George called again. 'Let nobody into the house – got that?'

'They're coming for us, then?' John asked.

'What do you mean?' Lucy demanded.

'George will be here soon. He'll tell us what—'

The crash of bullets against the kitchen window drowned Lucy's scream. The staccato explosions of an automatic weapon and the smashing of bullets against the glass were deafening. They flattened themselves to the floor.

Then – silence.

'What the …' Lucy started.

Another hail of bullets hit the other kitchen window, this time a more sustained burst.

Lucy put her hand on top of James's, straining to hear the slightest sound.

John's phone buzzed again. Lucy jumped with the shock.

'You folks OK in there? He's gone. I'm at the door now.'

John got to his feet to let George in. 'Did you see who did this?'

'A little guy, about five foot seven, I'd say; white, slight build. I'll be checking police records.'

'Sounds like the guy who followed me out of Sotheby's, and on Harbour Island.'

George put some spent bullet casings on the breakfast bar in a plastic bag. 'I still have friends in ballistics.'

He approached the windows to inspect the damage. 'Impressive bits of kit, these windows. Are all three panes bulletproofed, ma'am?'

'Yes. Why?'

'Because the outer panes held up without yielding. You still have two bulletproof panes that were never touched. Very impressive,' he said. 'I'm going to check outside.'

Tears were streaming down Lucy's cheeks. John held her tight to him.

'I can't do this, John. I don't have your nerves. How long will we have to live like this? What do we do about the kids? I'll never forgive myself if anything happens to any of you.'

'I know.'

'John, we're out of our depth. They're vicious and capable of killing – even each other. What chance do we have?'

John looked into Lucy's face. He had never seen such sadness.

'John, I've been thinking for a while I'm endangering you. This isn't your fight. You have your kids to protect on the other side of the Atlantic, I have mine to protect here. That's what we have to do.'

'What are you saying, sweetheart?'

'John, can't you see – we can't be together; it's too dangerous for all of us. I'm so, so sorry.' Lucy paused. 'I just don't think this can work.'

'Lucy … I don't think my heart will beat without you.'

'John, you're so sweet. But you're no good to your children dead. Can't you see – you have to go back to England.'

So - this is your sacrifice, Lucy – your happiness – to save his life.

Lucy sat down and sobbed.

30

The doorbell chimed. John checked it was George before opening it.

George could sense the sadness in Lucy's kitchen. 'Sorry, folks, I can see you need some time …'

'It's OK, George, don't mind us,' John replied.

'The precinct's just called. The food last night had two different poisons in it – sodium cyanide, and thirty-five grams of ninety-five per cent pure sodium pentobarbital. More than enough to kill a horse.'

'Why do you say horse?' John asked.

James heard the question. 'Sodium pentobarbital is Nembutal. It's used by vets to euthanise animals.'

They all looked at James.

Lucy wiped her tears. 'Why use two different poisons?'

'Most likely to confuse us,' John started. 'The Blacks realise that we know Andrew is a doctor and would know about Nembutal. By putting only Nembutal in the food, they know that we would think of Andrew. Let's assume that the killer is halfway bright. They would know that by implicating Andrew so obviously, we would suspect that someone was trying to load suspicion onto him. In effect, we would know Andrew was not the murderer.'

Lucy picked up on his train of thought. 'But if they use cyanide as well as the Nembutal, we might believe it was a clumsy killer trying to make sure of it.'

'Perhaps you could have this talk on the way over to the Ridge,' George said. 'I can follow you a little way behind.'

Lucy, James and John set off for the ranch together in Lucy's silver Mercedes.

They drove for a minute or two before John broke the silence. 'George seems to know what he's doing.'

Lucy nodded. 'James – does Simon still work out on the ranch?'

'Horses don't like him, and one of them died when he was there. He works in the gallery now.'

'Is that how you know about Nembutal, James?' Lucy replied.

'There were no injuries or signs of any illness,' James said.

125

Lucy looked at John, horrified.

Lucy probed further. 'Which gallery are we talking about, James?'

'The Sunset Gallery, on Newbury Street.'

John searched the gallery on his phone. 'We ought to visit, sweetheart.'

'Why's that?'

'Lots of early American … some Frederic Church and some Cropsey.'

'James? How would you fancy staying with your mom, back at the ranch for a while? Just till John and I get back to Boston in two weeks?'

'They'll know where I am.'

Lucy persisted. 'I have the feeling, if you're with Ma, they won't attack either of you.'

James looked to his right out of the window. The glorious yellows and reds of the New England fall would have distracted anyone. John and Lucy let him have his thoughts for a while.

Lucy turned her head so James could hear her clearly. 'If Simon poisoned a horse, the last place you should be is in the Boston house with him.'

'There's bad people in their phones,' James said. 'But I have all the numbers.'

'Whose phones?' Lucy asked.

'Jack and Billy,' came the answer. 'Just like black Simon – they leave their phones around.'

'Black Simon? James – you called Kelly black earlier. Is that something you can share?'

'Jack is red, Billy is green, Simon and Kelly are black.'

'Is that how you see them, James?' Lucy asked.

126

'Everyone has colours – it's who they are.'

A question occurred to Lucy. 'What colour am I, James?'

'Same as John.'

'And what colour is that?'

'Purple. Same as Ma, but she's in a bubble of her own. You and John are always in the same one.'

'Wow, James. You see all that?'

Lucy pondered a moment.

Then her thoughts turned to the less obvious reasons for her visit to the ranch today.

What we really need are the phone contacts of John Black.

Lucy took a right turn off the road. A hundred yards ahead of them were the gates of the Ridge Ranch. The dark-blue gates, fully twenty feet wide, sported the words 'THE RIDGE' in gold-painted characters a foot tall, set in a huge elliptical frame, high above the driveway.

The avenue of trees either side of the approach to the ranch were ablaze with the yellows, reds and browns of the New England fall.

'Why are the autumn colours so much more beautiful here than anywhere else?' John asked.

'It's a combination of the soil here in New England and the way the air turns cold, so suddenly. No other landscape with so many deciduous trees has such a sudden drop in air and soil temperature at this time of year.'

She wound the car around the four hundred yards of circular driveway, past six large grey weather-boarded family houses that fringed two acres of lush green grass. The homes, all exclusively occupied by the Black siblings who worked on the ranch, were built in the same style with grey roof shingles and white-painted Georgian window- and door frames. Each house was slightly different from its neighbour – and two of the chimneys gently effused woodsmoke, giving the cluster of buildings a kind of old-fashioned peace.

Outside the circle of houses was a larger concentric arrangement of four long stable blocks, a house specifically built for the full-time equine vet, a state-of the-art veterinary surgery, a building housing a circular pool for the rehabilitation of injured horses, three hay-barns, a huge grain store, and sheds that housed tractors, trailers, reels of hose and several large mowing machines.

'Wow,' John smiled. 'How many horses do they keep?'

'About a hundred and twenty,' James replied.

'It's like a village. Which one was yours?' John asked.

'That one.' Lucy pointed to the building opposite the main ranch. John's gaze alighted on the house Lucy had lived in, a large one he guessed had at least six bedrooms. His focus then extended further from the Ridge, into the valley beyond. The vivid reds, strong yellows and golden browns of the autumn seemed to form a continuous blanket of colour extending the width of Massachusetts.

Mary Black emerged as they pulled up outside the main ranch house.

'Hi, Jim. Happy birthday.' Ma gave James a long hug. 'Hi, Lucy. Thank you for bringing Jim over today. And you must be John.'

John smiled at the kind face beaming up at him.

Mary grinned at Lucy. 'Girl done good. Come on in – it's not getting any warmer.'

They made their way into the house. 'Two packages came for James Black.' Ma turned to James. 'Someone knows it's your birthday, Jim.'

'Lucy knows,' James said.

Lucy and John laughed as James approached the parcels on the kitchen table. He unwrapped a small parcel containing the latest Android phone.

'I know you already have a phone,' Lucy said. 'But this one has the internet.'

James unwrapped it, excited. He looked at Lucy and put his arms around her, the first time they had seen any show of emotion from him. He looked back at the screen.

'Why don't you open the big one, Jim?' Ma said.

James reluctantly turned his attention to the larger parcel. He tore off the brown wrapping paper to reveal a small fir tree in a pot.

'I've never had a tree,' James said. 'Can we plant it, Ma?'

'Of course. Why don't we plant it in the middle of the circle out there?'

Mary turned to Lucy and John. 'Thank you, thank you.' She smiled at them, gripping Lucy's hands in her own. 'Will you folks be alright for a few minutes?'

Lucy waited till James and Mary had left the house.

'Now, Mr Baxter, you'll see why I got the tree.' Lucy accessed the contacts on her cell phone. Immediately a phone rang in the next room. 'Now we know where Ma's phone is.'

He followed her into the next room, a huge living room with a high vaulted ceiling of oak beams and a vast open fireplace at one end. On a coffee table was a ringing cell phone. But Lucy noticed John's attention was focussed on the two eight-feet-tall, red-granite Egyptian statues, one each side of the fireplace.

He approached the one to the right.

Lucy watched him. 'I know it's tempting John, but right now, I don't think we have time.'

Suddenly, his expression changed to incredulity. He took out his phone and took four photos of the inscriptions on the chest of the statue. He crossed the fireplace and took photos of the same area of the other statue. 'I don't believe it,' he said.

Lucy held out her hand to him. He backed away from the statues, still staring at them. He took another photo of the pair. 'I don't believe it,' he repeated.

He turned to look at Lucy. 'Sorry, sweetheart. You've got Ma's phone, I see.'

'We can always come back some other time,' she replied.

Lucy opened up the contacts in Ma's phone and copied two numbers into her own phone. She dialled one of the numbers and they heard a phone ring upstairs.

'That's Old Man Black's phone.' They followed the noise to a large bedroom upstairs.

'So obliging of him,' Lucy said. 'Black always claimed the cell phone was an evil machine designed by jealous wives to keep tabs on their husbands. So here it is – with all his business contacts.'

Lucy took the SIM cards from both phones, transferred the numbers from Old Man Black's card to the memory of her own phone, then replaced the SIMs in both phones.

'And you thought trees were only good for turning CO_2 into oxygen,' she said, extending her hand to him.

'Oh, I wouldn't say that,' John replied. 'But it reminds me I haven't bought the carbon offsets for our flights yet.'

'Do you always offset?' Lucy asked.

'Actually, I triple offset – and it's not that expensive. It's only £9.42 for a return trip from Heathrow to Boston in economy – or £28.26 if you triple offset.'

'Why triple offset?' Lucy asked.

'Because not flying in the first place is much better than offsetting the carbon. When you offset, you are helping the development of wind turbines etcetera, that will reduce CO_2 emissions in the future. When you fly, you create CO_2 emissions today. Because of the urgency to reduce global temperatures now, we should more than pay back the carbon because that payback is in the future.'

Lucy was thinking as they walked back downstairs. 'Can anyone offset their carbon emissions; I thought it was only companies who could do that?'

'No, anyone can do it – even as a private individual,' John replied.

'What happens to your £9.42?'

'I buy the Verifiable Carbon Standards. On the website you see the projects your money goes to. I choose the wind turbines and solar parks because the CO_2 savings are easy to calculate accurately – and happen much sooner than the savings from planting trees.'

James and Mary returned, their faces flushed from their exertions in the autumn air.

'It should do well out there,' Ma said. 'Firs like sandy soils.'

Lucy turned to James. 'You remember you said you liked the piano at the Beacon Hill house?'

James nodded.

'Why don't you show Mary what those lessons have taught you?' Lucy said.

James made his way to the piano in the sitting room and sat on the red velvet stool.

They recognised the music. Ma clasped her hands together in a mixture of delight and disbelief. She stared at her son as his fingers danced faultlessly over the keyboard. He was playing the piano solo of Beethoven's Fifth Piano Concerto in E flat major, a piece of music known as 'The Emperor Concerto' – and playing from memory.

'That's beautiful, darling. But don't you need any music to play from?' Ma said, as he finished.

'Let's go back to the kitchen, Ma,' Lucy said. 'We have some more surprises for you.'

They left James playing the piano. Mary, Lucy and John settled at the long oak refectory table in Mary's kitchen.

Lucy started. 'Ma, James has talents most of us only dream about. He has literally hundreds of phone numbers in his head. I don't remember you telling me about his memory.'

'Lucy – I knew he had a good memory – but I had no idea it was this good.'

'Anyway, John and I have to leave New England for the next two weeks. We've engaged an investigator. We believe it will be safer, at least for the next two weeks, if James stays here. George Bellows will keep watch round the ranch – he misses nothing – he's very proactive.

'Someone tried to use James to poison some food we had delivered. James tells us that his brother Jack arranged it.'

'Jack? Tried to kill you?' Ma held her head in her hands.

132

'Ma, we think Kelly organised it and used Jack to persuade James. We wanted you to have this information before we went away. I think you ought to know that Kelly tortures James. She burns him with her lighter and we've seen the scars on his back from what she does to him with electrical flex.'

'What?' Mary's face was screwed up in horror – struggling to absorb Lucy's words.

'Ma, George is ex-police – he knows how to protect people. This is probably the time to introduce you to him.'

'Before you do, sweetie, I have something for you. Look at it as soon as you leave today. Promise me?'

'I promise, Ma,' Lucy said.

Mary handed Lucy a small neatly wrapped parcel. 'Lucy, you and I never had a cross word. You need to read the first page very carefully.'

Lucy dialled George. A few moments later, the doorbell rang. John opened the door. 'Come in, George. We need you to meet Mary Black.'

'Nice to meet you, George,' Mary said, looking up at the imposing figure.

'Nice to meet you too, ma'am.'

Mary turned to Lucy. 'Do you think James and I are safe in this house?'

'George has already saved our lives twice. He is proactive and predictive; he is probably going to ask you a few questions about the family and their various comings and goings.'

Mary started to sob. John put his arm round her. There were no words for a mother who had outlived three of her sons.

She looked up and smiled wistfully at Lucy and John. 'We'll be alright. Knowing my husband, only someone completely mad would come here to hurt us ...'

Lucy shuddered. *That's what worries me.*

31

Monday – 22nd October

Lucy woke early. On three successive days, they had survived an attack on their lives. Her sleep was becoming shallow and intermittent. Would she and John become so tired they would cease to spot the next murder attempt? Something had to give. She had to survive, even if only for the kids. She and John had to gain the initiative – but how?

John started to stir. It was still dark, but Lucy's mind was preventing sleep. As she moved to leave the bed, John's arm curled round her and held her tight.

'Got to get up,' she said.

'Want to talk about it?'

'Do you want coffee?' she replied.

A minute later, they were in her kitchen, dressed only in bathrobes. John pulled out the seat that ran the length of the old oak table. He sat astride the end of the bench, side-on to the table, watching her make the coffee. She was aware of his gaze and knew how much he loved to watch her move around.

She put the mugs of coffee on the table and hoisted her bathrobe to sit facing him on his lap, her legs around his waist. She smiled as he undid the cord on her robe.

Tenderly, she took his head and nestled his face to her breasts. She allowed her hair to fall forwards around his head, forming a thick blonde curtain that excluded the world and all other thought. They sat in silence, eyes closed, content to hold each other in the beauty of the moment, certain in the knowledge they were the only people who had ever been this much in love.

'I love you so much, John.'

He cupped her face in his hands and reached up to kiss her. 'Come on, out with it.'

She smiled – yet again he had picked up on her thoughts. 'There is something we could do to gain the initiative. But we need to go into Boston – in office hours. You game?'

32

John opened the driver's door for Lucy. She kissed him. 'You might be the last gentleman in England, Mr B.'

'We're not in England, sweetheart.'

She smiled at him. 'Well, you're certainly the last one in the US.

'John, when Jane and I spoke about the flights, she got me first class to Atlanta, but only economy back to London on the twenty-eighth. Can you ask her if there's been any cancellations yet from first class over to Heathrow? Use my phone – Jane's number's in there.'

He dialled Jane, who confirmed that there were still no seats available in first class for Lucy's return to England. She would keep trying.

John was still thinking. 'Why did Mary not mention the jewel theft yesterday?'

'Maybe she was overwhelmed with James playing the piano, meeting you for the first time, losing three of her sons. We females are a strange emotional species, aren't we?' she smiled.

'Well, when you put it like that … So why all this use of poison?'

'Well, poison is usually a woman's murder weapon. Kelly probably knows that. Maybe she got Simon to use poison on the horse to make people believe he poisoned his brothers. In that way she diverts attention away from herself?'

John googled Kelly Black. 'You're right about Kelly. She played chess for Princeton.'

'We need to put the family under pressure – they may start to make mistakes. The painting I crossed the pond to see you about is probably a copy. Do you want to open the crossword book Ma gave us?'

'How do you know it's a crossword book?' John asked.

'Didn't you hear Mary say there was never a cross word between us? And don't forget how she allowed us to find Mount Chocorua?'

John opened the packet. 'Mmm – I think I know who Kelly got her brains from.'

'Well?'

John started to read.

Dearest Lucy,

I have no illusions about the family. Including my husband, there were ten, of whom only three were decent. Time is v short.

RXU became dishevelled and has bad stones. No one else knows.

I knew you would reach your peak. Other truths are not so beautiful and only available if you experience the pi zza, as the lady would say. I knew Her.

She loves you as I do: for your huge capacity to love. There was never an angry word between us. They lost Ruth too and we found communion together. Detach and destroy this.

I know you will find happiness and I know that your honesty and intelligence will be rewarded. Whatever happens in your search for the truth in the next few weeks, I will always love you and the delightful children you have brought into this Black world. Ma. X. 10.21.12.

'She's scared, John.'

'Yes, but why does she talk cryptically when she had us there in person?'

'I think she knows she's being listened to. She may be afraid for her life. When we made the call to Mary this morning, we gave her only two hours. If she was to write anything in plain words, she never knows who'll show up and seize it.'

'Also, sweetheart, this may be how she tells us we're all being listened to.'

'Especially as the stakes seem to be getting higher. Three brothers dead, three attempts on our lives and one on James's life. I hate to think of Ma being in fear. Let's do some of the clues.'

John agreed. 'Only the middle three paragraphs are cryptic.'

Lucy suggested he read it again slowly.

'Well, Mr B, I think reaching the peak is us uncovering Mount Chocorua.'

'Agreed. What's next? *Other truths are not so beautiful and only available if you experience the pi zza, as the lady would say,*' John continued. 'But there's a space in the middle of the "pi zza", as if a letter is missing.'

'Show me.'

John held the book so she could see it while driving. 'OK. So what are the next few words?'

'*As the lady would say. I knew Her.* But the "H" of the word "Her" is a capital, as if it's indicating a proper noun or a name,' John said.

Lucy smiled. 'I may not have mentioned this – you remember I inherited the Boston house from Tim Howard? Well – Lady Howard and I got on very well. I think Ma's telling us that she knew Lady H.'

'Probably – but I think she's saying more than that. She uses the word "experience" when she talks about the "pi zza", maybe to indicate she is not talking about pizza. If it was pizza, she'd have used the word "eat", or even "partake", and not omitted a letter,' John suggested.

He continued. '*There was never an angry word between us.*'

'Ah, I think I know this one,' Lucy smiled. 'What she is saying is …'

'There was a *cross* word, instead,' John replied. 'Looking at the next sentence, Ma is saying they had communion. Crosswords were how they communicated confidentially.'

'But what if she meant an extra use of the word "communion" as well? She didn't have to use that word; she could've used "connection", or even "rapport". What if she was talking about something ecclesiastic?' Lucy asked. 'How does she continue?'

'*There was never an angry word between us. They lost Ruth too and we found communion together. Detach and destroy this.*'

'John, if you're right about them using crosswords to communicate, then Ma is talking about the Howard family when she says they lost Ruth. I never heard about anyone called Ruth in either family.'

She paused. 'No, let's assume that the two families didn't actually have a person called Ruth to lose … that would imply *ruthless*. So, there are *two* ruthless families and that is why she and Lady H had to be careful with their communications.'

'OK. But let's go back to the start. There's still a couple of things we need to understand. *RXU became dishevelled and has bad stones. No one else knows.*'

'What do we reckon this is?' John asked.

'I'm starting to get this encryption. I think Ma used the word "dishevelled" to mean all mixed up. If we unravel RXU, there are only a certain number of possible permutations of three letters.'

John smiled. 'You're right. There's RXU, RUX, XRU, XUR, UXR, URX.'

'Say the last one faster,' Lucy urged.

'URX,' he obliged.

'Faster, much faster,' she insisted.

'I get it – your ex, Billy Black.'

'If she is referring to my ex, then what does she mean by "bad stones"?'

'Did he have kidney- or gallstones?'

'Not as far as I know – at least when I knew him.'

'Then I think she meant the stolen stones,' John ventured.

'Well, we know he steals and we know jewellery has been stolen,' Lucy added.

'OK, let's go with stolen stones … so there is only one more thing to sort out – why the space after the "pi" and before the "zza"? No consonant can be put before two "z"s, at least in the English language … and only one vowel – an "a". So we get "piazza". And we know which piazza she most admired, don't we?'

'We do,' Lucy grinned. 'Lady H honeymooned in Venice – she always had a soft spot for it … that's why Ma uses the word "communion". The Basilica San Marco.'

'Impressive – considering Ma only had two hours to put it all together. Don't tell me I have to take you to Venice. I couldn't stand it; what with all that fabulous art, the opera house, chocolate shops, beautiful glass and Italian leather everywhere … what *would* we find to do?' John grinned at her. 'And that's just the daytime.'

Lucy kept a straight face. 'Well – a few days in one the world's most beautiful places couldn't hurt, I suppose.'

He smiled. 'So, I'll take you as soon as you get back from Atlanta.'

'Wrong – I will take *you* to Venice,' she said.

'Why do you say it like that?' he asked.

'That's my surprise. Meanwhile, we need to know where to start once we're in Venice.'

'In Ma's crossword book.' John started to leaf through the book to see if he noticed anything.

Lucy was deep in thought.

We seem to be carrying on as if the attack yesterday in Concord didn't happen. The train's travelling too fast. How do we stop this before one of us gets killed?

'Lucy, what would I have in common with a Venetian gondolier?'

'Ooooh, Mr Baxter. I love the way you plant your pole – firmly – and beautifully.'

John smiled. 'You *are* quick.'

Lucy giggled and glanced across at him easing back in the right-hand seat.

I love you so much. How can this feel so right and so wrong at the same time?

'A question,' Lucy said. 'Why would Ma want us to know Billy has the stones?'

'Indeed.'

'John, let's call Ma and tell her in coded form that we've got the message.'

John dialled and switched the handset to 'speaker' so that Lucy could speak to Mary.

'Ma, it was great to see you again. We just wanted to tell you that we get it, and that we're planning a trip when we get back to England.'

'OK, then, Sweetie. Have a good trip,' Ma replied.

John ended the call and grinned. 'What could be more romantic? Great art, great architecture and great history. I want to stand where Canaletto stood when he painted the Piazza San Marco. Which reminds me – we never went to Walton Bridge.'

'Speaking of England, I wonder if Jane got me in first class yet. John, could you find 'Jane' in my phone contacts and put me on speaker again?'

John dialled again; after a few rings, Jane replied. 'Sorry, Lucy. There are absolutely no first-class or premium economy seats available on any flight from Atlanta to London. I'm so sorry.'

'OK, Jane, thanks for trying.'

Lucy turned to John. 'Let's go up to Beacon Hill and see what sort of commute Simon has. What harm could come of that?'

33

'Where we're going is the prettiest part of Boston,' Lucy said.

'You'll see why I chose this route when I turn into the next street – named after one of Britain's favourite sons. See if you can guess – he was born on Christmas Day, 1642.'

'Was he a mathematician and a physicist?' John asked.

Lucy smiled, as she turned into Newton Street, doubling back towards Columbus Avenue, where she turned right.

John was admiring the two-hundred-year-old black metal railings of the homes on Beacon Hill, and the uneven brick sidewalk on the north side of the street. His attention was drawn to the golden dome of the State House at the top of the slope.

'You're into number coincidences, John. The designs of the State House were agreed on the 28th of October 1797. Ring any bells?'

John thought for a moment. 'One hundred years, to the day, after Canaletto's birthday. And you fly back to me in England in a few days, also on the 28th of October.'

Lucy smiled. 'Now we turn left and we'll be outside the Black place on Chestnut Street.'

She pulled the car into the kerb eighty yards from the house. A broken window had been boarded up and the wall above the window was black from soot.

'Let's see why they never wanted me inside, shall we?' Lucy said.

'Are you mad? If Simon comes back, he may be armed.'

'That's why we're here in office hours. We'll be quick. I just want to see if there's any evidence of any of the art fraud. You were the one who said we have to get on the front foot.

'But first, we make sure no one is home. Look, John, the phone number of the house is in Black's phone.'

Lucy showed John the contacts list of her phone and pressed the green button. She let it ring for a full minute, got no answer and dialled again. She let the phone ring another ten times and got no answer.

'OK, then. No one home. You coming?'

She took John's hand and approached the front door. She rang the bell. There was no answer, so she inserted a key.

'How long have you had that?' he asked.

'Only since yesterday, at the ranch,' Lucy grinned, inserting the key into the lock.

'It works. Don't touch anything; keep your hands in your pockets; we *cannot* leave any fingerprints anywhere.'

Lucy stepped inside. 'I wonder how long the burning smell lasts.'

'Quick, then,' John suggested. 'You take upstairs, I take downstairs. See you back here in a minute.'

'OK, but before I check upstairs, I need a few freezer bags,' Lucy said, looking for the kitchen.

Realising she was not going to chat, John walked into the living room. Six small paintings were leaning up against the wall under a window, each neatly sealed in bubble wrap.

Lucy appeared, freezer bags in hand. 'Look at this,' John said.

'Stay here while I get the car a bit closer,' Lucy ordered.

'We can't hang about. What are you doing?'

'Taking out some life assurance. Chess is more fun when you're on the attack.'

John followed her to the front door. While she was striding towards her car, he looked both ways down the street.

Where is Simon? Why couldn't he come back any moment?

He went in search of some kitchen towel.

Why is Lucy taking so long?

The next two minutes felt like five. Finally, Lucy reappeared. 'Thank god. I was worried. Here. Use these,' he said.

He handed Lucy some kitchen towel to use when touching the frames. 'And give them back to me when we're done.'

She picked up one of the works. 'You get to carry two.' Lucy had left the trunk of her car open and they placed the three paintings in it. She looked around them on the street. 'Three more and we're away. Come on.'

Lucy marched back into the house. Less than a minute later they were loading the other three paintings. 'Let's get out of here,' she said.

John twisted in his seat to check if anyone was following them. 'Legal-Lucy, you amaze me. Now what?'

'Now we put Kelly on the back foot. But first, Newbury Street.'

'Is the gallery open at this time of year?' John asked. 'It's well past the tourist season.'

'Probably not. But we're so close, anyway.'

Lucy pulled the car into the kerb, a full hundred yards away from the gallery.

John googled the gallery. 'Their website says the gallery is shut on Mondays.'

They left the car and walked up Newbury Street. 'Look, sweetheart – there are people inside.'

The lights inside the gallery showed people coming to the inside of the front door on repeated visits. John guided Lucy down some steps to the lower ground floor level of a denim shop opposite. They had a good view of the gallery without being seen.

The door to the gallery opened and two young men emerged with a large frame covered in bubble wrap. A third person stayed just inside the door.

145

'That's Simon, the rapist,' Lucy said, looking at John.

John frowned, waiting for her to say more.

'That explanation comes later.' Lucy turned her attention back to the gallery.

'Definitely Simon. Can't mistake that untidy flock of blond hair. Why does he have to be here today when the gallery is shut?'

John recognised the smaller man carrying the painting. 'He's our little guy from the Ritz.'

They watched as the painting was carried to a gold Cadillac near the gallery.

'That's the car James told us about,' John added.

'Look, they're getting two more. If this is a robbery, John, the police will interrogate employees. Simon knows they'll search the house at the top of the hill. So they have to hide the paintings somewhere else. Have you got your phone with you?'

'Good idea,' John replied.

Lucy's phone beeped. 'Battery's low. I'll save it for one or two in a minute.'

John took a photo of the blue-grey front door. 'Cameras date and time the shots. I want to get some faces though – one or two with them carrying the frames.'

'Don't get too close,' Lucy said. 'Once they're back inside, I'll get one of the registration plates. But I don't know if Simon carries a gun these days.'

Simon and his accomplice made their way back up the steps to Number 238 and disappeared inside. Lucy and John crossed the street. Lucy took photos of the car, set against the gallery.

'Simon will recognise me. Meet you back at the car,' she said.

John walked a few yards beyond the Cadillac to the corner of Fairfield Street – and remembered to turn the camera shutter noise off on his phone.

He stood next to a delivery van parked in front of the gold Cadillac. A minute later, the two young men walked straight towards him. His phone already in camera mode, he turned to face them and took a picture as they held the frame.

The smaller man recognised John – who could not know that the assassin's next kill method had never failed.

34

Lucy waited in her car, unable to see John, concealed by the delivery van.

What's taking so long?

John crossed the street towards her, stopping three cars away. He checked behind him before ducking into the kerbside seat of her car.

'Let's go,' he said. As they passed the gallery, there was no sign of Simon but the Cadillac had not moved.

John's phone tone told Lucy that George was calling.

'How you doing, folks?' came his voice.

'Where are you, George?'

'On the way back from the ranch.'

'George, we think Simon Black is carrying out a robbery at one of the galleries on Newbury Street. What Simon doesn't know is that we have six paintings they probably stole earlier.

'The police will take Simon in for questioning and search the Black house at the top of the hill. Because he knows that, he'll have to go back to move the paintings he thinks are still there.'

'Is there anything else you're not telling me?' George asked.

'Oh, there is one thing. One of the guys loading paintings into the Cadillac is the guy who came to Harbour Island to spy on us – and who followed me out of Sotheby's.'

'OK, I'll get up there and come back to you.'

Lucy turned briefly to John. 'When Simon's left the Black house, we should put some paintings back inside, and some in Kelly's house, then let the police know.'

John nodded. 'The ones they still have they'll hide at the ranch. That way, if the paintings are discovered, Simon and Kelly are not caught with the art. I believe they'd choose Billy's place – especially if they're trying to implicate you. You could have planted them on Billy out of some old marital grudge, or something.'

John's phone buzzed again. 'Can you put it on speaker, John?' Lucy asked.

'George, Mr Baxter. I've just had confirmation that the brothers were poisoned. I searched the records for this gold Cadillac I'm following. It belongs to Jack Black, so young James was telling the truth. By the way, it looks as if we're headed back up Beacon Hill. I'll buzz you back.'

Lucy turned to John. 'The little barn at the back of our old house would be perfect 'cos it's not overlooked by any of the other ranch houses – especially on a dark October night. Today's Monday. Billy's probably down at the Little Bear Saloon – and they know that.'

'George again. There's a fairly animated chat taking place here at Beacon Hill. I assume it's because they've discovered that the paintings they stole are missing.'

'Perfect, George. Have you got your listening stuff with you?' Lucy asked.

'I'm already recording them.'

'Great. We think they're headed out to the ranch to hide the art at Billy's place.'

'You know where Kelly lives, I take it, George?' Lucy replied.

'It's just around the corner from where I am on Beacon Hill, on the next block. You can almost watch both houses at the same time.'

'Thanks, George. We're about to call Kelly to stir things up a bit. She might turn up there and then go on out to the ranch.'

John accessed Lucy's contacts list on her cell phone.

'Is that Kelly Black?'

'Who's calling?'

'I've just photographed your brother stealing the paintings from the gallery – all digitally timed and dated. When I end this call, I will call the police to tell them where to find your brother and the two stolen paintings.'

He cut the call to Kelly and dialled George again.

'George, you any good at picking locks?'

'I can get in most places – why?'

'OK, George. We'll be up there soon. We'll stop quite a way away. Keep recording what you can, and when they leave, meet us round the corner at Kelly's.'

'Will do.'

'Sweetheart, how quickly can we get back up to Beacon Hill?'

'Five minutes,' Lucy said, taking a left.

'Because we talked about two paintings and not twelve, Kelly might wonder if Simon is cutting her out of the theft. Hopefully, that's enough to get her out to the ranch to check.'

'And that's when we put the paintings in her house,' Lucy replied.

'We hide two paintings in her house while she's on the way out to the ranch. We put the other four we have in the Black house. We tell the police where the stolen art is. That way, the family are in possession of all the stolen goods, and we are not.'

Lucy smiled. 'If Simon and the little spy are still at the Black house when she arrives, the recording George is getting might bury them all. And I thought you were a respectable art collector.'

John smiled. 'All we've done is borrow some art for an afternoon to focus police attention on the people who actually stole it. And as I recall, this was your idea.'

'Let's hope George gets the recording we need.'

She pulled the car to the kerb a hundred yards from Kelly's front door. John texted George.

We're at Kelly's. How goes it?

You gonna love wot I got. B there in 2 mins. Boys left for ranch. Kelly just gone into Black place.

Lucy turned to John. 'We need to find out what they're planning to do with all this art.'

'Maybe William knows something – let's call him later.'

'Here's George,' Lucy said, looking in her wing mirror. She lowered the window.

'George, we need to get into Kelly's house.'

'I can't handle stolen goods, John.'

'Absolutely. You'll see nothing. If you can get the door open, you'll know nothing after that, because you'll be going back to your car. Is that OK?'

'OK then – Kelly is searching the Black house, right now, and quite thoroughly. There were lights going on upstairs when I left.'

'We're going to wait till she's gone to the ranch. You may as well hop in the back while we wait.'

The three of them waited in the dark. A figure approached. Kelly entered her house and they watched as lights were switched on along the length of the house. Less than two minutes later, the lights were switched off, and Kelly emerged, got into her car and drove off.

'OK, George – your turn,' Lucy said.

George crossed the road to Kelly's front door. In less than thirty seconds the door was open.

Lucy opened the trunk of her car. She and John each took a painting using the kitchen towels they had used earlier and crossed the road. 'Let's be quick.'

John followed her across the road and into Kelly's hallway. 'Let's see if she has a spare bedroom with the door closed,' he said. 'And let's not turn any lights on.'

'Just what I was thinking,' Lucy replied.

They placed the paintings in one of the bedrooms and re-closed the door.

'There's one little thing I must do,' Lucy said, striding along the landing. 'Just need Kelly's bedroom.'

151

'Sweetheart, we can't hang around – especially if the Blacks carry guns.'

'Thirty seconds, literally,' Lucy said.

'What the hell can be this important? We have to go – NOW.'

'I'll be very quick – meet you downstairs.'

George was standing in the unlit hallway. 'Old habit,' he said, pressing the 'play' button on the answer machine on the hallway table.

'Kelly, it's Tom. Let's meet at the Waterfront Restaurant tonight at seven.'

'No other messages, but she got this one – the light wasn't blinking any more,' George said.

'What message?' Lucy asked, appearing at the top of the stairs.

George pressed the 'play' button again.

As Lucy descended the stairs, she listened to the message and smiled.

Here's where we gain the third initiative …

35

As John watched Lucy descend in near darkness, he recognised something on the wall.

That should be in the Rockwell Museum over in Stockbridge.

He was looking at an oil-on-canvas portrait of John F. Kennedy. Only sixteen inches tall and twelve inches wide, it was widely regarded as the best likeness of JFK ever painted.

What the hell is it doing here? How did Kelly get it? And what is it with the 28th of October?

'Let's get out of here,' Lucy whispered.

They emerged onto the street, shutting the door firmly behind them.

'George, you may as well follow Kelly out to the ranch and tell us what happens.'

'OK, then, I'll catch up in a minute with the recording I got,' George said.

Lucy started the car and trickled it round the corner to the Black house.

'What were you doing upstairs?' John enquired.

'Just getting a bit more life assurance,' she said, handing John a freezer bag. 'There's four sealed bags inside the outer sealed bag. Please don't open them.'

A few seconds later, George called to play back the recording he had obtained outside the Black house.

'OK, George. Let me put you on speaker so Lucy can hear.'

'*They're gone.*'

'*Shit.*'

'*What we gonna do? She'll kill us.*'

'*She might've moved them somewhere else in the house.*'

'*Where would she put 'em?*'

'*Dunno?*'

'*She dreamt this whole thing up, so let's ask her.*'

'*No, wait. She might think we took 'em for ourselves. If she does, she'll kill us like the others.*'

'*What others?*'

'*My brothers. All poisoned. That's how we tried to get the English lot, but that moron, James, goofed it up.*'

'*Do you think she'll try to kill us?*'

'*Not if we tell her how it is. Anyway, she's prob'ly got the pictures.*'

Another pause ensued and Lucy and John could hear cell phone dial tones …

'*Hey, sis. The paintings have gone.*'

'*Which ones?*'

'*The ones we left in the house. They're definitely not here. All six. We looked everywhere, just in case you'd been in while we were at the gallery for the second time, getting the other six.*'

'*But you got the twelve from the gallery, like we agreed?*'

'*Yeah, we got them all, just like you said. We still have six in the car with us.*'

'*Let's meet up at Billy's garage. We stick to the plan.*'

'*OK. See you at Billy's.*'

'*One more thing, sis. We saw the tall English dude outside the gallery, so he knows we have the art.*'

Lucy and John could hear the click that signalled the end of the call. Then – Simon's voice again.

'*She wasn't as mad as I thought she'd be. Wonder why that was.*'

'*Dunno, let's get out there.*'

'*Talking of Billy, I wonder how he got on at the Rockwell place.*'

'*Call 'im. He must have done it by now.*'

'*I'm doin' it … Hey, Billy, did you get it all in Vermont?*'

'*Yeah, got the two Rockwells and put the little one back, like we agreed with Kelly. Simon, I'm about to get busy, if you get me.*'

'*What – the Middle Eastern girl?*'

'*Yeah, she bangs like there's no tomorrow. She's the wife of the curator at the Rockwell. Beautiful coffee-coloured skin. Look, I'll see you at the ranch later.*'

The recording finished. 'Obviously, I'll keep the recording, folks. But for now, I'll be getting on my way out there. Call you later.'

Lucy turned to John. 'Billy's still up to his old tricks. You'd think, in all the years since I left him, one of the husbands would have come after him.'

Lucy opened the door to the Black house with Mary's key for the second time that evening. They brought in the remaining four paintings, hiding them in the laundry room at the back of the house.

'You hungry, John?'

'Famished. I have an idea. We could make the Waterfront Restaurant by seven. Senator Malvito will be expecting to meet Kelly there – could be very informative ...'

Lucy looked at him. 'What's wrong?'

'I wonder what Billy meant when he said he'd put the little one back,' John replied.

Leila Rashadi looked across at Billy in bed. The robbery at the Rockwell Museum had gone to plan. He had replaced the small portrait of JFK he had stolen a month ago – and he had the two larger Rockwells in the trunk of his Chevy.

For the second time in a month, she had deactivated the alarm system and unlocked the trade entrance at the back of the building. Billy had removed the paintings from their mountings, sealed them thoroughly in three layers of bubble wrap, and locked them in his car. She and Billy had departed for a hotel in Ticonderoga, about thirty miles away.

Leila sat up, her skin wet with the exertions of the last half hour.

'You're great. Where'd you learn all that?' Billy asked.

She smiled to herself. *No education – no appreciation of other cultures.*

'Do you want to go again?' she asked.

'You still angry he didn't take you to London for the auction?' Billy asked.

'Of course. He is trying to impose his medieval ways on me, even though he chooses to live in the United States. It's ridiculous. But divorce is impossible for me in my country.'

'Am I just revenge sex for you, Leila?'

'Partly,' she said.

Billy grinned. 'My daddy always said revenge is sweet, but it's not about right and wrong – if you put the money in the right hands and you can right all the wrongs. And anyway, even if your husband found out, what's he gonna do here in the US?'

Leila shuddered. *You have no idea …*

36

John took Lucy's hand as they walked from her car to the Waterside Restaurant on Congress Street. He looked sideways at the left-hand side of her face and remembered their first meeting at the Ritz. Had it been only three weeks? That seemed impossible.

But now, even in the lights of the restaurant, he did not notice the scar. Her nose was slightly retroussé, her lips full and well defined. Her hair swept over her shoulders like liquid gold cascading to the small of her back. Her pink lipstick offset the dark-blue roll-neck sweater clinging so faithfully. It seemed to John that her extraordinary profile perfectly manifested her playfulness and generosity.

How can an angel be so mischievous, so physical – and so perfect for me?

'What?' she asked, catching his admiring glance.

'You make me glad I'm male.'

She grinned. 'Tonight, I want every last inch of your masculinity.'

They stood just inside the restaurant door. There seemed to be no one to greet them, so for a moment they took in the decor. Bamboo foliage and tropical plants created an Asian forest atmosphere, complimented by the sounds of screeching monkeys and exotic birds. A large video screen showed a waterfall cascading into a pool. John smiled at the thought of making love to Lucy in this paradise, as they had in the sea only a week ago.

Lucy interrupted his reverie. 'He's here.'

Senator Malvito was sitting alone at a table at the far end. Over six feet tall, powerfully built, and with a thick mop of dark hair, he was an ex-Boston Red Sox pitcher who had kept in shape. He had served two consecutive six-year terms as senator and had learnt how to pull the levers that achieved what he wanted. A good-looking man, he was proud of his Sicilian father, who had moved to the US in 1946 to start a new life.

They made their way over to the senator.

Lucy started the conversation. 'Senator Malvito?'

'Yes.'

'I'm Lucy Howard. I used to be Kelly's sister-in-law. I was married to Billy Black. This is John. May we join you for a second?'

The senator gestured to the empty chairs at the table. 'Sure.'

'Senator, John is an art dealer and I'm a lawyer handling an art fraud. We know the way the business is manipulated from time to time; the art world is very well connected.'

'OK – so what's your point?'

'Senator, we believe you're being used by Kelly,' Lucy replied.

'And how is that exactly?'

'We don't know her motives yet, but we believe she killed three of her brothers recently. And she tried to poison us the same way.'

'She did that?'

'Matthew, Christopher and Peter were all poisoned.'

Malvito stared hard at Lucy, then John.

Lucy persisted. 'We hired a detective to listen in on Kelly's conversations recently.'

The senator sat up. 'Which conversations?'

'Don't worry, Senator; our only aim is to damage Kelly. You could distance yourself before it's too late. The recordings can be destroyed ten minutes from now.'

John looked Malvito in the eyes. 'The tapes are the only thing we have.'

Lucy continued the thread. 'If you could tell us where the next robbery will take place, we'll take the necessary steps. You can see the tape being destroyed and we all move on.'

'Hold on a minute, lady. What robbery? I don't know anything about a robbery.'

John could see Malvito was contemplating Lucy's suggestion. 'We know about the auction at Christie's next week. She's due to take some art there and sell it.'

'I don't know anything about Christie's either,' Malvito retorted. 'She was going to do it all from auction houses here in New England. She told me it was only going to be the Norman Rockwell stuff.'

Malvito paused. 'Look, I'll tell you what I know. I was to put up the money to purchase a few key pieces – legitimately. Kelly was going to get the pictures copied and sell the copies, as copies – again legitimately. At least that's what she told me. That's why she wants me to bankroll it. She couldn't afford to buy more than one or two Rockwells from her own cash.'

'I take it then you're aware how much Rockwell originals fetch these days? One fetched forty-eight million pounds recently in London,' John said. 'Perhaps Kelly's planning to take the copies to England where she'll get the best prices.'

'She told me she was going to get them copied, then sell 'em here in New England to collectors.'

'Did she tell you who this copier is?' John asked.

'No, sir. But he's so good he gets fifty thousand dollars each one, apparently. She has another twelve we're going to be able to sell or copy soon. She says that on three of them, fifty thousand could turn into five hundred thousand when they are sold. I know you can't buy the originals for less than ten million at auction – which is why people pay five hundred thousand for a really good copy.'

'Or ten million if they think the copy's an original,' John added.

Lucy continued. 'Senator – Kelly organised an art robbery that took place in Boston this afternoon. She thinks that her brothers may have taken six of the twelve paintings they stole

– and hidden them. She's on her way out to the Black ranch to sort it out.

'Senator – she's not just getting you to bankroll purchases; she's also stealing art and getting copies made. Which art was stolen, which art was purchased legitimately? It's going to get complicated – and you cannot come out of this well.'

Malvito stroked his chin, deep in thought.

John continued. 'We have photographic evidence of the robbery committed by the Blacks today.' He showed the senator the photos of Simon loading paintings into Jack's Cadillac. 'If you're connected with Kelly Black when this gets to court, you're guilty in the eyes of the law.'

'Can you guarantee to eliminate my communications with Kelly?'

'Of course,' John said.

'How do I know you're not just messing with me?'

'Senator, I can assure you – the last thing we need is two sets of people on our backs.'

The senator studied the couple. 'You folks are English, aren't you?'

'Is it that obvious?' John grinned. 'Actually, the Baxters came from Islay, just off the coast of Scotland, although I live just outside London. Lucy is English though.'

'And what kind of stuff do you trade?' the senator asked.

'Mostly the Italian Masters and the early Americans – Frank Cropsey, Frederic Church, Hopper – that kind of thing,' John answered.

'I guess you folks really are the experts. How 'bout I buy you dinner? I have a proposition for you.'

37

Senator Tom Malvito related how he had studied law at Dartmouth.

'Lucy and I have to be on planes tomorrow, Senator. I wonder if we could get to why you wanted to eat with us tonight?'

'You're right. I have some early American art here in Boston. I need information and you collect art. I have a couple by Frederic Church, three or four by Cropsey ... oh, and a Bierstadt. Could any of those be any use to you?'

Without looking at Lucy, John replied. 'Well, Tom, it's always interesting to see nice collections.'

Malvito continued. 'Here's the truth, folks. My wife, Monica – she's a lot younger than me. Great-looking woman. Used to be Miss Texas, way back. But she comes from a wealthy oil family and I kind of keep her interested with the art, if you get me.'

'It'd be good to see your collection, Tom. Did Monica buy the art herself?' Lucy asked.

'I'm not giving away any of my wife's art. But you could look at the stuff I bought myself.'

Lucy and John followed the senator out to Concord, then up a long drive through some woods. When the house came into view it was illuminated from the ground in the dark, its chalk-white walls giving it the presence of a stately home. With two Corinthian columns at the front, it resembled a version of the United States White House. John wondered if the house echoed the senator's political ambitions.

He continued to gaze at the house as they approached. 'It must have fifteen bedrooms.'

'John, we're less than a mile from home.'

They followed the senator into his house. 'I apologise, folks. My wife has taken one or two of the help to London, so we'll have to pour our own drinks.'

John laughed. 'Tom, we're used to pouring our own drinks.'

Malvito led the way to a huge sitting room with three sofas arranged in a semicircle facing a large stone fireplace. Above the oak mantelpiece was a large painting of a striking raven-haired woman wearing only a purple silk wrap that grudgingly covered her bust.

A fire had been made up in the grate and Tom stooped to light it. He turned to face Lucy and John, who were looking up at the painting.

'That's Monica, if you're wondering.' He gestured to a sofa and asked the couple what they would like to drink.

John looked at Lucy. 'Have you any red wine?' she asked.

'I think we have some Bordeaux, if that's any good?'

Lucy nodded, smiling.

'And what about you, sir? I have some single malts.'

The senator took the lead seal from a bottle of wine and proceeded to uncork it.

'Well, if I'm going to share your Scotch, you'll have to call me John.'

The senator nodded. 'Spoken like a Scotsman – if your family comes from Islay, you might like some Laphroaig? I have a brand-new bottle here.'

'Perfect.'

162

Tom Malvito sat down. 'Hope that's to your liking, ma'am. Perhaps it's as well Monica is away for a few days. It allows me to be completely frank.'

Lucy interrupted. 'Did you say a brand-new bottle?'

Malvito looked at Lucy. 'Ma'am?'

'You said a brand-new bottle – the Laphroaig – but when you uncorked it the seal had already been broken.'

'Don't drink it, Tom,' John said, putting his own glass on the table.

Lucy continued. 'Tom, our food was poisoned recently; we think the Blacks organised it. Could any of the Blacks have got in here recently? Has Kelly been here recently?'

Tom looked at his drink suspiciously. He put it on the table in front of him. 'Perhaps we stick to the Bordeaux this evening. You have sharp eyes, young lady.'

Tom poured some red wine into two more glasses and offered one to John. He looked at the whisky tumblers still on the table.

'Tom, we have a private investigator who is ex-police – he could verify if the bottle is poisoned. I could have him take it to forensics if you like?' John replied.

'I think you'd better – here, take the bottle,' he said, re-inserting the cork.

Tom shook his head. 'Hell's bells – who can you trust these days?'

He paused. 'Monica is doing Billy Black. Ma'am, you were married to Billy. I know the Blacks; Billy's always stolen things – often other men's wives. My people tell me he's even been seeing another woman at the same time as my Monica

– Middle Eastern woman by the name of Leila – Leila Rashadi. Do you know her?'

'Can't say I do.'

Malvito continued. 'Most of the Blacks play dirty. My idea is this … if the family is self-destructing, we ought to help them do it.

'But before all that, I would like you to see my collection.' He led the way to his dining room; it was thirty feet long, its walls covered in a rich red velvet, and John was reminded of La Fenice Opera House in Venice.

His gaze went straight to a painting depicting one of the New England peaks in autumn. As he noticed the signature *Cropsey '58*, it was as if an electric charge had jolted him; he hoped Malvito had not noticed.

He looked at the frame and knew immediately it was the missing one in Mrs Markham's set.

'Look, Lucy, this one reminds me of my early start in the art world.'

'I see what you mean,' she said, noticing the signature, but giving nothing away. 'But I like this one too, and George would like it.'

'He certainly would,' John smiled, noticing the signature, *G. Bellows*.

'How about the Rockwell?' the senator interrupted.

Baxter looked afresh at the lush, rich colours painted photo-accurate by Norman Rockwell.

'I've always liked him,' John started. 'What did you have in mind, Tom?'

'I want enough information to bury the Blacks. You folks know what's happening in that nest of snakes. No money has to change hands. You get to walk away with my picture and a proper bill of transfer of ownership.'

John looked at Malvito. 'I have to tell you, Tom – this Rockwell's worth millions. Nothing we could do would be worth that much. But we could discuss one of the less valuable ones. Tom, do you mind if I have a word with Lucy for a minute?'

'Sure. Give me those glasses. I'll get you a refill. Come through when you're ready.'

Lucy looked at the Cropsey again. John put his arm round her as they gazed at the painting of a stream emerging from a forested hill, a young deer, its antlers still forming, standing in the foreground. The exquisite colours of the New England autumn leaves were masterfully applied in painstaking detail.

'Cropsey makes it look so easy,' John remarked.

'We're not taking payment from a possible crook?' she asked.

'No. We buy the painting so he makes a fair profit on it. In that way we never accepted any favours. At the moment, we only have superficial evidence. If we destroy the phone tapes in Kelly's house, which George could do, there's nothing to connect Kelly to Tom.'

They re-joined the senator.

'Can I ask what you paid for the Cropsey, Tom, the one right by the door?' John asked.

'Fifty, I think. Let me find the bill of sale.'

He rolled up the shutter on a magnificent inlaid bureau made mostly of walnut. Pulling out a receipt, he announced 'Fifty-five thousand dollars – back in 1999.' He handed John the receipt.

'Tom, I will give you seventy-five thousand for it,' John said.

Lucy interrupted. 'John, in view of what's happening in the art world here in New England, might it be indelicate to ask if there is any way the painting is a copy?'

'Hold on, lady. Are you accusing me of dirty dealing?' Tom retorted.

'No – please don't get me wrong ...'

'Listen, lady – if you think I would sell you stolen or copied art, I'd rather you left right now, and we forget the whole deal. What is this – some kind of double act you guys do to get the price down?'

John shook his head. 'Tom, I assure you we don't play games like that. It's not your fault you don't know me better. If you did, you'd know I'm known for playing it straight. But here's what I'll do, so you know this is not some ploy to drive the price down. I will check it's not a copy. If it's not, I'll give you eighty thousand dollars – and you still get all the info we have on the Blacks, ongoing.'

Tom Malvito stared hard at the couple.

Lucy broke the silence. 'Tom, I'm sorry I offended you. We've all been a bit wary in the art world in the last year. It seems every tenth piece of art we look at is copied. It's the reason I met John in the first place.'

Tom Malvito looked at John.

'I'll be straight with you, Tom. This painting is priceless to the lady who gave me my start in the art world. We destroy all evidence of your links with Kelly, and we give you everything we know about the Blacks.'

The senator smiled. 'Go, take a look then.'

'Tom, you might like to look at the painting with me. It might help when you next buy any art.'

The three of them returned to gaze at Cropsey's depiction of the New England fall.

John smiled. 'I have the advantage of having owned Cropsey's summer landscape for twenty years now; I know his brushstrokes, and the colour tones he uses for skies. This one is totally consistent with the other work he did. And, if you look very closely, you can see the tiny cracks in the paint.

'This is a hundred and fifty-four years old, and tiny little fissures are inevitable in oil paint this old. But a copier cannot replicate cracks a tenth of the thickness of a single bristle in a brush; there's no way to paint these cracks.

'So – we look at colour tone, brushstrokes, style, age, how much the paint has faded, everything combined. And – not that you could have known – it's in the right frame too.'

'Interesting … I have an idea.'

John and Lucy looked at Tom.

'If this picture is so important to you – why don't I hold onto it till we know if the whisky is poisoned. If it is – and you can help me put Kelly away – you can have it for your original offer of seventy-five thousand, but only if she hasn't poisoned us all.'

'We have a deal,' John replied.

'OK, then,' Tom said. 'I hope it makes her happy. How quickly can you send me any tapes and photos you have?'

John dialled George.

'Mr Baxter. What can I do for you at this hour?'

'What's the situation?'

'I'm watching Kelly and the other two here at the ranch. You were right – they went to Billy's place to hide the paintings. But Kelly doesn't seem upset that the guys have lost six of them.'

'OK, I need you to get back to Boston and find out if the answer machine we accessed earlier is tape-recorded or digitally recorded.'

'It's tape-recorded. I could see the tape through the perspex window.'

'OK, George. Could you go back and get that tape? Nothing else, just the tape.'

'Is there any overtime for doing twenty-hour days, Mr Baxter?'

'I think I've come up with something, George, but can we talk later? I'm with someone at the moment. See you at the house – I have a bottle of whisky that may have been poisoned. Can you do your forensics thing on it?'

John turned to the senator. 'All evidence taken care of, Tom. And by the way, how much would you want for that Bellows in the dining room?'

38

Lucy and John climbed back in her car.

'Shame we can't take the Cropsey yet, John. But earlier this evening we had no idea of its whereabouts; it could have been anywhere on earth.'

Once more they were interrupted by George. 'I have Kelly's tape, John. Hang on – Kelly's calling Malvito – I'll turn the volume up on "my ears" and put the speaker near my phone. Hopefully, you'll be able to hear them talking.'

'*Tom, the tape's gone. It was here this afternoon while the boys were down at the gallery. That's when I got your message. I think it's those meddling English messing us about.*'

'*Meddling English?*'

'*Billy's ex – and her boyfriend. They're art dealers. We have to be careful, Tom.*'

'*What do they actually know?*'

'*They know about my involvement in the art scheme, but not much else.*'

'*Where are the paintings now?*'

'*Out at Billy's place, on the ranch. Nobody goes in that empty old garage, and it can't be seen from any other property on the ranch; that's why we chose it – that, and because the police might think Lucy stole the paintings to implicate Billy.*'

'*So everything's safe for tonight, then?*'

'*I suppose … except that they know we were going to meet tonight at the Waterfront.*'

George's voice broke off his broadcast. 'Did you get that, folks?'

'Yes. Listen, George. Get some sleep. I'll call the police to-morrow to tell them where the paintings are. Could you be back at Beacon Hill by nine? Might be some more useful recordings to get,' John said.

'Will do. G'night folks. Have a good trip to Europe.'

Lucy and John were thankful they could drive straight into her garage. They allowed the door to shut electronically before getting out of the car and entering the house.

John opened his browser. 'I wonder if Kelly's entered any paintings into the Christie's sale catalogue for Thursday's auction. Let's see … very little early American unfortunately … but two Rockwells.'

'John – suppose she's not going to Christie's at all. Kelly was surprisingly cool when she discovered they'd lost six paintings. Let's suppose she only wanted the paintings missing – no sale, no delays with copying the paintings. What would that tell us?'

'Well, she could take the fifty thousand dollars for each copying process from Tom Malvito. If he bankrolls a few of these, she could collect several lots of fifty thousand.'

Lucy grimaced. 'She may not be able to buy several Rockwells at thirty million each, but she's not short of the odd fifty thousand. It doesn't stack up.'

John paused. 'Apart from anything else, from an artist's perspective, how the hell is their copier going to paint several highly detailed paintings? It'd take years.'

'So – what the hell is she up to?'

39

Tuesday – 23rd October

By eight-thirty, Lucy had slept only two or three hours. How could she and John survive the Blacks' attempts on their lives? What if the Blacks decided to target their four children?

As gently as she could, she left the bed, went downstairs to her kitchen and turned on the local Boston news. Reports of a storm out in the Atlantic suggested it was the biggest of the year. She watched the projected path of the storm towards the east coast of America.

Finally, there were pictures of a reporter standing outside the Sunset Gallery.

'*This is the largest robbery ever committed in New England. Art worth millions of dollars was stolen yesterday. Police are trying to trace the whereabouts of Simon Black, who works at the gallery.*'

John entered the kitchen rubbing his eyes.

'I tried not to wake you,' she said.

'You didn't – how's my angel this morning?' He looked at the screen for a second.

'So, they've not connected Kelly with it yet,' he said. 'And there's no mention of the police finding any of the art. George will be on his way to Beacon Hill to get his recording. Now's about the time, don't you think?'

John went to his overnight bag and took out an old pay-as-you-go mobile phone. He held it up for Lucy to see. She joined him as he texted the words:

Police – Mising panetings – 2 at hows of girl who took 12 and called you – 196 biron st – becan hill – serch good – you find last 2.

John then picked up his Android. 'George, did you get any sleep last night?'

'Yes, eventually. I left the long-distance mike on so I could go to sleep. If there's noise coming from the ears, I always get woken up. At three a.m., Kelly calls Billy. She's telling him that there's pictures in his garage and Simon has put them there to incriminate him. She suggests that he takes the paintings over to the family place on Beacon Hill, since Simon has disappeared and won't be there. That way, it will be Simon, and not him, that will be connected with the theft.

'Well, remember, folks, I've still not moved from Kelly's. So, all I have to do is go round the corner in the dark and record what's being said. The police turn up and arrest Billy, who's now in Boston Police Station behind bars. And there's a warrant out for the arrest of Simon, who's a prime suspect in the theft from the gallery.

'But I tell you, folks – Billy was screaming when they put him in the police van. He kept shouting "I'm gonna to kill that Kelly."'

'So Kelly's got her brothers to incriminate each other,' Lucy said.

'Seems like it,' George replied. 'I got all the crucial stuff recorded.'

'Great result, George. So, the police are only missing two paintings now. From six tonight I'll be in the air for seven hours. I'll call you tomorrow.'

Lucy and John continued to watch the news. Another storm report was predicting where Hurricane Sandy would hit land.

Lucy felt uneasy but couldn't work out why. 'John, let's take the pressure off and get out to the airport nice and early.'

'Sounds good,' he replied.

Lucy dialled her local limousine company. 'Limo will be here in fifteen minutes. I always check the strongbox, before I go. You coming?'

Lucy's safe room was thirty feet long. They approached the far wall to within eight feet, to fully appreciate *The Piazza San Marco* for all its detail and subtle hues.

'Even though it's a copy, it gives me so much pleasure … I always make sure the strongbox is open when I leave, especially when the kids could be in town.'

'So, if they need to enter in a hurry, they can.'

Lucy nodded.

Minutes later, they climbed into the limousine. 'Delta Airlines, miss?'

'That's it, Steve, thank you.'

At the airport, they headed for the VIP lounge and found seats from which they could watch the news. A reporter was standing outside the gallery on Newbury Street.

'*Police have issued only limited information. Simon and Billy Black, both heirs to the Black oil and coal fortune, were found to be in possession of some of the stolen art, and Billy is being charged later on today. Police are trying to find Kelly and Simon Black. Kelly Black is not thought to be involved in any way, although her home near the gallery was searched thoroughly this morning.*'

'That's odd,' Lucy frowned. 'How come they found nothing at Kelly's?'

'Do you think they searched it properly?' John asked.

'Very odd. What if the art wasn't in her house by the time the police got there? Who could've told her it was there?' Lucy replied.

'Or if she moved it …' John continued. 'Where did she put it?'

'Apart from her brothers, who else would she want to incriminate? John, are you thinking what I'm thinking?'

173

'If you're right – then the safest assumption is your place out in Farmington. Concord's too secure; she'd have to put it somewhere outside.'

John called George. 'You've seen the news, John. They can't find the paintings at Kelly's so I'm on my way out to Concord, just in case the police get the tip off it's there.'

'George – you read our minds. If the art's not at Concord, would you mind a little trip to Farmington?'

'I figured that next. But have you folks figured beyond that? If it's not there, what do we do then?'

'Not our problem, George. If we're not incriminated, and the kids are OK, then it's not our problem. And don't forget – we only discovered the robbery accidentally. It was just an opportunity to put Kelly under pressure.'

'OK. I'll go out to Concord and Farmington. But I'd sure like to know who moved the paintings.'

'Let us know what you find, George? We'll be at Logan for at least another three hours.'

Lucy dialled Mark and Oliver. Neither were answering so she left instructions on both phones to call George if they found anything strange inside or outside the house.

'When you think about it,' John said, 'Kelly knows we're watching the news and learning that no paintings have been found. She knows we'll suspect she'll try to dump the paintings on us. So, she won't … not for another few days.'

'You might be right, John. But then, where would she keep them in the meanwhile?'

They continued to watch the news. There was no other information on the art. Most of the reporting seemed to be about the storm brewing out in the Atlantic.

Lucy and John chatted. 'With the robbery and everything, we've hardly had time to think about the four seasons.'

John smiled. 'You know Cropsey probably never saw them all together.'

'How so?'

'Because at that time of his life, 1858, his stuff sold like hot-cakes. He could never keep any of them for long. He could easily have sold the first before finishing the second, let alone finishing all four.'

'So, we could be the first people ever to see the set – actually as the set he intended?' Lucy said.

'Absolutely.'

'I wonder if we could find out when he sold the first one – and when he painted the last?' Lucy pondered.

'Lucy … if we could prove they were never seen as a set, even by the artist himself, and a hundred and fifty years later show the entire set together – that would make them priceless.'

'But you're never going to sell them?'

'Course not – nor will Mrs Markham – it's taken me half a lifetime to get them all back together for her.'

Lucy was curious. 'When we discussed the other four-season sets that exist, you said the Poussin set was in the Louvre and insured for a hundred million euros.'

'Correct.'

'If the Cropseys are six times larger – more accomplished – totally unique – and we collect the set never even seen as a set by the artist himself, how much do you think they'd need to be insured for?'

John smiled. 'I discussed this with William. He's never seen or heard of a set like it in his thirty-five years in the business. He reckons the Cropseys would need to be insured for two hundred and fifty million euros. That's if he could get a company to take the risk at all.'

'John, you don't suppose …'

At that moment, the screen above them started to report on the art robbery in Boston.

'News is just coming in that John Black, the chairman of Black Industries, and father of Billy arrested this morning in Boston, has himself been arrested by police for possession of some of the art stolen from the gallery here in Boston yesterday.'

John looked at Lucy. 'Now I've heard everything …'

Lucy nodded. 'So that's probably where Kelly stashed the missing paintings – actually in the main ranch house – in the garage – almost under Mary's nose.'

'Would all passengers bound for London Heathrow on Delta flight 402 and who hold preferential boarding passes or first-class tickets, please come to the gate for boarding?'

'I'll miss not waking up with you, Mr Baxter … but I'll be in London soon and we'll make up for lost time.'

He held her in his arms. 'I love you so much.'

He kissed her and walked to the door of the lounge. He turned back to see her still on her feet watching him. Her smile, as usual, lit up the world around her.

As he walked to the gate, Lucy's unease increased. Consciously at least, she had not yet accounted for the murderous power of the largest storm ever to hit the east coast of America.

Lucy sat in the lounge thinking about John.

Why, oh why is the man you've fallen for living a third of the way round the world? How can we ever make it work? Maybe it would be kinder on both of us if we end it before our lives become too entwined?

A single tear traced its way down her cheek – then another – and another.

When was the last time you cried for love? When did anyone make you feel this complete? When were you ever so excited, just to be with a man?

And why are they operating flights when this storm is so dangerous?

40

Wednesday – 24th October

A rapid tailwind shortened John's flight to Heathrow by more than an hour. When he turned his phone out of flight mode, a text from William was waiting.

2 pntgs stolen from Rockwell Museum. Call me.

He texted Lucy to find out if she was awake. She called him. 'Hi, John. How was your flight?'

'Good. How was yours?'

'It was fine. John, there's been another robbery.'

'I know. William texted me. I'm seeing him at the auction tomorrow. We'll catch up on it. Do you have any photos of Kelly or anyone else who might be at the auction?'

The following day John arrived early at Christie's Auction House on King Street in London. Lucy had texted him some pictures of the Black family, which he now studied on his phone. He enjoyed watching the characters as they assembled: the professionals, the nervous, those with money to spend for the first time. As usual, he took a seat at the back corner furthest from the door.

A tall, dark-haired woman in her forties walked into the auction room. *Old money*, John thought to himself. It was not a face that Lucy had sent, although it was familiar. Monica Malvito. The painting of her in the senator's living room – that was it. He remembered the senator saying she was going to an auction – and that she and Billy were having an affair.

Just at that moment, Billy came in and sat down with her. *Why is he not in a police cell – in Boston?*

John's watch told him the auction would be starting in a few minutes. It was only five o'clock in the morning in Atlanta where Lucy was. He texted so as not to wake her if she had already got back to sleep.

U awake, lover?

Yes, how's bidding?

Not started yet. Is Billy still held by police?

No, bailed on condition he stay in Boston. Why?

I believe Monica Malvito here with Billy. Two Rockwells for sale. Can you look at online catalogue and see if u recognise Rockwells from night at Malvitos? I think one of them is the one we saw.

Will do.

A couple of minutes later, Lucy texted back. *Yr suspicions right. Rockwell is the one she had on wall in dining room. Must have moved quick to get it over there for today.*

Can u get Malvito and ask him if painting is still on his wall?

Give me 2.

178

William Ritchey walked in. He glanced around him and John raised his bidder's paddle to attract his attention.

William sat down next to John. 'Is the art world getting smaller or have I done this too much?'

John smiled. 'It's good to see you again, William.'

'Likewise. What are you looking for today?'

'There's an early American landscape – and a Rockwell.'

William lowered his voice. 'We believe the fraud is not limited to the early Americans.'

John studied his friend. 'You're serious, aren't you?'

'Totally. We know the people who own the Rockwells here today. We believe this is part of the wider fraud going on all over New England.'

'You're not going to believe this, William – but I was in the house of the current owner of this one,' he said, pointing at the catalogue. 'Lucy and I were there only two nights ago. She texted me a minute or so before you sat down to confirm what I thought.'

'You were at the Malvito place?' William whispered.

'Yep. And they have some great names decorating their walls.'

John's phone buzzed with a text from Lucy. The senator had confirmed that his Rockwell was still in place in Concord. Anticipating John's next question, Lucy added that Tom Malvito was definite that the version he was looking at was the original; he had personally attended the insurance valuation.

John kept this to himself. He would enjoy this day. Apart from the knowledge he had about Monica and the fake painting, there was another advantage he always enjoyed whenever Crispin was the auctioneer: they had known each other from school. Crispin had since had a stellar career in the army, serving some time in bomb-disposal before being awarded his CBE and taking early retirement after twenty years of service.

They had evolved a set of bidding codes that made their lives much easier. A good portion of the financial benefits Baxter derived from this relationship went to Crispin's favourite charities, the RSPCA and the Military Veterans Association. In the previous year alone, these donations had totalled more than £2,000,000.

John smiled whenever he thought of the 128 veterans now using prosthetic limbs, only possible because of this money.

He smiled again when he realised today was the 25th of October – the birthday of Pablo Picasso.

You'd think someone in Sotheby's would have mentioned it before the start of an art auction.

But today's auction was going to be the most unusual that Christie's had ever staged in its two hundred and fifty years.

41

Thursday – 25th October

'Lot 16. This is a rare chance to acquire one of the last paintings done by Norman Rockwell, one of America's most sought-after artists.

'Ladies and gentlemen, we have a reserve price of two million, five hundred thousand pounds. I hardly need to remind the distinguished collectors in the room that "the other place" recently sold a Rockwell for more than forty-five million dollars … who's going to start the bidding?

'Thank you, sir – one million pounds.' Crispin, known affectionately as 'Crisp', gestured to the furthest corner from John, at the back of the room.

John decided it was too soon to enter the bidding.

'Two million, at the front, thank you … Three million.' Again, Crisp gestured to the back. 'Four million, to my right … Five, at the back … Six … Seven million to a new bidder in the centre. Good morning, sir. Was six million not enough to wake you up?'

Slight sniggers followed. Crispin knew the new bidder personally and his combination of gravitas and good humour allowed him the luxury of comments like this.

'Eight million, at the back … Ten? Ten, thank you … Do I have twelve? … Thank you … twelve million …' A slight pause followed as Crisp looked at his bidders for the slightest clue as to their intentions. 'Do I have thirteen million …?'

A longer pause followed and Crisp raised his gavel, threatening to close the bidding. Monica Malvito raised her paddle.

'Thirteen million, to a new bidder,' Crisp announced.

John gave the very slightest of nods to Crisp. 'I have fourteen million … yet another new bidder.'

William looked at John in amazement.

Crisp went on. 'Fourteen million, at the back … Fifteen, in the centre,' he announced, looking again at Monica Malvito.

John nodded again, winking twice to indicate to Crisp his raise of two million. This code had been agreed between the two of them back in 2006 over a cream tea in Fortnum's.

'Seventeen million, it is … Eighteen, from the front … Nineteen, anyone? Am I bid nineteen million? Anyone? … Nineteen, from the centre … Am I bid twenty?'

Crisp looked at John and the other bidders in the room. The dealer at the front shook his head. John watched the reaction of the person towards the back on the other side of the room. The bidder was unknown to John but was gesturing to Crisp that he had finished. Crisp looked at John again. 'Do I have twenty?'

John nodded again. This set up a murmur in the room. William's face turned white. 'Twenty, I have – thank you. Twenty million, five hundred thousand anyone? Am I bid twenty and a half?' Crisp looked at Monica in the centre of the auction room. Monica raised her paddle. 'I have twenty million, five hundred thousand pounds in the centre.'

Crisp looked at John, who shook his head. Monica had not seen the other two bidders signal their exit from the bidding. John had Monica where he wanted her – the highest bidder, for her own painting, with no further competition in the room.

'Am I bid twenty-one?' Crisp looked at the bidders one last time, raised his gavel …

'Going … going … gone to the lady in the centre – twenty million, five hundred thousand pounds. Congratulations.' Monica looked back at Crisp and smiled. The room applauded and the inevitable murmurs continued for a minute or two.

'Let's get a coffee; there's a thing or two you need to know, William.'

The auction assistants brought in the next lot, placing it carefully on the old easel that Christie's had used for over two hundred years.

'William, it's over to you now,' John said, as they left the auction room.

'What in heaven do you mean?'

'William – you have just witnessed two crimes – the owner of a lot bidding for it at a publicly sanctioned auction and … entering a copy as if it were the original.'

'What? That doesn't make sense. Why would she buy her own painting, especially a fake?'

'She may not have been intending to buy. But if she was – she wanted the price up as high as it could be. I saw the original two nights ago and it's still on the wall in Senator Malvito's house in Concord. And that lady with the unforgettable head of hair is Monica Malvito.'

'I still don't understand … in all my years …' William searched John's face for any sign of insincerity.

John continued to look him in the eye. 'You were the one who said this fraud went a lot wider than the early Americans. I wonder what happens when Christie's finds out who she is. Even if the painting is owned by her husband, what she's done is still illegal.'

William extrapolated. 'But if he knew a copy was going to auction, then he's guilty of fraud.'

'So – what now?' John asked.

'Well – I could not be expected to know who the successful bidder was. We could play the long game and see where it leads.'

William paused. 'What would you have done if you'd won the bidding?'

John looked puzzled. 'Surely you know I can withdraw if the painting is proven to be a fake? The auction houses guard their reputations fiercely; they can't be seen to sell fakes.'

'I did hear about this happening some years ago, but I thought their processes were so good now, it couldn't happen anymore,' William said.

'It's why they have their experts scrutinise every piece. The copy must be so good it fooled them. Personally, I think it demands as much talent to copy a painting as creating the original. If you're copying, you have constraints on brush-strokes and colour the original painter didn't have.'

'Let's check the register,' William said. 'We can see if Monica's listed.'

The usher took Monica through to the 'Bidding Room'. This gave William and John vital seconds. They moved quickly to the green baize table with its list of registered visitors arranged in alphabetical order. Monica Malvito's name was absent. The name that stood out was 'Kelly Black'.

'Kelly's name is here, but Monica's is not,' John affirmed.

'I can see Kelly's name, John, but she's definitely not here in person.'

'How do you know?'

'Because we've had our eyes on her – same as your other investigator – before I forget to mention it. I can tell you she never left the US.'

Billy Black edged nearer to John, who was checking the list. Although John recognised him from the photo Lucy had sent, Billy did not recognise him or William.

Raised voices were coming from the Bidding Room. A large man in a dark-blue uniform nudged his way between William and John and pulled the door open to go through it.

At that moment, Monica tried to rush through, but the guard was too quick. He caught her round her waist and lifted her clean off the ground.

'Put me down,' she shouted. 'Billy, do something.' She was perched like a baby on its mother's hip. 'Put me down.'

The guard kept hold of her wrist while he let her slide off his hip. This had the effect of lifting her dress to her waist. 'Billy, you gonna just stand there while this ape humiliates me?'

Billy was fully eight inches shorter and a hundred pounds smaller than the guard. He froze.

The guard used his free hand to get onto his handset. 'Roger, call the police and get up to 2A, soon as you can.' He steered Monica back into the Bidding Room and closed the door behind him.

Billy was now separated from Monica and the guard by the closed door. The eyes of the crowd were on him. He ran for the stairs. In trying to avoid collisions with the assembled collectors, he tripped and fell, hitting his head on a marble column. He lay unconscious, his blood spilling onto the carpet. Roger, the second guard, was followed up the stairs by a police constable.

'This one's going nowhere,' Roger said to him. 'But he's gonna need stitches. Can I leave you with him?'

Roger headed towards the Bidding Room door. As he arrived, the door crashed open towards him, its edge hitting him hard in the face. He stood there, dazed, struggling to maintain his balance. Monica dashed past him and rushed towards the stairs. She sprayed mace directly into the eyes of the policeman kneeling beside Billy.

Surprised and in pain, he put his hands to his eyes. Monica made her way deftly past him, down the stairs, weaving her way between the few people on their way up. She walked out onto King Street and noticed three London cabs lined up. She came to the one at the front of the line, opened the rear door, climbed in and was driven away.

'Aren't you interested in where Monica is going?' William asked John.

'Not much,' he said. 'I'm more interested that Billy was bailed two nights ago on condition he stayed in Boston.'

'You serious?' William asked.

'Absolutely. He's been implicated in the theft of art from the Sunset Gallery in Boston on Monday afternoon, where his brother Simon and an associate stole at least twelve paintings.'

'He can't be,' William said.

'Why not?'

'You remember that theft I told you about from the Norman Rockwell Museum?'

John nodded.

'John, Billy is implicated in that theft – he can't have done both, can he?'

'Actually – now I think about it – we didn't see him at the Sunset. We only saw Simon and his little spy friend.'

'Little spy friend?' William asked. 'Does this little spy friend have different eyes – one green and one brown?'

'He does. Do you know him?' John asked.

'Oh, yes. His name is Paul Adams – freelance killer – slippery as an eel – nobody's ever caught him. The police all round the world call him Letu – short for Le Tueur, "the killer" – because the French were the first to put him on the international "most wanted" list.'

John wondered: *How do we trap this guy? How do we get rid of him before he gets rid of us?*

42

The policeman had called for backup and a colleague was coming up the stairs. The large security guard tottered towards them, his eyes streaming.

'His name's Billy; he's with the woman who ran out,' he said.

The left-hand side of Billy's face was covered in blood. He was regaining consciousness.

'My head … what happened?'

'What's your name?' Roger asked.

'Black,' William said. 'He's Billy Black, recently bailed by Boston Police on condition he stays in Boston. He's charged with art theft in the Boston area and in New York.'

'And you are …?' the policeman asked.

'William Ritchey, insurance investigator. We've been watching Black and his family for weeks. He's also being investigated for a jewellery theft.'

The policeman looked back at Billy. 'Are you Billy Black?'

Billy said nothing.

'I'm going back in, William. Let's catch up later,' John said.

John reclaimed his seat. The auction room was still occupied by almost everyone who had been there a few minutes before.

He smiled. *Nothing like the enthusiasm of the art collector.*

Crisp was making an announcement. 'We're most sorry for the delay, ladies and gentlemen. If you'd like to take your seats, we'll begin again in two minutes.'

The painting John wanted was brought in and placed on the easel. It looked like a Cropsey; the colours were vivid without being artificial.

John walked to the front of the room to study the painting close up. It was signed simply 'L', but its frame was identical to the one on his Cropsey painting of summer.

Few people had left, but the bidding was restrained. John had only one competitor. Crisp put his hammer down on John's final bid of £65,000.

As John left the room, he took his phone off silent mode and noticed a text from William. He had gone to Kensington Police Station to give a statement and wanted John to meet him in the Ritz in thirty minutes.

John accepted the invitation and entered the Bidding Room. Felicity sat at the huge desk between them, filling out the form. They had sat on opposite sides of this desk several times over the years, and she apologised for asking, yet again, for John's passport and a secondary form of ID.

'Quite a morning, Felicity,' John ventured.

'I've never seen anything like it. All very distressing … mind you, that family was trouble last time they were here.'

'Which family?' he asked, nonchalantly.

'The Blacks. I'm sorry – I should never have mentioned it,' Felicity said.

'Oh, yes, the Blacks … Did you get as far as filling out this form with her?'

'Yes. Kelly Black has purchased here once before. The scene started when we were going through this process. She produced her passport, but the photo didn't match the one we photocopied last time she was here.'

'So, what happened?'

'Well – the two passports were different people entirely, even though they both said Kelly Black. It all got nasty.'

'So, what happened next?'

'She suggested we check her bank details; she would clear funds electronically, she said. Alistair explained that their processes were not to check payment – it was to comply with the money-laundering regulations in the UK. That's when she ran out.'

Felicity finished filling out the form. 'Where would you like the painting delivered, Mr Baxter?'

'Esher, please. You have the address.'

'Will we see you again soon?'

'I hope so. Thanks, Felicity.'

John made his way out onto King Street, relishing the short walk in the fresh air to the Ritz.

If Monica was trying to impersonate Kelly, did she seriously expect to be able to use Kelly's bank details to steal money from her? Apparently so, if her insistence that Christie's check the bank details was any indication of her confidence.

189

John turned right onto St James's Street, then left onto Piccadilly, arriving at the Ritz a minute later. He remembered his first night with Lucy – and marvelled that it was less than a month ago.

He found William, sitting on the same blue sofa that he and Lucy had used at their first meeting.

'John, you'll never guess what I've just learnt …'

'Go on then, your news first,' John said.

'Kelly Black never left the US at the weekend; still in Massachusetts. The Boston Police never found two of the works stolen from the Sunset Gallery.'

'Did they search the houses at the ranch?' John asked.

'Yes – they found the ones stolen from the Rockwell Museum at Old Man Black's house, in one of the stable blocks – it's why they took him in for questioning. They also searched the Black properties in Boston.' William paused.

'Anyway, they found nothing.'

'So – if two are still missing, William – where are they?'

'Perhaps the private chap you hired could shine some light on that?' William searched John's face for any reaction.

'William – we hired our "private chap", as you call him, for protection purposes. You two have different backgrounds – George is ex-police. We see you as the inside info from the art world. There's no overlap at all.

'You may as well know – the Blacks tried to poison us the other night. Kelly used her brother Simon to borrow their brother Jack's car to incriminate him. She then had Simon intercept the takeout, poison it and use James, yet another of the brothers, to deliver it to us. In one neat move she had three of her brothers implicated in a conspiracy to kill.'

'A real piece of work, then, this Kelly,' William replied.

'And she did it again,' John added. 'She set up Billy outside the Black place and organised the police to be there to arrest him.'

'So – four brothers and her own father implicated in theft. Who do you reckon put up Billy's bail?'

'Malvito told Lucy and me he reckons his wife and Billy are having an affair. Monica is wealthy in her own right – came from an oil family near Midland, in Texas.'

'Interesting,' William replied.

'Now I have to give you my news from Christie's,' John said. 'I bought what I think is a kind of Cropsey. I'll explain in a minute. Anyway, I got talking to Felicity who takes the payment. Monica was trying to use the financial details of Kelly Black to prove that she was Kelly.'

'But it didn't work,' William replied.

'No. But when she won the bidding, she seemed unperturbed. I think she planned to repossess the copy she had commissioned herself, use Kelly's money to do it, damaging her financially as much as possible, then sell it back home for a profit. She could sell it quite cheaply – maybe five million dollars – and still make a handsome profit, since it only cost her fifty thousand to get it copied in the first place.'

William was puzzled. 'It means that Monica has enough information about Kelly's bank account to know it could stand a twenty-million-pound hit. Which begs the question – if Kelly is that rich, why do all this art theft? And anyway, how the hell did Monica get Kelly's bank details?'

'Maybe Billy. He steals everything else; maybe he found a way to get his sister's bank details for Monica, who he thinks is in love with him? If Billy was robbing the Rockwell Museum, then Kelly must have offered him some cash. If he helped Monica get Kelly's bank details, it's probably also for cash.'

'So – why bring him to London?' William asked.

'Well, if Monica is just using Billy to ruin the Blacks, she may as well get him locked up when his usefulness has expired. One way to do that is to make sure he's seen to jump bail.'

'Let me get this right,' William said. 'Monica tries to use Kelly's money to pay for a painting that she owns anyway and has copied in order to sell at a public auction as if it was the original. All the while she is carrying on with Billy Black, whose sister she is trying to ruin. You couldn't make it up.'

John nodded. 'Meanwhile, Kelly is even worse. She has implicated her brothers Billy, Simon and Jack, more or less seeing them into prison single-handedly. She got young James involved in murder and she's probably the killer of three of the remaining four brothers. She's implicated her own father because two paintings were found at his place. That's eight lives she's ended or ruined. I'd love to know what she did with the missing two paintings. And if the paintings found at the ranch were not the missing two from the Sunset Gallery, but were from the Rockwell Museum robbery instead, then who put them there?'

'Hang on, John. Billy lives on the ranch and presumably had to go back there to sleep that night – why couldn't Billy plant the Rockwells in the Old Man's stable block?'

'Well – it would mean that Kelly has turned Billy against his own father. If Kelly is so rich as to have the odd twenty-five million dollars in a spending account, I think we can assume this is not about short-term gain.'

William was frowning his indignation. 'Are all wealthy people this nasty, do you think?'

He looked at John, realising what he had said. 'Sorry, John. I know you're no crook.'

'No worries, William. Anyway, in terms of wealth, I'm not in their league. And in my case, I've never been ruthless – just incredibly lucky. I try to remember that every day.'

'John, how does Kelly expect to get away with this when the rest of her family are in jail or have died in suspicious circumstances?'

43

Sunday – 28th October

'John – it's the worst storm ever to hit North America. They're predicting 210 mile an hour winds all the way from New York to Boston.'

He could feel her anxiety. Lucy was to fly from Atlanta to Heathrow, arriving in London to join him the following day. Her home in Farmington, Connecticut was a hundred miles north-east of New York and 400,000 people were being evacuated on meteorological predictions of imminent carnage.

'Sweetheart, they won't fly if it's too risky.'

'It's not me; it's the guys. You've seen where Oliver sleeps – the garden room's no protection if those big trees come down.'

'But sweetheart, they don't know where Sandy's coming ashore yet.'

'John, it won't matter; it's nine hundred miles wide. When it's fully ashore in New York, the other side is hitting Chicago. You know what they said when I asked how much dog food they have in the house? One can. I can't get hold of Mark – and all Oliver can say is "Just chill, Mom."'

'Has Mark got gas in the car?' John asked.

'I'll call you back. Give me two minutes.'

The phone rang again. 'John, they have a website for Sandy. It hits land tomorrow. There's going to be major casualties; people are being pig-headed and staying put.'

Through the phone, he could hear the announcement in her hotel reception and paused while she listened.

'The bus is leaving. I'll call you from the airport. I love you, John; can't wait to see you.'

John googled 'Sandy' – and shifted in his chair uneasily. He checked CNN News – even worse. His mind went to Lucy's younger, seventeen-year-old son, Oliver. A good-looking young man, Oliver was proud of his Viking forebears and John had liked him immediately.

He slept in a ground-floor room made mostly of glass. John hesitated to call the young man – but did it anyway. No reply.

John Baxter liked the Farmington home Lucy had created – a traditional, weather-boarded house in a quiet, leafy road, its pastel-grey boards offset by white window frames and dark blue-grey slate roof tiles. John remembered vividly his first ever visit. Oliver had a log fire going in the large open-plan reception area and it bathed the house in a cosy glow. Either side of the fireplace was a floor-to-ceiling bookcase, reminding him of his own home in England.

Lucy arrived at the airport and called John. 'I thought about going to Kennedy and being with the guys instead. But they've cancelled all flights into JFK and Mark just laughed when I suggested it. He asked me what I could do against 210 mile an hour winds. He said he wouldn't sleep tonight if he knew I was trying to get to JFK.

'They're still flying to London though; they go west of the storm over the Great Lakes, and then over the Atlantic to London. There are huge tailwinds, so you might want to get updates on arrival times. It's TAA flight 006. This week's been too long. I love you so much, John.'

'Me too. And don't forget to ask for a seat upgrade.'

Within two hours of Lucy's take-off, Hurricane Sandy was being described by CNN as 'vicious.' John called Oliver again.

'*We're unable to connect you to this number.*'

New England looked like a war zone. Fallen trees were blocking the progress of emergency vehicles. Most of the power was disconnected. People were staring at piles of wood and brick that hours earlier had been their homes. He could barely watch a couple looking at the ruin of their home, the wife in tears.

He tried to reach Mark and Oliver again. Same messages. Then he remembered that he had the number of one of their friends, saved into his mobile. Colin had moved into their home while searching for a place to rent.

'It's John, Colin. Are you alright? Are the guys OK? How's the house?'

'Good ... don't know ... and bad, very bad ... Just getting to the house – call you back.'

The next fifteen minutes seemed like an hour.

Finally, Colin called back. 'Beth from next door called the paramedics 'cos Oliver's room's all caved in. Wolfie's in the house barking but the medics are stopping me going in; it's not safe. Call you back when I know anything.'

John paced his office, wondering what he could do to help from three and a half thousand miles away. He put his phone on charge, although the battery was ninety per cent full. He sat on the sofa.

When John next looked at his watch it was 04.45 UK time. *I must have fallen asleep.*

Lucy would reach the arrivals hall in Heathrow's Terminal 3 at about 07.15. He could update himself on the storm, get to the airport and have a coffee near the arrivals barrier.

He turned on CNN News again. Homes in New England were being washed away in the floods. Cars were being tossed about like toys in a bath, colliding with each other and with buildings still standing. One young woman with a child on her back was holding onto a telegraph pole, struggling with the strength of the current. John watched in horror as she and her child were swept away.

He could find no details of flight TAA006 to London. This was odd. He accessed the airline website. Again, nothing. He clicked onto Yahoo News.

The blood drained from his face. A flight had gone down on the shores of Lake Michigan. He felt sick. He had to get to the TAA desk.

In the car he had time to think. How would he tell Oliver, if he was still alive, that he had lost his mother? How would he tell Lucy, if she was alive, that she had lost her son? Or, worse – how would he tell Mark he had lost both?

John parked and wove his way as fast as he could through the crowds. Reaching the airline desk was impossible; there were too many people. He had never seen panic like it.

What of Lucy? He could not imagine life without his best friend and lover. John pulled back to the cafe.

Then the coffee shop TV flicked to a fresh bulletin. TAA flight 006 had crashed on the shores of Lake Michigan, leaving no survivors.

John felt the strength leave his legs and found a chair just in time to prevent him from collapsing to the floor. Completely overwhelmed, he wept.

He thought of Lucy's two boys. Then he heard a voice. 'Excuse me, mate. We have this table – can't you see my coat there?'

'I'm sorry,' he heard himself say to them. 'I didn't realise.'

He struggled to his feet, tears in his eyes. The woman whose chair he had fallen onto looked at him in contempt.

For the first time in his life, he had nowhere to go. He walked, and then walked in the opposite direction. He changed direction again and realised the people clustered around the airline desk had not been told of something already on the national news.

Then the full realisation hit him again – that the love of his life had been taken from him – untimely ripped – as if life had no use for the kindest and brightest soul he had ever met. He couldn't bear the thought of her last few seconds – the time when she knew she would die – what she must have been thinking. Had she died immediately – or had she suffered?

He reached for his phone but found instead the cinema tickets for *Skyfall*. Lucy had said she would like to see it,

197

although he suspected it was only to please him. Then the enormity of his loss hit him again, but this time like a railroad train. There would be no *Skyfall*, no life with Lucy – just a great emptiness where once she had been. His tears started again.

There was a surge in the crowd, and John saw the airline had issued a piece of paper. *FLIGHT TAA006*, read the heading at the top.

People were weeping; some had let it fall to the floor. He picked up one of the sheets to notice it was printed on both sides with the passenger list. Near the top of the list was the name *Howard – Lucy Elizabeth*.

His phone buzzed; it was a text from Lucy. *Can't wait to see you, Mr Baxter.*

It seemed so cruel to be getting a text from her, but he couldn't bring himself to delete it. He would hold onto everything about Lucy.

I should go to Mark and Oliver. They have no one else now. Their father, Billy, is in jail. Lucy's gone. But Charlotte and Emma are expecting me home. Here it is – the reason it was always going to be tough – the times we're needed on different sides of the Atlantic.

John folded the passenger list and put it in his back pocket. Slowly, he made his way to his car in the short-term car park. He felt twice his normal weight, as if his legs were made of lead. He slumped into his Jaguar and felt the tears coming again.

As if you needed reminding, Baxter – money cannot buy you happiness.

He started back for Esher.

Would Lucy's sons blame him for her death? She was only flying to see him. If he and Lucy had not met, she would be alive.

When John arrived home, Charlotte and Emma were at school. The house felt cold and empty – empty of Lucy – empty of love – empty of meaning. He turned the heating up.

44

Lucy walked into the arrivals hall of Heathrow's Terminal 3. *Why so many people? Why the confusion? Where is John? What's all this paper on the floor?*

She stooped to pick up one of the sheets.

FOR WHOM IT MAY CONCERN – TAA006.

Why publish a passenger list? … Oh, my God … Is my name on it? … Yes. John doesn't know …

Lucy pulled out her phone and dialled.

'John?'

'Lucy! I don't understand. Thank God! Where are you?'

'In the arrivals hall. I've just seen the passenger list. I got on a different flight; I'll tell you all about it when I see you. Where are you at the moment?'

'At home. I can't believe it. I'll come back and get you.'

'John. I'll get a taxi. By the time you get here, I could be at Esher. You stay put. I'll see you in thirty minutes. I love you so much. Can't wait to see you.'

'Text me when you get to the entrance of the close; I'll open the gates from here.'

The taxi ride gave Lucy time to think.

Perhaps this was not the time to tell John about her doubts. And yet she'd put it off so long already. Why, of all days, did the traffic have to be so bad today?

The bad traffic turned a thirty-minute journey into an hour-long one – which felt like it lasted two hours. John opened the security gates to Whitehills Close remotely, and a few seconds later the sliding gates to his driveway. He was waiting outside his front door as the taxi pulled in.

He gave the driver a fifty-pound note for the thirty-five-pound fare and thanked him. They retreated into the house, shutting the door on the autumn chill.

'You never got my text – that I'd swapped my flight.'

Lucy hugged him, tears in her eyes.

He held her tight – to make sure she was still there – to tell her how much he loved her – to make sure she *knew* how much he loved her.

'Why weren't you on that flight?' John asked at last.

'You reminded me to ask to be upgraded …' Lucy's voice cracked.

'Today, for the first time, I asked. The lady behind the desk told me there was nothing on TAA006, but because of all the air miles I'd accumulated she could get me on an earlier flight in business class. I had to go straight to the gate as they were on "last call".

'I was rushing to the gate and trying to text you. I knew they'd need my cell turned off as soon as I got on the plane. I must have made a mistake.'

John gritted his teeth. 'I have to tell you about the house, sweetheart.'

'Are the kids OK?'

200

John paused. 'Sweetheart … the tree's come down on Oliver's room. The paramedics can't get into the house.'

Lucy burst into tears again. She put her head into John's shoulder and sobbed unashamedly. 'He's too young, John, he's just too young.'

All John could do was hold her.

Just then, Lucy's phone beeped with a text from Oliver. Laughing through her tears, she gave John her phone.

bdrm like car wreck. yr bdrm demo site. slept in garage under oak bench dad delivered. figured it was strong enough to hold house up. catch u later.

John held her. 'Well, he has the resources of his mum.'

Lucy's tears were falling on her phone as she dialled Oliver.

'Hey, Mom, how was your flight?'

'Oh, Oliver – it's so good to hear your voice. I got your text. We thought you were in the garden room. You alright?'

'The house is wrecked our side. The tree came through your bedroom and the floor right down into the garage where I was, underneath your room. If I'd not been under the bench … My battery's almost out. Give me a four-digit number you won't forget.'

'But is Mark OK?' Lucy was frowning her confusion.

'Mark's good. Quickly – a four-digit number you won't forget.'

'Oh, I don't know … 0312, I guess.' Lucy looked puzzled.

'Cool – catch you later. Got to go, battery …'

Lucy looked at John. 'What on earth is going on?' she murmured.

45

Monday – 29ᵗʰ October

Lucy's tablet pinged. 'Mark's asking me to call, John. It's three-thirty in the morning in Connecticut.'

Mark picked up immediately. 'How you guys doing?'

'We're fine, how are you?' Lucy replied.

'We're OK. The garage door looks like a crumpled Coke can. Oliver crawls out from underneath it. The first thing he said is "Let's see if the gas station has any food."'

Lucy dissolved into tears again.

As if you needed reminding, Lucy – money can't buy you happiness. This is motherhood – a lifetime of worry.

Through her tears, she smiled.

'What's the matter, Mom?' came Mark's voice.

'Oh, Mark, we thought we'd lost you both … we're just so happy you're both still alive … tell me about the house.'

'Oliver's room's all caved in; the largest bit of the tree came through your bedroom. If you'd been in bed, Mom …'

Lucy shuddered. 'Where did you sleep last night?'

'We came up to stay with Colin. We're there now.'

'OK, sweetie. Listen, stay in touch. Let me know if there's anything you need. I'm so happy no one was hurt. Hang on – Oliver's just texted me. I'll catch up later, I love you both.'

Lucy studied her screen.

isobel would say – (81) / 18 (0) 21 (6) 5 (0) / 4 (8) 21 (8) / 16.15.14.20. You and Mark will understand this, but not Billy.

All at Colin's again tonight, found package in garage, explain later.

John was curious. 'Why the code?'

Lucy transcribed the text onto a piece of paper. 'It must have something to do with the numbers he asked me for.'

'Why did he say you and Mark would be able to understand it, but not Billy?'

'That's 'cos Billy speaks no French. Isobel is the boys' Norwegian great-grandmother, but she speaks fluent French.'

'Wait a minute – she doesn't own a vineyard in Bordeaux, by any chance?' John replied.

Lucy smiled.

'Isobel owns the Château Largaux? No wonder you know so much about wine … wow, it all makes sense now … why didn't you tell me?'

'You never asked. It's been quite a morning, John. Is it too early to open a nice cold bottle of that pink stuff?'

Lucy was beginning to relax, but suddenly sat up straight. 'We forgot Wolfie. I have to text Mark.'

John arranged the champagne and two glasses on the coffee table in the living room.

A minute later, Lucy sat down beside him, phone in hand. 'Wolfie's with them up at Colin's house on the shore. Apparently, he loves running about on the beach. So they're all safe.'

Lucy suddenly stopped smiling. 'Jane. She thinks I was on TAA006. Better let her know before they all see it on the breakfast news.'

She texted Jane: *Reports of my death grossly exaggerated – got on earlier flight cos they had bus. class seat. Call you in office hours. Heard today we got the Atlanta case. Bye for now.*

John read her text. 'So, sweetheart, my gate combination really is our lucky number.'

'Mr B?'

'You avoid a disastrous flight – you land a hugely lucrative divorce case – Canaletto's birthday – all 28th of October.'

Pensive, Lucy put her head uneasily on his shoulder. *If a transatlantic relationship is going to be this stressful, how can we possibly sustain it?*

46

Lucy and John were exhausted from the emotional roller-coaster of the last twenty-four hours. They slept for large parts of the day, content merely to be together.

By six o'clock they were hungry. Lucy suggested a quiet, romantic meal, somewhere close, somewhere they could say the things only lovers say.

He smiled. 'In that case, it's Le Coq au Vin, next to the cinema in the high street.'

Half an hour later, they parked outside the Odeon in Esher. John opened the passenger door for her.

'I'm sorry about *Skyfall*, John. I know you wanted to see it.'

'Bit too hectic for this evening, methinks,' he smiled. 'This evening we need to slow things down a bit, *n'est ce pas?*'

The maître d' radiated his genuine liking of people. 'We have not had *le plaisir* to see you recently, monsieur. Have you been travelling so much?'

'I have, Pierre; collecting beautiful treasures.'

Pierre smiled at Lucy. 'I can see that, monsieur.'

'This is Lucy. We seem to have collected each other some-where in the last month.'

'Would you care for a drink madame, monsieur, while we prepare your table?'

He ushered them to the bar and the high stools arranged along it. Lucy perched herself up on one of six black leather stools. As she crossed her long legs, her dress revealed more of her thighs.

'What can I get you?' the barman asked. John looked at Lucy.

'Have you any single-malt whisky?' she asked.

The barman nodded. 'How do you like it?'

Lucy looked away from the barman and straight into John's eyes. 'Large and straight up.' She looked back at the barman, who was grinning.

'And you, monsieur?'

'Large and neat for me as well, thank you.'

He looked at Lucy, elegantly poised on her bar stool, her honey tresses draped over her bare shoulders. 'This is the dress you wore when I first laid eyes on you, in the Ritz.'

Lucy grinned. 'When you first laid me, you mean.'

'Is it coincidence you're wearing it again tonight?'

Lucy smiled. 'Why change a winning game? It had the desired effect.'

'It certainly had an effect on my desire.'

'Well, it is a cock-tail dress,' Lucy grinned.

'Titillating – would be the best word, I think.'

'You made very little attempt to disguise your appreciation.'

'I am used to looking very closely at beautiful works of art.'

Lucy grinned, glad there was no one near enough to over-hear the conversation.

John continued. 'Talking about expansive and beautiful works of art – I picked up something at the auction. I believe it's a kind of Cropsey. I think you'll see why, when you see it.'

Laurent, their waiter, approached. '*Suivez moi, s'il vous plaît?*' he said. Before Lucy sat down, John slid his hand from the small of her back to her bottom. Lucy turned to kiss him before sitting down.

'I like it when you do that – but I wish you'd keep it there longer.'

'Why's that?'

'It makes me feel owned by you. It's a strong declaration to the world that I am yours – I love that.'

John put his hand on hers. She looked into his eyes. She felt protected, engulfed in an ocean of love.

'Tell me about the picture,' she said.

'It's titled *Sugarloaf Mountain*, but was previously titled *Mount Chocorua and Railroad Train*. You remember when we first discovered *Mount Chocorua*, we talked about the confusion between Cropsey's depictions of different mountains?'

'I do,' Lucy smiled.

'Well, that's because when Cropsey was drawing, he drew his subjects very faithfully. He was very religious and he regarded accurate drawings as honouring the gifts his "creator" had given him. But when it came to filling a painting in, he sometimes used a bit of licence. This has led to confusion as to which mountains he was actually painting. Which is why the one I got at Christie's is interesting. It's signed "L", not "J. Cropsey".'

'So, if it's not Cropsey, then who?' Lucy asked.

'The day after the auction, I did a bit of research. Cropsey had a daughter named Lilly, one of two daughters he had with his wife, Maria. Lilly studied with her father for two years. Unfortunately, she died very early.'

'You think this was done by Lilly?'

'Well, if it is – it'd be a unique addition to a set already in a class of its own. It's very good. The commotion Billy and Monica were causing outside the room gave me a few seconds with the painting on the easel. I used the time to look at it close up. The painting – and its frame – are identical in size and style to the ones we already have.'

'Right,' Lucy said. 'But whether it's Sugarloaf Mountain or not, it's a real bonus for the set – especially if it's Cropsey-school.'

As she gazed into his eyes, Lucy realised she was more in love than she had ever been.

John raised his glass. 'Welcome home, sweetheart.'

Forget hurricanes; how can he and I survive the Blacks? How can we make the relationship work? Actually, those are the best questions we can ask. After all, this is the man you've been looking for all your life. He's actually here with you – right now.

'Well, Mr Baxter – if you want to welcome me home, promise me you'll take all the opportunities presented.'

Laurent approached. 'I am so sorry. We are under the staff tonight.'

'What's the house red?' Lucy asked.

'I sink it is somesing from Médoc, madame. Pierre is most happy when he tastes it.'

'Sounds lovely.'

A few minutes later he returned to show them the bottle and its label.

'This is your domain, sweetheart,' John said.

She looked at the wine, then up at Laurent. 'This will be great,' she nodded to him. She turned to John. 'It's not Granny's. But it's from the same side of the valley, same soil, same grape.'

'You know a lot more about wine than you let on,' John replied.

'I used to take the guys down there when they were younger. They loved the château. Jean-Luc and Isabella adored them and we spoke a lot of French.'

'You said Isabella. But the clue Oliver left used the name Isobel,' John observed.

'You're right. Isabella is her real Norwegian name. The kids called her Isobel when they were tiny, and it stuck. Oliver used the French version, Isobel, to tell us the clue is in French and not Norwegian.

'Anyway, we spent a month down there each summer. Billy never came with us – couldn't stand the food. So the trips became a sort of magic journey they only made with me. They could run around the vast garden, hiding in all the nooks and crannies. They loved it.

'To answer your question about the wine – Jean-Luc used to take us for drives. We'd all load up into his great old camion and visit his neighbours, all of whom had vineyards.'

Lucy and John continued to chat over supper. As they rose from the table, his hand went to her bottom. He kept it there as they wove their way through the tables to the front of the restaurant. A minute later, John seated her in the privacy of his Jaguar.

'That walk through the restaurant was quite something, Mr B.'

John smiled. 'The unconditional gift you make of yourself is an act of trust I treasure more than you can know.'

Lucy kissed him. 'I need you to own me. You need to know that; it's the most intimate knowledge we could ever share. I love that you know me that completely.'

John started the drive back to Esher.

A few minutes later, they were inside the house. 'Are you as naked under that dress as you were on our first night?'

'Completely.'

'In that case, come with me.'

He led her into the living room and put a match to the ready made-up log fire.

He took her in his arms. His kisses were gentle, then more urgent. The part of her still separate from him was melting. Her lips parted in symbolic anticipation.

Firm hands cupped her head, caressed her neck, her bare shoulders. She pulled his hips to hers and let her head fall back, her eyes closed. Then, his kisses again – his hands at the top of her dress – the pulse in her neck. Now, her very essence was being unzipped. She followed his gaze downwards ...

47

Tuesday – 30th October

Lucy and John woke early. 'You never showed me the painting last night.'

They descended the stairs and John led her into his study.

'It's gorgeous, John. You're right – it's as good as anything Cropsey did himself.'

Lucy paused. 'Mrs Markham must have it. You're right about the frame, it's the same as the others. We could put them side by side.'

'Funny you say that.' John picked up their recent acquisition of *Sugarloaf Mountain in Winter* and led Lucy through to his living room, where he had already taken Cropsey's summer off the wall. The one he was carrying, he placed to the right of it on the floor. He stood back to admire the two paintings, side by side.

'Stunning,' Lucy said. 'The styles match perfectly. We *have* to get the Cropsey Winter picture they're restoring at the gallery – and Senator Malvito's Autumn.'

'The frames definitely match,' John said.

'What if the frame on Mrs Markham's Spring doesn't match these?' Lucy asked.

'It matched the one she gave me. It's one of the reasons she was convinced there was a set. So, unless she's changed the frame in the last twenty years, the frames are identical.'

'Well, what are we waiting for? Have they finished the restoration of Winter yet, do you think?'

John grinned. 'The gallery called me to say they'd had a cancellation and had completed our project early. I hope you don't mind, but I had them deliver it here, as I knew the kids could take the delivery.'

'Course I don't mind. Where is it?'

'I'll get it. But you should be dressed as you were when we first saw *The Piazza San Marco* in Wimbledon.'

Lucy smiled. 'I'll get some coffee on.'

John fetched the newly restored Cropsey Winter from the dining room. He took it out of its delivery case and unwrapped the soft moisture-proof covering. He arranged the painting on the floor to the right of the two already lined up against the wall.

In the kitchen, Lucy made coffee and took off her robe. Completely naked, she carried the two mugs of coffee into the sitting room.

John turned – and laughed.

'Black as night, strong as death and sweet as love,' she said, repeating his words from the coffee shop. 'As you like it,' she smiled. 'And as you like me – Piazza San Marco.'

'Well, gorgeous … looking at how generous the offering is … I think you've raised the bar to impossible heights for all baristas everywhere.'

Lucy giggled and looked at the row of pictures. 'Wow. I can't wait to see Mrs Markham's face – especially if we can get Autumn from Tom Malvito.'

'I know. It'll be quite emotional to show her the four lined up with her own. It's been more than twenty years. Let's get the gallery to clean Mrs M's Spring.'

Lucy was thinking. 'You mentioned that your friend William estimated the set to be worth two hundred and fifty million euros. How much more do you think the set's worth now you have the fifth one done by Lilly?'

'Anyone's guess. I don't believe the art world has a precedent for this. The set is totally unique, even with only four canvasses. If the right people were in the auction room, the very minimum would have to be a hundred million US.'

'John, just think of the environmental lobbying a hundred million dollars could do. It's almost enough to overturn some of the vested interests you talked about when we met in the Ritz. Can you imagine the media penetration and social media that we could get for those bucks?'

John wondered …

'Anyway, I think you should take me over to see the wonderful Mrs M who got you started in all this.'

'Let's get them cleaned first. But something is still intriguing me … if Lilly did the Winter that she signed – why did she sign the Autumn she painted only 'L?'

'Six paintings – five different canvases – four seasons … we have to find out about Lilly Cropsey.'

I have more urgent needs, Mr Baxter.

Lucy moved to the side of the sofa.

'If you're not taking me over to see Mrs M … perhaps you will take me over this?'

She leant over the side arm of the sofa and put her hands on its seat.

She watched him move behind her – and closed her eyes.

Then his voice. 'Right now – media penetration can wait.'

48

John called Mrs Markham to ask her if the gallery could pick up her Cropsey for cleaning.

'What've you been up to, John?'

'Let's just say I've got something I think you'll like.'

'I fear you've done something extravagant, John. You must come for lunch and bring that lovely Lucy I've been hearing about?'

John's phone buzzed. 'George, Mr Baxter. Got some news – Billy has been extradited back into the US on multiple charges. One is skipping bail. One is possession of stolen art. And the last one is attempted murder – of Kelly.'

'What?'

'When he was apprehended for theft, courtesy of Kelly, Monica bailed him out. He went straight round to Kelly's place and tried to strangle her. Lucky for Kelly, Malvito was there and managed to pull him off. Monica and Billy jumped on a plane to England – but he's now been extradited.'

'Is Billy in custody, then?' John asked.

'Too right. I think the wheels are falling off his wagon. No one can bail him out this time. He's in till the trial. It'd be a miracle if he sees natural light in fifteen years.'

'So, the Old Man, Simon, Jack and Kelly are all still free to do whatever they want,' John replied. 'Have you heard anything else, George?'

'Oh, yes – they never caught your little spy. He's been connected with seven murders in North America and two in Europe. But he never leaves any evidence that can lock him away.'

'OK, George, thanks. Let's catch up later. And by the way, William tells me our little spy is called Paul Adams; is that the guy?'

'That's the one,' George replied. 'Apparently, they call him Letu.'

213

Lucy was thinking. 'Let's look at this code Oliver left – and Ma's crossword book.'

Lucy read Oliver's clue again. 'It's better if you can see it, I think, John.'

He sat down next to Lucy at the breakfast table and studied the text.

Isobel would say - (81) / 18 (0) 21 (6) 5 (0) / 4 (8) 21 (8) / 16.15.14.20.

'Why don't we go over to Walton Bridge and stand where Canaletto stood to paint your picture – we can solve the clue while we're there?'

'I don't think the current version of the bridge will be much inspiration,' he smiled. 'It's a rusty old piece of crap they're about to pull down.'

Lucy studied Oliver's text during the ten-minute car ride to Walton. The sun was making a last attempt to break through grey clouds on an autumn afternoon. John pulled off the main road to trickle the car down to the Thames on the south side of the river.

'This is known as Cowey Sale,' he said to Lucy.

The ice cream vendor smiled at them. 'What can I get you?'

John bought two of her chocolate Cornettos. 'You from round here? I seem to remember your face,' she said, looking at John.

'I used to bring the kids here to feed the ducks,' he said.

'That's it,' she replied. 'Kids all grown up now, I expect.'

'Too fast.'

'So - what brings you down here now?'

'We came to stand on the spot where Canaletto painted a picture of the old bridge,' John said matter-of-factly.

The ice cream vendor eyed them up. She laughed. 'Now that is original.'

'The painting is actually original. And Canaletto would've loved the idea we were eating Italian-style ice cream on the exact spot he painted his picture.'

They all laughed, together. The ice cream lady shook her head. 'You folks – honestly.'

Lucy giggled as they retreated. They stood where they judged Canaletto had set up his easel. 'I think we're here.'

A hazy sun broke through dark-grey clouds. On the river, a small motor cruiser passed slowly. The tranquillity of the scene was completed by a pair of swans, gliding together near where Lucy and John were seated. He reflected that swans mate for life and turned to look at Lucy, who was admiring the pair. He wondered if her thoughts matched his. For a few moments they sat, enjoying the peace in the sunshine.

'Aren't they beautiful?' she said. 'Beautiful – graceful – content – together.'

John turned to Lucy. Very gently, he kissed her forehead. 'That's just what I was thinking.'

Lucy put her head on his shoulder. They sat for a few moments more.

Eventually, she broke the silence. 'Let's have another look at the text,' she said, retrieving her phone.

isobel would say – (81) / 18 (0) 21 (6) 5 (0) / 4 (8) 21 (8) / 16.15.14.20.

'It may not be that sophisticated,' Lucy said. 'Remember – he had to do this after getting out of the house and before going to work.'

'Only one of the numbers is more than 26,' John said. 'They're probably letters of the alphabet – and "81" actually *is* a number. Suppose the four sections are parts of an address … if that were true, and the first "81" kind of tells us that, then it's at Number 81, somewhere.'

'OK,' Lucy said. 'The next bit's three words then. But why the brackets round the five digits in the middle?'

John looked again. 'If those are three words, what do we have … three or eight letters, then two or five letters, then four or eight letters – with the bracketed digits interspersed. Let's take out the brackets and set them aside, as it looks as if that's what he's suggesting. That would mean we have three words, most likely three, then two, then four letters.'

John made out an alphabet down the left side of the paper napkin they had been given at the ice cream van. Next to the letters he wrote the digits 1 to 26.

Lucy started to read off the code. '18 is "R", 21 is "U" and 5 is "E". "RUE". If 4 is "D" and 21 is "U" again, we have "DU". If 16 is "P" and 15 is "O" and 14 is "N" and 20 is "T", we have "PONT". Rue du Pont. So, we have 81 Rue du Pont.'

'So why the bracketed digits?' he replied.

'Take them in sequence, then,' Lucy suggested.

'OK then, 06088.'

'It's a zip code – 06088,' she said.

Lucy typed the zip code into Google Earth, but the indicator placed it in a field.

'If he translated it into French, why don't you type in 81, Bridge Street, 06088?'

Lucy looked at him. 'Clever clogs.'

216

'Seems funny we're at Walton Bridge – solving a clue that takes us to Bridge Street, a third the way round the world.'

Google brought the answer. 'It's the Bank of America, John. That's why he asked me for a four-digit code. He used a safety deposit box.'

John scratched his chin. 'What was so important it had to be put in a bank vault … and so urgently?'

49

'Let's see what Ma has to say in the crossword book.'

'One thing is obvious – both Mary and Oliver feel the need to talk in code,' John replied.

'Let's assume Ma believes she's being listened to. She probably feels the Old Man wants to know what she knows.'

She paused. 'And as for Oliver using code – he knows three of the Blacks have been killed.'

'And that the Blacks have tried to poison us,' John added.

Lucy retrieved the book from her bag. They reread the inscription Mary had put in the book.

Lucy's phone buzzed with Mark's photo. 'Hi Mom. Got some missed calls. How's it goin'?'

'Fine, sweetie. It's good to hear your voice. How are all of you?'

'Everyone's OK.'

'How's the Brown family – and their house?' Lucy asked.

'It's OK. No trees came down here. His dad says we can stay as long as we like – you know how big the house—'

The call dropped out.

John was thinking. 'I'd suggest we went back there, except that Sandy's still preventing flights over the Atlantic.'

'You're right,' Lucy said. 'No point flying west till Sandy has blown out.'

Lucy's phone buzzed with a text from Mark.

Got onto first mutual. claim number 976358. i go to house in two days to meet them for claim check etc. keep u informed. all cool. Don't fly yet. not safe. luv u. xxx

'Hold on – you said "no point flying *west*".'

Lucy smiled. 'Yup. The kids are obviously healthy – and with friends. Sandy will take three or four days to blow over. The airports on the east coast will be crazy catching up with delayed flights. We should go *east* for a few days instead. We have some pizza to eat, I think.'

'OK, then. Let's see what Ma wants us to find in Venice, then go back to Farmington to get your house straightened out. In about three weeks, the paintings will have been cleaned by the gallery and we can visit Mrs Markham back here in England, with the set.'

They looked at the sky above Walton Bridge. 'Look, John. The sky's the same as when Canaletto painted it – all dark-grey and threatening … What else did he paint?'

'Canaletto spent several years in London – and he painted prolifically. They have a permanent exhibition of his in Venice, just a few yards from the Rialto Bridge, and not far from a restaurant that does excellent home-made pizza.'

The dampening air made Lucy pull her collar up.

'Let's go home,' he said. 'We could hunker in with a film and some chocolate. We've been living at a hundred miles an hour recently.'

'Sounds dreamy … but we can't keep putting our chat off.'

'Dare we order takeout?' he asked, avoiding her question.

They returned to the car and drove into Walton along New Zealand Avenue. As they passed the Aston Martin forecourt on their left, Lucy remarked, 'If ever you want to make me feel like a Bond Girl, you should buy one of those.'

'Only when they make an electric version,' he replied.

The light was starting to dim as John pulled up thirty yards from the pizza shop. As he got out of the Jaguar, he noticed a Mercedes pull in a few yards behind them, outside the funeral director. All he could see of the driver was that he was very short in stature.

John got back into the car and started the engine.

'John?'

'Letu's here,' John said, lurching the car out into the traffic.

'What – in Surrey?' Lucy frowned.

'Yup – via Sotheby's, Harbour Island and Boston – kind of proves why our flight off Eleuthera exploded in the air.'

'John … how are we going to protect Charlotte and Emma?'

Approaching Whitehills Close, John glanced in his mirror. There were no cars behind him to see him make the turn. He pulled through the opening gates as soon as the gap was wide enough.

Now inside Whitehills Close, he pulled into the kerb only twenty yards in. The light was fading fast. He twisted in his seat to watch the entrance to the road behind them. It was fully thirty seconds before the Mercedes trickled slowly past the closed gates.

'We turned in before he got to the brow of the hill back there,' John replied.

'So?'

'He knew about us turning in here without even seeing us.'

'He's got a tracker on this car,' Lucy ventured.

John looked in his wing mirror to check for cars at the entrance to the close. The gates had closed and there was so sign of the Mercedes. Then, in the twilight, he noticed the faintest of red glows from behind him. He checked his dashboard – no indicators – no lights at all.

'Run that way, Lucy, NOW,' John shouted, grabbing the keys and the fobs.

They ran the hundred yards to the left-hand dog-leg in the road. They slowed to a walk and glanced back at the car.

'It could be a third-start bomb. Crispin told me about them after he came back from a bomb-disposal tour once. Goes off when the vehicle is started the third time.'

Lucy was intrigued. 'We started the car at the river to come home, we started it again outside the pizza shop. So if we'd got home, the next time would have been when we started it in your garage tomorrow.'

'The bomb would have taken the house then – along with the art.' John was dialling the police, as they neared the gates of his home. He keyed in the codes to the sliding gate. As soon as they could, they slipped through the widening gap and John pressed the close button. In a few moments they were enveloped in the warmth of the house.

'Is that Walton Police? I need to report what I believe is a car with a bomb ... where? ... Whitehills, just south of Esher on the Portsmouth Road ... my name ... Baxter, John Baxter ... my address is "Giza", Whitehills, Portsmouth Road, Esher ... yes, "G.I.Z.A.", as in pyramids, yes ...'

John put his phone down. 'They're asking if they can collect the keys at six p.m.'

'Maybe it *was* only a tracker,' Lucy said.

'Yes, but sweetheart, we'll only survive this by being too careful, not too careless.'

Lucy reached up to kiss him. 'You're right. I could do with a finger or two of that single malt.'

John poured two generous whiskies. 'When we met Vanessa Thompson at the gallery – she referred to three nicknames they had for you – The Mona Lisa, Isis and Boff.'

Lucy grinned. 'I wondered when this would come up again.'

'I think I get Isis; she was the Egyptian goddess of fertility. But why Mona Lisa – and why Boff, unless it was short for boffin, because of your scholarship?'

'Well, let's take one at a time. This seems the right moment to tell you about my time at Oxford. Just in case you get the wrong idea.'

'I'm all ears,' he replied.

'I got to Oxford very young. I was seventeen and fairly immature. But I was not underdeveloped physically, if you get me.'

'I get you,' he laughed.

'Exactly so, Mr B. But I was totally focussed on my degree. I went through the entire three years a virgin … I only lost my virginity on the very last day of my last term.

'Isis is how my peer group saw me – some kind of idealised, fertile goddess – but not how they experienced me, if you see what I mean.'

'Fair enough,' John replied.

John lit the fire and watched it spread in the grate. He turned to Lucy. 'Undress – right here by the fire.'

50

Twenty minutes later, Lucy and John were cuddled up naked on the sofa by the fire, under a huge grey faux fur. They watched as the fire crackled, mesmerised by the flames. He was sat against the end of the sofa, one leg extending along its length. Lucy was leaning against him, her back to his chest. His arms were crossed in front of her, enveloping her. She had mentioned how safe she felt when wrapped in his arms.

'This is my idea of domestic bliss,' he said softly.

'Me too,' she whispered.

Words were coming to him, words he knew he had to share with her.

'You are my sunrise, my sunset, the source of my bliss – You're *why* Aphrodite invented the kiss.'

'That's beautiful – and very poetic,' she replied.

He kissed her blushing face, slightly salty with perspiration. 'I love the taste of your afterglow.'

'Only you could say something like that,' she replied.

'It's the taste of a goddess who has poured herself into an act of love.'

'Perhaps when we've solved these clues here, you could pour some more of yourself into me.'

'Is there a goddess of sex?' he replied. 'Because if there is, that's what I'll call you.'

'The nearest would be Aphrodite, I suppose.'

'Calling you the goddess of love doesn't quite do it.'

'Aphrodite was supposed to be the Greek goddess of sex *and* love, I believe.'

'That'll do, then, sweetheart,' he replied.

'We should get some chestnuts to roast on the fire,' Lucy said.

Forty minutes later, they woke.

'We'd better watch the time. The bomb guys will be here in half an hour,' John said.

'Just two minutes more, lover,' Lucy replied. 'It's so cosy here with you, the fire and everything. We should do this more often.'

They gazed into the flames for a few moments. 'D'ya fancy another finger?' he said.

'How could I refuse an offer like that from you,' she grinned.

'While we're waiting, we can have a go at Mary's clues,' he replied.

Lucy opened the crossword book Ma had given them. 'The first clue is: *To snobs, this town in (New) England is the only place to mix.*

'OK, what's the second clue?' he asked.

Professionally speaking, it's a year with no tease.

223

'And the third?'

'Let's see.' Lucy turned three pages before finding another clue that Ma had highlighted. 'Ah, here we are.'

In this orange place, one trade is in a spin.

'Keep going,' he said, as he poured.

'That sounds good,' she said. 'Ah … the next clue is interesting: *The world's longest, in 1985, and the rest is hard.*

'She's put a kind of emphasised full stop after this clue,' Lucy added. 'It looks as if she's come to the end of a sentence or something.'

'Got the first one yet?' he asked.

Lucy frowned at him and looked again at the first clue.

To snobs, this town in (New) England is the only place to mix.

'Seven letters,' Lucy added.

'I think the word "mix" indicates another anagram,' John said.

'So, if it has seven letters, it can't be "BOSTON" then,' Lucy replied. 'Except that it fits perfectly, especially as the word "new" is bracketed – kind of suggests it's a town in England and in New England,' she said.

'Let's go with "BOSTONS",' he replied.

'OK, next one … *Professionally speaking, it's a year with no tease.*'

'So we're talking about a profession,' he said. 'The last bit tells us it's a mixture of "a year and no t's".'

'Oh, I see … it's no "t"s, as in "n", then "o", then "t" and another "t".'

John was thinking. 'So, it's likely to be one of the professions. And then we have to take the letters 'a, y, e, a, r, and add n, o, t, t.'

'ATTORNEY, then,' Lucy said. 'So we have "BOSTONS ATTORNEY". What's next?' Lucy read out the next clue as John put a pizza in the oven.

In this orange place, one trade is in a spin.

'Orange place ... could that be Seville?' Lucy suggested.

'Definitely, especially when you get the answer. If you look at the trades and then play with the word "spin" ...' John said.

'Pins? ... no, it's snip,' Lucy announced. 'Barber of Seville – snip – "BARBER", then.

'Now we have "BOSTONS ATTORNEY BARBER". What's next ... Oh, yes. *The world's longest, in 1985, and the rest is hard.*'

'Sounds like one of those composites, this one,' John said. 'When I say to you, the world's longest, how do you instinctively carry on the sentence?' he asked Lucy.

'Bridge? ... railway? ... river? ... Those are the obvious ones, I suppose,' she said.

'Usually, it's the geographical ones in *Times* crossword clues,' he replied.

'Geography was not my strongest ... but I would guess Amazon or Nile,' Lucy said.

'Nor mine, but I think the Nile goes through nine or ten countries.'

'OK, then ... Nile. But what has 1985 got to do with anything?' Lucy asked.

'These random dates usually refer to literature or when something was published ... 1812 would refer to an overture, or music or something. Sometimes it's a date of release of a book or a film.'

'You know the answer to this one, don't you?' Lucy frowned.

'If this is a book or film release, think of something with the Nile in it.'

'*Jewel of the Nile.* And it came out at about that time, didn't it?' Lucy asked.

'Well, you get confirmation when you look at the last few words of the clue.'

'*And the rest is hard,*' Lucy continued. 'So, we have "BOSTONS ATTORNEY BARBER JEWEL". I can see why people get hooked on crosswords.'

'Let's search for an attorney in Boston called Barber,' John said, joining Lucy at her side. 'Ma Black says she knows Billy stole the jewels. Is she trying to tell us to go to this attorney with the jewels, or just to tell him?'

'It's only twelve-thirty in Boston, John. OK, Google – phone number of attorney Barber in Boston.'

Lucy's screen showed a phone number. She tapped it.

A few seconds later, a voice said, 'David Barber.'

'I believe you're expecting my call, David. My name is Lucy Howard.'

'Indeed, Mrs Howard. What a pleasure – you've been solving clues, then?'

'Well, yes. I'm in England at the moment. Do we need to meet?'

'Can I put it this way? My client wants to know you're on the right trail and has to be very careful with communication. I'm told you'd understand.'

'We understand. You can tell your client we're going to Italy.'

'Excellent. You're doing just fine. She holds both of you in the highest regard. Good luck in Europe.'

'Thank you, David. See you soon.'

Lucy was puzzled. 'How many English lawyers practise in Boston? The way he talked, he sounded English.'

'You're English, sweetheart, and you're in Boston,' he replied.

'Mmmm – maybe ... Let's have a look at flights, then,' she said.

'OK then ... BA006 to Venice tomorrow at twelve-fifty?' he asked.

'Not 006, if you don't mind. Don't think I could handle that, just yet.'

'Oops,' he smiled. 'What about ten-fifty, flight 004, arriving lunchtime?'

'That's more like it – and we can have lunch in the piazza.'

'Good. Then Venice to Boston. Shall we say ... three days later?' John asked.

'I suppose it depends on the clues,' Lucy replied. 'Ma must be petrified if she couldn't even leave clues in the US.'

'Hence Venice,' John said. 'Perhaps we can stand where Canaletto painted yours?'

'If you're booking the flights, I book the hotel. I know just the place,' Lucy said, looking in Ma's crossword book. 'The next clue leaves no doubt where she wants us to go next.'

51

'Impress me,' John said.
'*Endless discipline and faith cover you in gold.*'
'How many letters?'

'2, 5, 8, so this one's not too tricky,' she replied.

'You're getting this very quickly.'

'I took it that the reference to faith steered us to St Mark's Church. If you've ever been inside, you'd know why you feel covered by gold. Then I worked it back to the word discipline without the ending and got "discipl".'

'So … St Mark's Basilica, then.'

'There are more clues,' Lucy replied.

'Are they in some kind of sequence?'

'She's put numbers to the left of them in the margin. I assume we take them in order. And she's made up a few of her own – presumably because she couldn't find a clue that suited her purpose.'

Lucy turned her attention to the next clue as John took the pizza out of the oven.

'This one, she wrote herself,' Lucy said. '*A sinister looking post office delivers Dutch flowers.*'

'You should be able to get this one – especially with your knowledge of Italian,' John said.

Lucy looked puzzled.

'What flowers do you think of as typically Dutch?'

'Tulips, I suppose,' Lucy replied.

'Right. Now we see how Mary cleverly doubles up her use of words. What is the old meaning of the word "sinister"?'

'Left-handed,' Lucy replied. 'From the old superstition that lefties were unnatural.'

'So, if we look at the left-hand side of the two words "post office", what do we get?'

'P and O. What's the significance of that?' Lucy asked.

'If you "deliver" the letters "P" and "O" to the word "TU-LIP", what do we get?'

Lucy wrote the seven letters on a piece of paper. 'She likes her anagrams, doesn't she?'

'You need your Italian, sweetheart.'

'*Pulpito.*'

'Yes, but Ma is even cleverer than that. In the Basilica, there are two pulpits, unique in all the Catholic churches on earth. I think she's using the word "sinister" in more than one way. I think it's the left-hand pulpit she wants us to visit.'

'Wow,' Lucy replied.

'Well, we'll find out soon enough. Why don't we make the Basilica our first stop?'

Lucy looked for the next number in the sequence. 'Here it is. But this one's all numbers and she's obviously written it herself. Look at this, John.'

16/3/4, 22/5/1, 12/10/1, 24/16/4, 34/12/1.

She slid the book along the kitchen bar and took a bite of pizza.

'Interesting – all the crosswords from page twelve onwards are completed, look,' she said.

John studied the five sequences of numbers and noticed that all five pieces of code ended in either a '4' or a '1'. He pointed this out to Lucy.

Lucy grinned. 'There are only two sorts of clue – across and down. I think you'll see what I mean.'

'Of course. The ones ending in four denote a "D", as in "down", and the ones ending in one denote an "A", as in "across".'

Lucy carried on. 'So, if we look at crossword 16 and at the clue 3 down, we should get another word. She must have been pretty scared to be doing it like this. I wonder how long ago she laid all these clues.'

Lucy and John discovered the five words.

BLACK – BRIBES – GOVERNMENT – ENVIRONMENT – OFFICIALS.

Lucy looked at John. 'No wonder Ma's scared … what do we do now?'

'We involve a third party to help us – someone investigating for a living – and who enjoys the protection of the organisation they work for.'

'Like who?' Lucy asked.

'An investigative journalist – motivated by a real scoop, a career-boosting scoop. Maybe someone who also has a personal axe to grind.'

I love your thinking, Mr Baxter. Maybe we can start to turn this round.

John's phone buzzed. 'Bang on cue – I need to meet the bomb guys outside. After I let them into the close, they won't let me near the car. I'll call you if they make any discoveries.'

'If we're not going near the car, I'm coming with you.'

Five minutes later, they stepped through John's grey front door. Lucy pulled the four-foot-long steel bar to shut it.

'The door's really heavy – what's it made of?' she asked.

'The insurance company insisted it was made of six laminates of hardened steel. The frame it's mounted in weighs nearly six hundred pounds and had to be fixed into a solid concrete frame built into the brickwork. Same for the back door. They refused me insurance otherwise.'

They walked the hundred yards to the dog-leg in White-hills Close. From there they could see the orange flashing lights of the bomb-disposal vehicle outside the gates. John activated the fob and two men entered the close. One of them slid an illuminated mirror under the rear of the car.

It was ten minutes till John's phone buzzed. 'All clear, Mr Baxter. The car is safe now. Forensics have checked the car but there's only two sets of prints. Do you mind if we come and collect your fingerprints to eliminate yours?'

'No problem, Officer. We'll be back at the house waiting for you. It's just two hundred yards down here to your right.'

A minute later, Lucy and John opened the door to the bomb-disposal crew.

'Come on in, gentlemen. I take it you found something then?'

'Two kilograms of Semtex, Mr Baxter. The third start of the engine. Anyone in the car would have been turned into what we call "The Red Mist".'

Lucy shuddered. 'I feel sick.' She quickly left the room.

Two minutes later, Lucy reappeared, the colour gone from her face. John wrapped his arm around her as they took it in turns to roll their fingers on the imprinters for the police.

John showed the two men to the door. 'Thanks for coming out so quickly, gentlemen.'

He turned to Lucy, as he closed the front door.

'We have to get much more proactive. We can't spend our lives waiting for the next attempt – we have to take the fight to them.'

52

Wednesday – 31st October

Lucy and John landed in Venice and took a private river taxi to the jetty nearest St Mark's Square.

They settled into their seats on the riverboat. 'It'll be nice to experience Venice with a romantic.'

'How so?' John asked.

'Well, Tim did all the right things; he tried very hard – but "romantic" was not something he did. He was a true gentleman – but he never really got who I am. Not like you; it was almost spooky how fast you knew what I needed.'

'Talking spooky, sweetheart,' he grinned. 'Today is Halloween – and guess whose birthday it is.'

'Dutch or Italian?'

'Dutch.'

'Bruegel?'

'Vermeer, actually. The 31st of October 1632.'

'How many other birthdays have you got stored in there, Mr B?'

'Only the important ones.'

Lucy stretched up to kiss him. 'The room I've booked is one of the most romantic you could imagine.'

'I hope you've not done anything too extravagant.'

'Extravagant, compared to what exactly – bidding twenty million pounds for a fake painting?' she asked.

They laughed. John pulled her tight to him.

Arriving at the Hotel Laguna, they approached reception.

'Signora. Welcome back. It's so nice to see you again. Are you here to buy art?'

'Not this week, Marco; we're just here for a break. This is John Baxter.'

'Nice to meet you, Mr Baxter. Please follow me – we have the room you asked for.'

Outside the suite, on the wall, was a plaque proudly presenting the room as *The Presidential Suite*.

John looked at Lucy, eyes narrowed, saying nothing. She grinned. They followed Marco in.

'As you will see, signora, there is something in the ice bucket, with our compliments – and we managed to achieve the white orchids you wanted.'

Marco withdrew discreetly. The eight-foot-wide four-poster bed was dwarfed by the main room. Two writing desks with chairs were placed on opposite walls. The sofa, two large armchairs, and a chaise longue were arranged around a coffee table even larger than the bed. The vast bathroom and separate dressing room created a feeling of uncompromising extravagance. The classical French windows in the main room extended from floor to ceiling and were dressed in grey-and-pink-striped drapes, matching the canopy of the bed.

'You did the white orchids – to remind us of our first night in the Ritz,' John said. 'And what have we here?'

He took the bottle from the ice bucket placed on the table in the large bay. 'Another shade of pink – this time Laurent-Perrier. They seem to know you well.'

'Well – nobody has ever known me as you do. But if you feel there are any hidden depths you need to explore ...'

'We'll be doing lots of exploring, sweetheart. But we did say we'd go straight to the Basilica for the clues.'

Hand in hand, they walked across the Piazza San Marco in the sunshine, towards St Mark's Church. Halfway across the square they stopped to admire it.

'I've never seen a building with this arrangement of ten arches in the front,' Lucy remarked.

'And I've never noticed the golden lion at the top there,' John replied. 'Or the four horses below it.' He paused. 'The sheer opulence ... actually, the curves of the arches give it a kind of voluptuous feel ... more than generous ... like your curves, sweetheart.'

'It's a good thing I'm not "Piazza San Marco" now, or we'd be arrested.'

'Sweetheart, if you were Piazza San Marco now, no one here would be admiring the buildings.'

Lucy squeezed his hand three times as they entered the Basilica.

'Even if you're not religious, you have to admire the artwork,' Lucy whispered. 'I'd forgotten how uneven the floor is. The church is built on top of a million vertical tree trunks to support the weight of the building out of the sea. But after hundreds of years some of the trees are rotting.'

They walked up the middle of the Basilica, the famous Pala d'Oro altarpiece drawing them in, as it had others for nearly a thousand years. The ten-foot-wide panel, made of gold and silver, was decorated with more than three hundred garnets, three hundred emeralds and two hundred sapphires. A further five hundred pearls of varying sizes completed a backdrop depicting the major events in the life of Jesus.

'There can't be anything like this anywhere else on earth,' John said.

They paused to admire the interior of the Basilica, decorated in a mosaic of gold leaf covering all parts of the ceilings not boasting a religious scene.

'Talk about "covered in gold",' Lucy said.

John spotted a church official standing near the left-hand pulpit. 'We need a distraction for the official.'

'Mmmm,' Lucy pondered. 'The sun is shining in the square. Why don't we get some hot chocolate and look at Ma's book? We can plan our distraction.'

'Good idea.'

Emerging into the sunshine again, Lucy took his hand and led him to the middle of the Piazza San Marco. 'I don't know how many times I've imagined us standing here together, in the middle of the square, just like this in the sunshine.'

John kissed her. 'Do you fancy a ride in a gondola?'

'I do.'

'Let's do that tomorrow, shall we?' he asked.

'Yes, 'cos a hot chocolate's what I need right now.'

'Let's go, then.' He put his arm round her as they crossed to the Caffe Florian on the south side of the square. They were joined by a waiter.

'*Potrei avere due cioccolate calde e due pezzi di torta di ricotta?*' John asked.

'Full of surprises, Mr B. When did you learn Italian – and why am I only finding this out now?'

John shrugged. 'You never asked. I took a sandwich year in the middle of my History of Art course – spent most of it in Italy. Florence, Naples, Rome, Venice – the Vatican even – in 1990.'

She shook her head and returned to the crossword book. 'The next clue's in the pulpit. I assume that one will give us the next.'

Lucy looked up at him. 'D'you have any other surprises in store?'

'Not really … my French isn't too bad, I suppose,' he replied.

Lucy continued to look at him.

He looked up from the menu. 'What? … OK, my knowledge of Egyptian hieroglyphs is pretty much total. But even if you count that as a language, which most people don't, that's only four. According to Dr Thompson, you left Oxford with nine, including Mandarin – before your twentieth birthday.'

'John, what got you interested in the hieroglyphs?'

'I was given a book by my mother on my tenth birthday. It had lots of paintings from the Egyptian tombs. I just loved the colours and the way the symbols seemed to be trying to say something. I asked my mother what they meant. She didn't know. She said only a handful of people on earth could decipher them. From that moment on, I was hooked – have been ever since.

'When she saw how fascinated I was, she started to give me books about Egypt. Several of them were by Sir Flinders Petrie. Most archaeologists think of him as the father of modern archaeology. His surveyor's attention to detail and his meticulous recording is still used as a model today. I wish I could have met him.'

Lucy studied John's face. *He doesn't know of my Scottish Petrie cousins.*

They sat in the afternoon sunshine. Although it was autumn, the square was filled with lovers holding hands, others simply standing in the middle, embracing.

Lucy and John looked towards the north side of the square and admired the shops in the colonnade extending the length of the piazza. At first- and second-floor levels, columns formed an elegant façade to the rooms set slightly back from the front of the building. The regularity of the architecture along the square contrasted with the uneven spread of shoppers eager to take home luxury leather souvenirs, chocolate and locally blown glass in all shapes and sizes.

John broke the silence. 'This café, the Caffe Florian, was the very first coffee house opened in Europe – in 1720.'

Lucy's mind was elsewhere. 'So – having rowed in the boat race in '89, you couldn't row in 1990, then?'

'They didn't need me – if they ever did; they had Matt Pincent at Number 4 in 1990 – and they won again – by two and a quarter lengths.'

The waiter appeared with the drinks and ricotta cake.

'I could come here just for the chocolate,' Lucy said. 'Oh … and I think I have the distraction we need. They don't allow photography in the Basilica, right?'

'Right.'

'Well, everyone's taking selfies. What if I approach the official inside and ask her for a selfie of her and me? She'd explain there is no photography allowed. I'd plead with her and that would give you a few seconds to search the pulpit.'

'That could work.'

They walked back over to the Basilica and made their way forward to the pulpit.

The official had moved. John quickly climbed the oak stairs of the pulpit and crouched down below the visible height of the lectern. He searched the only shelf underneath. In the dim light, his hand brushed an envelope. He tucked it into his jacket pocket before standing up. He re-joined Lucy and led her to some seats arranged for prayers.

They opened the envelope. 'This is Ma's writing,' Lucy whispered.

'*Where Buddhism meets Christianity in this place … there's a church outside a church.*'

'Why would Ma refer to Buddhism in a Christian church? And what is a church outside a church?'

Lucy glanced around. 'Now, we could use the help of that official. There she is.'

Lucy approached the guide. '*Dove il buddismo soddisfa il cristianesimo in questo posto?*'

The official looked puzzled, so Lucy asked her if she knew of a church outside the church.

'*Dove c'e una chiesa davanti a una chiesa in questo luogo?*'

The guide's face lit up. They followed her to a small private chapel in the corner of the Basilica itself. She opened the heavy iron gates and smiled at Lucy.

'*Ciò è la cappella di Zen.*'

'*Grazie mille.*' Lucy smiled, turning to John. 'The Zen chapel – where Buddhism meets Christianity.'

They entered the small chapel. The guide was now answering questions from another tourist, just outside. A bronze figure of St John the Baptist was laid out on top of a tomb.

John looked behind the columns on the north side of the chapel – nothing. Lucy looked around the figure of the Virgin Mary at the south side of the room – nothing. Then she noticed a long gap between the bronze figure laid out horizontally and the marble slab supporting it. She slid her arm in and moved it in the direction of the feet. She could feel another envelope. She slid it out. On the front were the letters *FAO – LH*.

'John,' she whispered. 'I've got it; let's go. Stick it in your jacket pocket. I can't wait to see what Ma has written.'

53

They stood in the middle of the square admiring the architecture.

'Canaletto must have loved this place,' John said. 'He painted more than one version of the piazza.'

'Don't you want to read what we found in the chapel?'

John looked around them. 'I'd rather read it when we're alone in the hotel. Let's get up to that balcony while the sun's still shining on the front of the Basilica. I've been looking forward to being up there ever since I first saw your painting.'

They climbed the steps to the Museo Correr on the west side of the square. Reaching the top, they turned left through the souvenir shop, then right, along the corridor to gaze eastwards out of an open window overlooking the piazza and directly facing the Basilica.

'This is it,' Lucy said. 'This is where he stood to paint the picture.' She shook her head in disbelief. 'Pinch me, John. Can it really be that we own the painting?'

'Better than that, sweetheart. You own two of them … but then again, some of your greatest assets come in twos,' he grinned.

'Well – perhaps it's time you conducted a really thorough audit, Mr B.'

As the face of the Basilica slowly became dressed in shadow, they stood mesmerised.

Lucy eventually broke the silence. 'You and I have seen some beautiful buildings in our travels – but the Basilica has to one of the most memorable.'

'*Canaletto era qui*,' John replied.

Lucy turned to look at him. 'So, it *was* you. You painted the words on the ceiling of the Baxter Laboratory. I did wonder if it was a coincidence the words were painted in the same cobalt-blue as your car.'

John grinned. 'You miss nothing.'

They continued to stare until the sun gently lifted from the face of the church.

'Let's get back to the room; it's suddenly got a lot colder,' John remarked.

They took one last look at the Basilica before idling back along the corridor to the steps down to the square.

John was thinking. 'As far as our young are concerned, the more they move about the safer they are.'

'You started talking about a third party to do the investigation for us,' Lucy replied.

'A thought came to me in the church. The reason we got together initially was to solve the fraud of the painting left to your client. It's all got out of hand. We should work this from a distance.'

Lucy agreed.

'We should solve Ma's clues here in Venice, then get some additional help in Boston.'

Back in the room, John opened the envelope Lucy had found in the Zen Chapel. They sat on the chaise longue and started to read.

To my beloved daughter, Lucy –11th September 2011

I am sorry to fetch you here. The family kills people that threaten it and they have ears all over the US.

He is involved in heroine and weapons, both large and small. This p art of the business is kept very secret as are huge cash incentives from foreign operators with vested interests in keeping wars going. The chaos of wa r prevents g ood border controls – especially in poppy-rich Afghanistan.

John pointed to the 'p', the 'r' and the 'g'. 'I can't believe these are errors.'

He has tens of millions of dollars in cash in the vaults only he has the combinations to. He paid $12,000,000 *in cash for the property out on Cape Cod, for example. He's built a war chest to run for President.*

But I see the fear he creates in the companies he runs.

His energy business buys land in fossil-fuel-rich Montana and Wyoming and bribes government officials who otherwise would never grant mining rights on such beautiful landscapes. They ruin the land with open-cast mines and kill p eople who raise objections, both locally and on Capitol Hill. I can hear y ou asking why this is an issue for me now, years after marrying him.

Early on, he downplayed his energy interests to the naïve girl I was. He owned groups of companies, all completely legitimate as far I know, even now. It allowed this twenty-year-old to be convinced that the business was ethical. He had not started the company, I told myself; his father had. He merely continued it while he built the property business. I knew little then of his w idth of interests and nothing of his part in the w eapons trade.

But I cannot pretend any more. Even though you could uncover enough detail to ruin the whole empire, I'll survive. My family is rich enough in its own right. They have offered me a helicopter lift out if I need it. But I have my children and grandchildren in New England and I cannot imagine leaving them.

I believe now my only exit is to a secure gated community Andrew has identified for me. I could see my children as often as they want to see me. Yo u and whoever you meet in the future should unveil the truth in such a way so as not to implicate yourselves.

By the time you read this you will know my attorney. He is honest – and u nder instruction to help you. He knows no more than he needs to; this protects him and his family.

I thank God for yo u – your integrity, your kindness, your generosity, your brains, and for giving me two beautiful, strong grandchildren in your own image. The last thing I want is for them to be orphaned. Please do not forget – Oil and Coal has very deep roots right at the top of government. So be very, very careful and protect yourself and the children above all else. I love you all.

He who has the stones may also have the combination to the Boston vault; he installed it and, knowing the character, may have figured a way of obtaining part of the combination. I know it's date sensitive, although I don't know how. Reading between the lines you will see I need this letter destroyed (and then s ome) as soon as you have extracted all you need from it. My guess is that today you would have to think about birthdays and how to wrap them up.

In the safe is all the information you need to collapse it all. His little 'Black Book' of connections contains killers all the way to the top of governments. If anyone can do this, you have the intellect, ability and courage. From the moment I first met you, I believed that the world would be a bette r and cleaner place for your time in it.

Tears were rolling down Lucy's cheeks. 'No pressure, then.'

As she put her head into his shoulder, John knew her emotions had not stopped her thinking …

54

Lucy looked up. 'The *Boston Times*. We talked about getting a journalist to do the investigation. We need a respected broadsheet that will be taken seriously when it outs the truth.'

John moved to his laptop.

'*Boston Times* – here we go – there's a reporter called Anita Smith.'

He paused. 'This is more like it. One of Anita's colleagues is a Facebook connection – reports on environmental issues and the 1.5 degrees centigrade limit ... she has a column with a global warming agenda.'

'What's her name?'

'Patricia Dixon ... let's see ... ah, yes ... sweetheart, she's *definitely* the one we start with.'

Lucy was curious.

'Her father died from miner's lung.'

John obtained the number for the *Boston Times* while Lucy wrote something on a piece of paper. Her phone buzzed. 'Hi, Oliver.'

'Mom, we're being watched up here at Colin's. Colin's dad is having the place scanned today. The package I took to the building you know about has some serious stuff in it – must be worth a fortune. You need the four-digit number you gave me to get the kit and you need to have someone with you.'

'Listen, sweetie, you did the right thing – I'm very proud of you. Were you hurt in the garage?'

'No, I'm totally fine. Something hit my head. The paramedics say I was probably unconscious for a while. The company doctor checked me out this morning. The house will need major work though. Wolfie was in the lounge so he's good.'

'I love you, Oliver. I'm very proud of you guys.'

'OK, Mom. Can't talk too long now. Have a good one.'

John's phone interrupted. 'Mr Baxter. Pat Dixon. What can I do for you?'

'Thanks for coming back so quickly. Before I say too much, we're being listened to. Have you got a discreet email address I can talk to you on? It's better if you text your address to me.'

A minute later, John was typing an email to Pat.

Three of the Blacks have been poisoned and we can prove they're stealing art and making fraudulent copies. They're also bribing government officials to give them mining rights on some of the beautiful wildernesses in the Midwest. The wives in the family dare not speak out because of what happens when they try. We've been reading your column so we thought you might like to use your investigative skills to see what you can find out. We have a great deal of information that we could give you – exclusively.

Pat replied immediately. *I'm interested.*

We're back in the US in two or three days. We'll put a hefty reward in a safe for you in Boston. You'll be absolutely free to walk away if you feel the reward is not generous enough. Is that fair?

I think so. But why can't we meet – it all seems so underhand?

We're being followed – and listened to. For your own protection – if you want to meet us to check us out – we should meet for only the briefest of chats. Speaking on the phone should be minimal – texting is best.

Is there anything you can tell me to give me a start?

Lucy pointed to her screen. John nodded at her.

There's a fundraising reception in aid of the Republican Party next Monday at the State House in Boston. Some senators and several very senior congressmen and -women will be there. You'll find the more moderate conservatives in New England very willing to spill the dirt on the ultra-right. There's potential to scoop yourself some high-level dirt.

What kind of ultra-right?

Big oil and coal.

Will you be there?

Our faces are known to people involved in the art fraud. That's the main reason we need outside help – and someone with your skills for investigation.

OK, then. I'll see you when you get back to Boston. But I have to say – this sounds dangerous …

'Let's hope Pat's on board. To help her, we can stir things up between Kelly and Monica.'

'Well – both Black and Malvito have to be at the State House reception,' John replied.

'And Kelly has got to have been invited.'

'I should think so. Her father will want her and Mary there. He can make his entrance with the two women at his elbow. If Monica is there with Senator Malvito …'

Lucy continued the thread. 'Early in the evening of the event we get a message to Kelly that Monica tried to use her bank details to buy a copy of the Rockwell in London – and steal twenty million dollars from her. That should mix things up a bit. We make sure Pat is hovering, ready to watch and record what plays out.'

Lucy grinned. 'And just to make sure – we tell Monica that Kelly is sleeping with her husband.'

'Monica may not mind – especially if she's been sleeping around herself.'

'But – from what you told me about the auction, Monica has a temper,' Lucy replied.

Lucy and John were waiting for their room service meal. Lucy wore her favourite pink satin pyjamas and was sitting, feet up, on the Renaissance sofa, searching Ma's crossword book. John was searching for the gaps in the letter Ma had left in the Basilica.

Lucy broke the silence. 'I've found something. It's not really a clue; it's more of a statement … *I keep six honest serving men, of whom "why" is my most trusted servant.*'

'D'you know the poem?' John asked.

'What – the Kipling? "*I keep six honest serving men. They taught me all I knew. Their names are What and Why and When and How and Where and Who.*"'

'Just so, Ms Howard. Just so.'

Lucy shook her head, smiling.

'But Ma is focussing us on "why",' John said.

Why, Mr B, have you not undressed me yet this evening?

There was a knock on the door. 'Supper is here. You hungry?'

'Yes and yes,' Lucy smirked.

'Me too,' he announced, striding to the door. The waiter put the tray on the table in the huge bay window. While John's attention was on finding his wallet for a tip, the waiter stared at Lucy. John thanked him and put a ten euro note in his hand. The waiter shot a last look at Lucy before leaving.

'Are you OK with that, sweetheart?' John asked.

'I'm fine – they can't help themselves – young men – too much unrequited testosterone.'

'If you could see yourself, undressed as you nearly are …'

Lucy looked down at her chest. 'The satin does cling a bit. Let's eat … and you can tell me how you'd like your testosterone requited – for dessert.'

John uncovered the food on the tray. 'The gaps in Ma's note have been intriguing me. Let's have another look while we're eating.' He put the two sheets of paper between them.

To my beloved daughter, Lucy –11th September 2011

'Let's get these isolated letters down so we can destroy the letter.' He wrote in silence the letters P R G P Y W W U U U S R.

'That's interesting in itself,' he said, looking at Lucy. 'Twelve letters. Ma says the safe had a twelve-digit combination.'

Lucy was thinking. 'So – a thousand billion possible combinations. This could delay your dessert somewhat.'

'As Garry Kasparov once said – the art is not in calculating all the different chess moves possible; it's in choosing between the few sensible ones.

'What if this was going to be easy, not difficult at all? Where would a genius like Kasparov start, knowing what we know?'

Lucy looked at John with new respect.

He does 'critical thinking' instinctively – always finds the right question.

'Well, John – Einstein once said that genius is not in getting the right answer; it's in asking the right questions to begin with. So – if Mary is suggesting birthdays – we should ask which birthdays and which order.'

'OK then – looking at the sensible possibilities, there are nine Black children, Ma and the Old Man himself. That's eleven, not twelve,' John said.

'But Ma said, *My guess is that today you would have to think about birthdays and how to wrap them up.* I wonder if she's suggesting we use the date at the top as a starting point.'

'We can see what we come up with. She wrote it on the 11th of September 2011. You don't think that has any significance?' John said. 'It's the tenth anniversary of 9/11.'

'Just do the numbers for now and see what they translate as.'

John wrote the letters of the alphabet down the page. He put the numbers next to them, with A being 1, Z being 26.

'P would be 16, R would be 18, G would be 7, P would be 16, again.

'Nothing like 09, 11, then,' he said. 'Let's try upside down. She had plenty of time to concoct this one.

'P would be 11, R would be 9, G would be 20, P would be 11 again. 11/9/2011. Let's do the rest of it.'

Lucy smiled. 'So, she's told us which way up the alphabetic code is to be used.'

'Y would be 2, W would be 4, then 4 again, U would be 6, then 6 again, then 6 again, S would be 8 and R would be 9 again.'

'Those eight are months,' Lucy replied. 'After the year 2011, there's none bigger than 12; it has to be months.'

'You're right, except we have far too many digits to use. We have 11, 9, 20, followed by 11, 2, 4, 4, 6, 6, 6, 8 and 9; that's fifteen digits in all.' John paused.

'If it really is birthdays and today's date, what would be the easiest thing for him to remember?'

'Seeing as he has so many offspring – probably just a four-digit date for the day and the other eight digits for birthdays,' Lucy replied.

'So, if he uses four digits of the date as the time-sensitive part, then he is only using eight birthdays of the eleven in the family. Which ones would he choose?'

Lucy's face saddened. 'I have this horrible feeling he left out James.'

'We know James's birthday is in October and the number 10 is not in this list of months. It looks like you're right,' John replied.

'OK, so let's see how many I know. Well, Billy is June; that's one of the sixes. Peter, the painter was February – 'cos it's Valentine's Day; that's the only number two. Kelly is April the first; her father always used to say that Kelly was never going to be anyone's fool; that's one of the fours ... how we doing? That's three birthdays; we need five more ... Jack was always exactly a week after Kelly; so that's the other four ... and the eldest, Andrew, is June; Ma once confided in me when we were talking about our firstborns – it took her longer to deliver him than the entire night – the night being the shortest of the year.'

'June, then. So that's one of the other sixes. So, we only have to get Matthew's, Christopher's and Simon's birthdays and we know the code being used in the combination. But the fact that five of the birthdays coincide with Ma's idea kind of confirms we're on the right track. I'm fairly sure the other three birthdays will be June, August and September.'

'I'll get onto Mark and Oliver and see if they can find some birthday months on Facebook,' Lucy replied. 'We should have all eight fairly soon.'

'Why don't we just find them ourselves?' John ventured.

'Well … you know what gondoliers do? I was hoping …'

John laughed. 'On one condition: you tell me why the nickname "Mona Lisa".'

'Fair enough. The name started off as Mona Lucy because my roommate, Anne, was doing History of Art for A-level. She reminded me that I'd been dismissing the attentions of the boys all through the sixth form. "Mona" is the abbreviated version of Madonna, meaning virtuous and beautiful woman.

'Anyway, I was studying hard for my Oxford entrance exams. I was doing sixteen-hour days in the library for most of the autumn. Apparently, I was in a daze of exhaustion and the biggest smile I could muster was a kind of half-smile.'

'Fair enough.'

'Funny thing was – Oxford had interviewed me and made me an offer contingent on my A-level results. They told me not to worry too much about the entrance exams. So when I got my results and knew I had my place, I cried for two days. Not exactly Mona Lisa.'

'So … why did you work so hard for the entrance exams, if you knew you had a place?'

'Didn't want to be the anomaly who got in with bad entrance exams. I decided I would not just pass the entrance exams; I would blow them away.'

'Which you must have done, 'cos you got the scholarship.'

'Yes – well – there's a story behind that too …'

'Well, come on then, you can't stop now,' John said.

'OK, then. All my A-levels were languages. When the dean at Somerville interviewed me herself, she asked why I thought

I deserved a place in one of the most rigorously intellectual colleges in Oxford.

'I asked her if she was going to see my entrance exam papers. She told me she would. So I told her that the last nine paragraphs of my paper would be written in nine different languages – just for her.

'I told her that in my time at Oxford I would become totally fluent in the two most recent languages I was studying. She asked me which ones. I told her Mandarin and Cantonese. She looked at me and asked me why both, when most people would be happy to speak Mandarin.

'I told her that the most common of the Cantonese dialects would access another thirty-five per cent of the Chinese people. I said I thought China was going to be the world's largest economy within the next generation.

'She asked me why, when most of my time would be studying law, did I believe I could become fluent in both languages within my three years at Oxford. She laughed when I gave her my answer.

'I told her that most six-year-old Chinese children are pretty fluent and that I have a three-year start.

'She told me that most Oxford undergraduates would be happy just to gain a first-class degree. She laughed again at my reply: "Yes, I'm sure you're right."

'She checked my year of birth. At the time of the interview, I was only just sixteen.'

John laughed. 'You probably scared the hell out of them.'

Lucy undid the top button on her satin top. 'Earlier, we discussed a really thorough audit of the assets …'

John was frowning.

'What's bothering you?' she asked.

'If one of your nicknames was Isis, the goddess of fertility ... and your other name, Mona Lisa, implied virtuous woman ...'

'How were the two names reconciled?' she continued.

'Well, yes?'

'The name Isis does not imply promiscuity, only that I looked extremely female. I've not discussed this with anyone before, but the name Mona Lisa, implying virtuous, was probably less misleading.'

'Why?'

'Because until my very last day at Oxford, I was still a virgin.'

John smiled. 'Wow – there must have been gallons of unrequited testosterone around you.'

'Let's just say, had you done an audit back then, you'd have found me much the same as today.'

'In that case, you were standing way out from the crowd.'

Lucy grinned and undid the second button on her pyjamas. 'Perhaps it's time for a bit of asset-stripping.'

'The pleasure will be all mine,' he replied.

'I doubt that. I doubt that very much.'

55

Thursday – 1st November

'I've been thinking, John. How could we use our information on the Blacks to achieve environmental wins for Planet Earth?'

'Great question.'

'If the evidence on Kelly is as damaging as it looks, maybe we can force Black Industries to generate wind power instead.'

'Or solar power – I love it.'

'Let's get dressed and develop that idea over breakfast,' Lucy said.

'Before you get dressed – there's something I need to do.'

Lucy looked at him. *What's he up to?*

'Come over to the window,' he ordered.

He took her hand and they stood together, bathed in the morning sunshine.

He put his hands on her hips.

'You are my sunrise, the source of my bliss;
You are the only true love of my life;
You're why Aphrodite created the kiss;
I'd be so honoured if you were my wife.'

'John … I don't know what to say. I love you so much. We haven't had the chat we promised.'

'Sweetheart – with our mindsets and resources, we can do anything.'

He reached for a little box he had left on the window table.

She put her hands on the box. 'John, I'm sure it's absolutely beautiful. Let's discuss whether this is even possible. But I know I love you.

'Maybe it's the uncertainty … whether we'll even survive this?'

Lucy watched the first tears descend his cheeks – the sadness in his eyes too intense to cope with. She put her head to his shoulder, her own tears wetting the skin on his chest.

As thousands of couples had done before them, Lucy and John walked through the streets of Venice to the Rialto Bridge. They paused to admire the six arches arranged each side of the central, more elevated arch. Lucy asked John how many arches he saw.

'Thirteen,' he replied.

'That's my point.'

'How so?' John asked.

'Most people miss the whole picture. People see the arches as symbolising Jesus and the twelve disciples at the last supper. They see thirteen arches, but they rest on the biggest of them all, the reason the bridge was built, the one enabling boats to pass.'

'You're suggesting we look at the bigger picture.'

'Yes, but for now, let's just enjoy the moment.'

John clasped her hand and squeezed three times. She smiled and reached up to kiss him.

'I'm looking forward to *La Traviata* tonight. Have you ever been to La Fenice?' John asked.

'No.'

'Then you're in for a treat.'

They returned to the piazza and sat in the late morning sun, idly watching the passers-by and the birds waiting for the food left behind.

'It's been a lovely few days,' Lucy said at last. 'But I can tell your mind is back in Boston.'

'Am I that easy to read?' he asked.

'Only for those keen enough to interpret,' she answered.

John smiled. 'I've just noticed – we've not seen Letu.'

'You're right. He'd have got pretty bored. All we've done is shop, eat, go to art galleries, Vivaldi's *Four Seasons*, and drink coffee here in the square.'

'Yes – but could this be the calm before the storm?'

Lucy squeezed his hand. 'I have the same feeling.'

At six-thirty Lucy and John walked through the Piazza San Marco and out of the northern side of the square towards La Fenice Opera House. They settled into their seats in a box just above the left-hand side of the stage. The interior was rich red: red velvet on the walls, red velvet seats. The building was unapologetically opulent; generous chandeliers and gilded plasterwork extravagantly applied to the ceiling completed the classical and traditional decor. The romantic intimacy of their box was perfect for Lucy and John this evening.

The orchestra was warming up below them. John pulled Lucy's chair towards him, an act which seemed suggested by the intimacy of the box they occupied.

'I love hearing the orchestra tuning up. It kind of builds the sense of anticipation,' John remarked, looking down into the orchestra pit.

Lucy looked at the side of his face as he gazed down. Tears were descending his cheeks again. She had never witnessed such unguarded emotions in a man. Nor had she ever aroused this depth of passion in anyone. She became aware of the responsibility this bestowed. Someone as much in love with her as he was deserved honesty and care; his feelings deserved to be treated gently.

She knew she would never love anyone this much, could never be who she needed to be with any other man. No other man had ever deserved what she needed to give him.

She had never seen such sadness …

56

Friday – 2nd November

John squeezed Lucy's hand three times as they landed at Logan International in Boston late the following evening. George had left a text on John's phone.

'Hi, George. Thanks for looking after things. Was Kelly in Boston all the time?'

'Yes, John. In the daytime she's at Black Industries and at night she's at home or with Malvito. No way could she have taken a flight without me knowing.'

'Thanks, George.'

John turned to Lucy. 'So – it was definitely Monica impersonating Kelly and trying to use her money to buy a fake Rockwell.'

The next morning, John and Lucy drove to the bank to retrieve whatever Oliver had deposited. They approached one of the bank tellers, who fetched the manager.

'I'm Paul Marks, the manager. We can talk confidentially in my office just here.'

They sat down and Marks continued. 'The young man who made the deposit was insistent that only someone who could answer these questions would be allowed to access it.'

'I understand,' Lucy replied.

'So, what is unusual about your driver's licence, Mrs Howard – that's the first question.'

'It's not a driver's licence; it's a driving licence, because that is what they're called in the UK. My driving licence was issued in Oxford, England on the 29th of September 1988.'

'So, the second question then. What is significant about that date?'

'It was my nineteenth birthday.' Marks nodded his head.

'Lucy! The date we met. You never said.'

'You never asked,' she replied.

'OK, then,' Marks said. 'Final question. What is the name of the place in the painting in your hallway in Boston and who did the painting?'

'It's Ketcham Farm and George Durrie painted it,' Lucy answered again.

The manager smiled. 'Good – sorry to have to put you through that. If you could follow me. The number of your box is listed as 3-25-6.'

They followed him down the stairs to the vault. Marks punched in a twelve-digit code on a keypad.

'Twelve digits … date sensitive … all the latest technology; it'll only be a few seconds.'

The huge steel door started its electro-mechanical sequence.

John noticed the name 'Armstrong' advertising the safe manufacturer on the door.

'I suppose the date's at the front, followed by the other eight digits,' John remarked.

'Not necessarily,' Marks said. 'And anyway, there's twin-layer verification.'

He took out his mobile and accessed the code arriving. Each character he input into the safe keypad had a different tone – indicating there were six characters to the code.

Just then the safe door started to open. Lucy looked at her piece of paper and the numbers she had written on it: *3. 25. 6.*

'It must be Section 3 over here,' John said. 'Then column 25 across here and sixth drawer down. Here it is, sweetheart. 3-25-6.' Lucy took a deep breath.

'Here goes,' she said. She punched in 0312. The door clicked open an inch or two and Lucy opened the door wider. John pulled out the steel drawer and put it on the table in the middle of the vault. In the open-topped drawer was a heavily built box made of oak, about twelve inches long.

John prised off the lid.

Lucy gasped.

The bright lights in the vault created myriad brilliant co-lours from scores of immaculately cut emeralds and diamonds fashioned into the most spectacular necklace. The largest twenty-carat emerald was the size of a grape, and several of the seven-carat diamonds were almond-sized. The matching earrings each boasted a seven-carat diamond, hung below an emerald of identical size and cut.

John smiled. 'That's a first, sweetheart.'

'Why?'

'Because I've never seen you with your chin on the floor.'

Lucy whispered into his ear. 'You have actually – several times. You just couldn't see my chin.'

John grinned.

'John, they're absolutely beautiful.'

'So beautiful, I can think of only one neck that deserves them.'

Lucy looked into his eyes. He was being genuine.

'So, this is what Billy stole from Mary, then hid in the oak bench,' she remarked.

John picked up the necklace. 'This has to be ten million pounds; it's really heavy. There must be more than a hundred stones here, most of them diamonds; must have taken ages to put together.'

Lucy and John continued to stare at the jewels, mesmerised.

Eventually, John took a deep breath. 'I hate to spoil the fun, lover… but we said we'd meet your guys at the house.'

As they exited the bank, they looked around for anyone watching them.

They strode quickly to Lucy's sports Merc. Once inside, Lucy activated the door locks. She wound the car out of the parking lot to connect with Route 90, taking them south-west towards Hartford and Farmington. 'It's about a hundred and ten miles to the house.'

She glanced quickly at John. 'What's the matter?'

You don't know how beautiful your engagement ring is – or that the stones were taken from rings that have been in my family for three hundred years.

'I was just thinking … why is this box so heavily constructed?'

He held the necklace up to the light. 'This *would* look fabulous on you, sweetheart.'

'I don't think that'd be wise … you may never get it off me.'

Lucy's mind was elsewhere. 'I can't wait to see the guys. But I'm dreading what the house looks like.'

57

Lucy rounded the corner into Wyndham Street. Mark, Oliver and their friend, Colin, were sitting on the front steps of their home in the sunshine.

Lucy looked up at her home, its western half demolished.

'Well, sweetheart, it happened the right way round.'

'How do you mean?' Lucy replied.

'The house is damaged but the guys are unharmed,' he said, as they pulled up.

Lucy kissed him briefly, her hand already on the door catch.

She ran to greet her sons, who were moving towards her in the middle of the front lawn. Lucy, at five foot, eleven inches tall, was the shortest of the three.

A few seconds later, the group disentangled and Lucy gave Colin a hug. 'It's so kind of you to give the guys a home.'

'It's not been all our house,' Colin replied. 'We were up at yours in Boston for two days.'

'Someone's been following us,' Mark said.

Proud tears streamed down Lucy's cheeks. She grabbed her sons again. 'It's so good to see you guys. I'm so glad everyone's OK …

'Hi Wolfie.' Lucy squatted down to muss the dog, who licked her nose enthusiastically.

Lucy looked at the garage, its door completely buckled in the middle. Above it, her bedroom was open to the air, the roof crumpled from the front of the house to the back. There was a gaping hole where the roof joined the long west wall.

'How did you get out of there alive, sweetie? It's a miracle.'

'I looked at the storm warning and decided to sleep under the bench that Dad delivered. When I helped him take it off the pickup it weighed a ton. He said it was solid oak. It was like he'd built it to last forever. It never broke. That box came out from underneath. Have to hand it to him, the bench saved my life – especially when you see the garden room.'

They followed him to the back. The roof of the three-season room was smashed onto the floor, broken glass and splintered roof beams scattered in the mess.

'Oliver, did anything else come out of the bench apart from this box?' John asked.

'You didn't find the compartment in the base?'

John looked at the box he was holding. 'Keep it flat,' Oliver smiled.

John held the box horizontal while Oliver slid the base sideways. For some seconds, the five of them stared, mesmerised.

In the base of the box, stuck to a piece of double-sided sticky tape, were fifty diamonds, each a quarter inch in diameter, arranged in five rows of ten.

'That's why the bench had to be so heavy,' John remarked. 'It masked the weight of the contents so you didn't think of looking underneath.' They continued to stare.

'Each of these stones must be five carats. There must be at least two hundred and fifty carats in weight here,' John said.

'I'm starving,' Oliver replied.

Mark agreed. 'Me too. We could go to Cobblestone's for breakfast.'

'I've noticed that whatever time you have breakfast in this country, it's always breakfast, even if it's not,' John retorted. They piled into Colin's car.

Oliver looked at Wolfie. 'Come on.' The dog jumped in and settled at his feet.

'What are diamonds like that worth?' Mark asked.

'Depends on the four c's,' John replied. 'Cut, carats, colour and clarity. Diamonds in larger size categories are significantly rarer and disproportionally more valuable.'

'So, what are we talking here?' Mark was curious.

'Normally a diamond of good cut, colour and clarity and weighing one carat would be worth about fifteen hundred dollars. A carat is a fifth of an ounce. But if a diamond is just five per cent over the one carat mark, it might be priced twenty per cent more. Diamonds this large are so rare that each carat in a five-carat diamond could be worth ten times more.'

'So – if each carat in a five-carat diamond is worth fifteen thousand, not fifteen hundred, then each diamond is worth seventy-five thousand dollars. There are fifty diamonds, so that's … $3,750,000,' Mark replied.

'And don't forget the necklace and earrings,' John replied. 'They're worth over ten million dollars.'

'Cool,' Oliver replied. 'So how does a carpenter who makes kitchens get all this stuff?'

Lucy was nervous. 'Great question. We need to go somewhere we can't be overheard.'

Lucy led the four of them into Cobblestone's. They sat at a table in the window.

As Lucy sat there, surrounded by the four men, she became acutely aware of her gender – and her motherhood. She smiled.

Mother Bear still needs to protect her cubs. They're alive and well. No one has been injured in the storm. Thank heavens.

Then a sadness arrived. Lucy remembered when they'd first moved in, the kids only ten and eight years old. She recalled the painting, the sanding, the gardening, all the work involved in reclaiming the house from years of neglect by the previous owners.

John was seated next to her. 'Why so sad, sweetheart?'

'You're so sweet; you always pick up on my mood. I was just thanking our lucky stars all of us are alive and well – and sad when I remember all the work involved in making a home for the guys.'

John put his arm around her. She smiled at him wistfully.

The waitress appeared with the omelettes. Lucy turned to John. 'You're about to see a magic trick.'

John frowned inquisitively.

'Yes – three plates of food will disappear before you can say "wolfpack".'

John watched the three young men eating for a few seconds.

'They do look like wolves who haven't eaten for a week,' John joked.

A few moments later, Oliver finished his food before anyone else.

Mark looked at John, tilted his head towards his brother – and said only one word.

'Beast.'

Twenty minutes later, Lucy picked up the bill. 'Colin, I hope these two have left some food in your house.'

'Don't worry, Mrs Howard – I've stayed with you enough times over the years.'

Let's go up to East Rock; no one will hear us talking up there,' Mark suggested.

'You mean the Soldiers' and Sailors' Monument, over in New Haven?' Colin asked.

As Colin wound the car up to the top of East Rock, it was easy to check they were not being followed. They left the car and sat at a picnic table.

John looked at each of them in turn. 'By doing this investigation, we've made ourselves the focus of the Blacks' attention. So – someone else should do it, and we think we've found a journalist with the right motivation. She'll be putting herself in danger, so we need to incentivise her generously.'

John googled The Oaks Hotel on Boylston Street in downtown Boston. Within seconds he was reserving two large suites.

He turned to Lucy. 'How many chess players can the Blacks beat simultaneously – especially if we have a three-move start?'

What are you up to, Mr Baxter? What have you got in mind?

265

58

Monday – 5th November

Lucy led the convoy of three vehicles on the 110-mile trip back to Boston. Alone with Lucy, John asked her if there was a branch of the Bank of America near The Oaks Hotel.

'About four blocks away. Why?'

'We need some serious cash,' John replied.

'How serious?'

John smiled. 'You let me worry about that.'

Two hours later, Colin and Mark pulled their cars up behind Lucy's near The Oaks Hotel.

John gave the young men instructions to buy eight copies of a large and thick hard-backed book, but preferably a book called *Worldwize Living*. He stressed the importance of the books being hard backed. They were to take them to the post office two blocks away and buy six of the very largest jiffy bags, a roll of duct tape and two ordinary envelopes. They were to put two of the books into one of the jiffy bags, take the package, unsealed, back to the counter in the post office and ask them to price out the postage, but not post it. They were to ask for four more postage labels of the same value, pay for the postage labels, get them stuck on the envelopes and bring all six unsealed, unaddressed envelopes and the books to The Oaks Hotel at 3.00 p.m.

The three young men looked hard at John, then at Lucy.

'I don't know what he's up to either; just trust him,' Lucy said.

Oliver sighed. 'OK, then. See you at three.'

'Right – we need a briefcase with a combination lock – then the bank,' John said.

'There's a luggage shop only about two blocks from here on Boylston Street,' Lucy suggested. 'And it's almost next to the bank.'

John called Patricia Dixon and arranged to meet her at The Oaks at 5.00 p.m. in reception.

From the bank, Lucy and John drove the short distance to David Barber's office.

'It's good to meet you at last,' he said. 'Mrs Black has told me lots about you. How was Italy?'

'Wonderful,' Lucy replied. 'We stood where Canaletto painted his famous picture.'

'Ah, yes – the Piazza San Marco. But you didn't come to talk about far-distant places.'

'We did not,' John agreed. 'We came to deliver what belongs to Mrs Black.' He opened the heavy oak box that Oliver had placed in the bank vault.

'The necklace and matching earrings,' David affirmed.

'And then there are the little somethings in the base,' John said.

David frowned. 'I don't understand.'

John placed the emerald necklace and earrings carefully on the table. He slid the base to the side to show the diamonds stuck to the inside.

David sat back in his chair, thinking hard. 'Well, you've more than passed Mrs Black's test. She said you would. But she could not have known by how much margin. Mrs Black wanted to know you were as honest as she believed. She wanted to know you'd bring the necklace in. But that was all; there was no mention of diamonds. I think these were added later by whoever stole the necklace.

'So now I can tell you that Mrs Black wanted you to know that this necklace set is fake; she had it made as a copy. It cost half a million dollars to make, less than a twentieth of the cost of the original. She said you would make good use of it, Mrs Howard, whatever that means.'

Lucy asked David Barber the question she knew was in John's mind. 'David, how did Mary Black know we would find the jewellery? She didn't even know where they were.'

'I'm going to leave that one to Mrs Black to answer, if you don't mind. She said she would explain it to you herself.

'Anyway, congratulations are in order. The question now is – are the diamonds the ones stolen from a van in London some years ago in Hatton Garden?'

'David, presumably you would not wish it known you have any knowledge of the diamonds?' Lucy ventured.

'What's on your mind?' David replied.

'We estimate we could change them into about three million dollars in cash and donate it to good causes. In this way, neither you nor Mrs Black could ever be associated with them.'

David smiled. 'Mrs Black speaks very highly of you both. I trust you will use it wisely.'

Lucy asked her final question. 'David, before we go – did Mary mention anything about the Blacks' Boston safe?'

'Indeed, she did. She told me the safe "can never be opened without zen".'

Lucy smiled. 'In that case, David, our causes may benefit from a lot more than three million dollars.'

59

Lucy and John sat in her car to drive to The Oaks Hotel. 'Before we get going, John – I don't want the necklace. I'd worry who'd be coming for it – and what they'd do to get it. You know a bit about this family. Kelly thinks it's rightfully hers – she's Ma's only daughter.

'Perhaps this is the time to tell you about my scar. It will explain why the necklace could kill me – and my reticence to get married before all this is settled. You deserve to know; I owe you that.

'Billy stole a painting from his brother, Peter, to apologise to me for one of his sexual indiscretions. I told him I couldn't hang it up because the whole family knew it was Peter's.

'That night, Billy came back to the house with Simon and Jack – and some rope. They tied my wrists together and slung the rope between my arms over the beam above me in the kitchen. They hoisted me so tight I was on tiptoes.'

Lucy paused.

'Sweetheart – if it's too difficult, you don't have to tell me.'

'No. I promised to tell you – and it will explain lots about the Blacks.

'Billy said he was going to remind me why I shouldn't tell Peter he had stolen his painting. I still feel the panic when I remember it.

'He took a knife from the wooden block and cut the straps of my dress. Simon tugged my dress down. Billy cut through my right bra strap. When he did the same on my left, he tugged upwards and caught my jaw with the tip of the knife.

'Funny thing is – I felt no pain. Blood was running onto my chest but all I cared about was Billy using the blade to scrape the bra cups down. I was petrified. Jack and Simon had their hands all over me – even though my chest was drenched with blood – can you believe that?

'Then Billy held his lighter near my nipple. I was starting to faint. I reminded him that I had breast-fed our children. I asked him if that meant anything to him. I must have started crying 'cos he hesitated.

'Jack egged him on. "Billy? You gonna do it – or shall I?"

'Then something clicked in me. I heard my father's voice telling me to use my brain.

'"Billy, there's a way Peter never gets to know you stole his painting."

'"Oh, and what's that?" Billy sneered.

'"We tell him you found his painting in a local art shop. You tell him you bought it from the shop so you could give it back to him as a Christmas present."

'Billy hesitated. So I told him if he ever wanted to see my tits again, he would have to leave them unmarked. They stormed out, leaving me still hanging from the beam.'

'How did you get down?'

'The kids came into the kitchen. They must have heard me crying. I'm standing in a pool of my blood about a foot wide. When they saw me they both started crying. I had to reassure them that I was going to be alright. I looked like something out of a horror show. I was completely stripped – blood was draining down my body. I told Mark to go and get his grandma from the big house.'

Lucy paused. 'He was only five years old – can you imagine – brave little trooper went across the grass in the pitch dark, to save his mum … When Mary came in, she gasped; she knew who'd done it.'

Tears started down Lucy's cheeks. 'Little ones should never have memories like that.'

John put his arm round her. Lucy put her head into his shoulder and started to sob. 'I'm sorry, John – but you deserve to know. We have to clear the way to be happy before we marry.

'Anyway, Mary cut me down. She loaded me and the kids into the car and got me to Boston General to get me sutured up. It's why to this day, she's never taken sides with her son. It's also why the boys never call their father. They've completely disowned him.'

John took his hand from Lucy's knee and put it to the nape of her neck. He drew her towards him and kissed her.

'You're so sweet,' she said. 'Actually, it's been quite cathartic, telling you. I've never related it to anyone. Of course, Mary and the kids know … and I made sure we discussed it with the kids; I didn't want them feeling it had to be suppressed.'

'Well, sweetheart, thank you for explaining – it can't be easy reliving it. But it only makes me want to marry you even more. You shouldn't be on your own against the Blacks.

'We're going to see them buried – if it's the last thing we do. We *will* have our life together, unspoilt by the Blacks – mark my words, Mrs Baxter.'

Lucy laughed, certain that somehow – somehow – they would make it happen.

'We'd better get started for The Oaks, John. They'll be waiting for us.'

Lucy dried her eyes, blew her nose, started the car engine and looked at John.

'That's a first,' she said.

'What?'

'The first time you called me Mrs Baxter.'

'Do you think you could get used to it?'

Lucy pulled out of the parking lot. She grinned. 'I do.'

60

'OK, then, sweetheart – assuming Kelly will inherit the real necklace, why don't we give the fake to Patricia Dixon as part of the payment for her services?'

Lucy nodded her approval.

They walked into The Oaks Hotel to find the young men already sitting in reception. In front of them on a low table were three cups of coffee and a dozen or so chocolate truffles.

'You seem to have made yourselves comfortable,' Lucy smiled.

'Have you been crying, Mom?' Oliver asked.

'Yes, sweetie. I was just telling John about Billy and the kitchen knife. I owed him an explanation. But it's OK – we're good. Thank you for being you.'

'You know we'll protect you, Mom. If that creep ever tries anything, Mark and I will kill him.'

'You've discussed this?'

Mark nodded nonchalantly. 'Many times – Mom, you've got to check out the chocolate shop over in the corner. Absolutely awesome.'

'When I look at all of you guys – it seems I have the best protection I could ever wish for.'

John was uneasy. *It's going to take brains, not brawn, to protect ourselves. We need to be two steps ahead of the killers.*

'Let's take the tray upstairs; there's stuff we need to do,' John replied. 'I'll get the room keys.'

He walked to reception. 'I have two suites booked under the name of Baxter for two nights.'

'Yes, Mr Baxter, I have your booking,' she said, looking at her screen. 'Both suites till Tuesday night, leaving Wednesday?'

'That's great – could you get five more coffees taken up to 606 and put it on my tab?'

John walked back to where Lucy and the three young men were seated.

'The coffees are being taken up. You'll see why when we get up there. Don't forget the jiffy bags, guys.'

John opened the door to Room 606. He stepped aside to allow the group into the room.

They arranged five chairs around the large coffee table.

John set the briefcase combination to 2937.

'Watch, people … we need four more versions of this.'

John took the diamonds from the wooden case and put three in his pocket. He opened one of the jiffy bags and took out both copies of *Worldwize Living*. He then took ten of the diamonds and taped them onto the right-hand, curved, opening edge of one book, making sure the duct tape wrapped around the ends of the book. He held the single book up for all to see and put it into a jiffy bag. He sealed up the bag, double-sealed it with more duct tape for safety and wrote Lucy's Concord address on the front of the bag.

'Voila,' he announced.

John left them to it, walked the ten yards to Suite 608, let himself in and shut the door firmly. He put the emerald necklace and earrings, one five-carat diamond and one brand-new banded pack of bank notes into the last jiffy bag, which he folded to put in the safe. He used 1826 to lock the safe shut.

He took one of the smaller envelopes, wrote *Room 608* on the outside, placed the room key into it and wrote *1826* on the inside of the envelope flap. Putting the envelope into his inside jacket pocket, he re-joined the others.

'OK, you guys – could you go back to the post office and post the bags – and get back here as soon as you can.'

'What do we do with the extra three copies of the book?' Colin asked.

'Oh, they're for you. It's for the planet you'll inherit after I'm gone,' John replied.

Lucy watched as they left. 'You gonna tell me how much is in that briefcase?' she asked.

'One. Come on, let's have a drink in reception. What d'ya fancy?'

Lucy frowned her disapproval. 'Something long and stiff as a gondolier's pole.'

A tall woman walked into reception and stopped to look around her. From her online profile, Lucy recognised her as Patricia Dixon.

John stood up.

'I know I'm a bit early,' she said. 'I came straight from the *Times*.'

John made the introductions and asked if there was anything she would like to know about them.

'Why are you doing this, I suppose?'

Lucy looked at Patricia. 'Where do we start? The family we're talking about is decimating large parts of Montana and Wyoming with illegally obtained planning approvals – and ruining the atmosphere with the CO_2 emissions their fossil fuels produce. And that's just the mining operations.'

'My father died of pneumoconiosis – miner's lung. But then you probably already know that.'

'Yes. But there's more. The Blacks are stealing art in New England. If we can't get them locked up for selling oil and coal, we might get them locked up for theft. We have video proof of an art theft here in Boston. If you decide to help us, you could have this recording for your newspaper. We can even connect the art theft with one senator, possibly two.'

Lucy let that one sink in.

'Was that the robbery at the Sunset Gallery – one of my colleagues at the *Times* covered it?'

'Yes, and we'd give you all the information we have – exclusively.'

'This lot are pretty dangerous,' Patricia replied. 'They hire killers to do their dirty work.'

'Maybe more dangerous than you think,' Lucy said. 'We believe they deal in weapons too. So, we're prepared to reward you quite handsomely in cash.'

Patricia looked at the couple, trying to size them up.

'How handsomely?' she said at last.

John took the envelope from his pocket and put it on the table. 'In here is the key to Suite 608 upstairs. We've placed a few items in the safe and the combination is in this envelope. Everything you find in the safe you can keep – whether you help us or not.

'If you're with us, there is one hundred times more cash in this briefcase, waiting for you. Have a look in the safe upstairs. If you decide to work with us, you'll take this briefcase, and we'll take it as your agreement to help us.'

'Why don't you just make me the offer?'

'We want you to be able to take your time to decide, on your own, without any pressure from us. The room is paid for, by the way.'

'And if I walk away with the contents of the safe, I am under no obligation?' she checked.

'None at all,' John replied. 'But when you've worked out what one hundred times the cash in the safe is worth, I think you'll see we're serious. And if the mining rights are being awarded by the people we suspect, I'm sure your career will benefit from the book you could write.'

'The art world must be treating you well,' she said. She put her forefinger on the envelope in front of her and slowly drew it towards her edge of the table. 'How will you get the other information to me?'

'What's best for you?'

'My personal email – padixon@scoop.com.'

'Very good. We wish you all the best. Let us know if there is anything you need. And be aware – they're listening to our calls and occasionally following us.'

'I get you.'

'Oh – just one more thing,' John added. 'Tomorrow night, here in Boston at the State House, there's a fundraiser for the Republicans.'

'Yes, I'm going as "Press".'

'Excellent. I'm sure the sparkles in the safe will do the occasion justice. But if you don't want to drive home late, you have Room 608 for two nights including tonight, if you need it.'

Her heart pounding, Patricia Dixon unlocked the door of Room 608. As soon as she entered, she could see the safe in the opened wardrobe in front of her.

Turning, she shut the room door, opened the envelope and typed 1826 into the keypad. The safe clicked open to reveal a large jiffy bag folded in half due to its size. Pat retrieved it and walked to the bed to pour the contents out. What slid from the bag caused her to catch her breath ...

61

Pat Dixon had only faint memories of her parents. Coal miner's lung had killed her father when she was just six years old, and her mother had failed to cope with two young children and no income. Less than a year after her husband's death, Patricia's mother put a revolver to the roof of her mouth and killed herself. Patricia and her younger brother were taken into care, and she had not seen him since.

Pat hated fossil fuels – especially coal. But she hated even more the people legally allowed to sell it and the legislators colluding with the industry. Her research had shown that burning coal was by far the most polluting way to generate a unit of electricity. And she had long suspected a link between the fossil fuel industry and the gun-goons, as she called them. One day she would document the links in a book.

She arranged the necklace neatly on the bed. She placed the earrings and the five-carat diamond next to it. She fanned through the neat packet of brand-new hundred-dollar notes – its band read *$10,000* in bold, black capitals. Could there really be a million dollars waiting for her?

She started to think of the investigation. Could it be true that the art theft implicated senior politicians? Could this be the scoop she had always dreamt of?

Patricia found herself undressing, suddenly intensely aware of her femininity. She picked up the sparkling necklace and made her way to the bathroom. She had never seen diamonds or emeralds this large.

She stood in front of the large mirror, the emeralds around her neck. She smiled at the muscle definition her recent gym sessions had given her. She loved how the jewels hung low enough to draw attention to her curves.

The man whose attentions she craved would be at the State House the following night.

She wondered what a million dollars looked like and how much it would weigh. Grabbing her phone, she searched for the volume and weight of a million dollars in hundred-dollar bills. She picked up the phone on the bedside table.

'Reception.'

'Can I get a bottle of Laurent-Perrier pink champagne?'

Patricia lay back on the large double bed. The cool satin felt good on her skin. This is how it would feel tomorrow night.

What would she do with a million dollars? She looked around the suite, checking there were electric sockets near the dressing table that she could plug her laptop into.

She would invite him back here tomorrow night after the fundraiser at the State House. She would need a bottle of his favourite single-malt whisky, Laphroaig.

The buzzer to her room sounded. She pulled her dress from the floor and threw it over the treasure on the bed. She put on the white robe she had noticed by the wardrobe at the door to the room. Still wearing the necklace, she opened the door and let the young waiter in.

She watched as he stepped awkwardly over her underwear on the floor.

'Shall I open it, ma'am?' he said. Patricia nodded.

Embarrassed to be in the company of a woman wearing nothing but her robe, he opened the bottle quickly and crunched it deep into the ice bucket. As he retreated, she pressed a five-dollar bill into his hand and shut the door behind him.

Patricia poured herself a glass – and smiled.

Here's to pink champagne and diamonds.

Her next thought saddened her.

Mom would have been so proud to see me now.

She swallowed two large gulps of the fizzy liquid and took a third which she kept in her mouth. She threw off her robe and lay back on the bed once more, rolling the fizz around in her mouth as she anticipated the following night.

This investigation could finally earn me the professional respect I deserve. With a million dollars I could resign my job and write the book about the gun-goons and the fossil-fools. And I'll sue that pervert of a boss who keeps groping me and implying that my promotion to Senior Political Editor could be arranged with me undressed.

Patricia got dressed, put the money and the large diamond into her bag and removed the necklace and earrings, zipping them safely into the internal compartment.

Downstairs, in reception, Lucy and John were finishing their whiskies.

Patricia approached them and sat down. 'I've decided to work with you.'

'Congratulations. You'll need to check the contents of this case. The banks are now shut so you might want us to accompany you to your bank tomorrow – just to make sure you get there safely.

'It's not locked – if you want to take a look.'

Patricia looked around her to check if she was being watched. She opened the case. She had never seen this amount of money. She started to sweat and wondered if anyone would notice. She counted the piles of hundred-dollar notes. There were three rows of five piles: fifteen piles in all. Each pile was stacked seven deep in $10,000 packets: $70,000 in each pile. Shutting the case, she accessed the calculator in her phone which told her that fifteen piles of $70,000 totalled $1,050,000.

$1,050,000. At least eighteen months' salary more than a million.

Who was it who said, 'Wear a cheap dress, people notice the dress – wear an expensive dress and they notice the woman?

She opened the case again to make sure she was not dreaming. She would get it to her bank first thing in the morning, pay the money in, obtain a second recording of her boss making his lewd suggestions in exchange for promotion, resign her job and go shopping. She would colour-coordinate her dress, shoes, clutch bag and the emeralds.

Once the senator has removed my dress, how cool would it be if my underwear matched the jewels?

62

George called John. 'I told you I saw Kelly go out to the ranch recently?'

'George, do you mind if Lucy hears this? I'll put you on speaker.'

'Mrs Black's in Massachusetts General with severe food poisoning. And there's been no food deliveries to the ranch.'

'Has Mary been out at all?' Lucy interjected.

'Not for days.'

Lucy looked at John. 'George, do we know what the prognosis is?'

'The doctor said they were just in time. They've sent the contents of her stomach to the labs – they normally get the results within twenty-four hours.'

'Did the doctors tell you when she'd be allowed home?'

'They have to keep her under observation for at least three days. They only let her go when she's good.'

'OK, George. Thanks for letting us know.'

Lucy's fists were clenched. 'Someone's got to do something about that bitch. What sort of psycho tries to kill her own mother? … Massachusetts General is on Fruit Street; it can't be much more than a mile. Let's go to see her when the guys get back … That *bitch*.'

John nodded. 'I know how much Mary means to you. But it sounds as if she's going to be OK …'

John kept his next thought to himself, unaware that Lucy's thoughts were identical.

The only thing that will stop Kelly is a death sentence.

'Let's find out if William has any news.'

'Hi, John,' William said. 'Did you enjoy any art in Venice?'

'A little; we wanted a break. Any developments here?'

'Yes. You remember we talked about a robbery at the Rockwell Museum?'

'Go on.'

'Well, it turns out there was a previous robbery from the Rockwell a few months ago. For obvious reasons they were keen to keep it quiet. But there were two odd things about it: there was only one painting stolen – a small portrait, of John F. Kennedy – and it was returned unharmed a month later. I could swear I saw a copy of it at an auction in New York recently.'

'How can you be sure it was a copy?'

'Actually, I've seen the original in a private gallery, then again at the Rockwell. Sometimes you know exactly why it's a fake – and sometimes you just get a feel.'

'I know what you mean. But you had multiple looks at the original. That's why I wanted you on the team.'

John was thinking. *How many copies of this JFK portrait exist? Kelly has a version at the bottom of her stairs; Lucy has one in her office; William saw one at the auction in New York. Were any of these the same ones, but at different times?*

Mark and Oliver walked into reception. 'So, no chocolate then, Mom?' Oliver interrupted, pointing at several empty truffle wrappers on the coffee table.

Lucy smiled. 'I did have one or two. But you know how this one likes his chocolate,' she said, purposely not looking at John.

Oliver could see the question on John's face. 'Yes, we got it all posted.'

'Where's Colin, by the way?' he asked.

'He went home. Girlfriend, I think. Why?'

'Because we'd like to visit Mary in hospital,' Lucy said.

'Why – what's wrong with Ma?' Mark asked.

'Poisoning,' Lucy replied.

Ten minutes later, the four of them entered Mary's private hospital room. She looked pale and weak, a drip line taped into her forearm. Because of the surprise nature of the visit, she had not put on any make-up. She smiled at them and apologised for her appearance.

'This is not how I want you to remember me,' she said, turning to her grandchildren. 'I want you to remember me running round the ranch after you, playing hide-and-seek, when you were little.'

Lucy had tears in her eyes.

How could anyone harm a person with so much love in them?

'Now, come on, Ma. They say you're going to be fine.'

'But they don't know how sick I feel. I've got this horrible metallic taste in my mouth. This must be how their cousin

Larry felt before he died. He was the company financial director. You remember Larry, Lucy; he was such a nice man.'

She put her head back on the pillows.

Lucy looked at John, a tear descending her cheek, before turning back to look at Ma. 'They said you should be feeling better tomorrow. Perhaps we should let you get some rest.'

Ma squeezed Lucy's hand. 'It's good of you to come all the way out here. Did you get everything you need from Italy?'

'Yes, Ma,' Lucy replied. 'Now, you should rest.'

Mary smiled and turned to her grandchildren. 'It's very important when you're as bright as you are …'

Mary looked out of breath. 'It's very important to find what it is you're truly passionate about in your life … and when you do, just do it … don't be worrying about what anyone says or thinks … just follow your passions. Life is too short to do anything else.'

'But you're gonna be OK, Ma. The doctor told us,' Oliver replied.

'Remember what I said, will you promise me?'

As the four of them made their way back to the entrance, no one uttered a word. Finally, Oliver could hold it in no longer. 'If Ma dies, I'm going to kill Kelly with my own hands.'

'Get to the back of the queue, dude,' Mark said.

'I think Ma's going to be fine,' John asserted. 'But I promise you – when Kelly does get killed, someone else will do it for us.'

Lucy stared at the side of John's face. It was set in stone-cold resolution.

What in heaven's name are you planning, Mr Baxter?

63

Tuesday – 6th November

Patricia left her apartment building the next morning, briefcase in hand. Her heart started to pound; her hands were sweating. She had only to reach the safety of the bank two hundred yards away.

Two minutes later, she walked into the bank. The manager filled out a form. Patricia signed it and followed him down the corridor to the vault.

He left her alone while she opened the case. She knew she could not pay in more than $9,999 in cash into a bank account. She separated only one $10,000 packet of the banded notes, putting the remaining 104 packets neatly into the steel draw. She took ten of the hundred-dollar bills from the separated packet and put them in her bag.

As she closed the steel door, Patricia pondered the best combination to use to lock it. She could not use her birthday, since it could be connected to her if ever the Internal Revenue discovered her unofficial 'earnings'. She decided to use 1826, the combination of the safe she'd been given in Room 608 at The Oaks Hotel.

She followed the manager up the corridor again, walked briskly to the teller at the nearest counter, paid the $9,000 into her bank account and tucked the teller's receipt into her bag. She emerged from the bank into the sunshine. With $10,000 from the safe in Room 608, and with an extra $1,000 from the briefcase, she looked forward to the shopping.

Patricia Dixon – tonight you're going to look quite the millionairess.

At four o'clock Patricia strode confidently into The Oaks Hotel, laden with shopping bags. She asked reception to order a taxi for 7.00 p.m. and rode the lift to the sixth floor. She let herself into Room 608 and plugged in her brand-new laptop to charge it up.

She ran a bath, relishing the liaison she was planning with the senator. She took the bottle of single-malt whisky out of its white tube and placed it on the coffee table.

She called reception and asked for two crystal whisky tumblers to be sent up, along with an extension cord for her laptop. She laid out the dark-green dress and matching underwear on the bed. She arranged the necklace near the plunging V-line of the dress – and was pleased with the effect.

A knock on the door told her the tumblers were being delivered. She took a ten-dollar bill from her purse, opened the door to the young waiter, thanked him, put the ten dollars on the tray and took the glasses and cord.

She placed the glasses and bottle of Laphroaig on the coffee table and extended the cord on the laptop. Making sure the laptop was still charging, she faced the screen and the tiny camera towards the bed. She found her new revolver and its six bullets, loaded the gun, took the safety off, and placed it under the pillow.

Pat looked around the room, checking everything was ready. Satisfied, she slipped out of her clothes and into the warm bath.

Tonight, she could start the research she needed for the book, ready for whatever else might happen …

64

John called George. 'Everything OK for this evening, George?'

'We're all good. Old Man Black will leave about six to make sure of getting to the State House by seven. Why don't you park four hundred yards beyond the ranch, just beyond the corner, so he doesn't see you when he leaves. I'll show you where Kelly hid the Rockwells and you'll be back home in Concord by the time the Blacks arrive at the State House.'

Lucy was thinking. 'John … that still leaves the two paintings from the Sunset Gallery unaccounted for; we still don't know what she's done with those.'

'Let's see what George and William turn up in the next few days.'

Lucy changed the subject. 'So, with Mary in hospital, I suppose the Old Man will only have Kelly on his arm this evening. Senator Malvito will go with Monica, who won't have the complication of Billy being there. Pity we won't see how it all plays out.'

At six o'clock it was dark. Lucy and John pulled off the road a quarter mile around the bend from the Ridge Ranch. Two minutes later, George pulled up behind them and they climbed into his station wagon. He drove into the ranch around the circle, to the rear of the main ranch house. With

Mary in hospital and James staying with his brother, Andrew, the house was in darkness.

George took a stepladder from his car. He shone his torch at the ground a yard to the right of the garage door, lifted one of the paving slabs and retrieved a key. He unlocked the door, gave Lucy and John each a pair of latex gloves and put on a pair himself. He shone his flashlight up to the horizontal rafters above their heads. Half of the roof had been fitted out with a chipboard platform.

George opened up the stepladder and climbed its four steps. 'Wait a minute,' he observed. 'We have two new arrivals.'

John took the flashlight from George and climbed the ladder.

'They're probably the two we worried about being planted at our place,' Lucy said. 'But I still don't understand how they were never found at Kelly's house.'

'Well, they seem to be unharmed,' John replied, climbing down.

Lucy climbed the ladder. 'They're all wrapped in bubble the same way. Time to get the police, before she starts moving the paintings again. She'll be at the State House now. Nothing she can do for at least three hours.'

'We need one of the paintings as a piece of leverage,' John said. 'The small one at the front of the stack.' He climbed the stepladder again to retrieve the painting.

Lucy smiled. 'If you're doing what I think you're doing, we'll be two moves ahead of them before we leave the ranch tonight.'

'Two moves?'

'You'll see,' she replied.

'Do I need to be in on this plan?' George asked.

'Absolutely,' she smiled.

As they left the garage, Lucy told John she needed to make a couple of house calls to the other side of the ranch. 'George, I may need your skills in a minute. It's the house I used to live in over there,' she said, pointing across the grass.

'What you up to now?' John asked. 'Any of these nutters could come back at any moment.'

'Do me a favour, John. The main ranch house is completely empty. So is Matthew's house, 'cos he's dead and Andrea's gone back to Illinois. Ditto Christopher's house. I'll be alright. I'll only be a few seconds in each house.'

They rode in George's station wagon for the short ride to the other side of the ranch. Lucy approached the house she had shared with Billy. She inserted a key into the lock and let herself in.

She smiled. *All these years after our divorce – and he still has the same locks.*

Thirty seconds later, she emerged, an additional key in one hand, shut the door firmly behind her and walked next door to let herself into Matthew's house. Sixty seconds later, she emerged, shut the door behind her and walked back across the driveway of Billy's, to the house the other side. Again, she let herself in, and emerged a minute later. She returned to Billy's, re-entered it, replaced the bunch of keys and emerged, closing the door firmly behind her.

'All done,' she said, getting back into George's car. 'Didn't need your skills after all, George. Let's go.'

John and George looked at each other as Lucy removed the latex gloves that George had given her earlier.

'She's the attorney,' John said.

George drove them back to their car. 'I'll wait here for the police,' he said. 'That should get at least one of the loose ends tied up.'

'Actually – more than one,' Lucy said. 'When the police arrive, George, can you make sure they bring your old friends in the forensic team? Make sure they get into the houses I visited just now, but don't mention I've been in. They might just find something interesting.'

Lucy started the journey back to Boston. 'Patricia and the Blacks should be at the State House now. Why don't we visit Ma again to see if she is feeling better?'

'Good idea.'

They reached the hospital and Mary was all smiles. 'Lucy, John. This is so nice. I wasn't expecting you. You've only just missed Andrew and James.'

Lucy leant over the bed to kiss her. 'You look so much better today. It's good to see some colour in your cheeks again.'

'I feel a lot perkier. They've been checking on me every hour. They say I should be going home within thirty-six hours.'

Lucy beamed at her. 'When I first heard …'

Mary squeezed Lucy's hand and looked at John. 'You look after this girl. She's the nearest thing to an angel we have on earth.'

They chatted until it became obvious Mary was getting weary. As John and Lucy walked back to the car, Lucy mentioned she was hungry.

'I'm hungry too,' he replied. 'If we don't want to drive home, we can always stay at The Oaks. We do have the room booked next door to Patricia's.'

65

George Bellows had worked for the Boston Police for nearly thirty years. Many of the officers he respected still worked on the force. But one name came to mind as he re-entered the Black ranch.

He dialled Mark Foster, a young detective who had been keen to learn everything George could teach him. Despite the difference in their ages and seniority, George and Mark enjoyed a rare rapport – based largely on the respect they had for each other's abilities.

'George. How goes it, man? It's been a while.'

'Mark. It's good. But can we catch up later? I need a favour and I need you to tell nobody except your partner what's going down.'

Mark had always respected George's integrity. 'Sure thing. He's still with me outside the precinct.'

'You know this art fraud going on. Well, if you and Bob can get out to the Black place here in Marlborough, I can show you where the stolen art is. I don't want the credit – you keep this one – could be handy when the Chief is promoting the next round of seniors. And we need two forensics guys.'

Mark asked his partner if he could spare an evening.

'We'll be there, George. It's nearly six-fifteen. Allowing for the evening traffic, we should be with you by seven.'

'You'll need a van for this, Mark. And you'll need a digital camera with flash, 'cos we need to have the photos timed and dated.'

'Right. Give us an hour.'

'OK, don't forget the forensics boys – and whatever you do, keep this all quiet.'

'Got it – but why the hush-hush?'

'Mark, the Blacks are killing each other; they wouldn't hesitate to kill you. "Jack, the Maniac" is still a free man. Just be real careful – and tell Bob what I've said.'

George knew he had an hour. He poured himself a coffee from his thermos and dialled William.

'George Bellows, William.'

'Mr Bellows, what can I do for you?'

'I thought you might like to know we've found the missing paintings.'

'Excellent. I was going to call you – I believe the whole thing is about copying the art and selling the copies, not the originals.'

'How d'ya figure?' George replied.

'Well, I met up with John at Christie's in London. Monica Malvito was bidding on a copy of a Rockwell which she herself had brought along to sell. She was trying to use Kelly Black's money to get it. Anyway, Christie's didn't fall for it and there was a hell of a row in the accounts room. She stormed out, leaving Billy with the police, which is why he's in jail awaiting trial.'

'If the paintings are only being stolen to be copied, and they're only planning to sell copies, it would explain why so few have come up for sale,' George said. 'It must take a while to copy a painting?'

'Depends on the picture,' William replied. 'Depends on the detail and how much subtlety there is in the tone of the colours.'

'So, what's your best guess for a real fancy piece, six foot wide and four feet tall?'

'Each copy would take at least a month – if the artist had nothing else to do.'

'So – how long for a portrait about twelve inches wide and sixteen inches high?' George asked.

'Less than a week, probably, if it's the one I think you're talking about. Especially if the copier had to make several copies. The colours would be easier and easier to duplicate if you've already made one or two.'

'In that case, William, those Black killers have made one too many copies.'

66

John Black arrived at Kelly's home on Beacon Hill at six forty-five. From there, his chauffeur would take two minutes to reach the Boston State House. Kelly seated herself in the stretch limousine next to her father and kissed him on the cheek. Although she pretended to find these functions tedious, privately she relished the prominence her family enjoyed. Everyone present this evening would know that she was now CEO of Black Industries, a role made possible when her father relinquished it. He would remain as President, supporting Kelly only when she needed help in managing the colossal egos of the men and women on the board. Since the board had approved her succession a week ago, the share price had risen four per cent.

Kelly knew how proud her father was of her. She smiled as he complimented her on her appearance.

'For the life of me, I cannot understand why the most eligible, driven woman in the north-east is still single.'

'Well, now Daddy, I think you've answered your own question.'

As they approached the domed building, Kelly looked up.

'I always think they could illuminate the roof better; in the dark you can't see the gold of the dome. I think that's such a pity.'

They walked up the steps together, Kelly's hand on his fore-arm. Once inside, they crossed the entrance foyer and entered the much smaller circular lobby. Not for the first time, Kelly looked up at its six elevated stone characters seeming to watch over them. She knew their elevation was more than physical; these pillars of Boston society were raised for their contributions to the State of Massachusetts. Thirty years ago, aged nine, she had decided that one day she would be afforded the same respect.

Kelly made her excuses to her father to visit the ladies' restrooms. John had spotted an old business friend and seemed eager to catch up. Two minutes later she rejoined the throng gathering on the circular mosaic at the base of the steps outside the Flag Hall.

Who's this in green walking down the steps? She's gorgeous. Wait a minute – that looks like Ma's necklace.

She approached to look at the necklace more closely. This was the set stolen from her mother recently. Getting closer, Kelly recognised the perfume the girl was wearing as being Clive Christian No. 1.

That's odd. I know most of the women in Boston who can afford CC1. And two of those are now dead. Daddy's had an affair with this girl – he gave her the necklace.

Kelly collected herself – and donned a smile. 'Hi, there. I'm Kelly Black. What brings you here this evening?'

'Kelly. Congratulations on your succession. I'm Pat Dixon.'

'Thank you. What brings you here tonight?'

'I'm with the *Boston Times*. My boss wanted another angle on these fundraisers. So, I wanted to ask – how do you manage in such a male-dominated world?'

'Is this the reporter asking?' Kelly replied.

'The person, actually. I also work in a very male-dominated environment; I'm always interested to see how successful women handle it.'

Kelly smiled. *This Pat Dixon is good. How much does she know about Black Industries if she slept with the Old Man?*

'We have accountants, financial controllers and marketing teams in each region. They each have their areas of responsibility, but none see the whole picture.'

Pat was curious. 'But the whole picture is surely the job of the CEO? Tell me – how does the multitasking thing women do fit into your success story?'

'Women switch focus from one task to another much easier than men. It's handy when you run a company. More women should find out how good they could be.'

'How do you handle the negative publicity about the mining fatalities?'

So, this girl dares to be aggressive with me.

'We only had thirty deaths in the mines this year and ten on the oil rigs. It's all about balancing the fatalities with the US government demand for cheap energy in our economy.'

'Do you account for the deaths from pneumoconiosis?' she asked.

You – Miss Dixon – have not accounted for your own death.

'Miner's lung, you mean?' Kelly responded.

'Yes, I hear more than a hundred of your ex-employees die from pneumoconiosis each year, half of them before their sixty-seventh birthdays.'

'We can't worry about men who are off our books,' Kelly retorted.

Kelly knew she had said too much.

Damn this reporter. And how did she get the necklace?

Pat used Kelly's sudden cooling to change the subject. 'Your family must know most of the people here tonight?'

'I suppose. Tell me, my dear, I've been admiring your necklace.'

'Thank you – a present from an old friend of the family.'

'Really? Does your family come from Boston?'

'Originally, no. My great-grandfather came down the coast from Maine.'

Patricia spotted Senator Malvito over Kelly's shoulder. 'Isn't that the senator over there?'

Kelly looked around to see her lover with his wife. 'Yes. Do you know him?'

'No, never met him. Can you introduce him to me?' Pat asked.

Kelly had to think quickly. She did not want to introduce her lover to this attractive young reporter. On the other hand

– she'd be dead by morning, and she could use Malvito to get her father over, so she could watch his face when he looked into the reporter's eyes. She would know from his reaction if he had slept with the girl.

'I'd be delighted, my dear.'

'Senator,' Kelly started. 'I'd like you to meet Pat Dixon. Pat's from the *Boston Times*.'

'Well, hello, Pat. I'm Tom Malvito and this is my wife, Monica.'

Kelly left the group to find her father. Patricia seized her chance. 'How is the campaign going, Senator?'

'Just fine, thank you, Pat. Could always do with more funds, but then that's why we're here. Most of these folks have been extremely generous.'

Kelly re-joined them, John Black at her side. 'Meet John Black. Daddy, this is Pat Dixon, from the *Boston Times*,' she said, studying his eyes for his reaction.

She watched as her father settled his gaze on the reporter. No reaction.

'My, my, that's a mighty fine necklace, young lady. Where d'ya find such a wonderful piece?' the Old Man asked.

Why had he not recognised the girl? There was no way he would raise the subject of the necklace if he had given it to her himself – especially if he had bedded her. So how had this low-paid reporter obtained the multimillion-dollar necklace that should have been around her own neck this evening?

'Thank you. It was a present from an old family friend a long time ago.'

Kelly was still watching her father – he did not recognise the girl.

So how did she come by the necklace? What sort of stupidity enables a girl to wear a stolen necklace at an event like this – unless she was given it by someone else who stole it?

'That's quite some friend you have. Are you here on reporting business?' Black replied.

'I'm afraid so. I was hoping you might have some personal perspectives,' Pat replied.

Old Man Black laughed. 'Your material could be a little thin, young lady. Hell, everybody in this room knows it's all about business. Am I right, Tom?' he said.

'Just about,' Tom said. 'These folks here tonight, they're from some of the oldest families in America – some of the richest too. They know the golden rule: he who has the gold makes the rules – or the law – which is how it all works.'

Pat alternated her gaze from Tom Malvito to John Black. 'I'd be very interested in chatting with you both – that is, if you could spare the time?'

'I'm sure, if you call the office, we could give you a few minutes next week,' Kelly interjected. This was code her father understood; the reporter would never get past his very experienced PA.

Tom Malvito was even less enthusiastic to make an appointment with the highly attractive reporter; he knew what Monica would think. 'We're on the campaign trail, so it may be hard to schedule.'

To casual observers, Senator Tom Malvito might have seemed content as Monica, his curvy wife, the ex-Miss Texas, stood beside him. But Kelly's informers had told her that Monica had swapped in Billy as her lover recently. Like most new couples, Monica and her new lover spent most nights together.

So Kelly knew that tonight Senator Malvito would be lonely. She could also see that he liked the young reporter. Kelly knew that if she told him she could not see him tonight, he would want to spend it with Pat Dixon instead.

Kelly grinned. *They both die tonight.*

Kelly, along with all the evening's guests, had to leave her phone at the check-luggage counter. Bombs could be triggered remotely using a phone's time function. All phones were numbered and kept in lead-lined drawers at the back of the luggage store.

She made an excuse and went to the ladies' room. She knew that phones without SIM cards are inert to electronic scanners. Opening her clutch bag, she took the SIM card out of its tiny pouch and inserted it into the pay-as-you-go phone she had purchased for this purpose.

She texted Letu, activating earlier instructions. Soon she would be rid of Senator Malvito. The fact that Pat Dixon had shown up with the necklace was a bonus. She would have her necklace back. Pat and the senator would die together.

Kelly walked back into the Flag Hall as the Master of Ceremonies called the guests to supper. She glanced at her father just in time to see Pat slip her business card into his lapel pocket. Pat also slipped one to Tom Malvito. On this one, she had written a message on the reverse:

The Oaks Hotel – Room 608 – Midnight – xxx

Over dinner the assembled wealthy listened to speeches hinting at how funds given to fight the last election had gained a 'proxy vote' in Congress. One extremely wealthy donor had been able to influence a motion brought before the Senate on oil-drilling rights in south-east Montana. It had cost him less than a million dollars and would cover Malvito's campaign expenses for re-election to the Senate.

Forty minutes later, Kelly accompanied the Malvitos and her father to the top of the steps leading down from the front of the State House. Despite the throng of press photographers, Kelly observed Tom Malvito watching Pat lift her dress slightly to lower herself into her limousine. Kelly smiled to herself as Tom noticed Pat's stocking tops momentarily revealed – and that she was alone …

Stupid people all make the same mistake – they walk onto the chess board not knowing how the most dangerous players move. Tonight, I kill two birds with one stone.

67

Paul Adams had accepted twelve instructions to kill, through Kelly's intermediary. The English couple was his thirteenth and they were proving unlucky. They seemed very unlike the people he was normally tasked with eliminating. He had never seen two people so much in love. He would never forget the sight of her disrobing on the beach – nor the early morning sun catching the honey-blonde hair which stretched all the way to her lower back, nor the sensuous sway of her breasts as she moved.

On two occasions Paul witnessed John Baxter making love to her in the water. He watched as her moans turned to giggles of release. He watched them kiss – and wondered why anyone would want to extinguish the beauty of this union.

Watching Lucy enact her love in the water, it occurred to Paul that Kelly's motive for killing her was jealousy – and nothing to do with Lucy's investigation of the JFK copy-portrait, or the robbery at the Sunset Gallery. Nonetheless, his three attempts to kill them were frustrating; this threat to his success record could cost him dearly. It even occurred to him that subconsciously, he had never wanted to kill the love this couple enjoyed.

Paul wondered if he would ever find a girl to love. Everyone he had ever loved had abandoned him. His elder sister could have tried to find him when she turned eighteen. Yet she had not.

His father had died of miner's lung. His mother was looking Paul in the eyes when she put the gun in her mouth. He had always believed she was trying to send him a message that her death was his fault. In his twenty-eight years he had been intimate with only two women. Each had ended the relationship, accusing him of being 'cold'.

Paul knew that sadness would overwhelm him for the hundredth time if he allowed these thoughts to persist. So, for the hundredth time he wrapped himself in the cold blanket of indifference that would enable him to do his work – an art requiring detailed planning, meticulous attention to detail – and two different escape strategies on each kill.

Tonight, he had received his fourteenth commission to kill – the girl in the green dress with the diamond and emerald necklace. He was to eliminate witnesses and retrieve the necklace and matching earrings.

As Paul followed Pat from the State House, he was careful to keep his distance. He walked into the reception at The Oaks Hotel and heard her asking if there were any messages for Room 608.

When he saw her enter the lift, he sprinted up the six flights of stairs, proud of the fitness he had been careful to maintain. When he emerged from the stairwell onto the sixth-floor landing, he looked at the back of her emerald-green dress as Pat walked the last five yards of the corridor.

A green-back – the irony. I will add half a million more to my collection tonight.

As Patricia reached her room, she turned to look back down the corridor. Adams stepped back quickly into the stairwell landing to avoid being seen. He listened to the door at the end of the corridor shut. He counted slowly to sixty, emerged from the stairwell and walked the length of the corridor to check the room number on the door. In exactly eighty minutes, he would return to do what very few could – execute, and escape.

68

It was twenty-one minutes before midnight when Patricia walked into The Oaks Hotel. She was excited, apprehensive. Would the senator see her invitation?

Half expecting a message from John Baxter, she enquired at reception.

'No messages for 608, ma'am.'

She walked to the lift and once inside pressed '6'. Emerging from the lift, she walked the long corridor to her room and thought she heard something behind her as she approached her room door. She turned but there was nothing.

Pat opened the door to Room 608, shut the door behind her, waited ten long seconds and silently opened it to check again. The passageway was abandoned – but she double-locked the door.

She went to her laptop and tapped in a few notes. She wanted information from Tom Malvito about his friend, Old Man Black – hopefully enough to damage the company. Whatever she did or did not discover about the Blacks, she would enjoy the senator's affections. She would loosen his tongue with his favourite whisky – tantalise him with the promise of her body – hold him off for as long as she could while she dug for the dirt.

The buzzer to her room sounded. Her heart started to race. With meticulous attention to detail, she saved the file, turned on the webcam function, checked it was recording, faced the darkened screen to the room and walked to the door.

She glanced back at the room. All was in order. She opened the door.

'Mr Black,' she stuttered. 'How … nice to see you.'

How could the wrong man have got hold of my invitation?

'Come on in, won't you?'

Maybe I can get the dirt on him directly. And I do have the gun.

Old Man Black walked past her into the wider part of the large room.

Compared with the tall, athletic Senator Malvito, you are short, sweaty and repulsive.

'Will you have a drink, Mr Black?'

'Why, thank you. I see you have my favourite.'

'Your favourite?' Pat answered.

'Sure is. Tom and I discovered it on a whisky tour of Scotland way back.'

'You saw my card,' Pat said, trying to discover how the wrong man was in her room.

'Well, me and Tom got talking in the restroom. We got your cards out and laid them on the counter. But Tom had to go into the closet. When I turned the cards over, I saw your invitation. Tom is trying to get his marriage with Monica back together. So, I figured I would take the chance, seeing as I had fifty–fifty odds of being right. Did I do the right thing, young lady?'

'Absolutely, John. How do you take your whisky?'

'As it comes and no ice, thanks,' he answered. 'Do you mind if I smoke?'

You're disgusting.

She poured two generous glasses of whisky and sat on the adjacent chair, her knees within an inch of his. 'Have you always lived in Boston?' she asked.

'Pretty much. Started where my daddy left off. He was one of those tough old wheeler-dealers who could make money out of anything – Prohibition an' all that. But he did good.'

'He probably had to be pretty ruthless to survive?' Pat ventured.

'Sure. But he never got caught.'

'I expect there were things you had to do to defend the company?'

Black shuffled his chair nearer, bathing Pat in a stench of tobacco breath. She shuddered as he put his hand on her knee.

304

Why does he keep looking at my necklace?

Pat eased back in her chair, keen to hear more of Black's past.

'You mean the sordid details of building a business over thirty-five years?'

She put her hand on top of his. 'Well, it sounds so interesting,' she said, trying to sound frivolous.

'There was the time we had to get rid of the environmental lobby,' he said, hesitating.

'That sounds like an interesting little story,' she said, hoping her tone of superficiality would drop his guard.

'Yeah, well … they sent a delegation to meet Black Industries. We organised a party boat that could take us up the river for a meal. We got the whole delegation, all twelve of them, to meet us on the boat.

'Why don't you take off your dress, young lady? That would make the story a bit more interesting, don't you think?'

No way do you get to see me naked, Old Man.

'Why, John, I was hoping we would get to know each other a bit better first.'

'Well, we got 'em on the boat and we had the captain poison their drinks. It's amazing what people will do for ten thousand dollars.'

Pat remembered the $10,000 she had taken from the safe the previous evening.

Black moved his hand further up her thigh.

'So what happened to the captain of the boat?' she persisted.

'Funny thing – he was run down by a car soon as the boat docked at our stop. The police never found the driver. It was at night and he just sped off.'

You murdering shits.

'I think you call it "eliminated", don't you?' Pat asked.

'Let's just say, we recovered our ten thousand from the body in the street.' Black laughed. 'Kelly called it "the Black economy". She was always good with money.'

The Black economy – the death penalty is far too kind for you lot.

'Why, John, anyone would think that Kelly had planned the whole thing.'

'I wouldn't say it needed much planning exactly. When we saw the boat trips available, she looked at me and I knew what she was thinking.'

Black slid his hand higher. 'Just give me a minute, John. My contact lenses are getting a bit scratchy. It's been a long day. Let me take them out.'

Pat locked the bathroom door and removed the blue-tinted contact lenses she had worn all day. She put a couple of drops into each eye – and remembered the gun under the pillow.

Pat returned to the bedroom to see Black get to his feet.

'My turn for the bathroom,' he said.

The room door buzzer sounded.

'Why don't you get the door while I use the bathroom,' Black suggested.

Pat welcomed the distraction; this would slow things down. She opened the door to find a small man in hotel uniform. His gaze was fixed on her necklace.

He produced a gun, its silencer pre-fitted, and put it in her mouth. He put his forefinger to his lips to keep her quiet, then inserted the door chain. Keeping the nozzle of his gun in her mouth, he kept her off-balance, moving her backwards until they reached the bed.

He pulled the gun from her mouth, put it to her forehead and pulled the trigger. The lifeless body fell backwards onto the bed, and he fired another bullet into the heart.

Now the witnesses; there's light under the bathroom door.

He opened the door just as the man flushed the toilet. The first bullet went into the back of the head. The figure slumped forward, hitting his head hard on the wall, and collapsed on the floor on his back. Adams put the second bullet into the heart and backed away, satisfied with how clean both kills had been. He returned to the body on the bed, unclasped the necklace, unhooked the earrings, and put the jewels together into a cloth bag.

From habit and due to his meticulous attention to detail, he scrutinised the space for any clues he might have left. He noticed the bottle of Laphroaig and five half-smoked cigarettes in the ashtray on the table.

But something was odd about the body on the bed. Normally he avoided looking into his victim's eyes; it made it personal. But today he felt compelled. He knelt on the bed and looked at the face. Her left eye was brown, the other green – it was like looking into a mirror.

Just a coincidence – keep focussed.

He went to the door and listened for any sounds outside. Hearing nothing, he turned off the lights, moved the chain to the end of its slide, opened the door four inches and saw nothing in the corridor. He took the chain from the slider and shut the door behind him silently, but firmly. Using the fire exit door he had checked earlier, he walked calmly down the six flights of steel steps to the street below.

But the thought would not leave him – where had his protective elder sister, Pat, spent her life after they were taken into care? What had she done with her talent for words – and all the bedtime stories she used to make up for him when their drunken mother could not put them to bed herself?

69

Lucy and John finished their meal at the Waterfront.

Lucy kept a straight face. 'Tell me, Mr Baxter. Have you ever taken a girl back to a hotel room, purely for sex?'

He laughed. 'I have not. I take it you'd prefer the shorter trip to the hotel rather than the longer trip home?'

'I was just remembering our first night in a hotel room, and how horny it was.'

'Ah, yes – millionaire lawyer and part-time art collector meets strange man in hotel and beds him on first date.'

Lucy smiled. 'Or – hunky man gets extremely willing woman tipsy, albeit on excellent wine, and gives her what she hadn't had for years – a really good—'

Lucy stopped short when the waiter put the bill on the table.

John grinned while the waiter retreated. 'I take it you'd like me to take you back to The Oaks?'

'Tonight, you could take me anywhere – but as you ask, yes.'

A few minutes later, they walked into the hotel and straight into the lift.

'I wonder if Pat got any useful information tonight,' Lucy said, as they approached their room.

'Let's have a listen.' John put his ear on the door of Room 608, next door to theirs.

'There are voices, but I can't hear what's being said,' he whispered.

They entered Room 606 and shut the door.

'I wonder if they have Laurent-Perrier Pink on the room service menu,' Lucy said, sitting on the edge of the king-sized bed.

'The Blush?' John replied. 'Probably priced to make you blush too.'

'You'll have to judge if you think a girl is worth it,' Lucy said, coyly pushing one of the straps from her shoulder.

John grinned – and dialled reception. 'Could we have a bottle of Laurent-Perrier Pink?'

'No problem, Mr Baxter. I'll bring it up myself.'

'Yourself?'

'Yes – one of our young waiters has gone missing in the last hour – taking his uniform with him, apparently.'

'Oh, I'm sorry to hear that. We look forward to getting the drinks then. Thank you.'

As John put the phone down, they heard a loud thump. Lucy frowned as they looked at the wall.

They stood, listening. 'I'll listen at the door for a second. Keep the door open so if I have to come back quickly, I can get in fast.'

Lucy tugged at his arm as he pulled away. 'You sure this is wise, John? I get bad feelings about this.'

'I won't take any risks. Just don't be standing in the doorway; I may have to come back quickly.'

He opened the door an inch. Hearing nothing, he opened the door wider and moved quietly toward Room 608. The door chain was being moved. He retreated quickly to Room 606 and closed the door silently behind him.

John moved to the main body of the room to where Lucy was standing, tense, her arms folded. He whispered to her. 'Someone was coming out of the room, so I legged it. I only gave one room key to Pat; I still have the other.'

'You're not going in there? Why don't we dial Room 608? If Patricia is in, we can speak to her,' Lucy implored, holding onto his hand.

'Let's do that,' John said, dialling extension 608. He let the phone ring ten times. 'There's no way anyone can take ten rings to get to a phone in the confines of a hotel room.'

'Unless she's in the shower and doesn't hear the phone. Let it ring a bit longer, John.'

He counted another ten rings. 'And now?'

Lucy took the phone. After a few more rings, she replaced the phone on the receiver.

'I just don't want you going in there,' she said.

'If Pat got any info, she might have left, or the person she was with might have left.'

'Well, the manager would know if anyone had walked out, surely? Let's ask him?'

He dialled reception. 'Is that the manager? … Has anyone left the hotel in the last few minutes?'

'No, sir … Is everything alright, Mr Baxter?'

'Have you seen our friend, the lady in Room 608?'

'Not personally, sir. But one of our staff took a couple of whisky tumblers up to her room much earlier.'

'What time was that?'

'Mid-afternoon, I think. She wanted a taxi for later. She was going to the State House. She came back in alone a bit before midnight.'

'And she hasn't left the hotel since getting back?'

'No, sir. Why don't you dial her direct? I'll be up with the drinks in five minutes.'

'OK, we'll see you soon.'

He turned to Lucy. 'She's not left. I think she's on her own. Maybe she drank too much. You stay here and I'll be back in a minute.'

He knocked on Pat's door – no answer. He knocked again, louder – nothing. Using the spare key, he let himself in, shutting the door behind him.

He could see a woman on her back lying on the bed. He edged closer. It was Patricia, eyes wide open, staring, cold. Why had he not noticed that her eyes were of different colours when they met in reception? The two bullet holes left no room for uncertainty. He stood there, a chill taking grip of him. Why was the bathroom light on? He walked to the bathroom. Another one – Old Man Black. John recoiled back into the bedroom. He stared at the lifeless body. What was that lying next to his pocket on the floor? He looked more closely – a mobile phone. Instinctively, he picked it up and wiped his fingerprints off. He looked at Pat again. The killer wanted certainty and had done this before. Same method for each body.

He noticed Pat's laptop. He tapped the return key. The screen came to life. The webcam was still running. Everything had been recorded – including him coming into the room.

He turned off the webcam, took his phone and substituted Pat's for his at the end of the lead from the laptop. He shut down the file, saved it as 'Oaks' and downloaded it to his phone.

He walked back into the bathroom to get some tissue paper to wipe his fingerprints from Pat's laptop and phone. From the TV news bulletin, John recognised the body. It was definitely Old Man Black.

What was he going to tell Lucy? Should he tell her? Would she panic?

He stood, just outside the bathroom, looking through the door at Black's body.

Get a grip, Baxter. Get some proof. Get some photo evidence. Get it all recorded.

He took photos of Black and of Pat lying on the bed. He took some of the room, how the furniture was arranged, how the glasses had been left, the ashtray. Then he noticed an emerald-green clutch bag on the writing desk. He opened the bag – small mirror, circular powder case, keys. But then he noticed the five-carat diamond he had given her ... and two small receipts.

He looked at the receipts. Both of them had *New England Bank, Boston* printed at the top. One had simply the digits *3256*, with a biro addition of *8066281*; the other had *$9,900.00* printed at the bottom. He put the receipts and the diamond in his pocket.

He made his way to the door and remembered the safe in the room. Had it been opened? As he stood with his back to the main entrance to the room, he stared at the open sliders of the wardrobe. The room safe he had put Pat's money in the previous day was locked. He tapped in 1826. The door opened and the safe was empty. He shut the safe door and reset the code to the default of 0000.

Something told him to return to the bathroom. Why had he not noticed the eye drops and contact lens case on the bathroom shelf? He put the items in his jacket pocket, exited the room and returned to Lucy.

'What's the matter, John? You look as if you've seen a ghost.'

He took Lucy's hand and put her in one of the chairs by the coffee table.

'I've never seen a murder before.'

'What?' Lucy sprang to her feet and looked at the wall between the two hotel rooms.

'Who?' Lucy asked, before John could answer.

'Patricia and Old Man Black. Looks like a professional job.'

'My god! Poor Pat. It's all our fault. We can't stay here now, John.'

'We can't just check out in the middle of the night, leaving the bodies next door ... especially as I booked Pat's room in the name of Baxter.'

'No. We report it. Otherwise, we've committed a felony by not reporting a crime.'

'Well – the webcam got everything I think ... including me going in. If anything, the webcam proves I didn't do it.'

He dialled. 'Is that the manager? Something terrible has happened in Room 608. You'll need the police with you.'

John replaced the receiver. *Ye gods – what have I done? I hope I saved the files correctly. Will the police believe me if I haven't?*

70

John and Lucy offered to help the police and were taken to Boston Police HQ on Hyde Park Avenue. They were separated into different rooms for their statements. On hearing Baxter was an art dealer, Detective Mark Foster got up and left the interview room.

John was left to contemplate the last twenty-four hours. He wondered what Pat had discovered in her meeting with Old Man Black.

Detective Foster re-entered the room. 'Everything you say, Mrs Howard corroborates. That never happens. An ex-colleague of mine tells me he is working with you to investigate some art fraud in New England.'

'George? You know him?'

'We worked together for five years when he was still on the force.'

'George saved our lives. We had a Chinese delivery and George stopped us eating it. It was poisoned with Nembutal and cyanide.'

'Who would want to poison you?'

'By now, you know Lucy was married to Billy Black. Three of the Black brothers have been poisoned recently. So naturally, we have our suspicions.'

'Please. Enlighten us, Mr Baxter.'

'How long have you got?'

'I've taken an extra shift. So I have all night.'

John took a deep breath. 'OK, then, let's start at the beginning ... When I met Lucy, she was into early American art. A painting she owned had been covered up – washed over, if you like – by someone trying to conceal what we think is a crime.

'It was a painting of Mount Chocorua, by Frank Cropsey. He is only supposed to have painted one of these, but it's been missing for more than a hundred years. It was given to Lucy by Mary Black as a kind of leaving present when Lucy was leaving Billy. We think someone in the family covered it up to hide a crime that Billy committed. Billy was always stealing things.'

Mark Foster looked at his colleague, then back at John Baxter. 'Go on.'

'Well, this led us to the Black family and having Kelly followed. Enter George Bellows. James, the youngest of the family, had been tortured into delivering our Chinese meal by his brother Jack. The same Jack Black that your chief of police let go in mysterious circumstances after he ran a couple down in a rental car.'

Again, Foster looked at his fellow detective.

'Anyway, we accidentally stumbled into a little visit they were making to the Sunset Gallery a couple of weeks back – when the gallery is officially shut. And if you're looking for the paintings, I know where they are.'

'We already have the paintings,' Foster said. 'George has shown us already.'

'OK then … you may be wondering how these killings came to be in the room next door to ours at The Oaks.'

John continued. 'We decided to get help from an investigative journalist. Unfortunately for her, Pat Dixon was the one most motivated to investigate the Blacks.

'We struck a private deal whereby she would get the dirt and publish. Her father died of miner's lung, so she was particularly interested. We paid her substantially because of the risks.'

'How substantially?'

'A million dollars … And the only reason we had the room next door was that I booked the two rooms at the same time.

'Anyway, Detective – Lucy and I have conceived a plan to get all the facts about the murders and the art thefts out into the open …'

71

Wednesday – November 7th

Lucy and John returned to her home in Concord at five o'clock in the morning and fell into bed.

Five hours later, they woke to a sunny but crisp late autumn day. The phone was ringing.

'Hello, John. It's Mary. I thought you and Lucy would like to know the doctor said I can go home.'

'Mary, that's great.' John paused.

'What's the matter, John?'

'Mary, you haven't been told?'

'Told what, John?'

'Mary – are you sitting down?'

'Why, John – I'm still in bed here at the hospital.'

'Mary, I have the saddest news … John Black died last night.'

John waited – to allow Mary time to absorb the news.

Eventually, Mary spoke. 'Do I want to know the details?'

John paused. 'That can come later, Mary. Lucy and I think you and James should stay with us in Concord for a few days, just till things settle down a bit.'

'Well, I don't know – I don't want to be any trouble.'

'Ma – we'd be very pleased to have you here. We could pick you up. How would noon be for you?'

'Well, I appreciate it, John. But tell Lucy not to do anything special; you know what she's like.'

'Mary, do you think I could stop her doing something special after all you've been through?'

'I suppose not. I just don't want to get in your way. You can understand that, John.'

'Yes, but you won't be – and you'll both be safer with us here in Concord.'

'Thank you, John. That was a conversation I should have had,' Lucy said.

'I hope you didn't mind me volunteering to fetch her from the hospital.'

'Course not. We better get ready,' Lucy replied.

John dialled George. 'George. Lucy and I are going to the hospital to fetch Mary home. Can we meet you back here at about one o'clock? Does that give you time to get ready for tomorrow?'

'Good for me.'

'George, it occurs to me that you'll be missing the game tomorrow.'

'I wasn't going to mention it, John … but yes.'

'How many tickets do you have, George?'

'Four.'

'Can I take them off you for a thousand dollars a ticket? You've gone way beyond the call of duty, and I know you'll be disappointed not to be there.'

'Actually, it's kind of late to sell them, so I will accept your offer. I'll bring them later when we set everything up.'

'Great, George. I really appreciate it. The guys will be thrilled.'

John interrupted Mark, Oliver and Colin in the theatre room at the end of Lucy's long corridor on the ground floor. They were watching an end-of-season summary of the Baseball World Series on the ninety-inch screen Lucy had installed.

'How's it going?' John asked.

'Cool,' Oliver murmured, still staring at the screen.

John looked at the three young men, saying nothing till all three were looking at him.

'Guys … I have some really sad news for you … last night your grandfather … Old Man Black died.'

They stared at John. Colin looked at the brothers, waiting for their reaction. Mark and Oliver looked at each other and returned their gaze to the screen, saying nothing.

John studied the group. He decided to let them process the news.

'But I have good news too. Mary is recovered and is coming here to stay for a while – with James.'

All eyes were now on John again.

'Listen guys, we need you out of the house tomorrow night. We have a little party here.'

'Whooah. Wait a minute,' Oliver objected.

'What would it cost to get into the game?' John asked.

'Kazillions,' Oliver replied.

'How many kazillions?'

Mark and Colin turned to look at him. 'Are you kidding us, John?'

John smiled.

'He's not kidding,' Mark said.

'Here's the deal. Your mom and I will pick up Mary and your uncle James – they're staying with us for a few days. George will bring the four tickets. It'd be really nice if you asked James to come; you'd be amazed at the Red Sox game stats he has in his head. Anyway, we need you out of here by midday tomorrow.

'We'll give you some cash so you can get cabs and not risk your licences. Stay the night near the game and get back any time after midday the day after tomorrow. OK?'

'What can we do to thank you, John?'

'You can stay safe and don't drink too much. The last thing your mum needs is extra worry at the moment – got it?'

John returned to Lucy at the other end of the house. 'All sorted. I've told them about Old Man Black – and the guys are going to the game tomorrow night. So, we have only two guests to invite.'

John picked up his cell phone. 'Tom, it's John Baxter. We're about to get some information about the Blacks. We wondered if you and Monica would like a drink with us tomorrow evening.'

'Thank you, John; it'll make a welcome break from campaigning.'

'Shall we say seven then, at Lucy's place. You know the place up on Musketaquid Road.'

'Great. But is it OK if I come on my own?'

'Of course. See you at seven. Oh, and Tom – could you put your car in the garage? We have a number of other people coming.'

'I'll get Carlos to drop me off – safer if any single malts are on offer.'

'Well, Tom – there may even be cause for champagne …'

72

Thursday – 8th November

'It's a few minutes before eight – time to explain the plan,' Lucy announced.

'Have you reset the front door code to the birthdays, John?'

'Done,' he replied.

Lucy looked at her guests. 'We're expecting intruders who think the house is unoccupied. George will be looking at the screen over there. I ought to tell you he is armed – for your safety – just in case. He'll tell us when we can talk again, but until then we have to remain silent. All the downstairs room doors are now locked. Nobody can get into this room. In case you didn't notice, the double doors to this room are three inches of solid oak and they have steel bolts top and bottom. But from now on, we need to stay totally silent. And we need to turn the lights off throughout the house. In a few seconds, George will make a call. But the rest of us need to stay quiet.'

Lucy turned off the lights. A few seconds later, George accessed his cell phone. A female police detective with her hair in a ponytail started up Lucy's car outside the house.

Paul Adams knew where to park so he could not be seen. At fifteen minutes to eight, he pulled up fifty yards away, Kelly in the passenger seat to his right.

Ten minutes later, he and Kelly watched the lights go off and Lucy's car pull out of her driveway. Adams set up his listening gear and scanned the microphone from side to side in case sound was coming from any of the windows. There was complete silence.

'You sure it's working?' Kelly asked.

'This is the same equipment that got the information about the JFK in their bedroom from their private dick this afternoon. So it's working just fine, ma'am ... and besides, when those kids are there, this house is never quiet – especially when the Red Sox are playing.'

'Right. Let's get JFK back,' Kelly replied.

Adams eased the car into the driveway and pulled up outside the front door.

'Let me do this bit,' Kelly said. She stepped up to the keypad and tapped in 03-12-29, the birthdays of Mark, Oliver and Lucy. The light above the keypad turned green.

So sentimental, these English.

'Take your shoes off before we step off this entrance mat,' Adams said, removing his. 'They leave invisible footmarks that can be matched. We need to put these shoe covers on so none of our DNA gets on the carpet.'

He put a pair of the blue polythene shoe covers over his socks and handed a pair to Kelly. She walked on into the hallway, located the alarm and tapped in 92-21-30, which satisfied the box into silence.

'Don't touch the light switch, ma'am,' Adams instructed.

'Why not?' Kelly replied.

'They've started to link alarm systems to the circuit-breaker box. It detects any extra current being used and sets off the alarm – both here and back at the security alarm base.'

Adams shone his flashlight at the map he had prepared from the information he had overheard that afternoon. In the narrow beam of light, he led the way up the stairs and into Lucy's bedroom.

As Adams scanned the room with his flashlight, their attentions went to a small portrait of John F. Kennedy, leaning against the wall at the far side of the room.

'There it is,' Kelly exclaimed. 'Let's check it's the original.'

She took the flashlight from Adams and directed the beam on the canvas to check it close up. In near total darkness they became aware that the majority of the dressing room was to their right. She scanned the room and settled the light on another painting, some twenty-five feet away.

Adams followed her a few paces closer to the painting.

Kelly stared. '*The Piazza San Marco*. You are kidding me.'

The clunk of heavy bolts at the other end of the room made them turn in horror. Adams snatched back the flashlight. He rushed back and banged on the four inches of tempered steel. But the door, weighing seven hundred pounds, was never going to yield to the man weighing one hundred and forty.

Kelly watched Adams in the darkness. Panic started to grip her, a feeling she had almost forgotten. She knew where the terror came from. Her father had locked her in a dark cupboard when she was a child and left her there as a punishment for being rude to him.

As her body tightened in the darkness, a certainty overwhelmed her. She knew she could kill someone with her own hands. She looked at Adams. This little wretch had got her locked up – in the dark.

She rushed to the steel door. Adams had found a light switch. Thank God. Kelly scanned the safe room. No windows, two doors, the one they had entered through and one other. She strode quickly to the other door – it was a bathroom with shower and WC. She banged on the wall on the far side of the bath; it was solid, cold, as if made of concrete. She returned to the larger room. All of these walls were solid too. Cupboards ran the entire twenty-five feet of the opposite wall. She slid one of the panels to her right. Inside were four shelves completely filled with vitamin supplements, canned food, long-life milk cartons, cereals, cartons of apple and orange juice. There was even a wine rack stocked with twenty-four bottles of an expensive-looking red wine called Château Largaux, wherever that was.

323

She looked back to the wall to the right of the bathroom door. *The Piazza San Marco* was lit from above. She grudgingly admitted to herself that the owner of this room had excellent taste. On the solid wall opposite the cupboards were four other works – one, a portrait of Mother Teresa, one of Mahatma Gandhi, one of Nelson Mandela and one of Martin Luther King Jr.

Kelly slumped into one of four sumptuous armchairs and looked contemptuously at the gallery of Lucy's heroes.

That just about says it all; two of you were shot dead and the other two were losers.

Kelly had to admit that considerable planning had gone into this room. This made her feel queasy. On top of that, she hated small, confined spaces. Worse, there were no windows, no way of getting her bearings, of knowing whether it was light or dark outside. She quickly dismissed the next thought that ran through her head.

What if the rest of my life is destined to be this confined?

The next thoughts took the strength from her legs.

What if they could prove the murders she had commissioned? Would the lethal injection really be as painful as she had been told? Who would be watching her die? Would she see enjoyment on their faces? Would she be blindfolded?

73

George turned the lights on in Lucy's sitting room. 'Two foxes in the trap, ma'am.'

'Thank heavens for you, George! But you don't look too happy about it.'

'Ma'am, my precinct has tried for years to get Kelly and her little killer locked up. And now I've left the police, we've achieved it in weeks …'

'I can hear a "but" coming,' Lucy said.

'But – a word of caution, ma'am – Adams is really tricky. A killer only gets a nickname if he's been successful enough to get away with it – he's very careful, and even more crafty. Just because we have him in your strongbox doesn't mean it's over yet.'

'Gotcha,' Lucy said.

'Actually, ma'am, if you'll forgive me – I doubt it. Letu has the confidence to use the same gun for his killings every time – and I mean every time. He knows that police ballistics teams will know it's him – again. This gives you some idea of his confidence. It's not over yet, ma'am.'

Lucy stared at George – and nodded. She glanced at the others. 'OK, we can talk now. If you'd like to follow me upstairs.'

As Lucy started for the stairs, she wondered.

What tricks could Letu have up his sleeves this time?

Lucy led the way up to her bedroom and turned on the lights. Mary, John, Tom Malvito and Detectives Foster and Jefferson followed. George plugged in the screen he had hidden earlier.

'Now the lights are on in the strongbox, we'll see who's inside,' George said.

'The two-way microphone allows us to hear them – but they can only hear us when I press this button. We can always see them, but they can't see us at any time.'

He turned the monitor on. They gazed at the screen on the dressing table.

'Kelly!' Ma started to sob. Lucy put her arm round her.

Kelly was dialling on her cell phone.

'You calling Malvito?' Adams asked. 'I doubt the steel in these walls lets in any signal.'

'Lets in any signal?' she demanded. 'And in any case, you killed him two nights ago, if you remember.'

'You didn't say anything about Malvito.'

'I told you to kill Senator Malvito and the girl and get my necklace.'

The group in Lucy's bedroom all turned to look at Malvito.

'You told me to kill witnesses, not Malvito. I killed the girl, like you said, and I gave you the necklace.'

Kelly approached the steel door and banged on it herself. It felt like hitting stone a foot thick. 'So, who was the witness?'

They all watched as Kelly explored her prison. Her eyes settled on something above the sealed door. 'It's a fucking microphone. They've heard everything we've said.'

She reached into her jacket for some chewing gum. She chewed it for a few seconds then reached up and sealed it over the microphone.

'I'm going to kill that English bitch.'

'How are we still hearing them?' Tom asked.

George cleared his throat. 'Because Mrs Howard said Kelly would look for a mike and we ought to let her find one. The one Kelly covered up was a dummy; the real mike she'll never find.'

Kelly stopped at the painting of the Piazza San Marco as she paced, then longer at the Norman Rockwell painting of JFK leant up against the wall.

Adams sat down in the corner opposite the steel door, next to the Rockwell.

'You telling me you don't know who you killed?' Kelly demanded. 'Tell me what you saw.'

'Half-smoked ciggies in the ashtray.'

The realisation hit Kelly immediately. 'Describe the man you killed.'

'Wore a tux – short, fat, sweaty, balding … that's why I know it wasn't Malvito.'

'My father smoked only half a cigarette.' Kelly paused. 'So why didn't the police announce his death? Why didn't I hear this from Ma? … Crap – they set up this up days ago.'

Adams took a few moments to let the reality sink in. 'But you'll still pay my five hundred thousand dollars for killing the girl and getting the necklace for you.'

'You little shit – I was paying you for killing the senator.'

'Ma'am – if you'd said "senator", I'd have asked which one – especially as the two Massachusetts senators know each other, and one is your pa. Anyways, I like Malvito; he's a good man – not like you – and me.'

'Why do you say that?'

'One day when you told me to watch him, he came out in the freezing cold and told me he'd seen me. He said I must be cold. He offered me a coffee.'

'So what happened?' Kelly asked.

'So I went in. He told me to sit by the fire. No one's ever been nice like that. He told me, if I wanted to know things, just ask.'

'Did he say anything else … about any of his night-time activities, I mean?'

'You mean you and him? He said he missed his wife terrible. Said he was lonely. He said it was very painful when she went with your brother to Europe.'

'You mean Billy?' Kelly said.

'Yep. The senator said he was a carpenter-joiner here in New England and fitted kitchens an' stuff. Usually tried it on with the wives, he said, and some of the underage daughters too.'

Kelly started a search of the wardrobes. 'There has to be a phone. If someone's in here, they have to be able to get help.

'Got it.' Lucy's bedside phone rang.

'Do you want to trade?' Kelly demanded.

'What did you have in mind?'

'Indemnity for me ... in return for information.'

'What kind of information?'

'What do you need to know?'

'The combination of Old Man Black's safe,' Lucy said.

'Oh, that's as simple as A, B, C. If I'm guaranteed indemnity, I can give you any information you want, including today's combination of the safe.'

Lucy turned to John. She made a scribbling motion with her hand. George handed her a pen and paper.

She wrote several words and made sure only John could see them: *A, B, C. Andrew, Billy, Christopher – and she said 'today's combination'?*

John nodded. Lucy replaced the receiver and turned to Mary.

'Ma, we need to check birthdays. In your coded message in Venice, I think you were giving us details of the siblings' birthdays. Are we right?'

'I suppose now I can say things I was frightened to say before. But I don't know which order he put the birthdays – or the date.'

'That's alright, Ma. We have the likeliest options.'

Lucy put the birthdays down on the sheet of paper, using only the month digits of the birthdays of Andrew, Billy, Christopher, Jack, Kelly, Matthew, Peter and Simon.

'Mark, where are your boys now?' John asked.

Mark Foster looked at his watch. 'Should be at the Black place up at Beacon Hill by now.'

'Ask them if there's a brand name on the safe,' John suggested.

'Why?' he asked.

'A dwarf standing on the shoulders of a giant can see further,' John replied.

'Mr Baxter?' Mark frowned.

'Let's be dwarves standing on the shoulders of one of the giant, chess-playing intellects of our time.'

Mark looked at John as he called his colleagues. 'The safe is made by "Armstrong".'

John beamed at Lucy. They sequenced the months of the siblings' birthdays in alphabetical order of their names and followed it by the date in a four-digit format. If what Paul Marks had said in the bank was true, the date was not positioned first, but last.

John passed the code to Mark Foster, who relayed it to his colleagues. Less than a minute later the two police officers called Mark back.

'That combo doesn't work, Mark. Any other ideas?'

'Try it again; make sure you punch the numbers in really carefully.'

'OK, stay on the line ... ... same thing, Mark. I was really careful.'

Mark Foster turned to Lucy and John, shaking his head.

John scratched his head. 'Let's suppose the manager at the bank was unsettled that we had sussed the date part. What if the date really is at the front – but he was pretending we had it wrong?

'Mark, let's put the date at the front.'

Another minute later, Mark was shaking his head again.

'What other sequence could they use, Lucy?'

Lucy's face lit up. 'Sequence is exactly the right question, but not the sequence we've been thinking. John, it's not whether the date is before or after the birthdays.

'John, what if the A, B, C thing Kelly alluded to was only telling us it was about the birthdays, not about the order. If Kasparov is right, then why wouldn't Black go with the sensible option and use the birthdays in the order the siblings were born?'

'It makes sense,' John replied. 'Especially as outsiders would be unlikely to know the order.'

'The more so since several of them are so close in age. Almost impossible to tell which are older with some of them. So – let's ask the ultimate authority,' Lucy said, looking at Ma.

Two minutes later, John was handing the sequence of numbers to Mark Foster. The day's date he placed at the start, not the end.

The eight of them waited for Mark's phone to buzz; it was three minutes of eternity, as the group contemplated the implications of what could be in the safe.

Finally, Mark answered his phone. 'Still no good,' came the voice. 'Got any other suggestions?'

Lucy looked at John. 'I think I have it.'

74

'John, today is November the 8th in the US – not the 8th of November, as it is in the UK.'

John looked at her. 'Got it. I used 0811. Black would have used 1108.'

Mark was on the phone immediately. For the fifth time, the group waited …

Mark's phone buzzed; he looked at the group in Lucy's bedroom.

Seconds later, he frowned. 'There's a problem, folks. Bob tells me a window has popped up on the digital display on the safe door and it's asking for the verification they've sent to a mobile.'

John punched the air in triumph. 'That tells us our twelve-digit code was right.'

Mark was puzzled. 'But we haven't got Black's phone and even if we did, we don't have the phone's password.'

'Most people use anniversaries or birthdays for codes like this,' John replied.

He turned to Mary Black. 'Ma, what was the date of your wedding?'

'July 15th, 1976. But why would he choose that date out of all the dates possible?'

John grinned. 'Because, Ma, if my hunches are correct, you have just discovered one of the most valuable pieces of stolen art never recovered.'

Lucy frowned, looking at Ma and John alternately. 'You going to enlighten us, John?'

'Lucy, when you told me about the divorce settlement meeting, you said Old Man Black complained about you blowing in like the storm on the Sea of Galilee.'

'Yes, but what has that got to do with it?'

'Sweetheart – Rembrandt painted *The Storm on the Sea of Galilee,* and his birthday was July 15th. If your anniversary was July 15th – as in month 7 and day 15 – and you had a Rembrandt in your safe, and the birthdays of your first two grandchildren were 07 and 15, what would you guess his mobile password would be?'

'Wow, Mr Baxter, that is impressive. I didn't know you even knew the kids' birthdays. But even if that is true, we still don't have his mobile.'

'Oh really,' John said, pulling an old mobile from his pocket. 'And you mentioned 15 and 7 when you told me how you worked out the divorce settlement figure.'

Lucy frowned her disbelief. 'And where d'you get that?'

'The night he died, it fell out of his pocket when he fell to the floor.'

John turned the phone on and entered 0715. The screen lit up, displaying the latest text message.

'Mark, tell Bob to put 822753 into the safe keypad.'

Lucy shook her head in mock disapproval. They waited for Mark and his reaction.

'Hallelujah! It's open ... huge stash! ... and there's a black notebook with names and details of deals.'

The group listened as Mark talked to Bob. 'Empty it out, catalogue it, lock everything in the van, except the black book. Get here ASAP – when you're underway call me with the black book in your hands. Got it?'

'No, you don't understand, Mark. There's a stack of hundred-dollar bills, made up into a cube about one metre in all dimensions. We reckon it's more than fifty million dollars. And there's more diamonds than you'll ever see in one place. There's even an old painting of a really stormy seascape about five feet long.'

'OK, lock it all up except for the black book – get that over here ASAP.'

Lucy approached John. She put her arms around his neck and whispered into his ear. 'What do I get when I cross a mathematician with an art historian?'

John smiled. 'What do you get?'

Lucy whispered once more. 'Hopefully, I get an absolutely historic fucking.'

Lucy's bedside phone rang again. 'You didn't call me back,' Kelly said.

'We had to chat.'

'Well, you're the lawyer. Have we got a deal?'

Lucy paused. 'I'm not a criminal lawyer; I can't promise how the law will judge all this.'

333

'The law doesn't need to know. Maybe we compensate you for your trouble, if you get my drift?'

'What have you got in mind?' Lucy asked.

'I know you mean well by the kids. You could be secure for generations. Just the contents of Daddy's safe would do that.'

'I'll call you back,' Lucy said.

Mark held his phone up, hardly concealing his glee. 'The boys have been reading the black book. We've been trying to prove these connections for years; now we have them. Mining rights, oil rights, the politicians involved, planning applications, payments listed, details of who made the payments – everything.'

Lucy picked up the receiver again.

'You started to talk about trading indemnity for information. You've organised two robberies at the Rockwell and one robbery at the Sunset Gallery. You'd try to kill the kids and me if ever you get your freedom. We would need more than information.'

'Like what?'

'We would have to record an admission of your involvement in the art thefts – to be kept by the police as part of an officially ratified bargain. That record would trigger automatic imprisonment if ever any of us are harmed. The art can be restored to the galleries. They might be persuaded not to press charges.'

'And how will you persuade the galleries?' Kelly asked.

Lucy handed John the phone.

'The gallery owners don't need the embarrassment of vendors knowing that art placed in the gallery's protection is not safe. They need to keep this quiet – otherwise nobody would want to use the gallery to sell art. If the paintings are returned in good condition, I believe we could persuade them.'

Kelly remained silent for a few seconds. 'How do we get these assurances? This could take weeks, and I'm locked up in here with an assassin.'

Lucy smiled to herself. *I can't believe Kelly is walking straight into this trap.*

'The room can sustain four people for twelve months with food and drink.'

Kelly screamed. 'You little shit. When I get out of here, I won't be using this incompetent little killer anymore, I'll do you myself, do you hear me?'

Lucy kept her cool. 'Is that a threat, Kelly?'

'It's not just a threat, it's a guarantee. I will make sure your death is the most painful you can imagine. I'll even arrange for your kids to watch. You cannot begin to conceive how painful the last two days of your miserable life will be.'

'Threats duly noted,' Lucy replied. 'As there are only two of you in there, you have twenty-four months' food and water.'

'This is unlawful imprisonment,' Kelly spat into the phone. 'You can be prosecuted.'

'You need to do a deal before the police arrive with the book from your father's safe – which by the way implicates eight of your senators, two members of the Supreme Court and at least one ex-president. They left the ranch five minutes ago. That gives you about half an hour.'

'You got into his safe?'

'We did, thanks to your hints about birthdays. You've just made enemies of all the nasties in your father's black book. You helped get us into the safe. Talk about a painful death

– can you imagine those ruthless fossil-fool senators with their resources being any kinder than you are when they find out? That's assuming Adams doesn't kill you first for getting him imprisoned.

'And the police know you're here, so legally we are jointly responsible for your imprisonment. You need to cooperate with the police before they bury you … literally.'

75

Detective Foster smiled to himself. *How many times have we tried to lock up one of the Blacks?*

'Well, we have all the art in police custody, except JFK in the panic room upstairs. So, we need to tie the robbers to the crimes at the Sunset Gallery and the Rockwell Museum.'

'I have photos of the gallery being robbed,' John said.

'What the … Why didn't you tell us earlier?'

'Because there were rumours that certain police officers were taking bribes.'

'So where are the photos?' Mark asked.

'In my phone, along with the video footage of the murder of Pat Dixon and John Black.'

'Say that again.'

'I have video footage of the murder. Patricia Dixon left the webcam on her laptop running.'

'Where's the laptop now?' Mark asked.

'In police custody. But to make sure the video reached the proper authorities, I downloaded it into my phone and my laptop. It's now backed up into the cloud so it can never get lost,' John added.

'Well, did you see the footage?'

'Oh, yes. You can see Adams killing Patricia, you can see him go into the bathroom to kill Black. You can definitely see Adams's face.'

'Have you got it here, Mr Baxter?'

'Absolutely, it takes him only seconds to do the killings.'

Lucy turned to Ma. 'This could be upsetting, Ma. Would you rather go downstairs?'

'Lucy, it's very kind of you. But I think I'd rather know everything – including the bits I was afraid to admit to myself … and anyway, it might make a couple of decisions easier for me. But thanks, sweetie, I just think I'd better know.'

Lucy nodded to John, who proceeded to show Mark the footage of the murder in Room 608.

'That's definitely the guy we have locked up. So, all we have to do is link Adams with the Blacks.'

'Well, you have both of them in the strongbox. They arrived together, they broke in here together,' Lucy said.

It was George's turn. 'And don't forget the recording I have of Simon and Adams talking to Kelly about the stolen paintings and the poisoning of the brothers.'

'What?' Mark erupted again. 'Is there anything else?'

'Mark – we had a problem with coming to the police because a senior officer may have covered up a murder by Jack Black a few years ago. In a few minutes, the little black book will arrive. It may have a record of the money paid to one of your officers. I think a little understanding might be in order

– especially as we got you into a safe with a thousand billion combinations.'

Mark's senior officer took Mark to the corner of Lucy's large bedroom. A few seconds later they returned.

'We're prepared to proceed as if you have been working with the police all along,' Mark said, uneasily.

'And gentlemen, let's not forget we've actually delivered the criminals to you for arrest,' John reminded him.

Lucy had been thinking. 'And Officer ... we have recordings of what they said just now in the strongbox – when they talked about the killing Kelly ordered Paul Adams to carry out. Surely you have enough evidence to lock them up and throw away the key?'

Mark stroked his chin, deep in thought. 'Conspiracy to murder. Let's have a look at your phone again,' he said.

John located the correct piece of recording. They looked at the killing again. 'But there's also the bit where Old Man Black admits to the murder of twelve environmental scientists and told Patricia that Kelly organised it. Do you want to see that?'

Mark shook his head in disbelief. 'I think I'd better, don't you, Mr Detective?'

Don't knock it, Foster; after all these years of work, you could use a break.

John searched the recording for Patricia's chat with Black. Mark watched as Black explained how he and Kelly had organised the murders on the boat.

'And you have copies of this?' Mark said.

'Absolutely, we do – all over the place,' John added.

Mark grinned at Bob, who was clenching his fist in triumph.

Lucy turned to Mark. 'Kelly doesn't know we have this admission from John Black. If she knew, she'd realise she was in so much trouble she may not help us at all.'

The front-door chimes announced that Mark Foster's fellow detectives had arrived with the notebook from Black's safe.

George got to his feet. 'If Ritchey's here, it could jeopardise everything.'

'How so, George?' Lucy asked.

'Because he knows about my electronics. I'll sit in the next room.'

Mark went downstairs to answer the door.

Detectives Rooney and Sanchez entered the house, smiling as they handed Foster the book.

As Foster studied it, his eyes widened. *This is worse than we ever imagined. An ex-attorney general and an ex-president …*

As he turned to shut the door, an unmarked car pulled up in the driveway. Chief Detective Ritchey climbed out.

Mark frowned. *How the hell did Ritchey know about this?*

76

The bedroom intercom from the strongbox was buzzing. Lucy picked it up. 'Where the hell have you been?' came the voice.

'The police have just arrived with the black book.'

Kelly paused. 'Which police have you got there?'

'Why?' John asked.

'Because if Ritchey's there, I've had dealings with him when Billy needed bail.'

John released the button so Kelly could not hear him. 'Sweetheart, you don't think this Ritchey is related to William Ritchey?'

She shrugged her shoulders. 'Let's see who is downstairs. In fact, why don't we all go down. You've probably seen enough for one night.'

John led Mary and Tom down the stairs and into the sitting room. 'We'll organise some coffee.' He shut the double oak doors as he returned to the hallway.

'You going to introduce us, Mark?' Lucy asked.

'Chief Detective Ritchey – he's come straight from the precinct. And these two are Detectives Rooney and Sanchez – they've come from the Black place.'

'So, you're the most senior officer here then, Chief Detective?' Lucy confirmed.

'Seems that way. Why?'

'Well, John and I have just been talking to Kelly. We believe that you, as the senior officer, will get more from her on your own than if there was a crowd up there. I think it will be more productive.'

And if you're half as stupid as I think you are, you'll incriminate Kelly still further.

Ritchey looked at the other officers. 'You guys stay down here.'

John recognised the trap Lucy was setting. 'Sweetheart – why don't I show the chief detective into the bedroom?'

A minute later, John left Chief Detective Ritchey alone in the bedroom and closed the door. He entered the next-door room where George was sitting. He put his forefinger to his lips and pointed to the room.

George nodded. Quietly they made their way downstairs.

As they descended, John put his forefinger to his lips again. George was greeted enthusiastically in silence by his ex-colleagues.

'Ritchey's the spitting image of William, sweetheart. If that's not William's brother, my name's Tricky Dicky.'

'You probably know Senator Malvito,' John said.

'Sure do,' Sanchez said. 'I voted for you last time, Senator. See no reason not to again.'

'Well, I'm always glad to have the support of you boys in blue, don't mind saying. You probably know we've been trying to clean up City Hall.'

An awkward silence followed – so Tom Malvito continued.

'Don't I recognise that painting, John?' he said, pointing to the painting he had sold him.

John looked at Lucy. 'Maybe this is the time, sweetheart?'

Lucy nodded. 'If you like.'

John went to the painting leaning up against the wall. 'You're right, Tom.

'George has been helping us, literally day and night, discover the truth about what's been going on. On at least one occasion he saved our lives. George, this painting was done by your great grandfather in 1888 and we think it should be back in your family.'

John handed the four-foot canvas to him. 'Back where it belongs, George … and thank you for everything.'

George held on to the painting. 'This was the one they lost. My son will be choked; he's been trying to find it. We thought we'd never track it down, especially if it was in private hands. Thank you. I don't know what to say.'

He put it up against the wall again. He stood back from it to admire it from a better distance. 'What can I do to thank you?'

'You've already done it. Enjoy the painting.'

Lucy approached George and squeezed his hand. 'I always thought fast food could be the death of me; but I never dreamt it would be so soon. We owe you our whole future, George.'

George looked uneasy. 'Something tells me we're not done yet.'

Lucy Howard – something tells me George is right.

Suddenly, it felt odd to be calling herself Howard.

I should be Lucy Baxter.

She smiled at the thought – but her legal mind was still working.

'John, we have to apply to freeze all Kelly's accounts. We can't protect two children each side of the Atlantic from assassins if she can still access her money.'

'You're right – and do it before she can get any mobile signal. Now is the time we use our advantage to maximum effect.'

Ritchey entered the room. 'I heard voices; I figured this was where you were. You have quite a gathering here … Senator … Bellows!'

Lucy's gaze passed quickly from Ritchey to George. Instantly, she understood another dimension of their relationship. Ritchey's expression was a mixture of shock and fear. George looked like a fisherman landing a salmon he'd hooked.

'You going to tell us how the conversation went up there?' John asked.

'Need a word outside with you, Detective,' he said to Mark.

Mark Foster followed Ritchey out into the hallway. He shut the double doors behind him.

An awkward silence followed again. Once more, it was Malvito who restarted the conversation. 'On the subject of freezing Kelly's accounts, I'll talk to the district attorney in the morning.'

'Thank you, Tom. Maybe we'll all sleep peacefully again,' Lucy replied.

'This calls for a celebration, sweetheart. I think I know what yours is, Tom. Will you join us, Detectives?'

The police officers looked at each other. 'Are we off duty yet?' Sanchez asked.

John cut in. 'One beer won't do justice any harm. Unless you prefer champagne?'

'I'll see what I can find,' Lucy said.

She opened the doors to the hallway. Foster and Ritchey were having a heated conversation. Lucy looked back at John, her eyebrows raised, before shutting the double doors behind her.

Two minutes later, Lucy reappeared with a drinks trolley, followed by Mark Foster. He brandished the black notebook in the air. 'We still have it, boys,' he said to his colleagues. 'I refused to give it to him, and he's gone back to the precinct – to start disciplinary action against me.

'Now guys, we can get all sorts of nasties locked up – including Ritchey himself, maybe.'

Malvito was curious. 'What you mean by that?'

'Senator … Ritchey's in the book himself. Apart from that, he's been meeting an insurance assessor. We think they have something to do with the art thefts and they're probably brothers.'

'What makes you think that?' Tom asked.

'They're both Ritcheys and they look dead similar. William Ritchey is a fine arts assessor – and Chief Detective Ritchey was recently seen with him the day before an art auction at Christie's, in London.'

Lucy looked at John. 'Now we know why the two pictures in Kelly's place were never found.'

John was puzzled. 'I can't believe it.'

'There's millions at stake,' Mark replied.

'Yes, but I've known William for years – it doesn't stack up.'

'The conversation Ritchey has just had with Kelly upstairs – you don't record those conversations, do you?' Mark asked.

Lucy smiled. 'Why do you think I wanted her locked up in there, officer?'

Mark grinned at his colleagues. 'I think the celebrations have to wait. Let's get a hearing of those tapes before we have our chat with Kelly. Can we replay the tapes without Kelly knowing about it?'

George smiled. 'We can now – had to make a few mods.'

'George, you're a star,' Mark said, turning his attention to Lucy and John. 'I need you upstairs with us to corroborate what we hear on the tapes. Senator, Mrs Black, I need you to stay here in this room with the detectives. Rooney, you come with me,' he said.

Lucy asked Tom if he minded pouring his own whisky. He chuckled. 'You go do what you have to. We'll be fine.'

Lucy and John were followed by the two detectives and George as they climbed the stairs and entered the bedroom. George rewound the tapes …

77

' *Kelly.*'

'*Peter? Can't you get me out of here? Surely you can pull rank or something?*'

'*Unfortunately not. Only the Howard woman knows the combination.*'

'*What do we do now?*'

'*Kelly, what do they know about the copying?*'

'*I don't know. But they have the art we hid in Ma's garage in police stock rooms … all except the original JFK here on the floor.*'

'*That makes it really tricky to get you out of here.*'

'*Do a deal. Maybe we can pay her, like my stupid brothers.*'

'*Kelly, they have the black book from your father's safe. It'll crucify us.*'

'*How do you know?*'

'*Because your father showed it to me. He showed me my name in it with the two hundred-thousand-dollar payment I took to let his son Jack go when that couple got killed, remember?*'

'*He said he was showing me the book, so I'd always know I featured in it. It was his insurance that I would always want to protect him. He knew I would take the two hundred thousand to*' *pay off my mortgage and shut the case off. He also said he knew his son, Moron Jack, as he called him, would give him this opportunity sooner or later.'*

'In that case, we have to try something else. Go downstairs and offer Foster five hundred thousand for the book. Adams, how many bullets do you have in that gun?'

The five of them standing in Lucy's bedroom listened as they heard the receiver click the recording off.

'That's when Ritchey came back down and tried to buy the book off me,' Mark said. 'That's why the conversation out in your hallway got heated.'

Mark picked up the intercom. 'Miss Black?'

'Yes.'

'This is Detective Mark Foster, again. I am arresting you for the murder of twelve people in Beijing. You have the right to remain silent—'

'Quit the crap, Foster. If you let us out of here, you'll never need to work again,' Kelly interrupted.

Mark recited the rights from the start, this time uninterrupted. 'We need Mr Adams to put the gun in the basin in the bathroom, then return to where he is sitting.'

'You can see us?' Kelly replied.

'We have three cameras on you. Every word you have said has been recorded and will be used as evidence at trial.'

'Is that stupid bitch Lucy there? Put her on for me, while it's still safe for her.'

'Mrs Howard can hear everything you say.'

'Good. There are other killers who will hunt you down. You and those precious kids of yours. You'll never sleep easy

346

again, especially as a mother. Did you think of that, you clever piece of shit?'

Mark Foster took the receiver. 'Adams, there are three armed officers here. Each of us has a machine pistol that can let go of a hundred rounds a minute. You only get out of this alive without your gun. Put three inches of water in the basin and put the gun in the basin where we can see it on our monitor. Only then will we open the door. Do you understand?'

Silence followed. After what seemed like half a minute, Adams walked to the bathroom, ran some water into the basin, put his gun into the water and re-entered the main dressing room.

George continued to look at the screen. 'I believe he has another gun.'

'Where would he keep it?' Lucy asked.

'Strapped to his shin, ma'am,' Foster replied.

'So … forgive me being naïve, Detective … but surely he could have two more guns then?' Lucy persisted.

'You could be right, ma'am. I think this is where you and Mr Baxter get yourselves downstairs to safety. We'll be down when this is over.'

'If Lucy's right, Mark, he could have more magazines in his pockets.'

Lucy took the receiver from Mark Foster.

'This is the stupid bitch speaking – the one who outwitted you into this trap. None of the officers here have the combination to this room. Now that you've been stupid enough to record a threat to me and my children, in front of police witnesses, you're staying put. Adams has at least one other gun on him, maybe two. So, unless we see him naked, you'll die of starvation.'

'This is unlawful imprisonment,' Kelly shouted.

'No court in the land convicts anyone when they kill their attackers in self-defence. In self-defence, I'm keeping two families safe, giving you water and food. No court will judge me as doing anything improper in view of your threats.

'We have lots of time. John and I fancy another trip to Europe. You could think about your solution while we're in London.'

Kelly screamed. 'You fucking cow.'

'Oh, and one more thing,' Lucy replied. 'While you can't even consult your lawyer, I have access to the finest criminal lawyers anywhere – free of charge. They will tell me if the evidence in your father's book and the recordings we have can convict you in your absence. They'll take some weeks to reach a conclusion, especially as these offences will be tried in a federal court. You and Adams are now both on record as having committed multiple murders, one in Montana, one in Wyoming. A federal court is likely to use the death penalty on you both.'

'Do you expect us just to walk out of here into the custody of the police, with you watching?' Kelly shouted.

'No, I don't. Your arrogance will keep you in my strong-box till Adams kills you to prolong his own food supply. But he can't stop your body decomposing. Sooner or later, the stench of your rotting body will make him ill. Even with you dead, sooner or later his food runs out. Eventually, he'll lose so much muscle mass, he won't be able to lift his gun. But if you're still alive, you'll be tried in Boston and die from lethal injection.

'*That* – is what I expect.'

A long pause followed, broken eventually by Lucy. 'Checkmate, in two moves, against any defence.'

'You'll never get away with this, you bitch,' Kelly spat.

'We anticipated your next two moves – the first being to talk to Ritchey and your corrupt attorney. So, while you cannot consult lawyers, we will prepare the cases against you and Adams for the murders you did in Montana and Wyoming, both of which can use the death penalty. With the recordings we made this evening, Ritchey's sentence is likely to be about fifteen years' jail.

'Now I come to think of it – I think I will apply to the courts to attend your execution. In view of the threats you've made, I believe I could gain permission. I want to be looking at you when you feel the potassium chloride enter your veins. I'm told it feels like ice running through you.'

'Wait – Detective? Can you hear me?'

'Yes.'

'It's me, Paul Adams. If I give you all the information you need – on the whole Black family and everything – do you think they'll do a deal?'

'What kind of information?'

'The other art robberies planned, the other murders they had me do – stuff like that.'

'You bastard,' Kelly shouted.

'Shut your mouth or I'll do you like the girl in the green dress. Anyway, Detective, you still there? D'you think there's a deal?'

'Paul Adams, I'm arresting you for the murder of Patricia Dixon. You have the right—'

'Pat Dixon? For the murder of Pat Dixon?'

'Patricia Dixon – journalist at the *Boston Times*,' Foster replied.

Adams felt sick.

78

Lucy and John left Mark Foster and his fellow officer discussing how they would present Kelly's incarceration to the district attorney's office.

'We'll see you downstairs, gentlemen,' Lucy said. 'Can we get you anything to eat or drink?'

'No thanks, Mrs Howard. There's not too much more we can do here tonight. We'll have to come back in the morning, after we've spoken to the DA.'

As Lucy and John walked downstairs, she lowered her voice. 'What if we can get Kelly to tell us about the other mining companies? There might be some seriously incriminating information. There may never be another chance like this.'

'I like your thinking. It could make her competitors nervous. They may retaliate with even more damaging information about Black Industries.'

'Actually, there's some other good that could come out of this,' Lucy replied. 'If the oil companies, as it's alleged, operate a cartel, then maybe we could damage some of their trading relationships. If the US government won't take measures against fossil fuels, we could use the information about several US senators to persuade the government to exact colossal donations from the mining companies. The money could build wind turbines and solar parks and carbon-capture sites.'

As they stood in Lucy's hallway, John took her hands in his. 'Have I ever told you how much I love your brains, sweetheart?'

Lucy grinned. 'Later, Mr Baxter.'

They re-entered Lucy's sitting room.

'Sorry to keep you waiting. I hope you helped yourselves to drinks,' Lucy said.

Mary was worried. 'What's happening with Kelly, Lucy?'

Lucy sat down next to Mary on the sofa. 'Ma, I don't know how to tell you – on top of losing your boys and everything – but I think you'll lose Kelly out of all this. I am so sorry, Ma. If she ever regains her freedom, she has promised to kill me and the kids. If it could have been any other way …'

'Lucy, it's not your fault. I am sure you know, as a mother, we see the faults in our children. Kelly was Kelly long before you met her.'

'Oh, Ma. You know John and I will always be here for you, don't you?'

Tom cleared his throat. 'Look folks, you have family things to talk about. I'll get myself back up the hill. Thanks for the drinks.'

Mark entered the lounge.

'Anything new?' Lucy asked.

'As a matter of fact, there is. Kelly says she has evidence that will link you to the deaths of Matthew, Peter and Christopher Black.'

'Come with me, then. You need to hear how this plays out,' Lucy said, starting for the stairs.

Mark Foster and one of his colleagues followed John and Lucy up the stairs. Lucy picked up the receiver to the strong-box. 'Do you want to ask the questions, Detective – or shall I?'

'What have you got to say, Miss Black?'

'I had a forensic team from the Boston Police examine the houses where my brothers live. They found hairs from Lucy in both houses. I believe she killed both of the brothers and Peter too. I believe she is guilty of three murders.'

'And where is the evidence now?' Mark asked.

'In police custody.'

'Whose custody exactly?'

'Presumably the officer in charge of the investigation,' Kelly replied.

Lucy took the receiver from Mark Foster. 'I'm surprised you even made the chess team at Princeton. It seems I held them in too high regard.'

'What do you mean,' Kelly asked.

'You didn't do your research? This is the second move we anticipated you'd make.'

'What are you talking about?' Kelly replied.

'You didn't know that DNA ages over time? I lived with Billy for the duration of our marriage. Everyone on the ranch knew I spent a fair bit of time with Andrea – and with Laura, the other side. The only people who wouldn't know would be someone who lived off-ranch – someone like you.'

Lucy turned to Mark Foster. 'Andrea was Matthew's wife. Laura was Christopher's wife. They were my neighbours on each side. It would be astonishing if some of my DNA from fifteen years ago could not be found in their houses.'

Lucy continued. 'I left the ranch fifteen years ago. DNA deteriorates over time. Testing is accurate to 4.86 years. Fifteen years is more than three times the margin of error in the tests. I will ask you, Kelly – in the presence of the police here – if you want those houses tested thoroughly for all the recent DNA that might be found. Criminal lawyers have told me that a single hair from a hairbrush has convicted people of murder.

'As I said, checkmate in two moves. Everything you say from now on makes your lethal injection more likely. So please – keep talking.'

Kelly said nothing.

Mark Foster, Sanchez, Lucy and John made their way downstairs once more.

John broke the silence. 'What's interesting is how calm the senator was this evening. I wondered if he'd get nervous about any information that might emerge from the conversation. But there was nothing – just a kind of detached interest.'

Mark nodded. 'He's not mentioned in the black book, but we'll double-check overnight. Anyway, we have to get back here tomorrow. Can I say ten a.m.?'

Lucy and John let the policemen out. John made sure the door was firmly shut before grinning at Lucy. 'So that's what the freezer bags were about – and your dash upstairs in Kelly's house.'

'I knew she'd play dirty, John. I took enough hair from Kelly's hairbrush to plant a fair bit in every house we know about. I left the hairbrush on the floor, so she'd know it had been tampered with.'

John and Lucy re-joined George and Mary.

'All OK,' Lucy smiled. 'Threat dealt with.'

'Thank goodness.' Ma yawned. 'What else can Kelly possibly have in store for us?'

79

Friday – 9th November

The next morning, Lucy and John were drinking coffee, waiting till George and Mary got down for breakfast. Lucy could see John was admiring her country-style kitchen.

'I love this big dresser,' he said. 'I don't think I've ever seen one this wide.'

'I got it the same day I acquired the bed – from the Warren Store in Vermont. I knew it would look good in this kitchen; it had the feel I wanted to create.'

'It matches this oak table perfectly,' John observed. 'And it goes great with these old flagstones.'

Mary walked into the kitchen. 'My god. What happened to your windows?'

Lucy looked at the windows, made opaque by the bullets.

'That's Kelly's work – Kelly and her little shit upstairs. Ma, if you ever wonder how dangerous Kelly is to us all, forensics found more than a hundred and sixty spent bullet casings outside.

'Ma – we're serious about you coming to England with us. We can help with the funerals. But the trials won't be for at least six weeks, so we'd have plenty of time to get back.'

'Let me think about it,' Ma said. 'It's all a bit much at the moment.'

As they sat round Lucy's big refectory table, Ma asked Lucy what she thought of Tom Malvito.

'Well – he never takes his eyes off you,' Lucy grinned.

'But he's married.'

'Actually, Ma – not really,' Lucy replied.

'What do you mean, he's got Monica.'

'Except, she's been seeing your son, Billy – that is, until recently. And now she's carrying on with some other "fancy-boy", as Tom calls him. The marriage has been all but over for some time.'

'Our Billy, you say?'

'Yes, Ma – and Tom seems really nice,' Lucy smiled.

'Oh, stop your nonsense; this is ridiculous,' Ma said, blushing.

Lucy approached Mary from behind and put her arms around her. 'You deserve some happiness as much as anyone, Ma. All of us who love you want to see you happy.'

Lucy's phone buzzed. Lucy picked it up and grinned at Mary. 'No problem, Tom, we've been up a while. Here she is.'

'Senator Tom Malvito, for you,' Lucy announced.

'… Well, that's very kind of you, Tom … I hope to see you there, then … OK, then, bye for now.'

George arrived in the kitchen. Lucy poured him a coffee. 'Did you sleep well, George?'

'I haven't slept that well in years, ma'am.'

Lucy settled George with some toast and maple syrup. 'That syrup's local. I hope you like it.'

'It's great – nearly as sweet as the information Mark got from the black notebook.'

At 10.00 a.m. precisely, the doorbell sounded. Lucy opened the front door to Mark Foster and Detective Sanchez.

'Come on in, guys.' Lucy led them to the kitchen where Mary was sitting with John and George.

'Mark, what if Kelly has more than merely the information that implicates Black Industries. What if she could expose the cartels that might exist?'

'Why would she help us?' Mark replied.

'To downgrade the sentence from the death penalty to life imprisonment,' John replied.

'If we could break any links in the fossil fuel industry, it would have to compete on a more even basis with renewable energy, which gets nowhere near the government subsidies of oil and coal.'

Lucy continued. 'And if fossil fuels had to compete more equally, the use of renewables would be even more viable. Renewable energy use would skyrocket, prices would drop dramatically, use increases exponentially. You get the picture. It would massively reduce CO_2 emissions in the US.'

Mark Foster was thinking. 'The notebook caused us some problems last night ...

'There's a long list of senators and congressional commit-tee members who are on record as helping the sale of coal and oil. And here's the shocker – and I quote: "the total deaths of workers in the mining industries continue to be a thousand times greater than those working in renewables – a small price to pay for the wealth generated".'

'Are there any names to this declaration?' Lucy said.

Mark looked at them. 'One is an ex-attorney general ... and three others are ex-vice presidents and ex-presidents. One took a five-million-dollar payment for the crucial tie-breaking vote in that environmental ruling where they approved the oil exploration rights in Alaska.'

'No wonder the Blacks wanted this book locked up so tight,' Lucy said. 'This has ramifications for the US constitution. It looks as if there's been an agreement, not just in the US but also in Europe, to delay the deployment of renewables. We know at least twelve senators are heavily invested in fossil fuels.'

John took a sip of coffee. 'To indict attorney generals and senators for distorting markets would require the most brilliant legal mind – and someone who speaks enough languages to be able to relate to senior politicians in different countries.'

John looked up at the ceiling. 'Who do we know like that, Mary?'

Mark was puzzled. 'But even if you could find someone as brilliant as that – who'd be brave enough to fight the attorney general? It'd be total career suicide.'

80

Lucy was thinking. 'Only if we lose. Tom Malvito is a lawyer. A third of the Senate are lawyers. There must be at least a hundred lawyers in Congress. I wonder how many of them we could get on our side.'

'Sweetheart, this will be the fight of the century. You sure you've got the appetite for this?'

'I won't be on my own. We'll be a ready-formed team before they even know about us. This could force huge change.'

Lucy and John led Mary, George, Foster and Sanchez up the stairs to Lucy's strongbox.

'Can you hear me?' Mark opened.

'We can hear you,' Kelly replied.

'There may be a way for you to reduce the sentence to life imprisonment.'

'And how is that?'

'Tell us what you know of the other oil and coal companies.'

'What do you need to know?'

'Do you know much about the ways they do business?'

'The same ways we do. Get the right people on your side – find out who the key influencers are in the right government departments in the target markets – the usual stuff.'

'So, you can't help us with any fresh information, then,' Mark said.

'How can I know what the chances are?'

'I can't make any guarantees. We have more than enough information to convict already. You have nothing to lose by trying.'

'Daddy once brought me in on the meeting between him and the officials in one of our biggest markets. They made FIFA look ethical.'

'Can you be more specific?'

'I remember Daddy paying a hundred thousand dollars to one official in China. China are building fifty coal-fired power stations each year – their appetite for coal is vast.'

'I'm sorry … why is this relevant?' Mark was puzzled.

'Because the official is now on the governing council of the United Nations.'

Lucy handed Mark Foster a piece of paper. Mark read the question on it to Kelly. 'Who would know the people doing the same things for the other coal and oil companies, the people in Russia and India for example?'

'I do know we paid millions to get into India. The poverty there made it easy.'

'Do you have names?'

'Sure … Get me out of this cell, and I'll give you anything I can remember.'

George handed Mark a piece of paper. 'Would you be prepared to give us a list of the crimes that competitors of Black Industries committed in the US – with the names of the people responsible?'

'Sure.'

'OK then,' Mark replied. 'You make a list. There's a laptop in the cupboard to the left of the door. You can print the names into it and buzz us when you've done it. We'll give you the passcode to access the email.'

Lucy moved to her dressing table. She opened her laptop. 'This should be interesting.'

While they were waiting, Lucy started to read the news bulletins that appeared down the right-hand side of her screen.

'John, look. It's a picture of Grace and Joseph's boy, from Harbour Island. He's had his foot operation.'

Lucy started to type an email.

FAO Grace – Fantastic – hope it all goes well and that all is well on the island. Love – Lucy.

'Here's one from Carol and Mike, John. They've found a vineyard – apparently the soil is perfect for the white Sauvignon grape. They're very excited and want to know if we want a share in the profits in exchange for help towards the deposit.'

The intercom buzzer sounded. Mark went over to press the record and answer buttons. 'Just need the password,' Kelly said.

Lucy looked towards Mark. 'Tell her … "2Cis2much" - as in digit '2,' capital 'C,' lower case 'is,' digit '2,' lower case 'much.'

Lucy's laptop pinged again. She and John stared wide-eyed at Kelly's list as Mark and the others crowded round them. 'Eight more senators,' Mary said.

'But interestingly, still no Senator Malvito,' John remarked. 'Ask her what proof there is that these people are involved.'

The response came almost immediately. 'I can link the names you have in the black book with what's in this list – including the lawyers in Congress who keep the law favourable in the US.'

Lucy nodded. *Now we're getting somewhere – we could actually pull this off.*

Mark Foster had heard enough. 'Miss Black, Mr Adams – I need you to listen to my instructions. Can you both hear me?'

Two voices replied, 'Yes.'

'OK then. We have a camera that sees through the doorway to the bathroom. We need to see three guns and eighteen bullets in the basin, underwater. Otherwise, the door will not be opened. Is that clear?'

'Yes, but *she* had better not be there when I come out.'

Adams put his guns and magazines into the basin and returned to the heavy steel door. Lucy wrote down the combination to the strongbox on a piece of notepaper and she and John walked downstairs.

'Miss Black, Mr Adams – we are now alone, my colleague and me. There's no one else here. Stand by the door. Turn around so we can see you are carrying nothing with you.

'Now put your hands in the air. Adams knows the dangers of loading wet bullets into a wet gun. But if either one of you goes back for the guns, the door will be locked immediately. Because you have access to weapons, we can shoot to kill.'

81

Lucy sat beside Mary on the sofa and handed her a tissue. 'You need something to look forward to, Ma. It's all been so sad. Why don't we plan the trip to England, and you can meet John's friend?'

'Maybe after the funerals and when we have the dates of the trials,' Ma said.

The double doors opened. Mark, Oliver and James entered the sitting room.

'How was the game?' John asked.

'Awesome,' Mark replied. 'Mom, you would not believe the stats Jim has in his head.'

James walked to the grand piano, sat down on the raspberry-pink velvet stool and looked at the sheet music in front of him. He looked at Lucy. 'It's for four hands.'

Lucy smiled and sat beside him. Without a further word, they set their hands to the keyboard. Lucy nodded and they started to play.

Mary was transfixed. Six minutes later, they finished, and Ma started clapping. Lucy put her arm round James and gave him a hug. She left him at the piano and came to join Mary and John on the sofa.

'Ma, he has a real gift; he was playing without looking at the sheet music. It took me a year to learn that piece – and I still need the sheet. His ability is humbling.'

'What was the piece you were playing, sweetheart?' John asked.

'Mozart's Sonata in C, written for four hands.'

John's phone buzzed with a text. *John – got news for you on the art – give us a call when you can – will need to meet for this – can be in Boston – regards – William.*

'Sweetheart, I have to go into town to meet William. We could all have lunch on the quay afterwards. Ma, would you like lunch with us? And what about you guys?'

Mark and Oliver were not interested. 'We just got back from there. We're good.'

Ma looked at Lucy. 'I'll stay here with the boys, Lucy. I don't often get the chance these days. You and John go.'

As they were preparing to leave the house, Lucy went upstairs to change the combination to the strongbox.

'The police forgot to take JFK with them,' Lucy said. 'They'll probably call us.'

Thirty-five minutes later, Lucy and John walked into The Oaks Hotel. William stood up and greeted them cordially. 'What's the matter? Something wrong?'

'William, we've met your brother, Peter,' John started.

'That's why I wanted to talk – that, and certain shiny objects.'

William looked around to see if anyone could overhear. 'And I have some clarity on the painting left to your client, Lucy – the one you crossed the Atlantic to ask John about.

'First – my brother Peter. I've been working with Mark Foster to put him away.'

'What've you got against your brother?' Lucy asked.

'Peter forged my mother's signature to falsify her will, cutting me out completely. He has also taken bribes from the Blacks to keep them out of prison. Your tapes prove the link between him and the Blacks. We had to pretend to be doing some copying of the art to get the link proven between Kelly and the police.'

'Go on,' John said.

'We got approval from Malvito to create the impression that he was involved. It seemed the only way that people as well connected as the Blacks would believe the whole thing. It was all part of Malvito's election pledge to clean up the police.

'And thanks to you people, we can now put Peter away, but for a lot more than falsifying a will.'

Lucy was puzzled. 'So, what about the painting I thought was a copy?'

'Turns out it is indeed a copy; it was passed off as an original to make your client think she'd been compensated properly in the will you were expediting when you met John. The Blacks needed to hush her up after they had falsified gas-fracking rights on her land in Kentucky. She could have sold those rights for two and a half million dollars over ten years.

'Turns out your client is a well-connected Democrat – and well known as a Kennedy fan. The Blacks stole the painting of JFK from the Rockwell Museum – enter Billy Black – and had it copied. They tried to use a copy to compensate her for the fact she had lost two and a half million.

'Now here's where it gets weirder. The Blacks made two copies, effectively committing two crimes. They used Billy to break back into the Rockwell Museum to return the painting of JFK, but a copy, not the original. We think he had inside help because after the first break-in, the museum beefed up security substantially. But the copy was so good it fooled the curator, a Dr Rashadi, who must now feel like a royal fool in front of his colleagues.'

William continued. 'Mrs Howard, you have one copy you're keeping in your office. The Rockwell Museum has the other – pending the discovery of the real one. Only when it's found can we link the copying of it to the Blacks; no court would convict for copying without seeing the copy and the original side by side.'

'But William, there's one other version of JFK,' John said.

'What?' William replied. 'Where?'

'William, apart from the version in Lucy's strongbox, which we found in the roof of Old Man Black's garage, and the copy in Lucy's office, and the copy now hanging in the Rockwell Museum, there's also one at the bottom of Kelly's stairs in her house on Chestnut Street. I reckon that's four versions.'

'John, you never told me,' Lucy replied.

'We were rushing to get out of the house, sweetheart. I was afraid we'd get caught if we hung around.'

Lucy turned to William. 'We'd better find out if the one we've got in the strongbox is the real one. John, why doesn't William come back to Concord, and you can look at the painting together?'

Half an hour later, Lucy opened her front door. William followed Lucy and John upstairs.

'Shouldn't be too hard to tell if it's the original,' William said, as he turned the painting over.

'Why's that?' John replied.

'The copies don't have the little note that Rockwell scribbled in ink on the reverse. He normally wrote the actual day he finished the painting and signed the note. But on this particular painting, he put the actual time of day he finished as well. See ... "10.00 a.m. Friday 28th October 1960". This is the original. I recognise his handwriting.'

'That's another amazing 28th of October coincidence,' John said.

'Why?' William and Lucy said in chorus.

'I knew Rockwell finished his JFK on the 28th of October because it was going to be the cover of the *Saturday Evening Post* on Saturday the 29th – which it was. He did three hundred paintings for the magazine in all. But ten a.m. is what gets me; it is exactly – to the minute – exactly – two years before JFK safely concluded the Cuban Missile Crisis at ten a.m. on October 28th, 1962, with Khrushchev.'

'Wow. That gives it a kind of historic, prescient significance then, John. I'm pretty sure this is not something anyone else has spotted. It would have to make it even more valuable. Let's have a look at the front.'

William turned the painting over. 'As I thought – no brushstrokes evident at all. It's incredibly difficult to paint oil on canvas with this effect; it's so smooth. I still think he is under-rated as a draughtsman. Anyway – this is the original. I've seen the copy hanging in the Rockwell Museum – it's got very good likeness, but the slightest of brushstrokes in one or two areas.'

Lucy was thinking. 'So, guys – you're the art experts – tell me – what happens to the copies Kelly has on her stairs and I have in the office in Hartford?'

William smiled. 'Nothing.' He looked at John.

'Sweetheart, what William is saying, I think, is that Kelly will never be able to sell the copy since the two break-ins have now had so much publicity. She certainly won't want it known she has it. The Rockwell will not want to admit any other copies exist either, because it devalues the Rockwell brand – let alone the Rockwell Museum brand. And as far as your office copy is concerned, I'd keep it; it'd be a shame to destroy it.'

'But you can testify in a court of law that this is the original,' Lucy said.

'Certainly,' William replied. 'And to get a fraud conviction, we only need to prove one copy was made; we don't need to mention the other two that you and Kelly have.

'And in turn, I can now prove the Blacks were trying to defraud my client into thinking she had been compensated for lost fracking rights. That's the reason I went to see John in the first place.'

'So there is something to be said for art fraud, after all,' John grinned.

Lucy shook her head. 'But it's good to shine the light on the truth.'

'Talking of shining, William,' John replied. 'You were going to tell us about certain shiny objects?'

'Ah … about eight years ago one hundred very large diamonds were stolen from a safety deposit box in Hatton Garden. Rumour has it that the diamonds were five carats each. But no one claimed any insurance; possibly ill-gotten gains from some shady deal. Anyway, the owners never went to the police. So officially, the diamonds don't exist. They have huge value but only if cut down to more normal sizes that attract less attention.'

John avoided Lucy's gaze. 'If they don't officially exist, how does anyone know about them?'

'We started an investigation, listening in on the Blacks, long before the election campaign for Senator here in Boston. The Blacks had got hold of the diamonds somehow and were going to use them as campaign money.

'But then, all talk of the diamonds stopped. Art thefts started all over New England, including the one over at the Rockwell Museum. Putting two and two together, we figured that the Blacks lost the diamonds and decided to use the paintings instead.'

Lucy smiled. 'Actually, William, we wondered why Old Man Black needed any more money, with all his resources. This whole art thing only makes sense if we take him out of it. It's Kelly who wants the seat in the Senate. Her old man probably never knew about her involvement in the art thefts – just as he never knew how Kelly made her very first two and a half million when she left Princeton.'

'So where does this leave the missing diamonds?' John asked.

'Probably in good hands,' William replied, looking at Lucy and John in turn.

John studied William. 'So why do you come to us with this information, William?'

'Well, I wanted to set the record straight about myself. I wanted you to know the truth and that I do have the best interests of the art world at heart. I also wanted you to know about the diamonds because I think you will use them wisely.'

William paused. 'Look, you two … I know you have … All I am saying is that the diamonds cannot be used in their present form.'

'If we ever got our hands on diamonds like that, we'd want to use them for real good. Lucy and I are comfortable enough. I'm sure we could find some good causes that could benefit.'

'I felt sure you'd see it that way,' William smiled.

John looked at William hard for a moment or two. 'Actually, I'm bloody relieved, William. I thought I'd lost a friend. I'm sorry I ever doubted you,' he said.

'No worries, John. It's mostly my fault for setting up the deception in the way we did. It seemed the only way to get the result.'

'And do you have any causes that would benefit?' John asked.

'Well – there's a hospice here in Boston that's run as a charity. There's also a kid whose mother can't get the wheel-chair he needs for his motor neurone disease …'

'I can see you've given this very little thought, William.'

Lucy was grinning. 'Did you have anything else in mind?'

'There's the Hope Centre for disabled kids. I happen to know the kids in there get a huge kick out of hydrotherapy.

It'll take them about a year to raise the seventy-five thousand dollars to put in a pool of their own. The kids really love it. But they only get out once a fortnight to borrow another pool ...'

William's voice cracked; he paused to collect himself. 'If they had their own pool, the kids could use it two or three times a week.'

'This one seems to have got to you,' Lucy replied.

William swallowed hard. 'My little nephew's in there and I don't have the power to help him.'

82

Just as William was leaving the house, Mark Foster called. 'Are you going to be around today, Mr Baxter? We'd like to pick up the painting.'

'Come as soon as you can.'

John finished the call with Foster and turned to look at Lucy. 'Sweetheart, did you notice the numbers in our chat with William?'

'The diamonds you mean? Yes, he said one hundred were stolen in Hatton Garden, but we've only got fifty.'

'Exactly – so where are the other fifty? Has Billy got them hidden somewhere else?'

'Talking about numbers, this 28th of October thing is weird.'

Lucy grinned. 'I wondered if you'd bring that up.'

'Let's see what we have ... Canaletto's birthday in 1697, the day they finalised the designs of the Boston State House in 1797, the stock market crash in 1929, the day Norman Rockwell finished his portrait of JFK in 1960, the day of the end of the Cuban Missile Crisis in 1962 and – possibly the most important of all – the day you upgraded your flight and avoided the plane crash caused by Hurricane Sandy in 2012.'

Lucy smiled. 'If we're talking October 28th – we might also include Julia Roberts's and Bill Gates's birthdays.'

The doorbell chimed. Lucy and John greeted Mark Foster at the door together.

'This is Detective Roberts, Mrs Howard. He needs to check the panic room for fingerprints. We won't be more than an hour or so, then we'll be out of your way.'

'Come in,' Lucy offered. 'Would you like anything to drink?'

'No, thanks, ma'am; we can't bring anything into the area under investigation.'

Forty-five minutes later the detectives entered the kitchen. 'You'll need this receipt for what we're taking away: painting by Norman Rockwell, value – what shall I put here, where it says "value"?'

John smiled at Mark. 'What, the auction price?'

'I suppose … I have to put something in this box,' Mark said.

'Well, then – eight million dollars,' John replied.

'Crap – oh, excuse me, ma'am.'

Lucy grinned.

John looked at Mark. 'Ten million – if the right buyers are in the auction room. You'd better take good care of it on the way back to the precinct.'

Mark hesitated.

'You haven't brought anything to contain it, have you?' John guessed.

Mark remained silent. John searched the nearest Home Depot on his phone.

'I need two pieces of marine ply, three quarters of an inch thick, twenty-four inches by thirty inches, one piece of marine ply, same thickness but fourteen inches by eighteen inches, and eight cubes of wood each measuring four inches by four inches by four inches, sixteen three-inch-long screws – three-inch tens – five yards of bubble wrap. But here's the thing, I need it here yesterday … Thanks,' John said.

'You can probably tell – I've done this before. The wood's being cut as we speak.'

'Stay for some coffee, Detectives,' Lucy insisted. 'I have a question or two. When do you expect to get dates for the trial?'

Mark frowned. 'There's something else … Kelly told us quite a lot last night when we interviewed her … we'll be bringing charges against her brother Jack for the first-degree murder of five people.'

'Five? I thought it was two,' Mary said.

'It turns out, Kelly used Jack to kill anyone she thought threatened Black Industries.'

'Will Jack stand trial for the murder of his ex-girlfriend as well?' John asked.

'Looks like it,' Mark said.

'But that raises questions of the bribe that Ritchey took from Old Man Black and which we know is in the black book. That's going to be awkward for him, Mark,' John suggested.

'Yep. I reckon ten to fifteen years.'

The delivery of wood arrived. 'I get what the larger bits of wood and the blocks are for. But what is the smaller piece for?' Mark asked John.

'That's so we can test the whole thing comes together. That smaller bit will act as a painting substitute. We can see if the case works without having to take the painting in and out of the box. Art gets damaged with too much handling.'

John took them into Lucy's garage and showed them the tools they would need. John took the bubble wrap inside the house to wrap the trial piece of wood. Ten minutes later he emerged to find they had finished the casing.

'That's great,' John said. 'Let me go and get the trial piece.'

He went inside to retrieve the piece of wood securely taped up in several layers of bubble wrap. They slid it into the case and it fitted perfectly. 'OK then, now we know it fits, let me go and wrap the painting,' John said.

He went into the kitchen to wrap the painting. Five minutes later, he leant the painting up against the wall and rested the trial piece of wood up against it to make sure they were both the same size.

John's phone buzzed. 'Hi, George, what's up?'

'I've been helping Mark get the case details together. But I also checked a few other safety things, just in case.'

'Like what?'

'It occurred to me that Kelly may use more than one killer. So I tried to figure out what she could have done before we locked her up. I checked Mrs Black's car and found an explosive device attached to the ignition circuit. I need to come and check Lucy's car.'

'Thank god for you, George. Get over here as soon as you can.'

John took the painting out to Mark and slid it into the wooden case. Mark inserted the last block into the long side and screwed it into place using the last two screws. They loaded it into the police van.

'Thanks for your help, Mr Baxter. I'll come back to you when I have the case schedule. It could take four months to prepare for trial – especially when the death penalty is involved.

'Oh, by the way, some post came for you when we were putting the packing case together. It was five jiffy bags, all identical. I put them just inside the garage door.'

Mark and his partner drove away, and John closed the garage door from the inside. He picked up the jiffy bags and made his way into the kitchen to re-join Lucy, Mary and James.

'Mark is saying the trial will take four months to get to court. I think we should book flights and return in about a month. That'll give them loads of time.' John paused.

'I nearly forgot. George is coming over to check your car, Lucy. He found an explosive device linked to the ignition circuit on Ma's car. He wants to check yours.'

Lucy stood up, fury all over her face. 'She's never going to stop – she'll keep going till she kills us all – even you, Ma.'

Lucy paced the kitchen, her fists clenched. She walked to Ma and put her arms round her. 'I'm sorry, Ma. I'm so sorry – Kelly's your daughter.

'John, whatever we've paid George, it's no way close to being enough. No way *close*.'

The front door buzzed.

'That'll be him now,' John said, making his way to the front door.

John watched as George unfolded his electronic scanning device. It gave off beeps at intervals of a second. As soon as he waved it under the front end of Lucy's car, the beeps become more frequent.

'Have you got anything on for the next few weeks, George?'

'Nothing as important as putting that murdering bitch away.'

'Good, why don't you come inside when you're done out here. Lucy and I will have put a small deposit into your bank in five minutes – so we can see this thing through to completion.'

John went back inside to sit at his laptop and access his bank.

'Just had a chat with George about the next few weeks, sweetheart.' Lucy looked over his shoulder as he entered seven digits into the rectangular 'Amount' box.

'Wow,' Lucy said. 'That's more like it. I'll give you half of that; seems only fair.'

John looked up at her. 'You were right, sweetheart. Every single one of us in this room is only alive now because George was proactive. We would literally, all of us be dead.'

Lucy took a deep breath. 'Right. Why don't we break open some of that '78? Seems like the right moment.'

'Good idea,' John replied.

'And we have an opera in Venice to go to, I think, Mr Baxter.' Lucy looked from John to Mary. 'When we were in Venice, we noticed that La Fenice was about to stage *The Barber of Seville.* Thought that would amuse you, Ma.'

John smiled. 'Lucy has this fantastic place to stay – and there's hot chocolate to die for.'

'Does it have a piano?' James asked.

'Absolutely, it does,' John replied.

'I'll get Jane in the office to book four seats then,' Lucy said.

'No, you won't, sweetheart. You'll ask her to book four first-class seats instead, and on any flight that is not 006.'

'You're a – gem,' Lucy said, recognising the jiffy bags John had placed on the table.

George walked into the kitchen carrying a device with wires and a mobile phone attached to it. He put it on the table. 'It's old-fashioned, but it's powerful enough to kill everyone within ten yards. There would've been nothing left of anyone to identify as a body.'

They all stared at the device for a few seconds.

John broke the silence. 'Which brings me nicely to the little deposit we've made, George. I hope it's enough to procure your services for a few weeks.'

'I'm sure it will be – and thank you – but if you'll excuse me folks, I'll be getting home. I'll catch up with forensics in the morning about this thing.'

John accompanied George to the front door and returned to the kitchen.

'Speaking of tomorrow – we find out from Mark when we can fly. We need to find out the actual value of these diamonds too – and the likely value of the cut-down stones we could create from them.'

'Diamonds?' Mary asked.

What are you up to, Mr Baxter? I know that look ...

83

'Make us an offer,' John said to Zach Weinbaum.

'On all forty-seven diamonds? I'd have to get my partners to approve this kind of purchase.'

'I need to do a deal today, as we're leaving for England. Of course, I could take the stones to another jeweller if you felt too rushed.'

'Oh, I don't think there's any need for that,' Weinbaum said. 'Let me have a closer look.' He held up a stone to the loupe lodged in his eye socket. He punched a few digits into the large keys of his desktop calculator. After a few seconds of deliberation, he used his well-practised sigh.

This told John that Weinbaum thought he was dealing with a fool who could be deceived by such acting. So John knew the offer he was about to receive would not be the best price.

'Two point four million dollars is what I will give you. We won't be able to turn them over so quickly; it will take months to cut them, and they could be here for a long time on our stocks.'

'Well, we wouldn't want to put you to that financial inconvenience, Mr Weinbaum. I think I'll take them to De Beers in London, next week, and come back to you. But thank you for your offer.' He started to pack up the diamonds.

'Let's not get too hasty, Mr Baxter. Perhaps, if you could give me a minute to call Mr Weinbaum Senior, I'll see what we can do?'

He picked up one of the stones and pushed his chair away from his desk. 'Let me just make the call,' he said.

'If you could leave the stone here, Mr Weinbaum, while you make the call.'

Weinbaum's mouth smiled, leaving most of his face unmoved. 'Of course, Mr Baxter.'

He returned a couple of minutes later. 'Three million, if you want the money today.'

'We would need it transferred electronically before we leave the diamonds here.'

'Very good. Have you internet banking with you?'

Lucy opened her tablet. 'Should be good in a moment or two,' she said, tapping a few keys.

Weinbaum swung his chair ninety degrees to face his computer. 'What's the sort code, please? … and the account number? …'

Lucy showed John the latest entry to her account. 'Thank you, Mr Weinbaum. Enjoy the diamonds.'

Lucy and John had only three blocks to walk to The Oaks.

'Now for the fun part,' John smiled.

They reached the hotel and sat down in reception with Mary and James. Lucy accessed her bank again and John dialled the Hope Centre.

'If we were to donate towards the hydrotherapy pool, what account details would I need?'

A few moments later, John repeated out loud the numbers for Lucy, who tapped them into her laptop. 'How much?' Lucy asked.

'The whole seventy-five thousand, of course.' Without looking up at him, Lucy smiled, tapped in the amount and pressed the 'send' button.

'Then there's Mike and Carol, and the mysterious case of Sauvignon Blanc.'

'I'm on it. Mike. It's John. Hope it's not too late for you in Europe? ... Good. Look – about the vineyard. Are you still doing it? ... Great ... what do you need? ... A hundred thousand dollars for twenty per cent of the shares ... OK, give me your bank details and we can sort out the shares later ... no problem, it's a pleasure.'

Lucy tapped in the numbers again. 'This is great; who's next?'

John was already on the phone. 'Hey, William. It's John. Who's the person you said needed the wheelchair for their son?' ... No, I'm not kidding, William – get me the account number details ... where's it coming from? ... let's just say, diamonds are a boy's best friend.'

Lucy giggled. 'You kids gonna share it with us?' Mary said.

'We're doing a bit of recycling, Mary,' John said, grinning.

'Ma, when John says "recycling", what he actually means is laundering African conflict diamonds.'

Ma's face lit up. 'Conflict diamonds ... In that case there's a cause that matches perfectly: the Boston Safe-House for women suffering domestic violence. They get no government or state funds.'

'Could you ask them what their annual budget is, Ma?' John said.

John's phone buzzed. 'William, that was quick ... I know the chairs are expensive ... the details, yes ... thanks, William.'

Lucy sniffed while she pressed the 'send' button. Her eyes were full of tears. John kissed her temple. 'We're not even half done yet, sweetheart.

'I think some has to go the police charity for disabled ex-policemen and women injured in the course of duty,' John added. Some minutes later, he was handing Lucy the account details. 'How much?'

'Five hundred thousand,' John said. Lucy looked at him, eyebrows raised.

'Yep, they put their lives on the line every time they go out on the streets.'

'Can I play too?' James asked.

'Sure, you can. What you got in mind?' John asked.

'American Dog Rescue,' James said. 'That's where Andrew had to give my puppy when he tried to give it to me – when Matthew said he would kill it – you remember, Ma?'

Mary shuddered and put her hand on James's arm. 'I was going to call him Peter, after my brother – before Kelly burnt him, and killed him.'

Lucy frowned at James.

'Peter left his phone on when he went to see Kelly for the painting she promised him. I heard him being burnt down the phone.'

Mary started to weep. She buried her face in Lucy's shoulder, finally yielding to the accumulation of grief she had suppressed for three weeks.

As Lucy held her, she wondered how many more of her children Mary would lose.

John got up to ask reception if they could spare a box of tissues. When he turned round, Mary, James and Lucy were all huddled together, Lucy as tearful as Mary. Looking at Lucy at that moment, John was acutely aware of how much he loved her.

And then, the realisation hit him. The reason Lucy had refused the engagement ring was because she believed it was made from the three conflict diamonds he'd put into his pocket here in the Oaks Hotel.

I have to explain where the stones actually came from.

'Can I help you, Mr Baxter?'

'Oh, Alan, glad to see you. It seems we need a box of tissues,' he said, pointing to the tearful group thirty feet away.

'Oh, my ... whatever can be the matter?'

'It's quite a story, Alan. For now, we need tissues and a bottle of your very best house red – oh, and a lot of chocolate. Can you fix it, and bring it over?'

'Give me just a minute.'

John re-joined the group. 'Some comforts arrive soon,' he announced.

'You're very sweet, you two,' Mary said. 'You shouldn't have to put up with me like this.'

Lucy wiped her cheeks. 'You've had a horrible time, Ma. You shouldn't be alone.'

Alan Carmichael brought over a tray. He had arranged a box of tissues and large numbers of truffles on it, plus four wine glasses, all surrounding a bottle of red wine, which he proceeded to uncork.

'Enjoy. Compliments of the house,' he said, handing John the cork.

John looked him in the eye, sniffing the cork. 'Thank you, Alan.'

Then Ma's phone rang. 'Oh, Rose. How are you? ... Well, as a family we've had better times; I'm sure you've seen the news … Yes, we wanted to help the centre you run. We need your account details … I'll hang on a minute, yes.'

'See if you can get the annual budget, Ma,' Lucy said.

'Rose, what's the annual budget of the centre? … four hundred and twenty-five thousand … I think you'll find a modest donation tomorrow morning … it's no problem … look, I'll catch up next week, when I have a little more time to speak.'

Mary was smiling again. 'This *is* fun, isn't it?'

'Are you alright with this today, Ma?' Lucy enquired.

'Listen, this is exactly what I need. I need to feel there's some good in the world.'

'Well, there is, Ma, and you're sitting next to her,' John said. 'We still have the Dog Rescue.'

'Perhaps we could do some more tomorrow?' Lucy suggested. 'I think we've all had enough excitement recently. Let's go home and have some food.'

'Shall we get a Chinese?' James replied.

Lucy and John laughed.

Mary was curious. 'Am I missing something?'

'Ma, James is referring to the time Kelly and Simon bullied him into delivering a poisoned Chinese meal to us,' Lucy replied.

'She tried to poison you, Lucy – you and John?'

'You sound surprised, Ma. She came even closer to poisoning you.'

'Tortured,' James said.

Ma was curious. 'Jim?'

'Bullied is not right. I didn't want to do it. She had Jack and Simon hold me while she did the cigarette lighter thing again. She said she wanted to burn me herself. She said she would do it till I agreed to always do what she told me – for ever.'

'Oh, sweet Jesus,' Mary replied.

The mood was sombre as they climbed into Lucy's car for the ride back to Concord.

John interrupted the silence. 'Let's not do Chinese tonight. Sweetheart, I think it's high time your new kitchen is used properly. I will make us all jacket potatoes.'

'That sounds lovely,' Ma said. 'Some nice, hot comfort food to keep out the cold.'

84

Saturday – 10th November

Lucy awoke the next morning feeling refreshed, empowered and ready to begin new chapters. She looked across at John and knew she had never been this deeply in love.

His unique combination of sensitivity and strength delighted her. She relished his acknowledgement of her ability and that he was not threatened by it; he had even said that only really bright women had ever turned him on. She revelled in the double entendres they conjured together – sometimes in different languages. And she loved the mischief he incited in her.

John opened his eyes – and smiled at her.

'Do you feel loved, sweetheart?' he asked.

'I do.'

She and John descended the stairs together and entered Lucy's kitchen. As John laid the table for breakfast, Lucy wrote on a piece of paper. She folded the paper in half three times – and put it in the breast pocket of her blouse.

Mary walked into the kitchen, smiling.

Lucy kissed her and turned to John. 'You remember when we first met, I told you how Ma welcomed me into the family?'

'I do. You had some lovely chats. I remember you telling me at the Ritz.'

'Well, yes – but some of them were extremely intimate. I think it's perfect that she is here to witness my little note.'

Lucy pulled the note from her pocket and gave it to him. 'Read this side first,' she said.

He read the words aloud:

Your lover stands before you, a yearning in her heart.
She's ready for the world to know we'll never be apart.
Proudly and completely yours – your loving Lucy
– XXX XXX

John smiled. He leant over to kiss her.

Mary smiled at them. 'I've never seen two people so … coupled. I'm so happy for you.'

Lucy kissed him. 'Anyway – I know you like your crosswords, lover. So, there are two little clues for you on the back. I don't mind that Mary knows.'

Lucy darted a grin at Mary as John read out the clues.

'*Pray our love is mixed and that I've eaten too much chocolate.* 4, 4, 3.'

John smiled. 'Sounds interesting, sweetheart.'

She blushed as he read out the second clue.

'*Assume this busy lover ... gives you all you want. 4, 3-5, 7.*'

85

James entered the kitchen looking at his smartphone. 'The pollution from the burning of fossil fuels this year will kill more than three million worldwide – that's according to the World Health Organisation.'

Lucy peered over James's shoulder at his screen and put her arm around him as they looked at it together. 'In the USA, fossil fuel air pollution will kill more than twenty-eight thousand people prematurely this year.'

James was thinking. 'Two thousand eight hundred people died in the 9/11 attacks. So, that's ten 9/11 attacks each year.

'But the worldwide total deaths are three million. That's more than one thousand 9/11 attacks each year – three every day, of every year. And that's not including the damage done by global warming and the rise in sea levels.'

John shook his head. 'It's time I explain my wind farms in Scotland. Most people know that CO_2 causes global warming; more than two thousand universities have been collecting data on temperatures for more than fifty years all over the world. Global temperatures do go through cycles, it's true. We can quantify carbon dioxide levels in ancient ice at the ice caps. But temperature rises in the last fifty years have been a hundred times faster than at any time in the last hundred thousand years. So the cycle argument doesn't cut it.

'But it's more urgent we cut CO_2 than most people think …'

'Why?'

'CO_2 gets us to what climatologists call the tipping point. It warms the planet to the point where water evaporates off the oceans much faster. Oceans occupy seventy per cent of the earth's surface, so this accelerated evaporation is very powerful – and creates storms like Katrina, and Sandy. Water vapour in the atmosphere traps heat twenty times faster than CO_2. So once CO_2 has got us to the tipping point, water vapour will do the real lasting damage far faster than CO_2 alone. But even beyond the tipping point, CO_2 continues to warm the atmosphere. The resulting vicious circle gets completely out of our control. Our ecosystems may just be able to tolerate 1.5 degrees centigrade more warming. But 2 centigrade is *way* too much – and our targets for CO_2 reduction are *way* too relaxed.'

'Wow,' Lucy said.

'Climate change deniers remind me of the tobacco industry – the only people who deny smoking damages your health are people selling tobacco.'

Lucy was thinking. 'I don't believe the Blacks give a damn.'

The Dog rescue phoned back. 'James – you tell us – if the Dog Rescue needs five hundred thousand dollars a year to keep going, how much should we give them?'

'Two hundred and fifty thousand. We can do more next year if there's any money left over.'

John smiled at Lucy, who was pressing her 'send' button again.

'James, I think there'll be even more next year,' he said.

'What are you cooking?' Lucy asked.

'Sweetheart, the baking has been done. But I need you, James and Mary to tell me if it's any good.'

Mary smiled at John. 'Oh, good. I've baked a bit in my time, as I think you know.'

OK – the ingredients – we have thirty thousand air pollution deaths in the US each year. We have two million dollars still to spend from the diamonds. We have the New York Art School for kids who don't have the fees for a college education. We own enough art to inspire a generation of young artists. And – we still have an original Norman Rockwell in the hall by the front door, worth at least eight million dollars.'

'I knew there was something going on yesterday,' Lucy frowned.

'Apparently, the trial piece of wood mistakenly made its way into the crate – and not the painting. I don't know how that confusion could have taken place, Judge, except that there were phone calls coming in all the time. George called, etcetera. Between the police and myself, we must have made a mistake.'

'So – we really are art robbers, after all.'

'Not exactly. I talked to the curator at the Norman Rockwell Museum, Dr Rashadi. I offered him an idea. We return the original JFK to him immediately – we replace the copy that Billy put in its place in the second break-in. Status quo restored. As we know, you can't get hold of an original Rockwell these days unless you're either super-rich or acting on behalf of a large corporation. We take the copy Lucy has in her office, and the copy still hanging in the Rockwell Museum. We then sell the two copies and raise about two million dollars.

'Dr Rashadi asked me what the two million could be used for. I told him it was common knowledge that Rockwell liked to portray America in an idealised way. I suggested we set up two funds. The first, The Norman Rockwell Environmental Fund, to promote the use of renewable energy – the second, for the New York Art School for scholarships so that more kids can study art.

'He'd been thinking overnight about my suggestion. He didn't want any copies to be in circulation; it reduces the value of the Rockwell brand. He would seek the permission of The Rockwell Trust to sell the original, for its full value – roughly eight million dollars – if it was to be used exclusively for art scholarships and a Rockwell environmental campaign. He was excited about promoting renewable energy.'

John paused. 'What's wrong?' Lucy asked.

'Nothing's wrong – luckily. Dr Rashadi asked me if I was related to the sponsor of the Baxter Laboratory at the National Gallery. He'd visited the gallery and been very impressed with all the equipment. He implied that if I was related, it could sway the decision of his boss.'

'Ma – John donated two and a half million dollars to the laboratory to purchase state-of-the-art equipment for analysis. It's how we revealed the Cropsey you gave me.'

Ma looked at Lucy. 'I like this man, Lucy. He's a keeper.'

John continued. 'Anyway, Rashadi liked the general idea, but he had to ensure the robbery could not happen again.'

'Seems fair,' Lucy said. 'They can't be getting robbed every three weeks.'

'Exactly. So Rashadi asked me to confirm the identity of a man in a photo he had obtained. I told him I'd be delighted if it helped release a painting that could achieve so much. He emailed me the photo this morning. Guess who the photo was.'

'Go on,' Mary said.

'Billy. I knew the police already had Billy for the Rockwell robbery, so I thought nothing more of it.'

'Seems odd, though. If the police already have him in custody for robbery, why would this Dr Rashadi want confirmation?' Lucy asked. 'Anyway, the cake tastes pretty good to me. I guess it's going to come down to whether the Trust goes for it.'

John grinned.

'There's something else isn't there? I know that look,' Lucy said.

John nodded. 'Rashadi and I agreed that the original of JFK should fetch between eight and twelve million dollars. Norman Rockwell was brought up and educated in New York State. He only came to live in Massachusetts in his early adult life. I suggested Rashadi tell his boss at the Trust that he had negotiated something else into the deal with us.

'Rashadi will tell the Trust he persuaded me to set up a second laboratory either in New York State or in Massachusetts. It would restore paintings and be as well-equipped as the one in London. The technology would enable a degree of forensic examination of paintings in the US not possible at the moment. This would enable them to identify copies of paintings definitively. It would be state-of-the-art – and a major deterrent to copying.'

'The icing on the cake,' Mary said.

388

'So we'll have millions more to give these charities then, John?' Lucy asked.

'Between five and eight million, after we've set up the laboratory.'

'I'm so proud of you, Mr Baxter. I love this cake. What do you think, James?' Lucy asked.

'If the original JFK's back in the museum, then the police will just leave it there so everyone can look at it. If they'd got it yesterday, they'd have it locked away till the trial. Pictures should be looked at.'

'Isn't that exactly the point?' John smiled.

Lucy's face lit up. 'Ma – you talk about the icing on the cake. I'll have to talk to our corporate lawyers in London on this – but if I remember rightly, corporate malfeasance on this scale could prompt shareholders to force a restructure of Black Industries. With the two largest shareholders, Old Man Black and Kelly, now unable to vote, we have the potential to force changes in the objectives of the company.'

Lucy paused, a Mona Lisa smile on her face.

'What's in that beautiful head of yours, sweetheart?' John smiled.

'John, the names in Senator Black's notebook implicate eight other senators and two members of the Supreme Court. If that information got out, careers would end. More importantly, the balance in the Senate would change completely. The old white climate change deniers you mentioned would be less and less the issue; they lose their votes in Congress and the Senate if they're in jail.'

Lucy paused.

'I think I love where this is going,' John smiled.

'What if, under threat of prosecution, the crucial members of the board of Black Industries could be forced to restructure the company as an energy generator, not an oil and coal producer? The land they've decimated in Montana and Wyoming could be used for huge solar parks and wind farms. The shareholders could be issued shares at an initial offer price guaranteed to create huge returns. They would get shares in the new company in the same proportion they hold shares in Black Industries.'

'It's brilliant. But what if this could be repeated elsewhere in other fossil fuel producers all over the world?' John replied.

Ma's eyes were filling with tears.

'What's the matter, Ma?' Lucy asked.

'Lucy, do you remember my coded note you found in the Zen chapel in Venice?'

'Yes, of course.'

'Do you remember the last bit – where I said I thought that the world would be a better and cleaner place for your time in it?'

'Oh, Ma – you're so sweet – you've always had so much faith in me … come to think of it … I know just the legal team who could make it happen.'

Ma was grinning. 'Lucy, with what you've overcome in the last few weeks, somehow I have no doubt you can achieve this – and the world will be a better place.'

Lucy kissed Mary – then sat down, thinking …

There are three crucial lawyers – who are owed favours by a lot of people.

Mark Foster called to tell Lucy and John they would be free to go to England as soon as they could make full statements to the police.

'One thing is bothering me,' Ma said. 'Won't Mark Foster get annoyed when he discovers the painting is not in police possession?'

'Not when he discovers we lodged five hundred thousand dollars into the police charity, Ma,' John replied, keeping a straight face.

Lucy smiled. *That proactivity has kept us alive these last few weeks.*

John continued. 'And – can you imagine how pleased Foster will be when he finds out the new laboratory can be used to clean up the art fraud? This cannot harm his career in the police.'

Lucy's home phone interrupted them.

'Yes, Tom … Autumn … thank you … and you have sixteen senators and counting and eight congressmen, so far. That's great, Tom. Let me know of any other progress … Yes, Mary is sat with us. Thanks, Tom.'

Mary talked to Tom for a while, her blush gradually deepening. At the end of the call, she turned to Lucy. 'I think he does like me.'

'*Finally*,' James said.

John looked at them in turn. 'In that case, we should celebrate. Lucy seems to have enrolled the help of several leading environmentalists and Tom fancies Mary.'

'And …' Lucy said, 'Tom says he is delivering Cropsey's Autumn today – he's had it cleaned and packed. He wants no money for it – it's a gift, a thank you for saving his life. Apparently, the whisky he poured that night *was* poisoned.'

'You're kidding, sweetheart – great result! That's the whole set, finally! Wow – all four seasons – I can hardly believe it. You saved my life too then, sweetheart. Whatever can I do to repay you?'

Lucy whispered in his ear. 'You know very well what I want – and you can do it in the sea.'

'I do,' he replied.

He switched on the TV news – and the mood in the kitchen changed rapidly. There was news of a local prison break. Mary, Lucy, James and John watched spellbound as a reporter mentioned the name, Billy Black.

Lucy looked at John in horror. 'Great, that's all we need – Billy angry and out of jail.'

86

An hour earlier, Billy Black had been pacing nervously in the exercise yard of Massachusetts' Walpole Prison. His transfer from Boston Police Station had been organised when Chief Detective Ritchey recorded – falsely – that all holding cells were full. Billy watched as the prison staff in the exercise yard were called inside. The prison governor had convened an emergency meeting after receiving a call warning of a security risk.

Then he heard it – the unmistakable sound of a helicopter. Billy's heart was thumping as the helicopter approached and moved over the exercise yard. A rope with a loop in its end dropped down. Billy ran for it and secured his foot into the loop as the helicopter swept away to the north.

Twenty minutes later, Billy was lowered into the hands of two enormous men. He was handcuffed, blindfolded, shuffled into a black limousine and driven away. He could feel the presence of the men who had handcuffed him, seated either side of him.

'Where we headed?' he asked. 'Kelly never mentioned anything about all this. She just said she would get me out of jail.'

'You're our guest for a day or so, at least until the search dies down,' the driver replied.

'Who's we?' Billy asked.

'You'll see soon enough.'

Billy was hauled out of the car. The cold air of the Massachusetts fall was replaced by the warmth of a log fire. He heard a door shut out the cold. He was placed in a heavy wooden chair, a piece of rope immediately securing his neck to its high back.

'What's going on?' Billy heard the high-pitched zipping noise of cable ties as his wrists and ankles were tied to the arms and legs of the chair.

Billy wrestled with the ties, but they were far too strong and cut into his flesh painfully. He could feel panic rising in his chest.

Someone took his blindfold off. His lover, Leila, was shackled, facing the wall in front of him, stripped to the waist. Dr Rashadi walked into the room. Leila started pleading for mercy.

'Please, no, Artin. I will do anything. Please not this – anything but this.'

'Do you know what happens to unfaithful wives in my country, Mr Black?'

Billy said nothing.

'I thought not. I have decided not to take her home to be stoned to death. I have taken responsibility for her punishment myself. But you can watch what you have caused.'

Rashadi disappeared behind Billy for a few seconds and re-appeared with a heavy bamboo cane, six feet long. 'I did some research, Mr Black. You have caused many more than one wife to be unfaithful. You are about to see the consequences.'

Dr Rashadi placed the bamboo on Leila's back. 'Can you imagine what her back will look like in thirty minutes, Mr Black – after the bamboo has started to split lengthways?'

'Oh, god,' Billy pleaded. 'Please let her be. She will be a good wife.'

'Quite the noble lover, then, Mr Black? Well, then I will give you the chance to take her punishment in her place. One of you has to be punished. Who is it to be … my wife or you?'

Billy looked at the cane lying across his lover's back. He had seen images of the open cuts inflicted by the razor-sharp edges of bamboo canes splitting lengthways after several heavy impacts. Billy shook his head in silent panic.

'Well, Mr Black, who is it to be? Will you, for once in your life, put someone else's welfare before your own? Or will you, as usual, take the selfish path?'

Billy could say nothing.

'I thought so,' Rashadi continued. 'That is unfortunate for you – most unfortunate.'

Dr Rashadi pushed a trolley towards Billy, its top tray covered in a white linen cloth. He took off his jacket and put on a crisp white lab coat.

'You have stolen art, jewellery, Rockwell paintings from my museum, a US senator's wife, and now my wife. Oh, and Kelly specifically asked me to mention the emerald necklace you stole from her mother.'

'I'm going to kill that Kelly with my own bare hands,' Billy hissed.

'One thing I can promise you,' Rashadi said, as he pulled the linen cloth from the trolley. 'It won't be with your own hands.'

Billy gazed in horror at the trolley.

'My research told me you are a carpenter, Mr Black. So you will appreciate the tools I have assembled.'

'Oh, sweet Jesus, no. Please, no. I'll do anything. Please not my hands. I can pay you in compensation – anything you want. Please.'

Dr Rashadi adjusted the laptop slightly. 'As you can see, Kelly is with us. She specifically asked that the operation be filmed, live. She wanted to get a real feeling of being there with you to share these special moments.'

Kelly interrupted via the weblink. 'Hi, Billy. This is to reward you for stealing the necklace and the hundred diamonds from my house. We'll be recording sound too, so feel free to scream as much as you wish. It will make the operation much more interesting when we put it out on the internet.'

'Oh, see Billy,' Rashadi cut in. 'You can see Detective Ritchey sitting with her in her police cell on their webcam.

'My medical degree was done some time ago. I confess, I forgot to arrange any anaesthetic. The tools might seem a little crude to you, Mr Black. But since you appeal to a Jesus whose values you have forsaken, I think it appropriate that you are fixed to the chair for the operation in exactly the same way he was fixed to the cross.

Rashadi picked up one of the two six-inch nails and a hammer. 'Jesus was also a carpenter, Mr Black. Don't you find that ironic?'

Billy looked up, as if to appeal to some god he had long since left behind.

No please, not this. Jesus, please. Not this.

Rashadi placed the tip of the six-inch nail on the back of Billy's right hand. He placed the hammer slowly to the head of the nail.

'Yet again, Mr Black, you place your focus on the short term. By looking at the nail, you take your eyes from what will do real lasting damage – the saw. Yet again, you fail to see the greater harm done a little later. Can you see the parallels, Mr Black?'

'I'm sorry, I'm sorry, I'm so sorry. Please.'

'You have made your bed – but with other men's wives. You now have to lie in it. Once again, you put yourself before all others. You did not respect your own wife, the senator and his marriage, or my marriage. And like all the people involved in the dirty coal and oil industry, you enjoy the financial benefits that come from the suffering and death of thousands of people every year – not to mention the damage to the world's ecosystems. This is the ultimate selfishness. Your life embodies this selfishness perfectly.'

Rashadi paused. 'Anyway – now you have chosen to let Leila take the punishment, I can tell you I never had any intention of punishing my wife so severely. We will have meaningful discussions, her and I, but that is light-years away from what would happen to her at home.'

'I'm going to be sick,' Billy said.

'Well. Mr Black. I have decided to show you the compassion that was denied your carpenter friend. I am not going to take your hands, and your living. But I will make you a promise – a kind of suspended sentence for both your hands, and your feet. If I hear you have been near another man's wife, I will make sure no woman on earth would ever want you near them.'

'Thank you.'

'Don't thank me yet, Mr Black. The next thirty minutes will be the most painful of your entire life. And just in case Leila is tempted to stray with other men – she is unlikely ever to forget your screams.'

Rashadi looked at the webcam. Kelly was smiling.

'Your persistent infidelity, Mr Billy Black, seems to suggest we start with your wedding ring finger.'

Rashadi took hold of Billy's finger with his left hand – and the pliers with his right.

'Oh, god,' Billy whimpered.

Twenty-four hours later, a black limousine, its licence plates removed, pulled up outside Walpole Prison. The door opened and Billy Black fell out. The driver pulled him to his feet – and stuck a clear polythene bag between Billy's teeth. It contained all ten of his fingernails.

87

Sunday – 11th November

Lucy entered the nail salon on Newbury Street in Boston. It was the first of several appointments that day; she wanted to look her best when she returned to England to meet Mrs Markham with John and Mary.

John liked her long hair – so to please him she wanted it trimmed, not cut as much as usual. But the appointment she anticipated most eagerly was with Jandri Noewi, who had agreed to fly across the US to meet her. Lucy knew something of her work from the painting above John's bed in England. She grinned as she anticipated the piece she would commission Jandri to do.

Annabel started to make small talk as she took Lucy's hand in hers. 'I don't think we've seen you here in months,' she said.

Lucy smiled at her range of possible answers. 'No. I only come down here to watch art robberies and pose nude for artists these days.'

Annabel looked at Lucy uneasily. They were sitting only four doors away from the Sunset Gallery that Lucy had watched being robbed three weeks ago.

'I watched it happen,' Lucy said. 'We just happened on it – and we knew the robbers.'

Annabel looked at Lucy. 'You should get a job as a comedienne; you're really good – keeping a straight face and everything.'

But Lucy could sense Annabel's discomfort. 'Don't worry – they've caught the robbers now – we made sure of that.'

'Who's we?' Annabel asked.

'Oh, the man I'm having the naughty painting done for.'

'Honestly, I've heard some stories in here – but that really is original.'

'Funny you say that – someone else said that to us recently,' Lucy replied.

'No kidding.'

Two hours later, Lucy made her way to The Oaks Hotel where she had booked a room for the afternoon. Jandri was waiting for her in reception when she arrived.

Lucy smiled at her, recognising Jandri's face from her website. 'Shall we go up; I have a room with lots of light – it's a corner room with windows on two different walls.'

'Sounds perfect,' Jandri said, smiling.

'Thank you for coming,' Lucy said as they exited the lift. 'You've come a long way. Would you like some coffee or something to eat?'

'No, thanks. I just ate. I knew you only had an hour. We can get started straight away.'

Jandri set the camera up on the tripod. 'You told me the kind of picture you wanted.

'I think we should take some photos as you undress. You may find them as much of a turn-on as the final painting – especially if you look at them with him.'

Lucy smiled. 'Shall I start slowly then?'

Jandri watched closely as Lucy crossed her arms over her chest and pulled her roll-neck sweater slowly over her head.

'What's the matter, Jandri?'

'Nothing, honey,' she smiled. 'Maybe I'm bi, after all.'

88

Mary, Lucy and John were in the VIP lounge at Logan International, waiting for their flight to London's Heathrow. James had gone in search of chocolate.

Lucy was pensive. 'I'm so looking forward to meeting Mrs Markham. John, you must be excited.'

John's phone buzzed. 'John, it's Tom. Can you speak?'

'Tom, let me move a little nearer the window; the signal's a bit iffy.' John moved away from the women, sensing Tom's need for privacy.

'John, you probably know, I kind of like Mary ... I mean ...'

'Tom, you don't have to explain. She's a very attractive woman.'

'Well, what I'm trying to ask is ... I don't know if I am getting the right signals – what with all the upset at the ranch recently?'

'Tom, you're right, she's had a hell of a year. Just be patient. If you can do that – I can tell you she's extremely warm-hearted and highly intelligent – well worth waiting for, if you ask me.'

'Thanks, John. I think Mary's great. Let's get together for that dram when you're back.'

'Tom, just before you go – what exactly happened the night that Old Man Black was killed?'

'You weren't there at the State House that night, but if you'd seen the hatred in Kelly's eyes when she saw Patricia with the necklace, you'd have come to the same conclusion I did.

'I've seen only one necklace as beautiful as that one – and I've seen some beauties in my time at these functions. The only

400

time I'd seen that necklace was round the neck of Mary Black on their anniversary. So I knew something was wrong.

'Anyway, Patricia wanted interviews with The Old Man and myself. She put her business cards in our lapel pockets. As she put her card in my pocket, I just caught a glimpse of some writing on the back of it. When John and I got to the men's room, I left my card with him as he stood at the basin. I went into a cubicle, pretending I needed to. I must have had my back turned to him for about five seconds or so. I opened my cubicle door a little to see what he would do. I could see him put the cards face up again. So I knew he'd looked at the backs. When I emerged from the booth, he handed me one of the cards. As I followed him out of the men's room and his back was towards me, I looked at the card he'd given me and there was nothing on the back.

'I knew he'd taken the card with the date on the back. I thought, if he's that desperate – let him have the date. I was not about to ruin the fundraiser by causing a scene that night.'

'So Old Man Black was in the hotel room, instead of you. Effectively then, Kelly had her own father killed,' John said.

'Very effectively.'

Lucy watched John tuck his phone into his inside jacket pocket and walk back towards her. She loved his enthusiasm, his strength, the fact that he was five inches taller than her, his unconscious competence, his humour.

John's phone buzzed again.

'It's George, Mr Baxter. I have a couple of bits of news. I don't want you to get alarmed because we have the situation under control.'

George paused, knowing how his news would land. 'Kelly Black escaped police custody while she was being taken away from the house in Concord.'

'What? We thought Kelly and Adams were in the police van.'

Lucy looked at John, her eyes wide with horror.

'I know. He was so embarrassed, he didn't want me to tell you – especially with all the trouble we'd gone to in getting her locked up. You should watch the playback of the CCTV over the front door.'

'OK, George – but we're at the airport and we can't run the CCTV back where we are.'

Lucy was puzzled. 'What CCTV?'

'The CCTV above your front door.'

'Yes, we can,' Lucy asserted, her body tightening with thoughts of what Kelly might do to her children.

'Someone's got to kill her.' Lucy took a deep breath. 'Let's play it back. The CCTV is all stored in the cloud. All I have to do is put the password in and we can see it all.'

John held his phone to his ear again. 'George – let us look at the footage and we'll come straight back to you.'

Lucy accessed the website and tapped in her passcode. It took her only a few seconds to enter the time and date of the recording.

'This should be about right,' she said.

The four of them watched the recording play back on Lucy's laptop.

Kelly and Paul Adams were handcuffed and led out of the house by Mark Foster and his assistant, Sanchez. Kelly glanced at her car, seeing the keys still in the ignition. She positioned herself so that Adams could reach beneath her skirt, his back towards her, and retrieve the gun strapped to her thigh. He pointed it sideways at Foster and Sanchez.

'Get your hands up, both of you,' he snarled.

Their guns long since back in their holsters, and with safety catches engaged, Foster and Sanchez had little option but to obey.

'Now take your guns and place them very slowly on the ground – very slowly – any tricks and I kill both of you.'

Sanchez looked at Mark for any ideas.

'Do as he says.'

'And do it now,' Adams barked.

The two officers slowly placed their guns on the ground.

'Kick the guns to me.'

Foster nodded to Sanchez. They kicked the guns towards Adams and Kelly.

'Now – unlock these handcuffs before Adams here shoots you dead.'

Sanchez unlocked the cuffs on Kelly's wrists.

'Now unlock his,' she hissed.

Foster uncuffed Adams who picked up the officers' guns with his free hand.

'Get on the ground, pigs, or I'll drop you right now,' Adams ordered.

Foster and Sanchez lay on the ground. Kelly opened her car door and climbed into the driver's seat. She turned the keys in the ignition – nothing. She tried again – not even the slightest noise from the engine.

She got out of the car.

'Think you're clever do you,' she said to Foster. 'We'll take your van then.'

Kelly moved to the side of the van, checked the keys were in the ignition and sat in the driver's seat. Before closing the door, she lowered the window to keep one gun pointing at the officers still prostrate on the ground.

'Get in Paul, we're leaving,' she said, starting the engine.

Adams, keeping his gun trained on the two police officers, walked to the passenger side of the van and climbed in. Kelly eased the van out of the driveway and drove off in the direction of Boston.

The two officers got to their feet. They stood – trying to come to terms with what had just happened.

Lucy's face had dismay and disbelief written all over it. 'So – after all the planning – Kelly is still on the loose, and armed with three loaded guns, and only two hours' drive from Mark and Oliver. I can't get on this flight, John. I need her cold and dead. *Very cold and very dead.*'

89

Lucy's phone pinged with a message from a phone not recognised by her own.

She and John gazed in horror as the video clip started.

Billy was sitting, his wrists and ankles tightly secured to a heavy chair with cable ties half an inch wide.

Rashadi took hold of Billy's wedding ring finger with his left hand. He held up the pliers with his right so that Billy and the webcam viewers would anticipate his imminent ordeal. Rashadi clamped the pliers to Billy's fingernail. Looking him in the eyes, he slowly drew Billy's first nail from his finger. Billy's head jerked back with the pain as he screamed at the top of his voice.

Rashadi held up the nail to the camera. 'As you can see, the nail-bed bleeds quite badly. Most nails grow back imperfectly after this treatment. It will act as a kind of permanent reminder to him. And as you can hear, it's extremely painful … Still … only another nine to go.'

They watched as Billy cried with the pain – and the horror of what was still to come.

Lucy's body tightened with tension, her face turning white.

The last thing Lucy remembered before blacking out was John's arms around her preventing her sliding off her seat onto the floor.

John looked at Mary. 'Could you get some water, Ma?'

Mary strode towards the juice bar.

Kelly cannot be my daughter. No daughter of mine could ever do that to another human being. If she can do that to her own brother, what could she do to Lucy and the kids?

John picked Lucy's phone up from the floor. A few seconds later, Lucy regained consciousness. She took her phone from John, read Kelly's text – and cried out in alarm.

This is what awaits Mark, Oliver, Charlotte and Emma. By the time you get this message, my men will be on their way to them. Next time you see them, I will be in posses-sion of all forty of their fingernails. This will continue all their lives. You have condemned each of them and yourself to a life of permanent fear. Sometime in the future, and you'll never know when, I will call on you. By the time I've finished, you will wish it had been my brother with his cigarette lighter. Imagine what a blowtorch can do to eyeballs – yours, and those of your kids. I have left instructions and huge rewards so that this will NEVER stop, even after your death.

Lucy's fists tightened. '*I am going to kill her – I'll kill her myself.*'

She dialled Mark. 'Mark, are you and Oliver still up in Concord?'

'Yes, Mom. We were going back down to Farmington tonight. Why?'

'Get yourself and Oliver into the strongbox, NOW… Please don't ask questions, just do it now … yes, NOW.'

'But why the urgency?'

'FOR CHRIST'S SAKE – DON'T ARGUE – JUST GET IN THERE – NOW.'

'OK, OK. I'll get him.'

'I'll call you in two minutes when you're inside.'

John dialled Charlotte, as Lucy texted Oliver. 'Sweetheart, are you and Emma at home?'

'Yes, Dad; it's nine o'clock.'

'Are the gates on the driveway shut?'

'Yes, Dad; they shut automatically.'

'Good, I'm just checking. Listen, sweetheart. I know tomorrow's Monday and you have school and everything, but this is serious, do you understand?'

'What's going on?'

406

'Charlotte – you and Emma are not to leave the house till I get there. Is that clear?'

'But why, what's going on?'

'All I can say is that Lucy and I have had threats made to all of us. It's very important you don't leave the house. I'll be back inside forty-eight hours. Do not open the doors or windows to anyone, no matter how credible they sound. Is that clear?'

'Yes, Dad. But what happens when my ASOS order comes?'

'Do NOT open the gate; the ASOS person will not be who you think it is. They will have to use the intercom from outside the gate. Just tell them to leave the parcel outside. Do not let them inside the gates. Is that clear?'

'But what about school? They'll wonder where we are.'

'I'll talk to them. You just stay put till I've handled this. I'll be back in a couple of days. No one gets in or out of the house. Keep the gates and the doors and windows locked. Do you get how serious this is?'

'Yes, Dad.'

'Will you tell Emma everything I've said?'

'Yes, but you know what she's like.'

'Sweetheart, this is life or death. Do I have to speak to her – or can you tell her how serious I am?'

'Actually, you can tell her 'cos she's in the kitchen with me now.'

Lucy was on her feet, agitated. 'I can't leave Mark and Oliver here in the States, especially locked up in the strongbox. I have to get back to them.'

John nodded. 'Let's get the limo back – Steve can take us back to Concord. Where's James, Mary?'

Lucy dialled Mark to make sure he and his brother were in the strongbox. 'Mark, we're coming back to Concord. We should be there in an hour or so. Just stay put, sweetie. Open the door to no one even if it's my voice telling you to. I have the combination. No one else does. Open the door to nobody – they might have a recording of my voice. You got it?'

90

Lucy, John, Mary and James sat in the VIP lounge waiting for Steve to return with the limo. Lucy was gazing out of the window watching the evening sun drop towards the Boston skyline. John held her hand and sensed something had changed. He looked at her, tears descending her cheeks. He squeezed her hand three times and said nothing. She continued looking out of the window, not engaging with him.

'I was going to say this privately, John, except that the whole family are involved – and I include Charlotte and Emma in that.

'We can't continue. This situation, Charlotte and Emma imprisoned in Esher – my two imprisoned in Concord, three and a half thousand miles separated – you needed in Esher – me needed here in New England – it's all too difficult logistically. As long as she is free, this won't stop; Kelly has other assassins, apart from Adams.

'The whole relationship endangers all of us. I realise now I'm being selfish. It's putting all our lives in danger, including yours, John. What good is either of us to our kids if we're dead? I'm so sorry, John. I'm so sorry.

'I think you have to go back to Esher – get your lives back to normal – get safe again.'

John put his arm around her.

He said nothing for a few moments. 'And it's selfish of me to put you and your guys in fear all the time. That's no life for anyone; you all deserve better. You don't need me – you didn't need me before – you were all doing great – and you certainly don't need this. Our relationship has probably even put your life in danger too, Mary. I'm so sorry. I never meant for any of this.'

John stood up and walked the five or six steps to the window. He stared out into the dusk. He knew he would love Lucy to the end of his life, wonder what she was doing, whether she was well, whether she had found happiness, whether she ever thought of him, whether any of their time together had meant anything to her. He knew he would carry her with him when he woke in the morning, when he laid down his head at night.

His tears started to fall. He had no thought of hiding them. This was the defining moment of his life. Pride did not matter. It was about saving the people he and Lucy loved.

He decided not to make it any more difficult for her than it had to be. He had to leave her in Boston. It would be selfish to drag it out. She deserved better. He would rebuild his life with Charlotte and Emma – thank heavens for them.

So, this was a dream after all – just as he'd suspected. He had never deserved a life with such a caring, loving, intelligent goddess; his selfishness in jeopardising their lives proved it.

John returned to the table. 'You're right; we have to be with our kids. You have to let Mark and Oliver out of the strongbox; they can't stay in there. And I have to be with Charlotte and Emma. I'll get on the flight we booked. You get back to Concord ... I just want you to know – I will never stop loving you as long as I live.'

'Hold me, John.' Lucy put her head into his shoulder and sobbed. 'And I know I will never stop loving you.'

91

Steve drew up just outside the arrivals hall. He stepped out of his limousine and watched Mary, Lucy and James approach.

'No Mr John?' he asked Lucy.

'No, Steve, no Mr John,' she replied.

It seemed so final to be saying it. As they handed their suitcases for Steve to load into the trunk, Delta flight 004 took off over their heads.

Lucy knew it contained one very special passenger. She broke into tears again.

There goes the man – with my heart. I will never be able to give it to anyone else.

They seated themselves in the limo. Lucy buried her head in Mary's shoulder, as she had on several occasions in the past. Mary knew no words could ease the pain. Her own tears fell silently but prolifically into Lucy's hair.

They rode in the darkness – darkness which seemed to symbolise her future. Where was the light, the hope of any kind of love, the possibility of the life she wanted with him? Where was the dream of what they could have been together, the places they had talked of visiting, the exploration of themselves in the relationship?

Would she ever see him again? Would it be too painful? Would he be thinking of her when he went to auctions, when he got back to his home to see his children, when he lay down his head for the night?

'Oh, Ma – what am I going to do?'

They continued in silence, gazing out of the windows. Mary held Lucy's hand as they negotiated the late evening traffic. James had been silent. He looked at the small mesh pouch loaded with Steve's business cards. Through the mesh he could see Steve's name.

'Ma, do you think Steve knows he has the same name as the guy who just ran the Olympic qualifying time in the four-hundred metres?'

'What do you mean, James?' Ma replied.

'Steve Freeman – that's a coincidence isn't it. He has the same name as the runner from the Bahamas.'

A few seconds later, Lucy wiped her eyes. 'Sorry James, I was miles away. Say that again?'

'Freeman – it's the same name as the runner guy from the Bahamas,' James said.

'What do you mean, James?'

'Look – Steve Freeman.' He handed Lucy one of the cards.

'I know, James. I have one of his cards at home.'

Steve had overheard the conversation. 'I hope you don't mind me interrupting, Miss Lucy, but that young man is my nephew. He just got a scholarship to Miami Dade – and that was just after an injury. He's four years ahead of his age group apparently. My brother, Joseph – he says all his son can talk about is winning a gold medal in the 2016 Olympics.'

Lucy smiled. 'That is good news, Steve. That sounds really hopeful.'

She turned to James. 'So there's your answer, James. Well spotted.'

James smiled his satisfaction and relaxed back in his seat.

They rode for another five minutes. Again, it was James who broke the silence.

'So where did Kelly go after she got away in the police van?'

Mary looked at Lucy, knowing James had touched the rawest nerve possible.

James continued. 'Everyone knows Kelly did the murders. So why can't the rest of the police in Boston find her and put her in jail? Why don't we call George?'

Lucy sat up straight with the sudden realisation that George could be in danger from Kelly and her assassin.

Lucy dialled George, hoping he had not switched his phone off for the night.

'Mrs Howard. I was hoping you'd call. You were going to call me back after watching the CCTV above the front door. I assume you've seen it.'

'Yes, George. It's caused quite a lot of upset – to say the least. James has just asked why the Boston Police can't go and find Kelly.'

412

'In that case, Mrs Howard, you might want to put me on speaker so you can all hear.'

Lucy pushed the little green speaker icon. 'OK, George, go ahead.'

'OK. As you guessed, I'd taken the distributor head out of Kelly's car. It's handy when you're dealing with vehicles that may be recovered by their owners after a crime. But that way, Kelly would have to use the police van.

'What Foster and Sanchez didn't know is that I made some mods to their van when they turned up to collect Kelly the next morning. While they were doing the negotiation upstairs, I took out a bit of insurance.

'I put a tracker under each of the front wheel arches of the van. Belt and braces, I think you call it in England – and I made one slight mod to the engine. Whenever the gearbox was first put into neutral or park after being driven away, the engine was going to cut out and the doors would be electronically locked. Normally, you can lock the doors from the dashboard on police vans. I just modified it so it wouldn't release from the switch in the front of the van. The main reason I wanted them in the van is that the glass is bulletproof – which works both ways. You can't break out using bullets.'

'So you disabled the van and locked her in it,' Lucy replied.

'I was hoping it would be Foster driving the van away, with Kelly and Adams in the back. I was going to follow the van and wait for the backup call from Foster when he realised he couldn't get out. In the end, I had to follow Kelly – so I took Foster and Sanchez with me while tailing her back to her place.

'By the time we'd followed her back into Boston, I guessed she'd need her passport. It was simple for Mark to arrange a

413

police ambush up at Beacon Hill and for me to get her out of the van. By the time Kelly had parked outside her place there were six or seven officers in unmarked cars, with machine pistols to take her into custody from there. I saw her and Adams locked into police cells with my own eyes – partly 'cos I knew you would ask me that question.'

Lucy broke into tears, unable to speak.

'Hello ... hello... Mrs Howard ... are you still there ... Mrs Howard ...'

'Yes, George. I'm sorry. Well done! You don't know what this means – I'll never be able to thank you enough – thank you so much.'

'Actually, ma'am, these last few weeks has been the most gratifying I can ever remember. And with the recent bonuses Mr Baxter paid me recently – I will always be in your debt.'

'Hold on a minute, George. You said bonuses. I knew about one bonus. He did another one?'

'Yes, I thought you knew. Just after he boarded the plane an hour ago, he called me to say he was travelling back to England on his own. He thanked me for everything – said he thought it was unlikely he would see me again. He was going to put enough money in my bank so that I could look after you and your children for the rest of your lives – whatever happened to him.'

'George – is it too indelicate to ask how much this second bonus was?'

'No, Mrs Howard. It was ten million dollars. He wanted to make sure we could use that military outfit – I think he said they were called A–Z Security. He said you used them for your divorce settlement meeting – he wanted us to be able to pay for them whenever we needed them. He wanted me to look after Mary and James as well.'

Lucy started crying again. James covered his face with his hands, his shoulders heaving in great heavy sobs.

'Mrs Howard … Mrs Howard?'

'George … I don't know what to say … except thank you, thank you.'

'My pleasure. I guess I'll be seeing you around then.'

'Actually, the kids are in the strongbox. Mary, James and I are coming back to Concord. George … I think if John were here, he'd say we have to be prepared for other surprises Kelly may have in store for us.'

Lucy ended the call to George, wiping the tears from her face. She turned to Mary.

'The crazy thing is, John doesn't know Kelly's in jail – and there's no way to tell him for at least another six hours.'

'You can stick 'im a text – so when he turns his phone off flight mode, he gets it while he's still at the airport in London,' James remarked.

Lucy smiled at him – and sent John a text.

I love you so much. Kelly in jail after all. George did his magic as usual. All secure, it seems. I love you too much … Call me now – even though it will be 03.00 here – I won't be able to sleep till I speak to you. Xxxxxx.

She then dialled Mark Foster. 'Mark, what happened when Kelly and Letu were locked up?'

'You heard all about the mess outside your house then?'

'Yes, George told. But I'm interested to know how the interviews went back at the precinct.'

415

'I wish you could have been there, Mrs Howard. Letu did a deal for leniency. He opened his heart – and his mouth for nearly two hours. Turns out, we didn't know the half of it. He attributed twelve orders to murder from Kelly, six of which he said he couldn't carry out. He said she wanted to specify how the victims were to die. Sometimes she wanted to watch it happen. Some of the deaths were to be so horrendous he couldn't imagine himself doing them.

'But he admitted to carrying out six instructions for Kelly, when he could do it his way. He gave us names, so we'll corroborate it all in the morning. They'll waive the death penalty, but he'll probably get six consecutive terms of thirty years.'

'And what of Kelly, Mark?'

'Massachusetts no longer has the death penalty and most of Kelly's instructions to kill were here in Boston. But two of the murders were done in Knoxville.'

'Knoxville, Tennessee?'

'The very same – and yes, it still has the death penalty, especially for double murders, which this one was.'

'But she'll fight to have the trial in Massachusetts then, Mark.'

'She will, but it will tie her up in legals for five years. This will delay the trial for however long she fights to have it in Massachusetts. Meantime, she's not going anywhere.'

'Thank you, Mark.'

Lucy looked Mary straight in the eyes as she made her next call.

'Delta Airlines? … Good. How is the ten a.m. flight from Logan to Heathrow looking tomorrow morning? … First class … Great. How many seats do you have? … That's OK then; I only need six.'

92

Monday – 12th November – 08.00 a.m.

John took hours to fall asleep on the plane. Just as he dozed off, he was woken by a bump. Delta flight 004 had landed at Heathrow.

He would restart his life as a single man. He thought of Charlotte and Emma and of how proud he was of them. He smiled as he recalled how often he had told them that. How fast these eighteen years had passed.

But John knew that this time next year Charlotte would be at university and that Emma would follow her two years later. They would be leaving home for most of the year.

John needed to fill the vast void left by Lucy – he needed a meaningful mission to pour his enthusiasm into. He smiled as he noticed the language of his thoughts. Lucy had once laid herself naked on her bed, drawn her knees to the sides of her chest, and then – with that mischievous look he found so sexy – invited him to pour his enthusiasm into her.

He needed to think about something else right now.

His fellow passengers in the first-class cabin were collecting their bags and coats, preparing to disembark.

Get on with it, Baxter. Life is what happens when you make plans.

John walked from the aircraft along the aerial bridge into Terminal 3. He wondered how many times he had walked these yards – and wondered how many times he would walk them wondering where Lucy was and how she was faring in the life they should have been sharing.

No time for self-pity, Baxter.

But tears were started to form again.

If ever you needed proof that money can't buy you love – here it is.

John walked briskly into the terminal. He took his phone out of his pocket and switched it out of flight mode to see if Claremont Cars had texted him. There was a text from Lucy.

I love you so much. Kelly in jail after all. George did his magic as usual. All secure, it seems. I love you too much … Call me now – even though it will be 03.00 here – I won't be able to sleep till I speak to you. Xxxxxx.

John pressed the little phone icon at the top of his screen. Was he numb with tiredness or from the grudging acceptance of what had happened?

He listened for her reply.

'John?'

'Sweetheart!'

'Oh, thank god. Did you get my text?'

'Yes, just now. I'm at Heathrow.'

He listened as Lucy explained how George had trapped Kelly in the van and arranged for Mark Foster to surround her with armed police when she got back to Boston. When Lucy had finished, John remained silent, wondering what Lucy wanted to happen next.

'You OK?' she said, at last.

'Yes, sweetheart. It's great – I just don't know what you want – it brings back memories of when I thought I'd lost you for ever on TAA006. It was in this same terminal …'

'Oh John. I want to see you. I want to be with you – for the rest of our lives – I couldn't have lived without you – the last few hours have been the worst of my entire life – I haven't slept – I can't stop crying.'

'Me too. Well … can you get over here? I still have my appointment with Mrs Markham. I think she knows what I've done. I'm reluctant to cancel that meeting because she's waited twenty years …'

'John. No worries. I'm booked on Delta this morning at 10.05 – if that's OK?'

'Of course. I can't wait. I'll pick you up this evening.'

'Ah … I have a confession to make … I've invited a few others to join us.'

'OK. Like who?'

'I hope you don't mind. I've invited Mary, James, Mark, Oliver and George, for protection. Is that OK?'

'Why wouldn't it be? It'll be great to get the whole clan together. Somehow it seems quite fitting that George will be there. We're only alive because of his proactivity.'

John knew that six passengers would have lots of luggage. He arranged for a stretch-limo to pick him up from Whitehills Close at 9.00 p.m. He would meet them personally, rather than wait at home.

Charlotte and Emma greeted him as he opened his front door. He explained that Kelly and her assassin were in custody awaiting trial and that he would keep them updated on the legal processes.

They would all stay in Esher today, make up a log fire in the sitting room, make sure the radiators were turned on in the four bedrooms not usually heated – and get some champagne in the fridge well in advance.

Emma asked why champagne was so important today. Charlotte rolled her eyes.

'Idiot child. Dad and Lucy have nearly died a few times. They thought they'd have to separate – and now they're not. They've got Kelly into prison. They got the set together for Mrs Markham. What have I forgotten, Dad?'

John smiled. 'You got most of it, sweetheart … We also solved an art fraud case that got Lucy and me together in the first place … and we think we can force Black Industries to create huge amounts of renewable energy on the land they ruined for oil and coal mining …'

'So basically, you've been swanning around, doing not much,' Emma said, matter-of-factly.

Charlotte shook her head. 'Like I said – idiot child.' She approached John and gave him a big hug.

'I love you both so much,' John said.

'I know, Dad; you tell us all the time,' Emma replied.

Charlotte shook her head again – and put three bottles of champagne in the fridge.

93

John stood in the arrivals lounge in Heathrow's Terminal 3. Painful memories of flight TAA006 came flooding back. Here he was again, standing in the same spot, looking up at the same electronic announcement board. Lucy's flight had landed safely. Baggage had been offloaded; he could only wait.

Ten minutes seemed like an hour. What would she be wearing? Could their life together really start again? Would the ongoing threat from Kelly persist, even if she was in prison? So many questions. He had looked into the abyss – a life without Lucy and her love. It was the blackest, bleakest place, a living hell on earth. This time he would never let her go.

Lucy walked through the double doors at the end of the hall. John felt tears welling again. He walked towards her. She broke into a run. She was beaming the widest smile. Their bodies collided; their mouths met, drawn together like magnets fastened for ever. Tears mingled, as if symbolically combining their fates.

Then – the awareness of the rest of the group, of not wanting to embarrass them. Lucy and John's mouths separated, their eyes locked. No words were needed.

As long as I live, I will never let him go.

'Did you get any sleep on the plane?' John asked.

'I did actually. I hadn't slept last night. So I must have been tired enough today.'

'Me too. Charlotte and Emma helped me get the house ready and I slept a bit this afternoon.'

John turned to George. 'I'm glad you could make it over, George. Lucy told me all about your proactivity with the police van. You're a star. Once again, we owe our lives to you.'

John turned to the group. 'I expect you're all hungry. I've booked a table for nine up at the Mitre at Hampton Court. We'll drop your luggage off at Esher, pick up Charlotte and Emma and go straight to the Mitre; they're expecting us late.'

After the main course, the waitress brought the dessert menus. They all ordered desserts except Lucy, sat beside John.

Lucy put her mouth to John's ear to whisper. 'I'm not having dessert, but I badly need compensating for my sacrifice.' She squeezed his thigh, three times in succession.

When they arrived back in Esher, everyone was tired from their travels. John showed his guests their respective rooms and walked down the landing into his own bedroom. He shut the door. Lucy was staring up at the painting above the bed.

'If we'd had to part for ever, John, the only regret I'd have had was that we'd never become everything we could have been. This last day has reminded me, if ever we needed reminding, that every moment we have is special. We should never take our time for granted.'

He took her head in his hands and kissed her. 'I love you so much.'

'If you truly love me, Mr Baxter, you will compensate me for my dessert sacrifice – and you will do it in the most demanding possible way.'

He looked her in the eyes. 'Get naked.'

94

Tuesday – 13th November

Lucy and John woke to the sound of voices downstairs. She looked at her watch on the bedside table. 07.15. 'That's spooky, John.'

'Mmmm?'

'That's exactly the time we woke up after our first night at the Ritz.'

John smiled at her. 'Perhaps it's a sign of new beginnings, starting afresh, dangers averted. Perhaps Aphrodite has been demanding a series of entry tariffs before we could enjoy a relationship like ours – almost as if she wanted us to prove we deserved what we could have.'

Lucy rolled on top of him, mischief all over her face. 'Could I exact an entry tariff from you, before breakfast?'

She sat up, knees astride his hips. 'Last night was so highly charged – so urgent.'

'It was,' John replied. 'But there's still something I've not solved.'

'Yes?'

'Why they called you Boff?'

Lucy grinned and leant forward. She put one, then her other nipple to his mouth.

'Probably easier for a woman to solve, Mr Baxter. You have to drop the very beginning – but you're as close to the finish as you've ever been.'

Forty minutes later, they started to descend the stairs. 'I'm worried about Andrew and Louise, John.'

'Well, let's see – Kelly, Jack, Simon and Billy – and Adams – are all in custody,' John replied.

'Kelly started this with eight brothers. She killed the three who were always going to be an electoral liability. She manoeuvred another three into prison. She tried to kill James. She's attempted to kill her own mother twice. She was prepared to pay five hundred thousand dollars to kill Tom Malvito. Why wouldn't she try to kill Andrew?'

'Because his respectability makes him an electoral asset?' John ventured.

'John, suppose she always had two agendas?'

They paused at the bottom of the stairs.

'OK – what's in that beautiful head of yours?' he replied.

'In Massachusetts state law, you cannot inherit money or property if you're in prison for a felony. To practise matrimonial law in the US, I've had to know the laws in different states, especially those in New England.'

'So, if all of her siblings are dead or in prison, Kelly inherits all money and all shares in Black Industries?' John asked.

'Yes, but only if her mother is dead as well – hence the two attempts on her life.'

'So, as long as Kelly is alive – Mary and James are still in danger. But where does that leave Andrew?' John asked.

'I believe Kelly was going to kill or imprison Malvito, her mother and all her brothers, except Andrew – until after she had won the seat in the Senate.'

'Except now she is in prison herself. So presumably she cannot inherit shares from Old Man Black,' John said.

'Her rights to inheritance only end when she is convicted. She already has quite a few shares. But she probably wanted a majority shareholding, especially as she's been the only sibling with any involvement in the company.'

John was thinking. 'So, when Kelly's convicted, Mary, Andrew and James could each have a one-third share of the entire wealth that John Black leaves behind.'

Lucy grinned. 'If it's one third each, James is worth several billion dollars.'

John laughed. 'Lovely – the first shall be last and the last shall be first. I believe the American Dog Rescue is about to get an absolutely enormous donation.'

Lucy grinned. 'Not just lovely – ironic too.'

'How so, sweetheart?'

'If you think about it, Kelly, who made it her life's purpose to be rich, ends up with nothing and in prison – while Andrew and James, who don't have a greedy streak between them, end up with billions. It's delicious.'

John grabbed Lucy and held her tight to him.

'Delicious – but kind of circular too,' she said.

John looked at Lucy, the question all over his face.

'John, on our first evening, I mentioned I knew how Kelly made her first two and a half million dollars.'

'I remember.'

'The conversation moved on and I never got to tell you. Billy told me Kelly did it by copying paintings and selling them as originals. It worked then, so she just kept doing it.'

John laughed again. 'Live by the fraud, die by the fraud.'

95

They entered the kitchen to find George, James, Mark, Oliver and Emma all sat at the kitchen table eating pancakes. Mary and Charlotte were standing at the grill piling pancakes in great heaps for the men to eat.

'Do you notice anything wrong with this scene, Mr Baxter?' Lucy asked.

John laughed. 'You sit down, sweetheart. I'll make the next two hundred pancakes. Mary, Charlotte – sit.'

Mary sat down gratefully. 'He's a keeper, sweetie.'

'Ma, you are the only other person alive who knows the full extent of it.' Lucy kissed John, lingering a little longer than their offspring wanted.

'Eeeew – get a room,' Emma winced.

Mary put her hand on Emma's forearm. 'I tell you, kids, what they have is more than special. It's the kind of love that overcomes the slings and arrows of outrageous fortune. I hope all of you find what these two have one day.'

Lucy stood behind Mary, put her arms around her and gave her a hug. Lucy straightened up, looked at the others, silently wolfing pancakes, and smiled.

'I hate to change the subject, but we have to be out of here by eleven if we're to make it to the manor by twelve. Perhaps after breakfast we can all make sure we're ready to leave a bit before eleven, just to be on the safe side.'

While Lucy chose what to wear, John and James loaded the boot of John's car with the paintings they were taking to the manor.

The pictures loaded, they entered the hallway to see Mary looking up at the landing. Lucy started down the stairs, her hair tied back in its usual ponytail. Her sleeveless, figure-hugging knitted dress, in cream, contrasted beautifully with her slim waist and generous bust. Its plunging V-line allowed full view of the diamond-and-emerald necklace around her neck. The matching earrings completed the effect. John stood, smiling.

Baxter – you truly are the luckiest man on earth.

'Ma ... the necklace,' John started.

'I've given it to her – it's the real one,' Ma replied.

'Wow. Look at you, sweetheart. I don't know which is more fabulous – your cleavage or the necklace.' John kissed her.

Lucy grinned. 'I only accepted the necklace on one condition – that Ma could wear it whenever she wanted. I don't know what to say, Ma. It's absolutely beautiful. Thank you.'

'I've always thought of you as my daughter, sweetie. You're far more my daughter than Kelly ever was. The love you have in your heart – I hope you can be my daughter for keeps.'

'Oh, Ma, you'll ruin my mascara.' Lucy hugged her and held her hand as they walked to the car parked outside the front door.

'What the hell is this, Mr B?' Lucy demanded.

'It's the only one with a boot big enough to take all the paintings, sweetheart. And bearing in mind where we're going, and that it marks the end of a twenty-year search, it seemed the most appropriate.'

'How is it I'm only now finding out you have a Bentley?'

John shrugged. 'You never asked.'

Lucy struggled to contain her grin. 'Are there any other surprises I should know about today, Mr Baxter?'

'I sincerely hope not.'

She really has no idea – she really does not suspect ...

96

The rest of the group were collecting outside the front door. The Claremont Cars driver spotted John and tooted his horn to be allowed through the electronic gates to the driveway.

John obliged him and addressed the group. 'We have too many paintings and people all to go in the car. Mary, James and Lucy will ride with me in the car. George, can you ride with the guys in the limo?

'James, I want you with me up front, we have some calculating to do.'

Mary interjected. 'Actually, John – do you mind if I sit with James in the back? I have something I need to discuss with him. You and Lucy should be together anyway.'

'No worries,' John said. He turned to the Claremont driver. 'Do you want to follow us – it's about forty minutes if we take it nice and easy.'

Lucy sat to John's left in the front of the car; Mary and James sat together in the back.

'James – we have some offsetting to do for the trips we've flown recently. We have forty minutes in the car. There's some paper in the glove compartment. Perhaps you could write down the flights I give you and you could research on your new phone how much carbon we need to offset? The website I use is worldwize.com.'

'I won't need to write it down,' James replied.

'I had a feeling you'd say that. OK then – Lucy from JFK to Heathrow, first class; Lucy and John from Heathrow to Miami, first class; Lucy and John from Miami to Eleuthera in economy; Lucy and John from Eleuthera to Miami in economy; Lucy and John from Miami to Boston, first class; John from Boston to Heathrow, first class; Lucy from Boston to Atlanta, first class; Lucy from Atlanta to Heathrow in business class – thank heavens; Lucy and John from Heathrow to Venice, first class; Lucy and John from Venice to Boston, first class; Lucy, Mary, James, John, George, Mark and Oliver from Boston to Heathrow, first class; Mary, James, George, Mark and Oliver from Heathrow to Boston first class. You got all that?'

Ten minutes later, James broke the silence. '66.12 tonnes of CO_2 emitted – including the altitude correction factor of 1.87.'

John looked at James in his rear-view mirror and smiled. 'Thank you, James. So, we offset three times 66.12 tonnes to mitigate some of the CO_2 I created on flights before I started offsetting. That way we're paying back carbon debt from the past.

'So – let's say two hundred tonnes, at six pounds per tonne – that's twelve hundred pounds.'

'Where does the money go, John?' Mary asked.

John's gaze returned briefly to the mirror. 'The gold standard offsets go to the World Projects Fund; it builds quantifiable assets – right now they're building solar parks and wind turbines, both in India. That will directly reduce their need for coal-fired power stations – which will directly reduce the CO_2 that would have gone into the atmosphere.'

'So, tell us more about this triple-offsetting, then, John,' Lucy asked.

'Environmentalists will tell you that it is better not to fly at all than to fly and then offset. They're right; flying puts CO_2

into the atmosphere now – whereas carbon offsetting prevents CO_2 being created in the future. Time is running out if we want to keep our planet cool enough to sustain us. So, because of the urgency, I tend to look for CO_2 reduction projects that make a difference sooner, rather than later: wind turbines, for example. By triple-offsetting I can make up for my flights before offsetting was a possibility.'

They all contemplated what John had said. Finally, Mary broke the silence. 'Talking of time running out – what I've got to tell you folks, I need you to keep completely secret between us. Are you OK with that?'

'Your secret's safe with me,' John replied.

'And with me,' Lucy said.

'Me too,' James added.

'OK, then,' Mary started. 'Back in 1973, I started to keep diaries of everything that happened on the ranch. There are things I recorded that you won't see in the little black book that my husband kept in the safe.'

Mary paused. 'If anything happens to me … In my library, I have three first-edition copies of *The Origin of Species*. It's perfect because they're leather-bound and almost exactly the same size as the ledgers I wrote my diaries in. "Diaries" come just after "Darwin".

'All you'll ever need to know is hiding in plain sight.'

Mary paused – and looked sideways at James. 'But some of the entries in my diaries concern you, James … there's something you need to know … the reason you're the only musical person in the family … the reason you were born so long after Kelly and your brothers … or should I say, your half-brothers.'

Lucy looked at John, who nodded.

Mary continued. 'James, you know how much I love you. And you know how much I love Venice. Well ... you were conceived in Venice, darling. It all started with a truly lovely, beautiful, romantic Italian man. We were so much in love, it was painful. His name was Leonardo Rossi. He had the most incredibly long fingers, fingers you've inherited. He was a concert pianist ...'

97

They arrived at the manor to be greeted at the huge front door by Mrs Markham herself.

'Let me make the introductions,' John said.

'Mrs Markham – Mary Black – Lucy – James – George – Mark and Oliver, Lucy's sons – Charlotte and Emma, my daughters.'

Lucy was beaming. 'It's so nice to meet you, Mrs Markham. I can hardly believe we're here at last.'

John stepped forward to greet Mrs Markham.

'Victoria – you never lose that twinkle in your eye.'

'It's good to see you again, John. Let's all go inside. November isn't getting any warmer.'

'You go on in,' John said. 'We'll unload the car.'

'I've got someone to help you,' Mrs Markham said. 'This is Michael, John. He's Simpson's grandson and Adam's eldest son.'

A young man, about twenty years old and dressed in a dark-blue uniform, emerged from the huge protruding porch that adorned the large house.

'It's nice to meet you, Michael.'

'It's nice to meet you at last, sir. They've told me all about the paintings.'

John smiled. 'I take it you're the chauffeur to Mrs Markham?'

'Yes, sir. I collect everyone from the airports too. But Granddad is helping me with the wine sommelier course I'm doing.'

'So – vintage in your veins, then,' John replied.

'Yes, sir.'

'Michael. I'd like it if you called me John. You can help me and James get these paintings and easels inside. Let's do the easels first.'

The vast drawing room was to the left, off the main entrance hall. After a couple of minutes, John set the last of the five frames onto its easel. Suddenly he realised he was alone in the room.

The drawing room was more of a gallery; John had always liked it. At least fifty feet in both directions, it boasted four huge stained-glass windows, each fifteen feet in height. John gazed again at the one depicting a visit to the house by Henry VIII. The ceiling was impressively ornate; gilded plasterwork framed three large frescos, one painted personally by Federico Zuccari. The walls boasted the original oak panelling built in the sixteenth century and there were two huge fireplaces framed in Italian marble, each at least twelve feet wide. Above the fireplace at the north end of the room was the mounted head of an enormous stag, its antlers boasting twenty-five points.

John's attention returned to the present. He had moved one of six large sofas to enable him to position the five canvases in a straight line across the vast space. The paintings, arranged in season order from left to right, were each six feet wide and occupied most of the width of the huge room. John stood back to admire them, knowing he was the first person ever to see the set together.

Then, he became aware of people behind him. They started to applaud as they walked forward.

There was Mrs Markham, Mary, Mrs Markham's butler, Simpson, and his son Adam with his wife, Sophie. Lucy stood in the middle of the group, resplendent in her emeralds. On her left were Mark and Oliver. To her right were Charlotte and Emma. William Ritchey was standing to Emma's right with James and George. Michael put a glass of champagne into John's hand and re-joined the group. All of them were looking at John, smiling.

They raised their glasses. John reciprocated.

'Here's to your persistence, young man,' Victoria Markham said.

John's eyes were filling with tears. He backed away to the row of canvases arranged behind him.

'The paintings Lucy and I collected back together for you, Victoria … well, they are now all yours. It seems the very least we could do for the start you gave me. There were times I wondered how we could ever get them all together. But luck played a big part – as did Mary and Lucy and George here, who literally saved our lives on more than one occasion.'

He looked at Mary. 'If it hadn't been for your crossword clue on the back of Lucy's picture of Mount Chocorua, we'd probably never have found Winter – and if Lucy hadn't suggested we went to the Waterside Restaurant in Boston to meet Senator Malvito, we'd never have found Autumn.'

'They're absolutely out of this world, John, out of this world,' Mrs Markham said. 'Thank you doesn't seem anywhere near good enough. It looks as if he painted them yesterday.'

'We had them cleaned up at the gallery. I must say they've done a fantastic job. Finally, these paintings are with their rightful owner.

'You're wondering why there are five paintings – in a four-season set.

'Well, the fifth one, the additional Winter, on the very right, was done by Frank Cropsey's daughter, Lilly.'

'It's incredible,' William interrupted. 'It's every bit as good as the others.'

'Absolutely. I picked it up at Christie's. If you'd stayed that day when Billy knocked himself out, you'd have seen the bidding.

'So, finally I unravelled the mystery as to how these five canvases came to exist. It's quite poignant actually; it's all about a father losing his daughter.

'In 1858, Jasper Francis Cropsey set out to paint some famous New England scenes in each of the four seasons. Vivaldi had composed *The Four Seasons* in 1723. Cropsey decided to do it on canvas.

'He painted Spring, then Summer, which Mrs M later gave me as part of our deal. Then Autumn, when Autumn arrived in New England. And anyone who has seen the New England fall knows how incredibly beautiful the colours are on the trees.

'As you can see, Frank painted Autumn beautifully – and unsurprisingly, it sold immediately. It's the one we were given by Senator Malvito. In fact, Cropsey sold Autumn for two thousand dollars, just as he was starting Winter. Two thousand dollars in 1858 was a lot of money – gives you some idea how popular he was as a painter. But he continued with Winter, *Mount Chocorua and Railroad Train*, the fourth canvas here. So, although we can now see his four seasons, these four to the left, Cropsey himself never saw them all together.

'By the time the Cropseys finished their twenty-nine-room mansion in 1869, Cropsey's daughter Lilly was spending lots of time painting with her father in his studio. She was only ten years old – but she was becoming very good.

'But – the American Civil War had started to change the tastes of the art-buying wealthy. The demand for Cropsey's paintings was waning. Lilly witnessed the declining fortunes of her father. By the time she was twenty-six, they'd sold their large mansion and were renting a small place in New York.

'So Lilly painted Autumn to complete the set again. She probably thought the four seasons together could be sold for enough to improve their financial circumstances. But for the plan to work, she'd have to paint it so well that it could pass as her father's painting.

'But if Lilly was trying to create a set that would sell as four seasons, why paint her Autumn on the back of his Winter? The set wouldn't be seen simultaneously. The answer could be that she may not have believed it would be good enough to pass as Frank's Autumn; she may have believed this was to be a trial run. So, if this was a trial run, she would not have wasted an expensive canvas – and Frank's Winter here, on the front, could still be exhibited.'

John turned the fourth painting over – Cropsey's Winter canvas – to reveal Lilly Cropsey's Autumn.

'But I think you'll agree – she well and truly nailed it on her first attempt; her Autumn is absolutely stunning. But, exhibited like this, what you see is Frank Cropsey's Spring, then his Summer, then his Autumn, and Lilly's Autumn to its right.

'So, with Spring and Summer still in their possession, Lilly could have put her Autumn as the third in the sequence, even though it had Frank's Winter on the back. But that means Lilly needs to paint her own version of Winter – this fifth canvas on the far right – for the whole set to be seen as four seasons.

'Now for the second intervention – Frank Cropsey has a stroke. He does recover enough to paint – but he paints less prolifically. He earns enough to buy another canvas for Lilly. Which is just in time because late in the autumn of 1888, when she is only twenty-nine years old, Lilly gets the news that she is dying of cancer.

'Suddenly she is very motivated to paint Winter in her father's set, so that the four seasons can be seen on four different canvases, as intended initially. She never signed her Autumn – she could always sign it later if she thought it was good enough to show as part of the whole set. She paints Winter faithfully to her father's style, but on the new, separate canvas she now has – this fifth one here. It's almost as if she was painting in honour of her father's life, before she died.

'So, as we look at them here now, we have Spring, Summer, Autumn, all done by Frank Cropsey. Then we have this fourth canvas, a second Autumn done by Lilly, with Frank's Winter on the reverse – and the fifth canvas, Lilly's version of Winter.'

John's voice cracked with emotion. 'Lilly died in February 1889, the very next day after completing her painting of winter. Although they saw the set, as four seasons on four different canvases, neither Frank nor Lilly Cropsey ever saw all four of *his* paintings together, because his original Autumn – the middle one of five – had already been sold.'

John turned Lilly's Autumn around again so that the fourth canvas was showing Frank's Winter.

'And now you can see the four seasons done by Frank Cropsey again, followed by Lilly's version of Winter to the very far right. We, today, are the very first people ever to see the whole set painted by Frank Cropsey all in one place.

'What makes this set priceless, is that you have different methods of displaying the four seasons; you can mix up Lilly's with her father's in varying ways. It's totally unique in the whole of the world of art. This aspect of the father–daughter combination of six paintings on five canvases, depicting four seasons, may never be duplicated ever again.'

Lucy's tears were flowing freely. She started to applaud. The rest of the group joined in. John fixed his gaze on Lucy.

'The greatest beauty takes many forms – and sometimes requires the greatest persistence to achieve.'

Victoria Markham marched forward. She hugged John Baxter. 'I think the story restores one's faith in human nature. And you collecting them together does the same. How long's it been? Twenty-five years? Thank you, John – thank you. The set is absolutely gorgeous.'

She turned to the group gazing at them. 'And now – we eat. Let's go through, shall we?'

John interrupted. 'Before we go through, I have something important to ask …'

The party looked at John, who was approaching Lucy.

'Sweetheart – when I asked you before – I believe you thought the ring was made from conflict diamonds. I only realised this recently. But you should know I had it made from stones that have been in my family for three hundred years.

'Lucy, I have loved you from the day we met – sometimes, so much it hurts. I cannot imagine us not being together. Will you marry me?'

Lucy beamed. 'YES, YES, YES.' Lucy's kiss left the group in no doubt.

John grinned. *I am the luckiest man on earth.*

John reached into his pocket and retrieved the ring that Lucy had stopped him giving her in Venice. He placed the engagement ring on her finger, covering it with his hand as he did it. When he took his hand away, the group gasped their disbelief.

The ring was comprised of three stones: a four-carat diamond with a three-carat ruby each side of it.

They applauded again. 'It's absolutely stunning, John. It's fabulous.' She kissed him again.

'*Finally,*' James said.

They shuffled through to the dining room. Lucy took John's hand and squeezed it three times in quick succession. 'And by the way, Mr Baxter – I never thought this ring was made of conflict diamonds. You had the ring ready before we even went to Venice – we didn't even know the conflict diamonds existed till we got back to Boston, two days later.'

As they sat down at the long oak dining table, Charlotte handed John three envelopes, each one identical and with Italian stamps.

'They arrived every day for three days. They look important,' Charlotte said.

John knew immediately. 'It's from Domenico – from his solicitor – it's the letter Benito told me about after Domenico was killed.' John opened one envelope.

Dear John,

You may be the only person on earth with the persistence to find what is buried with Menkaure's pyramid on the Giza Plateau. I have discovered hieroglyphs which no one else knows exists.

I know your cousin was the great Egyptologist, Sir Flinders Petrie. I have observed your passion for many years. I believe you have his unique combination of curiosity and persistence.

My research tells me that Menkaure's treasure is vast – much greater than any buried in Egypt because he collected artefacts taken from the previous five hundred years, dating right back to King Scorpion. I believe no other tomb has come close to this kind of collection. It is five hundred years of history, all in one place – it has never been found.

Despite Flinders's huge contribution, the Egyptians refuse to acknowledge that anyone in the West could have anything more of value to add to their culture. But with your connection to Petrie, you may be the only person who could gain the exploration rights.

Because this knowledge cannot get into the wrong hands, I have set the clues so difficult that only someone with your determination, your fascination for solving puzzles, the comprehensive knowledge I know you have of all seven hundred hieroglyphs, and your family background could make the discovery.

Remember me when you open the tomb; I will be with you in spirit.

PTO – Important.

'*Lucy – we have to go to Egypt – it may be the most important find ever made.*'

'John – wait a minute, you never told me *you* were a cousin of the Petrie family.'

'You never asked,' he replied.

Lucy paused. 'So that explains your interest in Egypt – and the hieroglyphs.'

John looked at her. 'What's not being said here?'

'Turn it over, then,' she said. 'I think we're about to find out.'

John turned over the letter from Benito.

NB: You may be interested to know there is another cousin of Flinders who married a Norwegian woman called Isabella. They own a vineyard in Médoc so I have not been able to trace the family I believe they have.

Lucy grinned.

John stared at her. 'So, we're both related to Sir Flinders Petrie. Wow.'

'Seems so, Mr Baxter, seems so. What other surprises could today possibly have in store?'

98

Mrs Markham had opened up her great oak-panelled dining room for the occasion. As they took their seats, John looked at Mary. 'Did Lucy ever tell you she was booked on the only flight brought down by Hurricane Sandy?'

Mary looked incredulous. 'TAA006? It was all over the news for two days.'

'The night I met Lucy in the Ritz, I fell in love with her immediately. But we were being watched that evening. As Lucy and I chatted, I knew that for any relationship to work, we would need more than a little bit of luck – we would need our wits about us too.

'I couldn't have known the half of it: a bomb on a plane, poisoned food, machine-gun attacks, poisoned whisky, car bombs and Hurricane Sandy.

'Lucy got upgraded onto another flight … and I started to feel luck may be with us after all. Lucy escaped the crash caused by Hurricane Sandy on the 28th of October, Canaletto's birthdate. The omens were good – even the day we met was the birthday of two famous painters, Caravaggio and Tintoretto – the 29th of September – which I later found out was also Lucy's birthday.

'You never mentioned that before,' Lucy said.

'You never asked ... And come to that, I bought Lilly's Winter at Christie's on the 25th of October – Picasso's birthday.'

Lucy grinned and John continued. 'Anyway, we've sorted out the fraud that Lucy crossed the Atlantic about in the first place, we've had a two-week holiday on Harbour Island, we've survived at least five murder attempts, Black Industries will generate renewable energy, and we've collected the entire Cropsey set together at last. And what I find hard to believe – it all happened in only forty-six days.'

Victoria Markham looked at Lucy and John in turn. 'Talking of the Cropsey set – did Mary ever mention how she got hold of *Mount Chocorua in Winter*?'

Lucy and John said nothing.

'A long time ago, my husband Fred and I had a place in Boston. We were always dining the good and the great. One night, after one of our parties, Cropsey's Winter had disappeared from the library. Well, we're not short of art. But it's sad to think that someone has come to dinner and then stolen from you. Such bad manners, don't you think?'

The guests laughed.

'Anyway, Fred and I discussed it at breakfast. We decided to let it go; it seemed tasteless to accuse your guests of stealing. We never possessed Cropsey's Autumn. So now that we'd lost Winter, I never believed I'd see the whole set.

'Winter turned out to have been stolen by Victor, the brother of John Black, Mary's eventual husband. How did we discover this? Because Victor gave the painting to Old Man

Black as a Christmas present. Years later, when Mary married John Black, she recognised the painting in his study.'

At that moment, Simpson approached Victoria Markham.

'Shall I serve the wine now, ma'am?'

'Yes, thank you Simpson.'

John looked up at Simpson, remembering the time he had poured champagne at their first meeting. 'Time has been kind to you,' John said.

'Not as kind as Mrs Markham, sir. Madam has graciously allowed me to retire here, though I do help occasionally when we're busy. It's nice to see you again, young sir.'

Simpson smiled as he poured some red wine into John's glass. 'I'm reliably informed that you'll find this exceptional.'

John smiled. 'So we know it's Château Largaux '78, then.'

John looked at Adam and his wife, Sophie. 'For the benefit of the other guests today, Simpson's son, Adam here, served us this '78 in the Ritz the evening Lucy and I first met.

'I think we can all agree, Simpson and Adam look very similar. It's the reason – that first evening in the Ritz – I was convinced I'd seen Adam somewhere before. Lucy's grandmother Isobel owns the château and Adam and Sophie have just bought the neighbouring vineyard. It should produce a world-beating wine. And it's so nice to see Michael continue the expertise.'

Lucy was still thinking. 'But Ma, you gave me Lilly's Autumn – Winter was covered up. You had to tell us it was there with your clue.'

Ma looked at her. 'When I recognised Cropsey's Winter I knew it had been stolen by Victor. This implicated my husband in a theft. I could see the original Cropsey had been varnished

443

so I knew it wouldn't be damaged if I covered it with a light brown layer. That left the unsigned Autumn on the other side. And nobody would think an unsigned canvas would have much value.'

'So you knew you were giving me an original Cropsey when I drove away from the ranch that day,' Lucy said.

Mary smiled. 'There was never a cross word between us – and I knew you'd uncover it eventually. And we never believed we'd see the whole set together anyway; we'd never possessed Cropsey's Autumn. But to ensure you were curious, I wrote the clue on the frame.'

John looked at Victoria Markham. 'Talking about clues – a year after we did our deal, Victoria, you left a completed *Times* crossword on the table in the library.'

He paused. 'So, Ma, the reason you recognised Winter when you married John Black was that you'd grown up with it – long before it was stolen.'

He paused again, his face lighting up. 'So, Ma – you knew we were meeting your mother. Which means James and Mark and Oliver all knew as well.'

Mary smiled. 'John, meet Victoria Markham, my mother.'

John laughed. 'So, Lucy – you knew all along who Mrs Markham was. Why did you never say?'

'You never asked.'

THE END

Lucy and John continue their adventures in *You Never Asked* and in *Hearts or Minds*, set in Giza and Cairo, the ski resort of Avoriaz in France, the Bahamas, the whisky distilleries on Islay, the British Museum, the Petrie Museum at University College London, the Louvre, Boston, Cape Cod, Gettysburg, Rome and the vineyards of Bordeaux.